Alice in Deadland Trilogy

Alice in Deadland
Through the Killing Glass
Off With Their Heads

Mainak Dhar

As always, for Puja & Aadi

TABLE OF CONTENTS

GREETINGS FROM
THE DEADLAND

I N LATE NOVEMBER OF 2011, I uploaded my novel Alice in Deadland to the Kindle store using Amazon's KDP self-publishing program. I had first discovered the tremendous opportunity in reaching readers worldwide through the Kindle store in March, and after a modest beginning (I sold 118 ebooks in my first month), I was beginning to see some success, having sold some 20,000 ebooks by November. However, nothing had prepared me for the reception my story about a girl called Alice in a dystopian world called the Deadland got from readers. Alice in Deadland quickly became an Amazon.com bestseller and encouragement from readers like yourself led me to write the sequel, Through The Killing Glass, which was published in March 2012.

As of May 2012, the two Alice in Deadland novels had been downloaded by well over 100,000 readers on the Kindle store. This was the kind of reception most writers dream of, and certainly more than I had ever expected. I received more than two hundred reader emails and also started a Facebook group for Alice in Deadland fans (at http://www.facebook.

com/groups/345795412099089/). The feedback I got was pretty unanimous- readers wanted to know more about the world that Alice found herself in. How had our civilization been reduced to the Deadland? What was the story behind some of the characters readers encountered such as the Queen and Bunny Ears?

That feedback motivated me to write the third book in the series, Off With Their Heads, which was created as a prequel to Alice in Deadland, depicting the final days of The Rising through the eyes of some of the pivotal characters in the series.

In this special Omnibus edition, you get all three titles together to provide a complete immersion into the world of Alice. Hope you have as much fun reading the books as I did while creating them.

Mainak Dhar

ALICE IN DEADLAND

ONE

ALICE WAS BEGINNING TO GET very tired of sitting by her sister on the hill, and of having no Biters to shoot. Once or twice she peeped through her sniper rifle's scope, but could see no targets. 'What is the use of an ambush,' thought Alice, 'without any Biters to shoot in the head?'

Alice was fifteen, and had been born just three months after The Rising. Her older sister and parents sometimes talked of how the world had been before. They talked of going to the movies, of watching TV, of taking long drives in the countryside, of school. Alice could relate to none of that. The only life she had known was one of hiding from the Biters. The only education that she knew to be useful consisted of three simple lessons: if a Biter bites you, you will become one of them; if a Biter bites someone you know, it doesn't matter whether that person was your best friend; they were now a Biter and would rip your throat out in a heartbeat; and if you could take only one shot, aim for the head. Only the head. Nothing else would put a Biter down for good.

So here she was, lying on a small hillock, her rifle at her shoulder, waiting to pick off any stragglers who escaped the main force. The first few years of her life had been one of hiding, and of surviving from one day to another. But then the humans had begun to regroup and fight back, and the world had been engulfed in a never-ending war between the living and the undead. Alice's parents were part of the main assault force that was now sweeping through a group of Biters that had been spotted near their settlement. She could hear the occasional pop of guns firing, but so far no Biters had come their way. Her sister was lying quietly, as always obedient and somber. Alice could not imagine just lying here, getting bored when the action was elsewhere, so she crawled away to the edge of the small hill they were on and peered through her scope, trying to get a glimpse of the action.

That's when she saw him. The Biter was wearing pink bunny ears of all things. That in itself did not strike Alice as strange. When someone was bitten and joined the undead, they just continued to wear what they had been wearing when they were turned. Perhaps this one had been at a party when he had been bitten. The first Biter she had shot had been wearing a tattered Santa Claus suit. Unlike kids before The Rising, she had not needed her parents to gently break the news that Santa Claus was not real. What was truly peculiar about this Biter was that he was not meandering about mindlessly but seemed to be looking for something. The Biters were supposed to be mindless creatures, possessed of no intelligence other than an overpowering hunger to bite the living. She braced herself, centering the crosshairs of her scope on the Biter's head. He was a good two hundred meters away and moving fast, so it was hardly going to be an easy shot.

That's when the Biter with the bunny ears dropped straight into the ground.

Alice looked on, transfixed, and then without thinking of

what she was getting into, ran towards the point where the Biter had seemingly been swallowed up by the ground. Her heart was pounding as she came closer. For months there had been rumors that the Biters had created huge underground bases where they hid and from which they emerged to wreak havoc. There were stories of entire human armies being destroyed by Biters who suddenly materialized out from the ground and then disappeared. However, nobody had yet found such a base and these stories were largely dismissed as being little more than fanciful fairy tales. Had Alice managed to find such a base?

Her excitement got the better of her caution, and she ran on alone. She should have alerted her sister, she should have called for reinforcements, she should have done a lot of things. But at that moment, all she remembered was where the Biter had dropped into the ground and of what would happen if she had truly found an underground Biter base. She was an excellent shot, far better than most of the adults in the settlement, and she was fast. If there was one thing she had been told by all her teachers since she started training, it was that she was a born fighter. She could put a man twice her size on the mat in the wink of an eye, and she had shown her mettle in numerous skirmishes against the Biters. Yet, she was not allowed to lead raids far from the settlement. That had always grated, but with her father being one of the leaders of the settlement, she was unable to do anything to change that. He claimed that her excellent shooting and scouting skills were better used in defensive roles close to their settlement, and had promised her that when she was older he would reconsider, but she knew that was a nervous father speaking, not the leader of their settlement.

This could change all that.

Suddenly she felt the ground give way under her and she

felt herself falling. She managed to hold onto her rifle, but found herself sliding down a smooth, steep and curving slope. There seemed to be no handholds or footholds for her to slow her descent or to try and climb back up. She looked up to see the hole through which light was streaming in disappear as the tunnel she was falling down curved and twisted.

Alice screamed as she continued falling in utter darkness.

It took Alice a few minutes to get her bearings, as she was totally disoriented in the dark and also winded by her fall. She saw that her fall had been broken by a thick cushioning of branches and leaves. She had heard whispers that the Biters were not the mindless drones that many adults dismissed them to be, but those accounts had been dismissed by most people as fanciful tales. She wondered if there was some truth to those rumors after all. As her eyes adjusted to the darkness she saw a sliver of light to her right and crawled towards it. As she went deeper into the tunnel, while she still could not see much, the smell was unmistakable. The rotten stench that she knew came from only one possible source: the decayed bodies of the undead. Even though she had seen the aftermath of many a skirmish with the Biters and was no stranger to the stench, she found herself gagging. As she came closer to the light, she saw that the tunnel opened into a small room that was lit by crudely fashioned torches hung on the walls.

She could hear some voices and as she peeped around the corner, she saw that the rabbit-eared Biter she had followed down was in animated conversation with two others. One of them was, or rather had been in life, perhaps a striking young woman. Now her skin was yellowing and decayed and hung in loose patches on her face. Her clothes were tattered and bloodied. The other Biter with her was a plump, short man who seemed to have the better part of his left side torn off, perhaps by a mine or a grenade. Alice had been around weapons for as long as she could remember, and while all humans now needed to be able to defend themselves, Alice had shown a special talent for fighting, perhaps one her mother did not always approve of. Her mother had wanted Alice to do as the other young people did and stand on guard duty close to the settlements, but Alice had always wanted to be in the forefront, to feel the thrill that came with it. Now, Alice thought, she had perhaps got more thrills than she had ever bargained for. She was trapped in an underground Biter base, with no apparent way out.

The Biters were talking in a mixture of growls and moans, but they seemed to be communicating with each other. Now that she got a closer look at the rabbit-eared Biter she had followed in, she realized that he had been in life not much older than her. Perhaps he had been on his way to a costume party when he had been bitten. As he turned his head, Alice saw what may have once been a smile now replaced by a feral grin that revealed bloodied teeth.

Alice's heart stopped as Bunny Ears looked straight at her. For a second she hoped that he had not seen her, but he bared his teeth and emitted a screeching howl that sent a shiver up her spine. As all three Biters turned to look at her, she exploded into action.

Alice's grasp of the alphabet may have been tenuous despite her mother's many failed attempts to teach her the languages of yore. But after The Rising, Alice saw no use for them; there were no books to read, and no time to read them even if they had remained. But what Alice excelled in school at, and could do almost without conscious thought, was how to thumb the safety off her handgun and bring it up to a two handed hold within three seconds. The first shot took the fat Biter squarely in the forehead and he went down with an unceremonious flop. As the two others bore down on her in the slight loping, lumbering gait the Biters were known for, she fired again and again, the shots from her gun echoing in the underground cavern. She hit the female Biter at least twice in the chest and then knocked her flat with a head shot. Bunny Ears was now barely a few feet away when Alice's handgun clicked empty. She cursed under her breath at her horrible aim, realizing just how much easier it was to shoot at targets in practice or snipe from hundreds of meters away compared to being so close to Biters out for her blood, and with her heart hammering so fast she could barely keep her hands straight, let alone aim.

Alice heard footsteps and howls behind her, and realized with a stab of panic that she was now well and truly trapped between Bunny Ears and others who may have come behind her down the hole.

She looked around frantically and saw a small opening in the wall to her right. She ran towards Bunny Ears, diving down at the last minute beneath his outstretched fingers, which were crusted over with dried blood. Alice stood only about five feet tall, and was lean, but she had been top of her class in unarmed combat. She swept her legs under the Biter, coming up in one seamless motion as Bunny Ears fell down in a heap. She ran towards the hole in the wall and turned around to see at least four more Biters coming behind her.

Alice fumbled at her belt and took the lone flash bang grenade she had slung there. As she ran into the hole she pulled the pin and rolled it on the ground behind her, and then continued to run at full speed into the darkness of the hole. She heard the thump of the grenade a few seconds later, hoping that the intense flash of light it emitted would slow down her pursuers for a few seconds and buy her some time.

With that hope came a sobering thought. Time to do what? She was stuck deep inside what seemed to be a Biter base, and was running ever deeper into its recesses. She was well and truly trapped.

Alice ran till she was out of breath and stopped, going down on her knees, more tired and scared than she had ever been. The darkness and narrowness of the passage she was in did not help, as it made her feel disoriented and claustrophobic. At least she could no longer hear footsteps behind her. That did not surprise her. While the flash bang would not stop the Biters, she knew they hated very bright light, and it would certainly have slowed them down. Also, she was a very fit young girl who could outrun most of the people in their settlement, whereas the Biters pursuing her, while feared for their feral violence, moved with their characteristic stiff, loping gait, which meant she would be able to outrun them in any flat out race. The problem was that she was trapped in their base, and all they had to do was to tire her out.

When she thought she heard distant footsteps behind her, her fear gave her a second wind and she started running again, clutching her side, which had begun to hurt from the exertion. She ran into a wall, and fell hard on her back, realizing that the tunnel turned ahead of her. As she looked past the turning, she saw what appeared to be a door framed by light coming from behind it. She ran towards it, and as she came closer, she was stunned to see a familiar figure drawn on the door. It was a seal showing an eagle framed by letters that were barely visible in the light coming from behind it. She started trying to read the letters and got past the U, N and I before she realized she did not need to tax her limited reading skills to understand what it showed. She had seen a similar seal in old papers her father kept locked away in a dusty box. Once he had told her something about him having worked in the United States Embassy in New Delhi before The Rising. She had understood little of what he had meant, though other kids around the settlement had told her that her father had been some sort of important man in the governments of the Old World. They had told her that she and her family had come from another land called America, which was why her blond hair and fair skin looked so different from her brown friends. But none of that mattered much to Alice, or to anyone else anymore. The old governments and countries were long gone. Now all people, irrespective of their old countries, religions or politics were bound together in but one overriding compact: the need to survive in the face of the Biter hordes. She had heard tales of how human nations had waged wars against each other, driven by the gods they worshipped, or the desire to grab oil. Alice remembered laughing when her teacher at the makeshift school in the settlement had told her class about those days. She had thought her teacher was telling them some tall tales. What was it the old folks called them? The ones who had read the books before the undead rose and the world burned?

Yes, fairy tales.

When Alice heard footsteps behind her, she was snapped back to reality, and she struggled with the door in front of her, trying desperately to open it. She found a handle and pulled it with all her strength, and finally found the door budging. The door was made of heavy metal, and it sapped all her strength to open it enough for her to slip through.

She looked back through the open door and heard the roars before she saw shadows appear in the tunnel. She pulled the door shut, hoping that what she had heard about Biters being stupid was right. That old joke about how many Biters it took to open a door.

She took a look around the room she was in and saw that it was lit by a single small kerosene lamp on the ceiling, and was filled with papers and files that crammed the shelves lining the walls. There was a small desk in a corner and when she walked to it, she saw some old newspapers on it. She had never seen a newspaper in her life, and was fascinated by the pictures and words she saw. She didn't need to read the words to know what they showed. They were relics of the last days during The Rising and its aftermath. There were grainy pictures of the first appearances of the undead, which she imagined for those who had never seen before them must have been quite a sight. Then there were pictures of burnt and charred cities: the remains of the Great Fire that the human governments had unleashed on so many cities when it seemed like all was lost. That was the barren, bleak landscape that Alice had known as home: the wastelands outside New Delhi, where millions had died in the Biter outbreak and then millions more as governments tried to contain the outbreak by using nuclear weapons on the key outbreak centers. Man had proven to be the most jealous of lovers, preferring to destroy the Earth rather than give her up. But it had not been enough, and in the fires of that apocalypse was born a renewed struggle for survival between humans and the undead in the wasteland that was now known simply as the Deadland.

Alice had been so transfixed by what she saw that she had forgotten all about securing the other doors to the room, and she screamed in agony when she realized that there was another door, partially obscured by a chair, which was ajar. She heard footsteps behind it, and realized that what she had taken for escape was in fact nothing more than a death trap.

She took out her handgun from her belt and as she felt for the safety, remembered with dismay that in all the chaos she had forgotten to reload. As she saw shadows enter the door, she realized she had no time for that any more. She unslung the sniper rifle from her shoulders. As such close quarters, there was no hope of her putting it to much use as a long range weapon, but there were other ways to make it count.

As a child, Alice had forever been getting into scrapes, and her parents would never tire of telling her to back down once in a while, instead of wading into every fight. But once, after she had shot two Biters during a night-time raid, her father had got quite drunk to celebrate and told her that he loved her spirit and that no matter what the odds, she should never give into fear. To be afraid in the face of the undead was to die, or worse, to become one of *them*.

As Alice remembered her father's words, she felt her fear slip away. She knew that the Biters tried to bite and turn every human they found, but also that the humans who fought back the hardest sometimes enraged them so much that they ripped them apart, killing them instead of turning them into the undead.

Better dead than undead.

That had been the motto of the school where they had been taught survival and combat skills. Whereas little girls before The Rising may have been playing with their toys or watching TV, Alice had grown up playing with guns, explosives and learning the best way to destroy the undead. And she had been the best in her class.

She was now swinging the rifle in front of her like a staff, moving it around her fingers so it cut sharp circles through the air. Three Biters came in, and as the first reached for her, she cracked him across the forehead and leaned toward him, sweeping his legs under him as he went down. The next up was a squat woman wearing the tattered, bloody remains of a saree, and incongruously enough, a huge diamond solitaire earring on her left ear. The right ear was missing. Alice delivered a roundhouse kick that sent Ms. Solitaire stumbling back and then reversed the sniper rifle in her hand, firing a single shot that disintegrated the Biter's head. The third Biter, a tall man with his jaw missing, was almost upon her when she hit him hard in the face with the butt of her rifle. Biters might feel no pain, but it unbalanced him enough for Alice to jump back a few steps and put another round into his chest. Only a head shot would put down a Biter for good, but a high powered sniper rifle bullet did impressive enough damage and slowed one down no matter where it hit. A gaping hole opened in the Biter's chest as he slumped back. Alice knew he'd be at her throat soon enough so she tried to chamber another round in her rifle.

That was when she felt her right arm caught in a cold, clammy grip that was so strong she screamed and dropped her rifle. Bunny Ears was back and he was bringing his face back to bite her arm. Alice kicked him in the shin, but he did not even wince as he came closer to delivering the bite that would be the last thing Alice felt before she became one of *them*.

Alice did the last thing he perhaps expected. She head-butted him, and as he staggered back and loosened his grip on her arm, she vaulted over the desk and stood with her back to the wall. There were now no less than six Biters gathered in front of her, and Alice suppressed the welling panic within as she unsheathed the curved hunting knife that was always by her side. Bunny Ears snarled and screamed in rage, a hellish concerto that was soon taken up by all the Biters in the room. Alice had heard of this ritual before. It meant the Biters were going to rip some human apart instead of trying to convert them. Alice reversed the knife in her right hand and stood with her legs slightly spread apart, just as she had mastered in countless hours of unarmed combat practice. Her teacher there had been some sort of elite commando in the armies of the old governments, and he had told her she was his best student. She slowed her breathing, focusing on the creatures in front of her, trying to block out her fear, trying to still her mind. As Bunny Ears stepped toward her, she gripped the knife handle tight and readied herself. Better dead than undead.

TWO

WHEN BUNNY EARS LUNGED AT her, he was met with a sharp kick that had him rocking on his heels, and then Alice delivered a knife thrust to his chest. He just looked up and snarled through bloodied teeth before Alice kicked him again, sending him down on one knee. Alice knew it was a losing battle. She was hopelessly outnumbered and even if by some miracle she managed to drive the knife through one of the Biters' brains, that would still leave several of them to rip her apart. Be that as it may, she was not about to go down without a fight. A Biter with half his face torn off reached towards her with a hand that had several fingers missing. Alice put all her strength into it and drove the knife through his skull. The Biter fell back and did not get back up.

Now she had no weapon to defend herself with.

As two more Biters reached towards her, Alice overturned the desk in front of her, sending both of them sprawling, but she knew that at best she was merely delaying the inevitable. She felt a painful blow to the side of her head as Bunny Ears hit her, and she fell over hard against the wall.

As she scrambled to get up, she felt cold hands grip her legs and sharp nails dig into her jeans. She grabbed onto the bookshelf by her side and it toppled over with a crash, scattering papers and files all around her. She was now being dragged along the ground, and could hear the Biters screeching in anticipation of the kill, like a pack of wild dogs around their prey.

Alice looked up to see Bunny Ears looming over her, his eyes yellowed and wide, his skin peeling off in places and his stench unbearable as he bent over her.

Then he suddenly stopped. A couple of the other Biters tried to get to her, but he stopped them with an authoritative roar. Alice cringed as he grabbed her hair, but instead of attacking her, he seemed to be examining it, turning it around in his fingers. Alice was nearly paralyzed with fear, wondering what torture he had in mind for her, half wishing that he would just get it over with and grant her a quick death. As far as she had ever imagined Biters capable of emotions, she saw a flicker of doubt cross Bunny Ear's face, and something had clearly caused him to put his bloodlust on hold. Whatever that was seemed to be something right behind Alice since he seemed to be looking beyond her at the wall where the bookshelf had been seconds earlier.

He reached out with a torn and callused finger and Alice cringed, only to find that he was reaching for the wall behind her. The other Biters were now gathered around him, looking at her. A few of them were jostling and pushing, eager to get at her, but he snarled again, and they held back. Clearly Bunny Ears was in charge here. Whether that was a good thing or not was something Alice reckoned she would find out very soon. He grabbed her hair again, this time almost yanking them out from the roots, and Alice shouted. That got him focused on her again, and he brought his face close to hers. Alice tried hard not to throw up as she smelt his stench and saw his torn and decayed face up close. He was but a few inches away from her face when to her shock he said one word.

'A...a...lissssssssss.'

Alice thought she had imagined it but when he repeated himself, she recoiled in horror. Not only did this creature speak but it was calling out her name. She had not said anything, but her reaction must have given her away. Bunny Ears leapt back, as if he had been electrocuted, and the other Biters all took a step back. She was alone, unarmed and utterly at their mercy, but the tables had somehow been turned in an instant. They seemed to be terrified of her. No, as Alice studied them almost bowing down before her and heard a few more of them growling, trying to utter her name, she realized it was not just fear. They were in awe of her.

Alice scrambled to her feet, unsure of what was going on, when Bunny Ears pointed to the wall behind her. Now that she had got her first close look at Biters outside of the heat of battle when all that mattered was killing them or being bitten, she realized that while they certainly looked hideous and were capable of savage violence, they were also capable of some level of rational action. She hoped that if she did as they wanted, she had at least some chance of appealing to that part of them and getting out alive. As she turned towards the wall, it felt as if the world had stopped around her. On the wall was a drawing, with smudged lines and crudely filled colors, as if it had been made by a small child. But what it showed was clear enough.

It showed a blonde girl jumping down a hole. In front of her was a creature that was wearing some sort of coat but had the unmistakable ears and whiskers of a rabbit. Just above the drawing was, etched in a childish scrawl, 'Alice.'

Alice's reading skills may not have been great but one thing she did know well was how her own name was spelt.

She sat down on the ground, oblivious to the bloodthirsty Biters just feet away from her.

What was going on?

She felt strong hands grab her by her shoulders and pull her upright. The Biters were now in a state of considerable agitation and between grunts and screeches, Bunny Ears was trying to tell them something. Whatever it was, they seemed to agree on it soon enough, and Alice was pushed out of the room and into another tunnel.

She was too shell-shocked to resist or even ask where they were taking her. And so Alice was bundled off even deeper into the Biter base.

They continued in darkness and total silence for many minutes, and the only consolation Alice had was that if the Biters had wanted to kill her they would have done so long ago. They clearly wanted her alive, but to what end she had no idea. They soon began a steep climb and while the Biters seemed accustomed to both the darkness and the area they were going through, Alice found herself stumbling and falling more than once. Finally they rounded a turn and she felt hands holding her back as if asking her to wait. She saw a sliver of light open up ahead, gradually growing as the door out of the tunnel was pushed open. As she came closer, she saw that it was not much of a door but branches and twigs gathered together, which were now being pushed back into place as their group came out of the tunnel.

The bright sunlight hurt her eyes after having been in the dark for so long, and as Alice squinted and looked around, she saw that they were now very much in the heart of what had once been the bustling city of New Delhi. Now all that remained was rubble, but she recognized the broken edifice of what had once been some monument called India Gate. She had only heard about it from the adults, since this was an area that was firmly under the control of the Biters, and was avoided by humans. All around her, she saw evidence of that. There were small groups of Biters lumbering around, and when one or two of them saw her, they snarled and were about to launch themselves at her. Bunny Ears swatted one of them away, and growled a warning to the others. Whatever he said, she realized that her name had been mentioned more than once, and the effect on the Biters was immediate. They all backed away, as if fearful of her, and she continued with the group that was now herding her along to their unknown destination.

Alice subconsciously tried not to breathe too deeply. While the Great Fires had taken place years ago, nobody really knew how much radiation still lingered. When Alice had first heard of the Great Fires and the terrible weapons that had been unleashed, she had wondered aloud how much of the Biters' hideous nature was the result of the radioactive fallout and how much was due to whatever had caused The Rising in the first place. Nobody seemed to have much by way of answers. Most of the nuclear blasts had supposedly been air-bursts designed to incinerate the Biters but keep the ground as free from radiation as possible, but nobody could really be sure what their legacy had been. Her father had by all accounts been someone senior in the Embassy, but things had moved so fast that even he had no real idea of what had been the exact chain of events during the last days.

Alice saw that they were headed towards what seemed to be an opening in the ground. Clearly the rumors about the underground bases had been an understatement. Far from being an isolated base that she had stumbled upon, it seemed like the Biters had a fairly sophisticated network of underground tunnels and bases. She filed away all the details she could spot so that she might be able to help others when she got back. That kept her thinking positively that she would indeed somehow make it back and also took her mind off the growing fear about just where she was being taken.

She heard a dull whirring sound coming from the sky above and she froze. She had heard similar sounds before, and in the past they had always been an unwelcome omen. Today, they signaled hope for her liberation. Bunny Ears pushed her behind the walls of some ruins and they hid as the three black helicopters came into view. As they came closer to the ground, Alice could see that most of the Biters had taken cover. Most, but not all. Two Biters were running around frantically, as if in a state of panic, trying to find safety. A door slid open in one of the helicopters and two men leaned out with sniper rifles at their shoulders. Two shots rang out and both Biters went down, their heads split open by high velocity rounds.

Alice looked around her at the Biters cowering behind the ruins and she saw them in a totally new light. She had grown up thinking of them as rabid, vicious creatures who had to be destroyed because their only reason for being was to destroy humans. Now, as she looked at Bunny Ears and the others, she realized that they were absolutely terrified. They certainly did not display much by way of evolved intelligence, but they seemed more like a pack of terrified animals being hunted by humans than a band of evil, ferocious killers. She saw several of them shake in terror as the helicopters came closer to the ground.

She saw the golden trident and lightning bolt drawn on their side, and did not need to read the letters to know which group these represented. Zeus.

She had sometimes overheard her father talk about Private Military Contractors, and how much power they had begun to wield in the chaotic times before The Rising. She did not understand much of what had been talked among the adults, but knew that Zeus was the most powerful of those armies, and its power had only increased after The Rising and human governments had ceased to function. Nobody knew who really controlled them, but they were the only visibly organized, and certainly best armed, human army around. Every few months, they would visit the independent settlements like the one where Alice lived and try and ask for volunteers to join them, or try and coerce the settlements to accept the rule of the Central Committee. It was unknown who made up this Central Committee, but this group controlled Zeus and it was common knowledge in the Deadland, as the area where Alice lived had come to be known, that once you accepted their rule, you signed away your freedom.

Alice had been lucky to be born in a settlement that had been begun by her father and the remaining contingent of US Marines guarding the US Embassy in New Delhi. They had then linked up with a group of Indian Army officers and their families. So, unlike most other settlements in the Deadland that had proved easy prey both for human looters and Biters in the chaos that prevailed in the early days, their settlement had been able to repel the assaults, and quickly established a reputation of being a group not to be messed with easily. Even then, whenever the Zeus soldiers had come to visit, Alice had felt a stab of fear at their sight. The men she had grown up with were mostly professional soldiers, or men like her father, fighting to save their families. The Zeus troopers, in contrast, were guns for hire, and displayed little compassion or sympathy for those in the Deadland. If you didn't join them, they would turn their back even when you were under assault by Biters.

As snipers on the helicopters provided cover, men dressed all in black rappelled down from the helicopters and began fanning out. Alice was only too conscious of the reputation Zeus had, but right now between being herded to an unknown fate as a prisoner of the Biters, and getting a chance of going back home, even if it meant trusting the Zeus troopers, she would choose the latter in a heartbeat. She waited for the Zeus troopers to come closer, since she knew that if she tried to attract their attention too early, Bunny Ears and his friends would surely kill her. She kept waiting for the right moment, but then without her having to do anything, a distraction presented itself.

A female Biter near Alice lost her nerve and ran into the open, screeching wildly. Two Zeus troopers knelt and fired their weapons on full automatic at her, the crisscrossing lines of fire turning the Biter around like a puppet on a string, before she was thrown to the ground. When she tried to get up, a sniper on a helicopter shot her head off with a single bullet. Another Biter ran towards one of the doors leading to an underground base when several shots sent him down, and once again a sniper delivered the coup de grace.

Alice watched, realizing that this was no battle. This was a massacre. She saw Bunny Ears and the others with her huddling, as if deciding what to do, when she decided to make her move. She stepped out from behind cover, hoping that the Zeus troopers would not shoot her, and screamed at the top of her voice.

'Help me! I'm human!'

Alice's eyes widened in fear when instead of coming to

her assistance one of the Zeus troopers knelt down and aimed his rifle at her. She was pushed to one side as the bullets tore through the air where she had stood scant seconds before. She looked up to see Bunny Ears glaring at her before he grabbed her by her arm and dragged her behind cover.

The Zeus troopers seemed to comprehend what was going on, and the fact that a young human girl seemed to be held captive by this horde of Biters galvanized them into action. More troopers rappelled out of the helicopters and they began advancing towards the wall behind which Alice was now hidden.

Bunny Ears whistled, an ear piercing sound that made Alice involuntarily cover her ears. When she peeked out the side of the wall, she saw what his signal had meant. All around the Zeus troopers, Biters gathered among the ruins and advanced upon them. The troopers opened fire and Alice saw several of the Biters fall, but the others were now advancing at speed. The snipers on the helicopters took out a few more Biters with carefully aimed head shots.

Alice looked on in fascination. She had directly participated in more than a dozen skirmishes with the Biters and witnessed a dozen or more as a spotter or during her training. At that time, it had been but natural to think of the Biters as the ferocious, formidable adversaries everyone said they were, and she had not even thought twice before emptying her clip into the undead Santa's head when he had blundered into their path during a patrol.

Now, sitting among the Biters and getting a glimpse of what battle against humans looked like from their perspective, she began to see things a bit differently. Sure, up close they were formidable with their strength, seeming immunity to pain, and their single-minded dedication to biting human flesh. But in the open like this, against trained soldiers, they were cannon fodder. They could not use any weapons, moved slower than humans, and did not seem to have enough intelligence for anything more than the most rudimentary tactics.

The dozen or so Zeus soldiers were now tightly packed with their backs to each other, like a phalanx, and were moving steadily towards her position. They were still picking off targets at will, and dozens of Biters littered the ground around them. But the Biters kept coming, and Alice saw that at least two holes had opened up in the ground, and Biters were pouring through them, trying to get close enough to the soldiers to bring their teeth and nails to bear. It was a massacre, and Alice wondered what the Biters were trying to achieve by walking straight into certain annihilation. Or were they just such mindless drones that they kept going, driven by instinct or bloodlust, regardless of the odds that faced them?

She felt a tug at her arm, and Bunny Ears pulled her up and dragged her along. She tried to resist, but his grip on her arm was so tight that she could not shake him off. When she kicked out at him, sending him staggering back, he nonchalantly slapped her across the face. The blow was so hard it knocked her down and she felt the ground spinning around her as Bunny Ears picked her up and slung her across his shoulders. He screeched loudly, and in apparent response a dozen or more Biters stepped between them and the advancing Zeus troopers.

It became instantly clear to Alice that there was a method to what the Biters were doing. They were buying Bunny Ears some time so he could get her away. Why they wanted her so badly and what the drawing on the wall had meant were beyond her, but what was certain was that her hopes of a rescue were being dashed. She could now see the Zeus troopers falter and start to withdraw in face of the sheer strength of numbers of the Biters. Before Bunny Ears ducked into some ruins, she saw the first Zeus trooper fall under a group of clawing and slashing Biters.

They were someplace dark, and Bunny Ears was running through what appeared to be long corridors of some official building. There were doors lining the corridor, and Alice saw Biters hiding behind more than one of them. Even if any of the Zeus troopers got this far, in the confined and dark environment they would be easy pickings for the hidden Biters. She began to reassess the Biters based on what she had just seen. Yes, they were clearly not as intelligent as humans, but they were displaying some sort of planning and forethought. But the big question still remained: what the hell did they want with her?

Bunny Ears ducked low under a collapsed beam and finally stopped, unceremoniously dumping Alice on the ground. She swore with the choicest of obscenities she had learnt from years spent in the company of soldiers and glared at him, but he just looked at her with no expression in his yellowing, vacant eyes. He pointed to a hole in the wall that he motioned for her to walk through. When she hesitated, he slapped her, sending her crashing to the ground again.

'What the hell is it with you? Stop hitting me and I may listen!'

Again, her words seemed to have no effect on Bunny Ears, and so Alice, realizing she had no real options and no apparent means of escape, walked in through the hole and began a steep descent underground. Just a few minutes ago she had got her first glimpse of humans for the first time since she had been foolhardy enough to follow Bunny Ears down the hole, and had begun to entertain hopes of rescue. However, now she was again firmly in the clutches of the Biters, and headed back into one of their underground strongholds.

They walked for what seemed to be at least an hour in total darkness, and Bunny Ears finally stopped in an opening that was lit by a single torch. Alice grabbed her sides, with barely enough strength left to stay standing, let alone follow him any deeper.

'I need water, ok? I am not like you. I need to drink and eat.'

He looked at her, with no expression on his face, and she made drinking motions with her hands, hoping that he would get the idea. When he moved his right arm, Alice flinched, wondering if he would hit her again. Instead, he held out her backpack, which he had taken from her after the fight in the Embassy. She opened it and took out her water bottle, draining it as she drank every last drop there. When she put it back inside, she felt inside the bag for a second. She had her first aid kid, and one signal flare. While she had no weapons left on her, that flare might come in handy. When Bunny Ears growled, she handed the backpack to him, thankful that he was intelligent enough to understand what she wanted, but not quite smart enough to check the bag.

She followed him deeper into the abyss, going through several more descending turns before they arrived at a door. When Bunny Ears pushed it open, Alice saw that they had entered some sort of shelter that must have once been designed for use by humans. Metal bunk beds lined the room, in which dozens of Biters were sprawled. Some of them hissed and moved in her direction, but a series of growls from Bunny Ears sent them scampering back. Perhaps to keep her close and out of harm's way, he grabbed her wrist and pulled her behind him. Many of the Biters glared and spat at her, and she had no doubt they would have ripped her to shreds if her unlikely guardian in the form of a Biter with bunny ears had not been there.

They paused at an open door, and Alice froze when she heard a human voice coming from somewhere on the other side. It was a gravely voice, deep and slow, but it was unmistakably the voice of a human female, unless Alice was about to meet her first talking Biter.

'What have you brought down today? Let me see.'

Alice heard some growling and screeching in response, as the speaker continued.

'Two Zeus troopers? What on Earth would I want to do with them? Their papers show that they are but fresh recruits, so they could have nothing of use for me. Of course, you would have no way of knowing that, would you?'

Alice heard more screeching, and listened to this surreal conversation, wondering if the two parties actually understood what they were saying to each other.

'Oh well, you have brought them down, and I did have a chat with them. Unfortunately, they are totally brainwashed and unwilling to join us, and after what they've seen, I cannot let them go back up. I was hoping that they would have a more open mind. It's probably all for the better; these two are part of the unit that killed all the little ones a fortnight ago.'

The screeching now gave way to a blood-curdling roar, and Alice realized with a start that the Biter being talked to did understand what was being said to it. The next words from the female voice made Alice's eyes open wide with fear.

'Take them, and off with their heads.'

Alice heard the men begging and pleading as they were dragged away, and then Bunny Ears began to push her into the room. She pushed him back, now in a state of panic, wondering if she was being prepared for the same fate as had befallen the captured Zeus troopers.

'Let me go! Goddammit, let go of my hand!'

Suddenly she heard the female voice inside the room call

out to her in a soothing tone.

'It's quite all right, dear. I suspect you have nothing to fear from me. Come on in.'

'Who the hell are you?'

The voice tut-tutted, like a disapproving school teacher.

'Young lady, I had hoped for better manners from someone from one of the settlements. You are not one of the wild humans roaming and scavenging in the Deadland. Come on in, and we can talk like civilized people. As for who I am, these fellows down here think I'm their Queen.'

And so, shivering with fear, Alice was pushed into the room for her audience with the Queen of the Biters.

THREE

WHEN ALICE ENTERED THE ROOM, she found herself in what resembled an office of some sort, with a large couch at one end and a desk with a high-backed chair at the other. The Queen was sitting in the chair, but had her back turned to the door, so Alice could see little more of her than a gloved arm resting on the chair's side. Bunny Ears was standing behind her and making vaguely threatening growling noises. Alice had no idea how they communicated, but she thought a fair attempt at translation would indicate that he was reminding her not to try anything since he was right behind her. That suited Alice just fine, since she was so terrified that any act of bravado was the last thing on her mind.

'Dear, please sit down, and don't mind Rabbit there. He's just very protective but is otherwise quite gentle.'

Alice found it impossible to contain a dismissive snort as she considered how anyone could think of a vicious Biter as gentle. The Queen seemed not to notice, or at any rate, take any offense, and so Alice sat down on the couch and waited. When the chair swiveled around, Alice's curiosity was in overdrive and she was leaning so far forward that she was on the verge of falling off the couch. Then she got her first glimpse of the Queen, and to say that she was let down would be quite the understatement of the century.

The Queen of the Biters looked like a friendly librarian at the local library, complete with her grey hair tied in a neat bun, and dark tinted glasses perched on the edge of her nose, framing an aging, tired, but kind face. Of course, Alice had never been to a library, and had never seen a librarian, but the figure she saw in front of her was the farthest thing possible from the fearsome Biter leader she had half-expected to see. As the Queen got up, Alice saw that she was most certainly not a Biter, with her face unblemished, and that she was evidently Indian, for she wore a saree that hung loosely around her thin frame.

'Are you the Queen?'

The old lady smiled, as she came closer to Alice.

'My name was Protima, though nobody has called me by that name in a very long time. In our world, I guess I am considered the Queen, though what I rule over is something I myself am not very sure of. Now, young lady, let me take a look at you and see if what has got these fellows so excited has any basis in fact or not.'

When the Queen came closer and took off her glasses, Alice gasped and shrank back.

The Queen's face may have looked as unblemished as that of any healthy human, but her eyes were red, dilated and lifeless, the eyes of the undead. When she grinned, Alice saw crusted blood on her lips and around the corners of her mouth. Alice began to scream, but a gloved hand was clamped over her mouth.

'Shh, dear. There's nothing to be so terrified of. Yet.'

With that, the Queen grabbed a lock of Alice's hair and pulled on it hard enough to make Alice grimace.

'Well, it is real blond hair. When these fools came in

blabbering about a blond haired Alice, I was sure they had got it wrong. Who would have expected a young blond girl in the middle of what was once Delhi?'

Alice was sitting frozen in place. Somehow, the combination of her unblemished face and her ability to speak so articulately made the Queen even more fearsome than the most outwardly bloodthirsty and fearsome Biters Alice had ever encountered. Finally, she mustered up the courage to speak.

'Are you one of...'

She never got a chance to complete her question as the Queen snapped back.

'One of the undead? One of the Biters? What other hateful label were you planning to use? That's always been the problem with humans. You take anything you fear and cannot understand and make it an object of hate. So much easier to hate and destroy than to seek to understand.'

Actually, Alice had been about to just say 'them', but she was too scared to interrupt the Queen's rant, so she just sat in silence and waited for what was to come next. The Queen sat down next to Alice and took off her gloves. Alice saw that underneath the gloves were not the hands of a healthy human, but yellowed, decayed and blood crusted hands crisscrossed with open wounds and bite marks. When the Queen laid a cold, hard hand on Alice's wrist, she involuntarily flinched, but the viselike grip on her wrist prevented her from moving. In a brief moment of panic, Alice contemplated striking out, but a low growl behind her warned her that Bunny Ears was right there, watching her every move.

'Dear, you must be wondering what all the fuss is about, right?'

Alice noticed that the Queen's face was twitching and while her lifeless eyes betrayed no emotion, she seemed excited, like a little girl at a toy shop.

'It is the prophecy I had made. It is finally coming true, and that means that our days of suffering will come to an end.'

Alice had no idea what the Queen was talking about, so she just waited for her to continue.

'Don't you see? You must be the one the book told me about.'

'What book?'

The Queen got up, and Alice saw that she was virtually hopping in excitement. At that point, Alice realized that human or undead, one thing was for sure: the Queen was totally unhinged. The Queen walked back to her desk and fished in the drawers for a few seconds before bringing out something covered in a coarse cloth. As soon as she raised the package in her hands, Alice saw that Bunny Ears had gone down on his knees. Several thoughts were buzzing through her mind. Since when did mindless Biters get religious? How the hell was this so-called Queen partly human and partly Biter? How was it at all possible that she of all people had anything to do with any prophecy this crazed old Queen claimed to have made?

The Queen was now in front of Alice and holding the package in front of her.

'Do you realize what this is?'

Of course Alice had no way of knowing, but she was young enough to not know a rhetorical question, so she shook her head. Any response on her part was largely unnecessary because the Queen was in a trance like state, talking without a pause.

'When the mad human governments rained fire, I hid in the underground chambers that they had made as bomb shelters and old sewers, moving from one tunnel to another. Do you know how long I was down there?'

Another rhetorical question, and then the Queen continued.

'I kept my phone running as long as I could, turning it on for a few seconds every day to see the time and date. When I lost it, it had been three months. I had been bitten seven times.'

The Queen put the package on the sofa next to Alice and raised her sleeves, showing a bloody, mangled mess on her hands. Alice wondered again how this woman had retained some human faculties despite so obviously having been bitten by Biters. Also, she shuddered to think just how horrible it must have been to wander alone in the dark tunnels, surrounded by crazed Biters in utter darkness, with no easy access to food or water. Anybody would have lost their mind in such circumstances. The Queen continued.

'I would have given up and killed myself if I had been just a human, but as you can see, I was becoming something more. I did not have much to eat, so I scrounged around for herbs and leaves. And one day, I found this.'

She motioned to the package.

'At the time, I didn't know what to make of it, but when I came back to the surface and saw what the world had been reduced to, I realized it was perhaps the last book left in the Deadland.'

The Queen took a break and went back to her desk, bringing out a bunch of green leaves that she proceeded to chew raw. Alice could hear Bunny Ears growling in anticipation and the Queen threw him a couple of leaves that he gobbled down. Alice recognized the leaves as ganja leaves and remembered the warnings from the adults about never eating them. If this woman, or Biter, or whatever the Queen was, had been living on ganja leaves for months, no wonder her mind was a bit messed up with all the hallucinations it must have caused. That feeling was cemented in her mind when the Queen took out what was in the package and held it before Alice.

'Behold the prophecy I was given by the last book left in the Deadland. A vision of you coming to lead us to victory.'

Alice saw what the Queen was holding and saw a slightly charred book cover. It showed a blonde girl jumping into a hole after a rabbit, and Alice suddenly realized that it must have inspired the drawing she had seen and also explained why they had been so excited to see her. She could not immediately make out all the words, but saw her name on top. The Queen seemed a bit disappointed at the lack of recognition from Alice, but then she did not know that Alice had not read a single book in her life, and did not recognize the title on the cover.

Alice in Wonderland.

There must have been hundreds, if not more, Biters crowding the large underground hall in front of the Queen, all down on their knees. They kept up a constant crescendo of howling and screeching that made Alice want to put her hands over her ears. But her hands were pinned behind her by Bunny Ears and the Queen was now addressing her troops.

'Look at her! The prophecy is true! She will lead us to victory and we will throw off the oppression and savagery of those evil humans forever. They did not want to coexist with us but now we will have a chance to make them understand, to accept us, and let us survive side by side with men. Otherwise, we will wage our final war for survival and make them understand that we can and will become the dominant species on this planet.'

The Biters seemed incapable of speaking in any human tongue but they seemed to understand the Queen just fine, and soon they had worked themselves into a frenzy. The more Alice saw them, the more they resembled wild animals, and the Queen ended her exhortation by asking them to prepare for their missions that night.

Alice was herded back to the small room that was effectively her cell. She had no idea of how the Queen expected her to lead her forces to victory. What could one young girl contribute? Moreover, Alice had no intention whatsoever of playing out whatever role the Queen had imagined for her in her delusional prophecy. She was just biding her time, waiting for when she could escape, and so for now she decided that playing along with the Queen was her best strategy. Her chance came sooner than she had expected when later that evening the Queen sent for her.

'Alice, they look to me to be their leader, but I was an old woman even before I transformed, and while I had my skills, being able to fight and lead in battle was not one of them. You are the one who must take on my mantle and continue our struggle.'

Alice could take it no longer and blurted out, 'What struggle? Why don't you just leave humans alone? What harm have we done to you that you lead these creatures to attack us?'

The Queen sat down, and while a smile played at the edges of her lips, her eyes were as lifeless as ever.

'I don't blame you for believing what you do. You've grown up hearing only one side of the story, and from my old life I know just how good the powers that be are at propaganda.'

She saw the skeptical look on Alice's face and continued.

'I won't try and convince you because my words would be of no value to you. So I will let you see through your own eyes.'

She nodded and Bunny Ears grabbed Alice by her arm and led her out. She was dragged more than led up a series of winding tunnels and then suddenly she found herself outside again. It was getting dark outside and she was in a thickly wooded area. She saw a broken sign and she recognized the symbols from some of her training when they had been familiarized with the surrounding landscape. They were near the Yamuna River – or rather what used to be the river, but now was a dried up trickle after the nuclear firestorms and subsequent battles had destroyed the dams and reservoirs feeding it. She sensed movement around her and she saw that there were at least a dozen more Biters hiding among the trees.

After more than an hour of waiting, she turned to Bunny Ears, asking him what it was he had brought her here to see, but he merely grunted in reply, as if telling her to shut up and wait. Then as she watched, something strange happened. She saw a large group of Biters emerge from the trees, perhaps a hundred or more of them. They were all walking in single file, which was totally contrary to the image Alice had grown up with of them being savage, mindless brutes incapable of any act of co-ordination or reason. But what totally took her breath away was the fact that the Biters were not just a random group out to inflict violence, but seemed to be a social grouping of some sort. There were a handful of women, many of them carrying small children. The children themselves looked like something out of a nightmare, with their yellowed skin and many cuts and bruises on their blood covered bodies, but all the same, they were children. Alice had no idea if these were families formed and born after the adults had been transformed to Biters or if these were families that had retained some of their old bonds even after they ceased to be human. Either way, yet again irrevocable proof was in front of her eyes that there was much more to the Biters than she had been brought up to believe.

As the column came closer, Alice got a better look at them. With their bowed backs and trundling along slowly in single file, they looked more like a group of refugees than a band of marauding monsters. She heard Bunny Ears screech behind her, and two Biters in the group ahead responded in kind. What was the Queen trying to show her by sending her here? True, there seemed to be much more to the Biters than what she had grown up believing, but so far she had seen nothing that would change her mind about joining the Queen or fulfilling some deranged prophecy of hers. No, if there was one thing Alice was sure of, it was the fact that she would find the earliest possible opportunity to escape.

Just then, the convoy in front of her stopped in its tracks, many of the adults looking up at the skies. Several of children began howling, their inhuman cries making Alice's hair stand up on end. She didn't know what had suddenly brought about the change in their behavior, but within a few seconds the group transformed from an orderly convoy to a totally panic-stricken mob. The Biters were now screaming and running in such a panic that she saw more than one run into trees and fall down. Bunny Ears had now emerged and was howling, an ear-splitting noise that was taken up by the others who had been hiding in the trees with him. It almost looked like he and the others had been sent by the Queen to shepherd the group to safety through the woods, but now there was no more semblance of order. The Biters were running around, screaming like wild animals that have caught a scent of hunters, and one of them, a woman with a bloodied and mangled child in her arms, came within a few feet of Alice. She glared at Alice with hate-filled eyes, and baring bloodied teeth, seemed ready to pounce when Bunny Ears knocked her off her feet with a blow to the back of her head.

Alice still didn't know what had caused such bedlam when she heard a familiar sound. The whirring rotors of approaching helicopters. She looked up to see several black helicopters approach the clearing. Zeus had arrived.

The female Biter who had been knocked over by Bunny Ears was getting up unsteadily on one knee when her head exploded in a spray of blood. Alice screamed and dove for cover behind a tree as more snipers aboard the oncoming helicopters opened fire. She watch three more Biters caught in the open fall, their heads split open by high-powered sniper rifles, before the others scattered among the trees. The child the Biter had been carrying was now feet away from Alice, and looking at its hideous form, with its mangled face and bloody skin, it was hard to feel any emotion the way one felt towards human children. Alice was about to crawl away under the bushes nearby and try and escape, but something held her back. She looked back at the child again, and this time his eyes met hers. There was no innocence, no love: just the blank, hate-filled expression that was characteristic of Biters, and while he could not even walk, he began to crawl towards her, baring a handful of half-formed teeth. The rational part of Alice's mind told her to run, but she was transfixed at the sight of this little child who would no doubt bite Alice and transform her into a Biter like him given half a chance, yet who was little more than a child. A helpless child.

Just then, a huge Biter easily standing more than six and a half feet tall ran over in front of her. He was wearing a floppy hat and much of the left side of his face was missing. He picked up the child and ran towards the nearby trees as Alice heard a fresh burst of firing. This time it was not the distinctive pops of sniper rifles, but the staccato bursts of automatic weapon fire. That could mean only one thing: Zeus troopers were now on the ground.

Alice looked to her left and saw something was which no less than a miracle: her backpack, which Bunny Ears must have dropped there in the chaos. She remembered the signal flare that had been there and crawled towards the backpack, grabbing it before she again retreated behind cover. She unzipped it and breathed a sigh of relief as she saw the signal flare was still there. She looked around and saw that Bunny Ears was nowhere to be seen. Now was her chance. She popped the flare and soon a red light shot up in the sky. She watched it sail above the treeline and hoped that it would get the attention of the Zeus troopers and someone would come to get her.

She did succeed in attracting attention all right, but of entirely the unwanted variety when she saw two Biters homing in on her. They were screaming and coming at her with their teeth bared. Alice realized with a shudder that one of them must have claimed a victim in the fighting now going on all around her since his mouth was covered with fresh blood that was dripping onto his muddy and torn shirt. There was no time and no place to run, so Alice got ready to face her attackers. The first to reach her was the man with the bloody face, a thin man who was missing his left arm below the elbow and seemed to have half his hair burnt off. As he screamed and leapt towards Alice, she went down on a knee, sweeping him off his feet. She had no weapons with her, but she brought her foot down on the Biter's windpipe in a crushing kick. It would have killed a grown man, but the Biter screamed and began to get up again. The second Biter, a tall man wearing a blood stained vest and shorts, was now almost upon her. Alice ran towards him, dodging his outstretched arms, and then turned around on her heels to kick his foot from under him behind his knee. It shattered his leg, but as Alice well knew, that would hardly be enough to stop a Biter on the rampage. He got up unsteadily on one leg, as Alice tried to run only to come straight in the path of the first Biter, whose neck now hung at an awkward angle, but his mouth was open and he lunged at her.

Alice closed her eyes, bracing herself for the attack that never came. She heard a loud pop and when she opened her eyes she saw the Biter's headless body lying just a couple of feet from her. The second Biter, now limping towards her, met a similar fate as another round slammed into his head.

She looked into the trees ahead and saw a black clad man kneeling, a rifle at his shoulder. He wore the black battle dress of the Zeus troopers, but unlike the others she had seen, he had no helmet to cover his close-cropped black hair, which was covered with flecks of grey. He saw her and grinned and began to run towards her.

Alice took a step towards him, her heart racing in anticipation of her coming rescue, when three Biters jumped out of the trees and in the path of the Zeus trooper who was less than a hundred meters from her. He shot one in the head at point blank range before another Biter knocked the rifle out of his hand. Alice had been trained to fight since she was a child, but she had never seen anyone fight like the Zeus trooper in front of her. Unfazed by the loss of his gun, he unsheathed a large knife at his belt and jumped up, bringing it down into the skull of the nearest Biter, who screamed and went down, not to get down again. The third Biter was now almost upon him, and he rolled out of the way, taking out his handgun, and put three shots into the Biter's head.

Two more Zeus troopers now appeared, and judging by their salutes and the deference they showed the grey haired man, it seemed that he was an officer of some sort. He pointed to her and the two of them began to jog towards her. That was when the large Biter with the hat came crashing out of the trees. He grabbed the nearest trooper and snapped his neck, the sickening crunching sound carrying to Alice. The second trooper tried to bring his rifle to bear, but the Biter bit him on the neck, and he went down spurting blood. Alice knew what would come next. The trooper spasmed and went rigid, and when he got up again, Alice saw that his eyes were the vacant, lifeless eyes of the undead. His head exploded as the grey haired officer fired, preferring to kill his own man versus having him turn into one of the undead, as the Biter with the hat reared up to his full height and screamed. More than a dozen Biters now emerged into the clearing and the Zeus officer retreated into the trees, looking at Alice once. As their eyes met, he cocked his arm back and threw something at her before he disappeared into the trees, pursued by the Biters.

The object he had thrown landed a couple of feet away from Alice, and she ran to pick up what he had thrown just as Bunny Ears reappeared with three other Biters. He grabbed her arm to pull her away but before he yanked her off, she looked at the small blinking object in her hand. It was a radio beacon that would give away her position as long as she carried it. There was to be no escape today, but as she slipped the beacon into her pockets, she felt a new surge of hope.

Help would be on the way soon.

'So, what did you learn from your trip?'

The question had been asked as if the Queen were enquiring about a field trip to a museum instead of her having just been in the middle of a life and death struggle, so Alice wasn't quite sure what the Queen had in mind. That became clear when the giant Biter with the hat appeared and uttered a series of guttural growls.

'Hatter here tells me that you caused a fair bit of inconvenience, but if anything is to be learnt from today's experience, do learn that we are not fools. We did not send you out to offer you an easy and convenient escape route.'

'So why did you send me out there? I've seen enough battles and there's nothing I saw that I haven't seen before.'

The Queen turned on Alice with a fury, baring her teeth, and for a second Alice was truly fearful that she would attack her. But then the Queen seemed to control herself with a conscious effort of will, and answered in a soft voice, 'You just used your usual prejudices to filter out what you didn't want to see. I wanted you to see us as we are: a society, a group of sentient beings. Different from humans, but no less deserving of the right to exist. Not animals to be hunted down and exterminated.'

That did ring a bell with Alice. True, she had never imagined that Biters could be organized in some sort of social unit, and certainly had never bargained for the fact that she would see babies and what appeared to be their parents together. Still, that did not change the fundamental equation. The anger at all the cruelty she had seen Biters visit upon humans in her life came back to her as she answered the Queen with a bitter tinge in her voice.

'I have seen enough innocent humans slaughtered by

Biters. I have seen babies bitten by Biters. I have seen good, decent people turn into bloodthirsty Biters after being bitten. So it's not as if your precious Biters are innocent, helpless victims.'

The Queen hissed, though Alice sensed more regret than rage in her reaction.

'I had hoped you would begin to change your mind and embrace your destiny, but it looks like your mind is still too closed. Oh well, I hope you can reflect on it over the next few days.'

With that, the giant Biter referred to as Hatter gripped her arm and pushed her roughly out of the room. She was led to a small, dark room and the door slammed shut once she went in. Alice huddled alone in a corner of the cold, dark room, and took out the beacon from her pocket. She watched the small blinking red light till exhaustion overtook her and she fell into an uneasy slumber. She dreamt of a Biter baby having its head shot off, and she woke up covered in sweat. There was no more sleep to be had that night.

FOUR

I F THE QUEEN'S INTENT HAD been to torture Alice into submission, Alice thought she was doing a pretty good job of it. For the next two days, she got nothing to eat or drink other than a single glass of dirty water that was shoved into her room once a day. The room was totally dark all the time and Alice soon lost track of time. She screamed her rage out for the first few hours but then just sat in silence against the wall. She may have been trained as a warrior from an early age, but nobody had ever trained her on what to do if she were captured. It had never occurred to anyone that someone could be taken prisoner by the Biters.

Finally, hungry, thirsty and disoriented, she was on the verge of asking for the Queen and agreeing to whatever crazy prophecy she seemed to believe in. Anything to get out of the room. Anything to get a bite to eat or a drink of clean water. That was when Bunny Ears opened the door and pulled her out, leading her to the Queen's room. Alice found the Queen sitting at her desk, chewing ganja leaves and holding the charred book that seemed so important to her. When Alice entered the room, she called out loudly for food, and Hatter came in, holding a hunk of nearly stale bread. As disgusting as it looked, it was the first food Alice had seen in almost three days, and she hungrily wolfed it down.

The Queen waited for her to finish and then sat down in front of Alice, the book on her lap.

'Alice, I was wrong. In my anger, I thought that frightening and intimidating you would bring you to my side, but if you are to fulfill the prophecy, it cannot be through fear. It has to be because you believe in our cause.'

Alice, bitter and angry after what she had endured over the last two days, blurted out, 'Yeah, and locking me in a dark room and starving me will make me believe in your prophecy. Or will it be the bloody ganja leaves you gulp down?'

Alice saw the muscles on the Queen's face tighten, and once again she saw a glimpse of the rage she was capable of, but she controlled herself as she responded to Alice.

'No. You remember the old quote about the truth setting us free.'

Alice had never heard the quote, but listened as the Queen continued.

'Tell me, what do you know about what you humans call The Rising?'

Growing up, Alice had heard the story many times from her parents, and then it had been amplified and embellished by countless conversations with other kids, so the answer to her was obvious.

'Everyone knows about it. One day, something happened, and the dead started coming to life. Before anyone could do anything, they started attacking others, and those bitten turned into...Biters, I guess. They couldn't be killed other than through a shot through the head, and they soon overran most cities. Then the governments got desperate and bombed the cities after evacuating as many people as possible....'

She couldn't finish because the Queen had got up and screamed, an inhuman howl that shocked Alice so much that she got up from her chair, which clattered to the ground behind her. The Queen was now speaking fast and with such anger that spittle was flying from her mouth.

'It did not just happen. We made it happen.'

Alice wasn't sure what she was referring to and asked what she meant.

'Us. Human governments, or at least some elements in our governments. The US government had been experimenting with chemical and biological agents that would transform our troops into super-soldiers, into berserkers immune to pain. At the same time, there was research on modifying these to create agents that would drive enemy troops insane, a rage virus which would transform them into wild animals who would kill each other. We experimented with rats, with monkeys and...with humans.'

Alice found that hard to believe and gasped aloud.

'No, dear. We did all that. In secret facilities in Afghanistan and other places. We were drunk with our power, imagining what would happen if we could drop one single canister of this agent in the middle of an enemy army division. It would tear itself to pieces without us firing a shot. Then it all came apart.'

'What happened?'

'The Chinese found out what we were up to, and they knew that if we perfected this, we would be invincible. They infiltrated our program, and destroyed our key research lab in the US. We couldn't prove anything; it looked like an explosion caused by a gas cylinder, but we knew who was behind it. The American economy was in deep recession, China was on the ascendant, and this was our last hope in keeping them in check. We had extra stores of the agent the Chinese did not know about, and we decided to teach them a lesson, to show them that we were still the superpower. A covert mission was authorized and we dropped the agent into a village in Mongolia. It was the first time it had been used on humans outside controlled conditions, and nobody knew what to expect. I had pleaded against the decision, so many of us had, but we were overruled. Thousands fell, then tens of thousands as it spread.'

Alice knew only vaguely of the politics between countries of the Old Days, since national boundaries and the old countries now hardly mattered, but she found it hard to believe that people could have done this to themselves.

'What happened then? If you were in America then how did it spread there?'

The Queen sat down again.

'Hundreds of people were injured in the blast at the lab and were exposed to all the toxins and agents we were working on. The next day, they started transforming and biting all those around them.'

A chill went up Alice's spine, yet her mind refused to believe what she was hearing.

'Why should I believe you?'

The Queen went to her desk and fished out an identification card and some papers. Alice struggled to read what was on them, but the emblem of what she knew to be the United States Government was there.

'I was one of the head researchers on this project. I was born here in India but did my Doctorate in the US and joined the Department of Defense. I thought it was exciting, to be able to come up with new ways of treating our wounded, to make the world safer. But then we all got a bit drunk with our own power, and we started meddling with things we should have left alone. We tried to play God, and we were not ready for what we unleashed. When the decision to attack China was made, I quit and came back to India, but by then, nowhere was safe any more. At first, after being bitten, people changed after a few hours, so you had many cases of people being attacked in airport terminals and boarding their flights after what they thought were minor cuts. In days, all air travel was banned, but when you have tens of millions traveling by air every day, it spread like wildfire.'

Alice still refused to believe what she was hearing, so it was only harder for her to believe what came next.

'And the Great Fires, that too was of our making, of our petty jockeying for power. It began with the US and China using tactical nukes on each other. It had nothing to do with making the world secure from the so-called Biters. It was man destroying the world when it looked like all that mattered to us then – power, money, oil – were now going to be worthless. It was as if all the old rules and taboos were broken. Then Pakistan joined the party, and India retaliated. Iran and Israel nuked it out. Between the attacks and the spreading of the virus, the world became what it is, and nobody bothered to do the one thing that could have stopped it all.'

'And what was that?'

The Queen looked straight at Alice.

'We had a vaccine, Alice. We could have cured them all if we had chosen to co-operate and not turn on each other.'

Alice barely slept that night, despite being placed in a much more comfortable room with a mattress and a table with clean water on it. She didn't want to believe the Queen: she didn't want to believe that humans could have been so savage. All her life, the Biters had been the boogeymen, the monsters of our nightmares that had emerged from the dead to turn on humans. Her mind found it impossible to process the possibility that humans had been responsible for starting it all.

Unable to contain her curiosity, she went back to the Queen's chambers and found her sitting on her chair, reading the charred book that she held so dear. Did Biters never sleep? She looked up as Alice walked in.

'So, Alice, as the story in this fine book goes, have you become curiouser and curiouser?'

Alice had no idea what she was talking about so she got to the point.

'You have no proof for anything you've said. Maybe you did work in the Government, but everything else could be a story. I don't know why you think I have anything to do with this, or why your finding that book makes it a prophecy, but there's no reason for me to believe you.'

The Queen got up and went to her desk and brought out a small vial with a red cap that had a syringe in it. She held out the vial in front of Alice.

'Here is the vaccine. The last and only dose I know of. When the outbreak started, one of my colleagues in the US sent me a couple of vaccines. The Government had limited stocks and was starting to vaccinate key leaders, so it was a really big deal for her to try and save me.'

'If there is a vaccine, why didn't they save others?'

The Queen stopped, looking at the vial.

'Good question. Many of us believed that they did not want to.'

'Why would they do that?'

'There were always rumors – but nothing more than rumors – about how some powerful groups were actively manipulating events to create a New World Order. They believed the world was getting overpopulated and wanted to start over, with a select group of elites in charge. Powerful people, in Government, in the Military, in banks, engineering all this behind the scenes. The times before The Rising were one of chaos: many economies were in deep decline, and common people were starting to rise against the elite who seemed to get richer even as common folks lost their jobs and got poorer. The rumors said that these elites were seeing their grasp on power slip away and so they had a long-term plan to wipe out much of the population and start afresh. That's where people like Zeus come in. They could not rely on the Military to do all their dirty work, and that's why in the last few years before The Rising, Private Military Contractors were getting so prominent and powerful.'

For Alice, this was all too incredible to believe. Secret private armies, human elites trying to re-engineer the world and so on. What she had grown up knowing was so much simpler, and it was tempting to believe the simpler version than even consider such a possibility.

'If that was their plan, they succeeded, right?'

The Queen looked and Alice saw the hint of a smile on the corners of her lips.

'We came in the way. They had never bargained for just how...contagious this turned out to be, or indeed the fact that so many of us survived by going underground into sewers and bomb shelters. They thought we would be mindless animals who would wander around and get nuked, but I led so many of us underground and then we emerged.'

Alice now asked the question that had been on her mind from the beginning. 'Excuse me, but what happened to you?'

'As things unraveled, and I found out more about the possible conspiracy behind all this, I got very disillusioned and angry and started reaching out to people. One of my sources told me that there were elites in the Unites States who were colluding with elements in the Chinese government to orchestrate all this. They tried to kill me twice with the Zeus thugs and I went into hiding. But when the chaos took Delhi, I was attacked and bitten. I had two doses of the vaccine on me, and I injected myself seconds after being bitten. I was unconscious for several hours and I woke up the way I am. I don't understand it entirely but perhaps the combination of being bitten and than taking the vaccine within seconds left me this way. Many aspects of me were transformed, but I could still think like a human, and I was furious at what we had done to ourselves, and what we had allowed to happen.'

'What about the other Bit—'

'I saw them for who they really are. Yes, they are very unlike the people they were as humans. What the virus does, especially as it mutates over time, is activate the most primitive parts of the brain – so you get no sensation of pain, hyper aggressiveness, and an almost reflexive desire to reproduce. In this case, bite others to increase their numbers.'

Alice refused to think of the Biters as just innocent victims.

'Wait a minute, I have seen so many innocent settlements and groups massacred by the Biters. They aren't just scared innocent animals.'

The Queen sighed, a gesture that made her suddenly seem much more human.

'We are all animals. We all experience fear, and when scared, we lash out. That's what you and the other human survivors have been doing. I can't make them understand everything I know since their brains have regressed a lot, but they are in awe of me because I am like them yet I can speak and can think more rationally. I helped save thousands of them by bringing them into these underground shelters.'

'What about this prophecy of yours?'

The Queen now had the book in her hands again.

'Oh, that is very real. I found the book when I had lost all hope, and in that fevered dream, I saw you. I saw us finally reclaiming the world from the evil men who made this happen. I saw us and humans stop fighting each other.'

'It was just a dream.'

'Every prophecy is a dream, but if we believe in something, we can make it happen. The powers behind this conspiracy have a vested interest in keeping this war alive. Have you considered how they keep those helicopters flying? How do they get those weapons, and why do they focus so much on bringing more and more human settlements under their control using the fear of Biters as an excuse? We fight it out in these barren wastelands while the elites behind all of this are perhaps living in luxury somewhere, in their own settlements from which they rule over us, with all the wealth and resources of the world at their disposal. You've seen only the Zeus troopers since they patrol the Deadland, but I know they are commanded by Red Guards, Chinese shock troops. I have seen them myself near Zeus bases beyond the Deadland. How is it the Chinese still seem to have such an organized force?'

Suddenly a beeping noise came from Alice's pockets and she froze in fear. She had forgotten all about the beacon. The Queen reached out and took out the small sphere from Alice's pocket and recoiled as she saw the logo on the side.

'What have you done?'

Then Alice started hearing the dull thud of explosions overhead.

Alice used the distraction of the explosions to bolt from the room, narrowly evading Bunny Ears' outstretched arms. The Queen was screaming now, all human speech and civility replaced by the wild screeching of Biters. Alice heard footsteps behind her, and given the rage the Queen had flown into, Alice thought it more prudent to get to safety instead of trying to reason with her. The sound of explosions was now closer and Alice ran into a corridor that seemed to lead towards the explosions. Overwhelmed by panic and the hope that she might get back to her parents, Alice put aside all that the Queen had said and focused on finding whoever had come to rescue her.

She came across a group of four Biters huddled in a corner and realized just how foolhardy she had been in running out alone. Without the Queen or Bunny Ears to save her, and with the attack on the base unfolding outside, the Biters would tear her to shreds. The four of them took one look at Alice and stood, moving towards her with their teeth bared. In such a confined space, the only silver lining was that they would have to come for her one by one, and she used that to her advantage. As the first Biter, a fat woman with her scalp half shorn off, came within reach, Alice kicked her in the chest, putting all her body weight behind the kick. The kick sent the Biter stumbling back and into the path of the one behind her, and the two of them stumbled down in an ungainly heap. However, Alice had lost her footing and was now on the floor. She knew she was now in severe danger. There was no way she could fight off all four Biters in such a confined space, and with Bunny Ears and others likely chasing her, there was no question of her going back the way she had come.

As the first Biter reached for Alice, his head exploded and he fell to the side. The other Biters turned to face this new threat and within seconds, all three were down, with their heads split open by precisely aimed shots. Alice looked down the passageway to see three black-clad soldiers. She recognized one of them as the grey-haired officer she had seen in the forest. He waved at her with his assault rifle.

'Come over here!'

As she ran towards them, she heard howling behind her. The officer shouted to his two men, 'Set up Claymores here and let's withdraw.'

Both troopers set the anti-personnel mines and then joined Alice and the officer who were already racing up the tunnel. Alice saw some movement to her right and dove to the ground just as a Biter hiding in an opening jumped at them. The trooper behind her was not so lucky as the big Biter grabbed him and bit his throat. The trooper's screams soon gave way to gurgling pleas for help as he fell to the ground, bleeding from his throat and face. The grey-haired officer with her kicked the Biter off his comrade and then shot him in the head twice. He then paused and looked at the fallen soldier, and Alice saw him close his eyes as he shot him in the head.

They then continued running up the tunnel. Alice could now see the light ahead from the tunnel's opening as they heard the Claymore mines explode behind them. As they got closer to the opening, she saw more than a dozen Zeus troopers, each carrying an assault rifle and standing at attention. The officer shouted to them.

'Hold them while I call in the air strike! The Red Guard jet should be on patrol now.'

Alice stumbled out, slipping and falling on the grass outside, which was slick with the dew that came with Delhi winter nights, as the troopers took position and began firing into the tunnel. The officer pulled her to one side and asked her to wait while he reached into a backpack lying nearby for a handheld radio.

'Apache One requests immediate air strike at last reported co-ordinates. We'll be clear in five.'

With that, he ordered his men to plant a few more mines at the entrance and then get as far away from the tunnel as possible. It seemed like an eternity since Alice had been standing in front of the Queen, but in reality it had all taken less than five minutes. Alice was still in a bit of shock, and followed meekly when the officer pulled her along. It was now nearly Sunset and the sky was beginning to darken as they jogged to a nearby hill and then the officer pushed her down, telling her to lie flat. She saw the other troopers take up position next to them. She now had a clear look at the tunnel, from which Biters were flowing out. The troopers all had their rifles at their shoulders and were firing away. Many of the Biters were hit by bursts of full automatic fire and twisted and turned before falling. Alice knew only a head shot would take them out permanently, but the damage the bullets did would make sure many of them never walked, as she saw legs torn off by the land mines and withering fire. She had accurately read the officer's mind as he bellowed to his men.

'Don't bother with head shots. Take their legs off so they can't move away from the target zone in time.'

Suddenly Alice saw the entire tunnel disappear behind a giant cloud of smoke, and a split second later she heard the deafening boom of the explosion. The shock wave almost lifted her off the ground and as she looked again, she saw that the tunnel had largely caved in and there was a gaping hole in the ground, exposing the warren of tunnels underneath. There were dozens of Biters littered around, their bodies burning in the wreckage.

The officer spoke calmly into his radio. 'One more pass. Aim for the opening.'

Alice heard the roar of an aircraft flying overhead and looked up to see a dark shape silhouetted against the setting sun. It turned towards them and dove down, and Alice saw a small cylinder detach itself from the aircraft and track down towards the tunnel. It entered the hole opened by the previous explosion, and once again there was a thunderous explosion as the bomb struck home. Alice had never witnessed such an awesome demonstration of firepower and she was in total awe of what Zeus seemed to be capable of when the officer told her to keep going.

'Some of the critters must have got out and will be around among the trees. So we can't afford to wait.'

They ran through the forest, and Alice was soon setting the pace that the Zeus troopers were trying hard to match up to. When the officer yelled for her to stop in a clearing, she saw that he was panting a bit when he caught up with her.

'You sure are fast. Wait here while I radio in to confirm where our pickup zone is.'

The troopers set up a perimeter as the officer radioed in. It was now nearly pitch black and Alice was beginning to get worried. It was one thing to bomb the Biters from thousands of feet in the air as the Zeus forces or these so-called Red Guards had done, but it was quite another to contend with them on the ground in the dark. Alice had grown up in an environment where knowing how to best survive exactly in such circumstances was the difference between life and death every single day. As she scanned the Zeus troopers around her in the dim light thrown up by their emergency lights, she realized that for all their heavy weaponry and fancy equipment, they looked terrified. Only the officer seemed a bit composed, and as he finished asking for the helicopters to zero in on their lights, he smiled at her.

'I never introduced myself. My name is Colonel Dewan

and I am in charge of the North Indian operations for Zeus.'

'Hi. I'm Alice Gladwell.'

Dewan smiled as he packed his radio.

'Alice, everyone knows who you are by now. The only human to be a captive of the Biters and live to tell the tale.'

Alice felt more than heard something and whispered to the colonel, 'Should your men have those lights on?'

He replied, even as he was putting a scope on his rifle, 'All of them have night vision scopes like these on their rifles. We are quite safe here.'

Alice was not so sure. Having lived and fought in the woods since she was a child, she knew that in the darkness, victory went not to those with the most firepower but those who knew how to use the darkness to their advantage. The troopers, including the colonel, seemed to believe, as she had done just days ago, that the Biters would just mindlessly walk in to be slaughtered. But after what she had seen, she wondered if they even knew what they were up against.

Something rustled in the dark to her right and a trooper opened fire. Dewan screamed.

'Cease fire till you have a confirmed target!'

Another trooper screamed as a huge shadow leaped out and grabbed him. Alice noticed the floppy hat in the dim light as the trooper screamed while being dragged away into the trees. The other troopers were now firing wildly, and Alice saw that Dewan was now screaming on his radio for the helicopters to come in. More shadows emerged from the trees and two more troopers fell within seconds. Dewan had picked up the light and shone it to his right, revealing a blood-stained trooper who had now crossed over to the Biters and was walking towards him with his teeth bared. Dewan calmly raised his pistol and put two rounds in the man's head as he asked Alice to pick up a weapon to defend herself.

Alice needed no prompting and had a rifle in her hand and was on her knees, waiting as the Biters emerged from the trees. The remaining troopers were huddled in a tight circle and as the Biters came in sight, Alice selected single round mode and put a bullet into one's head. She then sought out another target and brought him down. Dewan was doing the same, and he had shot three Biters in quick succession.

The troopers took courage from Dewan and Alice and they began firing in a more disciplined way, covering each other, using overlapping fields of fire. As Alice kept squeezing the trigger, she realized this was turning into a slaughter. There were dozens of Biters down now and as others emerged from the trees, it was a matter of seconds before they were cut down.

She heard the sound of helicopters emerging and then the rattle of machine gun fire as one of the helicopter gunships opened fire, scattering the nearest group of Biters, many of them cut to ribbons by the heavy-caliber fire. One helicopter hovered overhead and lowered ropes which the troopers used to climb on board as other helicopters provided covering fire. Alice grabbed the rope when her turn came and then looked into the forest one last time. She thought she caught a glimpse of tall, pointed ears like a rabbit and a frail looking female form next to him. She then heard the Queen scream one last time.

'Alice, remember the truth! Don't believe their lies!'

As she scrambled onto the helicopter, Dewan sat down next to her.

'You're safe now. It's all going to be okay now.'

Alice sat in silence, thinking back to the Queen and everything she had told her.

FIVE

I T WAS THE FIRST TIME Alice had tasted chocolate and she licked the wrapper clean. Food for her had consisted of whatever could be hunted or scavenged. One or two men in their settlement had harbored dreams of growing their own food, but when you're constantly on alert and may have to abandon your position in minutes, you don't really have a lifestyle suited for agriculture. Dewan had walked in and sat down next to Alice. He had showered and changed and was wearing a simple khaki uniform. He seemed to epitomize all the ways in which Zeus was different from the life she had known. He was clean, wearing spotless clothes, and was not constantly looking over his back. He seemed to be about the same age as her father, and he asked Alice if she wanted to shower and change before she met anyone else.

Alice was instantly aware of just how she must have looked in the muddy clothes she had worn for the last few days. At the settlement, her mother had gone on and on about how young ladies should always appear well groomed, but when your big extracurricular activity is sniping at Biters and your favorite toy is a handgun, meeting such archaic standards was impossible. Alice's hair was cropped short (so that nobody could grab it in a close fight, as her instructors had said), and her face was lean with her cheekbones showing prominently. She was thin, but certainly not weak, since she had the wiry frame and strength that came with years of running and combat training every day.

After she changed into some khaki clothes Dewan gave her, she joined him in what appeared to be a cafeteria of some sort. There were long benches and tables which were filled with black-clad Zeus troopers. Most of them were men, though Alice did see several women. They all greeted Dewan with deference and he asked her to sit down and ordered dinner. Alice felt her mouth water as hot soup and chicken were put in front of her and Dewan smiled.

'Dig in and don't worry about formalities. You must be starved.'

After that, she needed no more encouragement as she polished off her food. Dewan told her that he would talk more to her the next morning and showed her the way to her room. As Alice was walking to it, she saw two young Zeus troopers looking at her and whispering among themselves. One of them, a young, pimply Indian boy, worked up the courage to talk to her.

'Are you the one from the Deadland who lived with the Biters?'

Alice looked him straight in the eye and saw him flinch at her response.

'The Deadland?'

'Oh, you know, the settlements outside our centrally administered zones where people are….'

'Free.'

Alice completed the sentence for him. Her father had told her about how Zeus tried to get more and more settlements into their fold, promising protection in return for the supply of young men and women for their army and effective control over their defenses and supplies. The settlements who signed up got security, but effectively became bonded labour, growing food in farms for Zeus and their masters, giving up their right to bear arms unless Zeus allowed them to, and supplying young men and women to serve in factories and mines that those who controlled Zeus ran. Nobody really knew who the real masters behind Zeus were, but the Queen had mentioned Chinese Red Guards, and she had heard her father sometimes grumble about how he would never submit to the Red Guards.

She walked back to her room, and lay down on what was a simple cot, but a luxury compared to what she had just been through, and also compared to the old sleeping bag that was her bed back home. She was fast asleep within seconds of hitting the mattress.

She was awakened by a light tap on the door and she found Dewan standing there, wearing a black uniform.

'Your father is on the way and should be here any time. I thought I'd let you know.'

Alice ran more than walked to the small attached bathroom to shower and change, and then joined Dewan in a small meeting room. There were two more men there with him wearing black uniforms covered in medals and badges. One was white and other Indian. The white man, who was bald and built like a bull, spoke first.

'Good morning, young lady. My name is General John Appleseed and I oversee all the Asian operations for Zeus. I flew in last night when we learnt that your extraordinary ordeal was coming to an end.'

The Indian, wearing the traditional Sikh turban, spoke next. 'I am Major Balbir Singh. I am in charge of the Indian subcontinent.'

Alice never thought she would get intimidated by any

man, but the way these men spoke and the way Dewan showed deference to them told her just how big and organized Zeus was. That feeling was intensified when her father walked in. He was tall, wiry and wore faded jeans and a crumpled shirt. At first sight one might have assumed that he would be awed by the men in front of him, but he gathered his sobbing daughter in his arms and looked them straight in the eye as he thanked them.

As he began to leave with her, General Appleseed spoke up softly.

'Chief of Mission Gladwell. It is a pleasure to see you after all we have heard of you. It is a pity that you choose not to join your old comrades again.'

Alice felt her father stiffen as he turned to talk to the General. There was a cold bite to his voice, very different from the gentle, loving father she had known.

'General, I served the United States of America and what she stood for: freedom, liberty and equality. That nation is dead, but the spirit lives on in all of us who refuse to bow to the new dictatorship of big business and hired guns and the Chinese tyrants who pay you.'

The General's eyes hardened but his voice remained soft. 'How long can you last out there by yourselves in the Deadland?'

'We've done well so far.'

With those words, he whisked Alice out of the room and walked her out. She wanted to tell him so much about what had happened, but he just hushed her, telling her that they would talk more when they got back. When they stepped out of the building, Alice saw that there was a sprawling air base outside and Dewan ran up behind them.

'Your helicopter is waiting there. Mr. Gladwell, you have an incredibly brave daughter. Good luck to you both.'

Alice's father seemed to size Dewan up for a second and then, seemingly liking what he saw, shook his hand, thanking him again as they walked towards the waiting black helicopter. Alice saw four boys whom she recognized from the settlement standing at a far corner. They looked miserable and scared and one of them glared at Alice as she passed him.

'Dad, what are they doing here?'

'They're here to join Zeus as recruits.'

'But we never...'

Her father stopped her.

'That's the price we paid to get you back. Four young, untrained boys for a trained combat veteran like you. We all agreed it was the best decision when Zeus demanded something in return.'

Alice felt like she had been punched in the stomach and felt sick that four boys would now have to live away from their families, in the murky world of the Zeus army, because of her. As they sat down in the helicopter, she looked at her father. He looked old and tired, as if he had aged years in just the few days she had been gone. He had implied that the leaders had decided on trading her for the boys, but she knew just how much it must have been gnawing at his own conscience. She reached out and took his arm, and he smiled at her. She saw Dewan waving to them as the helicopter took off and she sat back, wondering just what she had got herself into with that one fateful decision of jumping into that hole behind the bunny-eared Biter.

Alice's mother smothered her in hugs when she landed, and her older sister, Jane, ruffled her hair. That was as close as she had ever seen Jane get to a public display of affection. Jane was almost ten years older than Alice, and remembered enough of what the world had been like before The Rising to harbor bitterness at what she had lost. That bitterness had never entirely left, and if anything, it had acquired an even sharper edge with the years of fighting to survive.

For the last one year, they had made an abandoned village their home. The village was located near the crest of a small hill with a great view of all directions, and that made it both easily defensible in case of attack and also offered several escape routes if they had to abandon their settlement.

When Alice walked into the large building that had once been a school but was now the communal dining hall, she could feel many eyes on her. She had been well liked and also respected for her skills, but she saw that something had changed. Many of the men and women she had fought shoulder to shoulder with were averting their gazes. She sat next to Jane, who seemed to be in a foul mood as well.

'What's wrong?'

Jane took a small bite and then answered, 'Everyone's really angry about us giving into Zeus and sending our boys over. They think once Zeus has a foothold they'll be back for more. Some people are saying Dad made the others agree since you were the one involved.'

Alice ate in silence, realizing that whatever she said would not help.

She came back to her room and saw that a fresh set of weapons had been laid out for her. Whether they grumbled or not, everyone at the settlement knew that her skills could be needed at any time. She spent the next few hours cleaning her guns and then lay down to sleep.

She heard a knock at the door. It was her father.

'Alice, tomorrow some folks from Zeus will be here to

take you.'

Alice sat up in a panic, wondering if saving her life had meant sending her to join Zeus as well. Her father saw her expression and sat down next to her.

'No, no. You don't need to worry. I would never let them take you. But they want to question you about what you saw and heard while you were in the Biter base. Nobody's survived so long behind enemy lines and they want to know what you saw. Anything you'd like to tell me before you go with them?'

Alice thought about all that the Queen had said, and even as she began to say something, she realized just how ridiculous it would sound. A Biter Queen who could talk. A supposed conspiracy behind it all led by shadowy powers trying to bring about a New World Order. Biters who were not entirely the bloodthirsty monsters everyone took them for. Whichever way she tried to spin it, she thought it made her sound crazy or delusional. So she just shrugged and lay down to rest and was asleep within seconds.

She was awakened by the sound of helicopter rotors, and when she sat up, she saw her parents standing near her.

'Sweetheart, they're here to get you. They promised us that you'd be back by evening. Just tell them whatever they want to know and you'll be fine.'

Despite his reassuring words, Alice could see the strain in her father's eyes. She knew that he was dealing with a lot of compromises he had been forced to make to get her back: sending the boys to Zeus and dealing with those he had tried hard to avoid all these years. He had often told Alice that unlike before The Rising, when there was at least some form of order due to governments, the chaos and vacuum that had resulted had been filled by greedy, power-hungry men and their private armies. He had spent all these years keeping their settlement free of such men, and now, to protect his daughter, he had been forced to compromise with them. Alice was old enough to realize just how much of a sacrifice her father had made for her and she hugged him tight as she boarded the black helicopter.

The helicopter turned north-east, and flew over forests on the outskirts of what had once been Delhi, but was now simply called the Ruins. On her previous flights she had been too terrified or tired to notice, but now she got her first look from the air at what lay below. It was a depressingly familiar pattern: miles upon miles of wrecked buildings and debris, broken by the occasional small settlement of humans. Without many standing buildings, the sands from the Rajasthan deserts were now freely swirling over the cities nearby, creating a near constant haze.

She then saw a large fortified compound with gun turrets on the walls, followed by the airfield she had seen before. As the helicopter came to a rest, she saw Dewan run up to it. While he was a stranger by any standards, he was the one familiar face and she felt a bit more comfortable having him there. He spoke loudly to be heard over the helicopters and Alice leaned over to hear what he was saying.

'General Appleseed himself is here. From what I gather, what our Intelligence folks most want is tactical intel. So just tell them what happened when you went into the Biter base, what you saw, the numbers of Biters, and so on. Also, any clues as to where hidden entrances could be will be very helpful. That's really all they want, so it should be pretty simple, and then you're on your way home.'

It sounded simple enough and Alice was feeling much more reassured when she stepped into the briefing room. General Appleseed was the only one there and as Dewan saluted, he asked him and Alice to sit down. The big general folded his arms in front of him and smiled, trying to put Alice at ease. With his big neck, huge arms and bald head, it was hard to think of the general as anything other than a raging bull, but Alice smiled back, glad that he was at least trying to be nice.

'Ms. Gladwell.'

He paused, puzzled as Alice stifled a laugh.

'I'm sorry, nobody's ever called me Ms. Gladwell before.'

Appleseed grinned and continued.

'Okay, Alice. I know you've had a tough few days, but you know just how terrible our continuing war is, and any information that can help us strike a blow for all humans would be of great value.'

Alice didn't say anything, but she noted that Zeus was now claiming to represent all humans. She wondered what her father would have said to that as the general continued.

'So, please just let me know everything you saw and experienced. Don't worry about any detail seeming to be too small or insignificant; just tell me everything from the beginning.'

So Alice began her tale, starting with how she had seen a Biter jump down a hole and how she had followed. She watched Appleseed raise his eyebrows as she talked about the first confrontation in the caves and how she had managed to get away. He was scribbling notes furiously and stopped when she mentioned about the room she had entered and the seal she had seen on the door. He looked at Dewan.

'That can only be where the US Embassy was. I know we had underground bunkers, but who would have thought those mindless monsters would have used our own underground bunkers and the ones the Indians had built against nukes to hide? When we're done here, I'd like a recon group to go and check out the area.'

Alice continued her story, about how she managed to get into the room and saw old newspapers. When Appleseed asked what was on those papers, Alice replied that she saw the pictures of when The Rising first happened, but that she could not read fast enough. She thought she saw a flicker of satisfaction cross Appleseed's face as he continued.

'Now, these creatures were outside the door. How did you manage to get out?'

Alice started speaking and then wondered how she could possibly explain the drawing on the wall and why the Biters did not tear her apart or at any rate bite her to convert her into one of them. However, she had never been a good liar, and struggled with what she should tell the general. Her dilemma was solved when a trooper knocked on the door.

'Sir, we are serving lunch in the cafeteria now. Will you come and join us, or should I send it over here?'

Appleseed growled, his friendly demeanor gone in an instant. 'Trooper, we're working here! Colonel, can you ask them to arrange a bite here?'

Dewan walked out, resting a friendly hand on Alice's shoulder as he left. Alice looked back to see Appleseed looking at her with his chin in his hands, as if contemplating something. Finally he came around the table to sit next to Alice.

'Alice, we will continue the debriefing when Dewan gets here, but there is one thing I needed to ask you in private. It is a highly confidential matter that nobody else should know about, but if you helped me with this, it could make a huge difference to the war effort.'

He took out a photograph from his pocket and put it on the table in front of Alice. It was an old, faded photo, with some of the edges torn off, but the smiling face with greying hair in the middle of it was unmistakable. It was the woman whom Alice had met as the Queen. She tried to contain her reaction, but Appleseed must have noticed.

'Alice, I need you to tell me if you saw this woman.'

Alice was saved from having to answer by Dewan coming in with some sandwiches. As they ate, Alice told them about how after the encounter in the Embassy room, she had managed to hide in the underground caves and tunnels for the next two days. Appleseed was skeptical and his expression showed it.

'When our men first saw you, it seems you were in the company of Biters. How did that happen?'

Alice's mind raced. At the best of times, she was terrible at making up excuses; now she had to find some plausible reason for why the Biters around her had not attacked her when they first encountered the Zeus helicopters.

'General, I was hiding behind some ruins when your helicopters arrived. The Biters would have found me in minutes if they had not landed up when they did. I was hardly with the Biters then – but with all the fighting, I couldn't get to the troopers and I hid underground.'

'And what about the incident in the forest when we gave you the beacon? Or did you again just happen to be near the Biters? One of our men said that it looked like they had you in their custody.'

Alice saw that Appleseed was not going to be so easily convinced.

'Biters can hardly take anyone in their custody. They tried to get me in the forest and I was fighting them off when your men arrived. It was all so chaotic that someone must have mistakenly believed the Biters had captured me. I was scared and in the middle of so many Biters that I just dove into one of the openings in the ground. It seemed to lead into one of their bases and I hid there, waiting for you guys to get me.'

Dewan nodded at Appleseed and whispered that he had indeed seen her fighting Biters when he first saw her. The general just grunted as Alice continued her tale about how she had been deep underground escaping the Biters when the rescue mission was mounted. As she talked, she noticed that the general seemed to be relaxing a bit as he clearly got pieces of information that he deemed useful, such as the exact location of the tunnels near the old Yamuna river, and more than once he whispered to Dewan to get sorties out over the areas to check them out for any sign of Biters. Finally he closed the writing pad in front of him and asked Dewan to go and check if the helicopter to fly Alice back had been arranged.

As Dewan left the room, Appleseed was again right beside Alice, the photo in his hand.

'Alice, in my time I've interrogated many men and women, and I know that you're keeping something from me.'

He reached over and gripped Alice's knee hard, and then Alice felt his hand moving up her leg.

'In my time, we had many ways of persuading young, attractive women like you to co-operate.'

Alice cringed as the general's hand moved higher – and then, on instinct, she grabbed his hand with her left hand, and just as her instructors had taught her, she twisted it and brought her right palm hard against the flat of his hand. Appleseed's hand snapped back and he howled in pain as Alice stood up, ready to fight. The general towered over her and outweighed her by a big margin, but Alice's parents had not brought her up to give in so easily. She would go down fighting if need be. Appleseed was holding his wrist and his face was red.

'I should have known better than to reason with a wild girl from the Deadland like you. Savages like you aren't fit to be with humans anymore. The days of isolated settlements are going to be a thing of the past – and you need to learn how to live in human society again.'

Alice spat on the ground, knowing that there was no need to waste her effort on being polite any more.

'So that we can be slaves to you and your masters, whoever they are? Is the war against the Biters your mission or is that an excuse to get power?'

Appleseed smiled.

'The woman whose photo I showed you is a known traitor and a Biter sympathizer. We know that she lives among them and claims to be some sort of leader. We don't let that information get out because we don't want anyone to know that the Biters can be lived with after all. She is a traitor and the Central Committee has already condemned her to death. Anyone collaborating with her is also a traitor.'

Alice didn't flinch at the threat.

'I have no idea who she is, but it looks like you are the ones who are keeping secrets. How would your men feel if they knew that the Biters could actually co-exist with us, and that your war is based on lies?'

Alice regretted what she said next a second after the words left her mouth, but she was angry and wanted to lash out, to see Appleseed on the defensive.

'I cannot read fast, but I can read, and in the rooms below, I saw papers that I had lots of time to read. Papers that talked about experiments done before The Rising, about how the Great Fires were wars waged by elements in human governments to get power, about how people could have been vaccinated if your masters wanted to.'

Appleseed looked as if he had been punched in the gut, but then he smiled: not a smile born out of good humor, but that of a predator looking at a helpless prey.

'Your friend Dr. Protima had tried to reach out to her associates in the early days, telling them such stories, and I personally had the pleasure of breaking many of them. I never got her but I managed to stamp out these lies. My masters have been working for years to create a new Earth, one where there is no overpopulation, no poverty, no weakness. They selected those who were to be vaccinated and we would have repopulated our cities and started afresh. The spread of the infection and the way it mutated surprised us, but we would have achieved what we wanted long ago by wiping out those critters had it not been for that stubborn hag.'

Alice was suddenly very afraid. There was only one reason Appleseed could be sharing all this so openly: if he had no fear that she could give away these secrets. He loomed over her.

'And you, my dear, a wild girl from an inconsequential settlement, ruled by that delusional, idealistic father of yours. Do you think you can come in the way of the vision of the most powerful men in the world? The Central Committee is based in China, but unlike what your father believes, it's not just the Chinese. Elements of the Chinese government of old are there, together with the richest and most powerful bankers and politicians of the Old World. You are like an insect before their vision for a New World.'

He heard the door open as Dewan came back, and he leaned close and whispered, 'Be careful, my dear. Accidents are known to happen all the time in the Deadland where you live.'

Alice walked to the helicopter, numb with fear and dreading what was to follow. A part of her had wanted to believe that the Queen's rants and prophecies were nothing more than the product of a delusional mind. She had wanted nothing more than to forget about all that she had seen and heard while she had been among the Biters and to get on with her life. To have Appleseed so casually admit that it was all true chilled her. There was, of course, the realization that perhaps everything the Queen had said had been true after all, and that perhaps the Biters were not the only, or even the most dangerous, enemies ordinary people like Alice and her family had to fear. As the helicopter took off, she saw Appleseed standing on the flight line, waving to her.

Her first thought was that she would go and tell her father everything. She didn't know if he would believe her, but she was sure that he would have some ideas on what to do. After all, what could she do alone against someone like Appleseed, his masters, and all the force Zeus could bring to bear? Between the hordes of Biters, who regarded every human with fear and hatred, and Zeus, what chance did she have alone?

Then an even greater fear gripped her. Appleseed had known who her father was. He would know that she would likely go and tell him everything. She suddenly felt very afraid for what the coming days were going to bring for her and her settlement.

SIX

ALICE HAD A QUIET DINNER back at the settlement, but found it impossible to sleep. Jane was lying in her own sleeping bag just feet from her, and Alice considered waking her up, but then dismissed the thought. What could she possibly tell her older sister that would make the story she had to tell sound anything other than ludicrous? She lay in silence for a few more minutes, but soon realized that she was so on edge that there was no way she could sleep. Her ears seemed to be picking up every sound and magnifying it, mirroring her fears. A solitary footstep sounded like a full squad of Zeus troopers; the sound of a bird or bat flying made her wonder if a helicopter was on the way. Finally, Alice sat up and realized that the risk of her being laughed at or not believed was nothing compared to what would happen if Appleseed did carry out his threat and the settlement was taken totally by surprise.

She got up and quietly walked to the room her parents were in. Her mother was asleep, but her father was poring over some papers. The brutal fact was that everyone who had survived so long in the Deadland had to know how to take a life, and she knew her father had done his share of fighting and killing, but he always was more in his element as a man of peace. Which was why he was the de facto leader of their settlement. He was the person people knew they could rely on to get fair advice on how to solve a dispute. He was the one who was trusted to tally and apportion their stocks of food and fuel, which he was doing now. And he was the only person in the world whom Alice could contemplate trusting with her secret.

He looked up at Alice and smiled, motioning for her to sit down next to him.

'Dad, can we talk outside?'

He put the papers aside and joined her in the chill of the night. As they walked together around the settlement, he didn't say a word, choosing to wait for when Alice would be ready to say what was on her mind.

'Dad, I think I found out some stuff. It sounds crazy, but I think it's true, and because of it, we may all be in danger. I'm really scared.'

He stopped and looked at her.

'Alice, all those years ago when everything suddenly went to hell, I was just as scared. Your mom was expecting you and with all the chaos in the last few days, I had no idea how I could protect my family.'

'So what did you do?'

He smiled, the light from torches burning around the settlement's walls reflecting in his glasses.

'I got help. Sometimes the bravest thing you can do is to ask for help. I went to a general in the Indian Army who had become a friend, and he let us shelter with his unit in their barracks when the Biters came out. He and I started this settlement once we had to leave the cities after they became unlivable and we realized that there was no more government and no more help coming our way.'

Alice wrapped her hands around herself, not just because

of the chill, but because she needed to brace herself to tell her story. Her father put an arm around her and they continued walking as she spoke. He didn't interrupt her once, though he did see his face cloud over with a flash of anger when she related what had happened with Appleseed.

Finally, he stopped and seemed to be staring off into the distance. When he said nothing for several seconds, Alice tugged at his hand.

'Dad, I know it sounds crazy. That's why I was so afraid of saying anything to you.'

When her father turned to look at her, Alice was shocked to see his eyes well up with tears.

'Alice, when the first infections emerged and within a day or two all law and order broke down, a lady had come to meet me at the Embassy, pleading with me to pass on some information to my superiors in Washington. The Ambassador was in the US so she wanted to meet me. Just before she was to come and visit me, I got a call direct from someone in the White House that I was not to meet her or to entertain anything she had to say. I thought she was another wacko who had lost it in the madness of those days and I did not meet her.'

Alice felt her heart almost stop as she guessed what was to come next.

'That lady's name was Dr. Protima Dasgupta. She was an Indian-American researcher who had recently left the government. My background check showed that she had been working on some classified projects, which had such a high level of secrecy that I couldn't even find out what they were.'

'So everything she said is....'

Her father exhaled loudly, as if clearing his mind and trying to come to grips with what he now faced.

'Alice, I don't know if everything she said is true or not,

but what's clear based on what you saw is that there is more to the Biters than we've always been led to believe. In the five days after The Rising, when the media was still on, did you know what was on TV every single day?'

Alice had never watched TV but knew of it from her parents and sister, so she just shook her head.

'Reports about how horrible these creatures, these mutants, were. Reports about how our brave troops were fighting a new war on terror. Every single channel was screaming about how these creatures needed to be wiped out. But what was funny was that ordinary folks had no real protection; most National Guard units in the US were pulled back to barracks. Then all of a sudden, wars started breaking out all over. If I were a conspiracy nut, which I most certainly am not, I could start connecting all those dots and say that what this Queen or Dr. Protima has to say may well be more true than not. But that's not what worries me most. Something else terrifies me.'

'What, Dad?'

He looked at Alice, his eyes dead serious.

'If Protima lives, there is a chance that this secret could come out, and getting to her is the only chance Zeus and its masters have of wiping out the Biters as per their plan and then bring the surviving humans under their control. Appleseed now suspects that you know where she may be. He will be coming for you.'

Alice tried to put on a brave face.

'Dad, can we hold them? We have almost two hundred men and women who can fight. We can all shoot well, and we know this area better than they ever will.'

He shook his head sadly.

'No, sweetheart, we won't be able to hold them. You've seen a lot more death and evil than I would have ever wished upon a child of mine, but the most evil thing in this world is what one man can do to another. If Zeus comes here with their air power and heavy weapons, we won't last more than a few minutes. They will wipe us out and take you away.'

Alice didn't know what to say. Part of her felt guilty for having involved her father. The rational part of her knew that the dangers would have been just as great and just as real even if she had not told a soul, but telling her father and seeing how scared even he seemed made it even more real, and infinitely more frightening.

'Gladwell, we don't know if even a word of this is true.'

The speaker was Rajiv, a former banker who had become one of the pillars of their settlement ever since he and his wife had stumbled onto them while running from a horde of Biters. Alice had sat quietly for the half hour her father had taken to relate her story. He had thankfully spared her the ordeal of having to speak in front of more than two hundred people, most of whom looked increasingly skeptical as the tale progressed. Alice saw more than a few of them get up and leave. She knew they were among the many who had lost family and friends to the Biters, and even an insinuation that the Biters were anything but a mindless, bloodthirsty horde offended them. What made it worse was that the first accusation came not from one of the rabble-rousers but the normally placid Rajiv.

Alice's father looked at Rajiv, pleading with him. 'Why on Earth would Alice make all this up?'

Rajiv looked sheepish and shrugged his shoulders. 'She is but a girl. Maybe she just got scared in the tunnels down there and imagined things.'

'Or maybe this is just you trying to hold onto your so-called freedom!'

That stinging accusation came from the rear of the group, and Alice saw her father flinch as if he had been struck physically. His accuser was now standing up, and as three or four more men stood up, felt emboldened to continue his tirade.

'For years, Zeus has been coming to us. What they want isn't much: our boys to join their army, a share of whatever we find by way of salvage, and maintaining a tally of our weapons with them. In return, we get some fixed rations, ammunition and safety.'

Alice saw her father's face tighten.

'We are FREE! That counts for something. We all owed allegiance to others, and several of you served in government or in uniform, so we all know what that meant. But that was different: that was allegiance to a nation, to our identity. Zeus are a bunch of hired guns, and their real masters never reveal themselves openly. Have you forgotten about those settlements who signed up and then had their weapons taken because Zeus decided they were needed elsewhere? Who saved them from attacks after that? What about those who were re-settled into farms to grow food, half of which is taken away by Zeus for their masters with no payment? What about all those young people who are taken away and never seen again – and the rumors that they are being used as bonded labour in the factories and mines of the elites who control Zeus? Why become their slaves when we can be free?'

It was an old argument, one that had consumed many meetings before, but tonight the revelations about what Alice had found had given it a new, bitter edge. The man who had been arguing with her father refused to back down.

'We all know how you feel about it, and you also know

that there have been some of us who disagree. Some of us who are tired of fighting to survive every day, or scavenging for food every day for our families. And now you conveniently have this fairy tale from your daughter where Zeus and their masters are some sort of super-villains who destroyed the world.'

As the meeting disbanded, Alice's father took her aside.

'I tried, sweetheart, but their minds are closed. The problem is that if this general is indeed going to strike, we are running out of time. We cannot just sit here and debate and hope we convince these people.'

'Dad, what can we do?'

He hesitated, as if weighing whether to say what was on his mind.

'We need to meet this Dr. Protima. She's the only one who could convince them.'

Alice shuddered at the thought of going back to the Biters in their dank, dark underground world, and also of what they would do to her when they found her after her betrayal.

'Dad, I don't know if what they said is true or not, but that silly prophecy and that book she has freaks me out.'

'Darling, that's just an old fairy tale called Alice in Wonderland. I don't blame her if she has lost her mind a bit down there and believes it to be some prophecy. I guess they heard your name and saw the way you met them, and wanted to believe it was this prophecy come true, that's all. If that's what it takes to save us all, then just play along for a little bit.'

Alice could see her father's conflicted face, because he knew he was putting her in harm's way. But the sheer fact that he was willing to even contemplate that told her just how desperate their situation was.

The next morning, Alice walked along the woods where

she had followed Bunny Ears down the hole. They were a good five miles away from their settlement, and if there was trouble, they would not be able to make it back in time, and of course, there was no way they could expect help or reinforcements. Alice held a pistol in her right hand and a shotgun slung across her back, but she had already seen that up close, with the weight of numbers on their side, the firepower she carried would count for little if the Biters were intent on attacking her. Her father was sitting a hundred meters away, hidden in the trees, his face daubed with camouflage paint, his eyes glued to the scope of his rifle.

Alice had no idea if Bunny Ears or any other Biter would even show up again at this location, but as far as she knew, no other human had found this entrance, and now that she scanned the area, it was so well hidden that she could not spot it either. So if it had not been compromised, there was a chance that they would still be using it. Also, she reminded herself, they were probably looking for her. That thought made her grip the handgun in her hand even tighter as she waited.

They waited for what seemed to be an eternity, and as Alice was about to give up and go to her father and ask if they should just return to the settlement, she saw some movement in the bushes. She froze, both hands gripping the handgun, but she forced herself to not bring the gun up. If their plan was to work, she had to make sure that she was not seen as a threat. She held her breath as the bushes parted, reassured by the fact that at this very moment her father's rifle would be trained on whatever was emerging. She saw two pointy ears emerge first, and then Bunny Ears was in front of her. He growled, spitting in her direction, and for a moment, Alice thought that he was about to attack. He pounded his feet on the ground and raised his head to the skies, howling, but as

Alice watched she realized that his roar was not one of fury but more a plaintive wail.

She tucked her handgun into her belt and took a step closer. As she looked at Bunny Ears, she saw that he too was looking at her with his lifeless eyes. She had no idea if he would understand what she wanted, but she had no other choice. She spoke in a gentle voice.

'I am so sorry. I did not know what Zeus and their masters were up to, and I did not believe the Queen. I know now, and I need your help. The only way we can survive is if we help each other. Please tell the Queen that I need her help. We've tried convincing others in the settlement but many of them don't believe us.'

Bunny Ears just looked at her for a few seconds and then he disappeared back into the bushes. Alice wondered if he had understood a single word she had said.

Alice was sleeping with her shotgun near her head, and her parents had insisted that she and her sister sleep in the same room as them. It was hard to believe that things had got so bad so fast. It had begun with a fight between two young boys at lunch-time, one of them supporting her father and another insisting that they should just go the way of so many other settlements and do what Zeus wanted. When things had got more personal and some harsh words had been said about Alice, a couple of her friends had waded in. Soon words had given way to blows and before anyone could control it, the settlement had been neatly divided down the middle. What was apparent was that it had to do with more than whether they believed Alice's story, or even what they thought about joining Zeus. It had become a battle for power. A battle between Alice's father and some of the original founders of the settlement, and others who had joined them more recently and resented the authority the old-timers wielded.

Alice's father would have normally waved it all off as yet another of the countless arguments that had been inevitable over the years when you put strangers together in such a high-stress situation. But now things were different. He knew the imminent danger of Zeus moving against them, and he had also now seen first-hand that what Alice had said had some truth to it. He had been tempted to pull the trigger the moment he saw the Biter emerge in front of his daughter, and he had to fight years of conditioning to not blow his head away. But then he had seen it stand there, apparently listening, apparently understanding, and then walking away. With all the devastation the world had endured, if there was even a small chance that things could be set right, then it was worth fighting for.

He had called a meeting just after breakfast and as the entire settlement gathered, he noticed that the lines were drawn. People were sitting in groups, and those he knew supported his views were sitting around him and his family. However, an even larger group was now sitting around Rajiv, who had somehow taken on leadership of the splinter group. Better him than one of the rabble-rousers, he thought, as he began his account of what he had seen.

He was less than a minute into it when he saw the dissenters stirring. Rajiv stood up.

'Gladwell, we go way back, but you cannot seriously expect us to believe this. I understand you're trying to help your daughter, but this is too incredible to be true. After all the Biters have done to us, why are you doing this?'

He heard a few catcalls and a man's voice boomed out

from the crowd. 'He's just scared of no longer being the head honcho if we join Zeus, that's all. And if he hates Zeus so much, why did he strike a deal to save his daughter?'

Alice could see her father wither in the face of the criticism and he put his head down, defeated, knowing that nothing he could say was going to make a difference.

Just then one of the lookouts shouted, 'There's an intruder headed our way.'

Immediately, all differences were forgotten as guns were picked up, safeties switched off and men and women began taking their defensive positions. Those too young, old or sick to fight were herded to the middle of the village to shelter in the building that served as their communal dining hall. Everyone else was expected to fight. Alice was one of the first to reach the wall where the shout had come from, and she was on top of the boxes that served as the perch for snipers before many of the older and slower men had even reached the wall. She put her rifle to her shoulders and peered through the sniper scope. She could hear others take position around her and the nervous shuffling and swearing of those who had not seen combat before. As Alice waited, she found a clarity that had eluded her in the confusion of the last few days. This was what she had been trained to do since she could walk. This was when there was no ambiguity to deal with – where it was simple: kill or be killed. A familiar adrenaline rush washed over her, and she welcomed it, waiting for a target to present itself.

'Alice, got something on your scope?'

Alice grinned and asked the man to wait. It was one of the men who had been heckling her father just minutes ago. It was reassuring to know that they still realized and respected the fact that Alice was one of the best shots in the settlement.

'Ram, did you actually see anything or were you drinking more of your hooch again last night?'

That question from Alice's father brought laughter all around and helped to lessen some of the tension. Alice was still too young to fully grasp it, but she had an intuitive understanding of just why so many men and women had followed her father over the years. It was not because he was the strongest or even the bravest, but because he could keep people calm in a crisis; he could think when others were losing their heads. She peered through her scope once again and this time she saw someone emerging from the early morning mist. As the figure resolved itself, she saw someone covered in a full-length coat, one that seemed several sizes too big, and walking towards their settlement at a steady, almost leisurely pace. She moved the scope up and caught her breath as she realized who was approaching. It was Dr. Protima, or as she preferred to be called nowadays, the Queen of the Biters.

Alice heard one or two rifles being cocked so she called out, 'Hold your fire. It's just an old woman.'

Two men from the settlement unlocked the gate and went out, cautiously approaching the figure who was now just a hundred meters away. Alice watched them trade some words and then heaved a sigh of relief when they led her in.

When the Queen walked in through the gate, every man, woman and child in the settlement had gathered to see who this stranger was. In the early days they had often encountered solitary stragglers, but by now, people were either in groups, or dead. A single person, least of all an old woman, had virtually no chance of surviving on their own in the Deadland. Alice saw that the Queen had prepared well. The oversized coat covered her body and arms, and she wore long gloves to conceal her hands. She was wearing tinted glasses that obscured her eyes and as she came in, she glanced towards Alice once, but betrayed no hint of recognition.

As someone offered her a chair, she sat down and said that she had to talk to someone in charge. When Alice's father and some of the other men sat around her, she looked around at the dozens of people gathered, perhaps waiting for them to leave. But there was no chance of that happening: the entire settlement wanted to know what this strange old woman had to say. And then she began her tale.

'My name is Dr. Protima, and I was a Biologist of Indian origin who lived and worked in the United States for several years.'

Alice saw her father's eyes widen as he realized who she was, and saw several of the men stir, but they all sat and listened. And the Queen had indeed come prepared to meet a skeptical audience. Under the coat, she had a small bag from which she produced old faded passports, identity cards, official documents bearing the seal of the US Government. Some of the younger folks would not know what many of those were, but were suitably impressed, but all the older ones, the ones who had known a life before The Rising, saw and understood. Alice saw some of the men who had been opposed to her father pass the documents among each other, and saw several of them glance at her.

Rajiv finally worked up the courage to speak when the Queen concluded her tale, ending with how Alice had landed in their midst.

'Dr. Protima, we have heard some of this before from Alice, and it still seems incredible. How can we believe any of this?'

She did not say a single word in reply, but stood up and loosened the coat so it fell at her feet. Then she took off her gloves and glasses and looked straight at Rajiv. There were gasps all around her, and one or two women screamed. Rajiv stumbled back, holding onto another man for support as he looked into the decayed, lifeless eyes and the yellowing, bloodied arms of the Queen. No one said anything for a few seconds, and then Alice's father spoke.

'Dr. Protima, if this vaccine got into the right hands, could it save any more humans from being...'

As he fumbled with what to say, she answered, 'Yes. It would ensure that no more humans have to worry about the virus being transmitted through a bite. Imagine what that would do to the chances of people finally coming to grips with the fact that we are not just dangerous animals and an existential threat to be wiped out. What would that do to Zeus's fear-mongering, which they are using to wipe us out and bring all of you under their control?'

Alice heard many murmurs of approval in the crowd, as the Queen now looked straight at her.

'But there's more than that. Before it all went out of control, we were working on antidotes, not just vaccines. If I can get the vaccine to a good lab, we should be able to create a cure. It may take time, but I know it can be done. I don't know how much brain damage has already happened to those infected, or whether it can be reversed, but there is at least hope. Alice, I told you my prophecy was what would lead us to a way out.'

Nobody else present understood what she meant by the last comment, but they were all looking at Alice with a mixture of shame and awe. They had doubted and rejected her, but now they had proof before their eyes that she had been right. Moreover, they suddenly found themselves the bearers of a terrible secret. Many people began speaking at once, everyone with their own idea on what to do, but everyone in agreement that they needed to help get the vaccine into the right hands.

Alice's father spoke next, and what he said stunned everyone into silence.

'The men who caused all this will not let us succeed so easily. We know they have been hunting Dr. Protima and now they will come for us.'

Nobody said anything for a few seconds. Alice was about to say something when the silence was shattered by the sound of an incoming helicopter.

SEVEN

EVERYONE AT THE SETTLEMENT WAS watching, most down the sights of their guns as the black helicopter landed at the foot of the hill leading to their village. Alice had her sniper rifle at her shoulder and while many of the younger kids were babbling about this being an attack, she knew better. If Zeus had wanted to launch an attack, they would have come from the skies, raining rockets and bombs from high above, while Alice and the others at her settlement would have been impotent to do anything about it. By landing the helicopter in such a vulnerable position, whoever was coming was indicating that they came in peace, at least for now.

Alice put down her rifle to motion to some of the men behind her to not get trigger happy and wait for her signal before doing anything. When she looked back towards the helicopter, she did not need her sights to know who was coming. The imposing bulk and bald head of the uniformed man now making his way up the hill told her who it was.

Why would Appleseed be coming alone? Alice had spent the last few days in the fear that he would lash out with an unexpected attack, so why was he coming here like this?

When he reached the gates of the settlement, Alice's

father asked for the gates to be opened and Appleseed walked into the midst of two hundred armed, scared and jittery people.

'Gladwell, tell your people I pose no threat. You can all see that I am unarmed.'

Appleseed held up his hands to reinforce the point, but even that did little to defuse the tension. Everyone at the settlement had heard about Alice's adventures and the threats this general had made, and none of them was willing to take his words at face value. Appleseed looked around, and seeing Alice, he smiled and said through gritted teeth, 'So, young Alice, we meet again.'

Alice spat in his direction, and several people jeered. Appleseed didn't seem to be ruffled and addressed Alice's father.

'Gladwell, your daughter has grown up in the Deadland, so I don't blame her, but you were a diplomat. Surely you can sit down and talk in a civilized manner with an unarmed guest?'

Alice's father lifted the shotgun he was carrying, casually aiming it at Appleseed's ample gut.

'Any bastard who threatens my daughter is no guest at my home.'

All trace of civility dissipated from Appleseed's face as he pulled a chair and sat down, staring at Alice's father with undisguised hatred.

'Fine, let's play it your way. Give me Dr. Protima and all of you can go on with your miserable lives.'

There was a stunned silence, and as Alice's father started to say something, Appleseed cut him off. 'Don't waste my time. I've had unmanned drones watching your settlement ever since your darling daughter spilled the beans on her freak friend. So I know she's here. I just want her handed over. Oh yes, as per the rules laid out by the Central Committee, all of you are guilty of treason for collaborating with the Biter enemy, and I could have all of you executed for it. Instead, I'll settle for confiscating all your weapons and relocating you to one of our safe zones.'

There was a commotion among the group as Alice's father roared in anger.

'This Central Committee of yours, these rich men who hide in their bases together with the Chinese tyrants, do not rule us. They rule only their hired dogs like you, and what they say or want has no jurisdiction here. As for Dr. Protima, you have no authority here to take anyone away.'

Appleseed stayed calm, knowing that he held all the cards. 'One air strike is all it would take to turn all of you into smoking carcasses. Tempting as that is, I need that witch alive. That is the only reason I am sitting here and not sifting through your corpses after an air strike. The Central Committee has to make sure that she is not capable of spreading her lies and that we know where her hidden bases are. This is your last chance before you officially commit an act of treason.'

Alice saw Rajiv look at her father, and she wondered if there would be those who would be willing to give into Appleseed's demands. After all, how many of them would risk their lives and their families for an old lady with an incredible tale? Alice's father was perhaps thinking the same thing and he spoke aloud, addressing all those in the settlement.

'For years, we have lived a life that is little more than surviving from day to day. We have taught out children nothing more than how to kill and avoid being killed. All of us who lived before The Rising know that there is more to life than that. I had forgotten that life and I had resigned myself to a life where my only and biggest achievement was to see my family live one more day. But today, I realized there is hope. There is hope that the evil that has overtaken all our lives can be reversed. There is hope that once again we can live like humans, not wild animals. That hope is worth fighting for, and I for one will not give into someone who represents the same forces that destroyed all our lives in the first place. I will not choose for you. If you choose not to side with me, I will take my family and those with me and leave with Dr. Protima.'

Appleseed snorted derisively.

'His daughter filled your ears with fairy tales, and you have this delusional old woman who means nothing to any of you. Why throw away your lives for them?'

Rajiv walked up to Appleseed and looked him in the eye.

'When I was a banker, I thought the bloody stock market crashing was the end of the world. If there's one positive of all this crap we've gone through, it's that it has given me a sense of perspective, a sense of what really matters and what is worth standing up for. I will stand by the men and women who sheltered me when I had nothing and whom I have fought with shoulder to shoulder every day. You can stuff your Central Committee up your fat ass.'

If Alice's father's appeal had not done the trick, Rajiv's certainly did, and everyone gathered started cheering.

Alice walked up to Appleseed and tapped him on the shoulder.

'I don't think you're welcome here anymore.'

He glared at her and began to walk away, when the Queen emerged from the building where she had been hiding and stood next to Alice.

'General, wait. I believe you were looking for me.'

He stopped in his tracks and turned to look at her, and then recoiled in horror as she took off her glasses and gloves.

'I dare say, General, for a delusional old woman I still

have a bit of a bite.'

As she opened and snapped shut her bloody teeth, Appleseed stumbled back, almost falling down as he realized what the true nature of the elusive Dr. Protima he had been pursuing for so many years was. He ran more than walked out of the gate, as cheers rang out all around Alice.

The Queen looked around her and spoke to no one in particular. 'There is still goodness left in man. There is indeed still hope.'

Alice's father shouted above the cheering. 'Quiet, everyone! We've done enough celebrating; now we need to get ready.'

'For what?' shouted someone in the crowd.

'For the attack that is surely on its way even as we speak.'

Alice watched till the combination of the smoke drifting into her eyes and her own tears made it impossible for her to see much more. Jane was tugging at her arm and shouting something, but Alice did not hear a word of what she was saying. All she heard was the crackling sound of what had been her home for more than a year burn down to the ground. And yes, the sound of men screaming. Men she had trained with, men she had known all her life. Above all else, the one man she had loved with all her heart: her father.

Soon after Appleseed had left, Alice's father had asked for twenty volunteers to stay on in the settlement, both to slow down the Zeus forces that were surely on their way, and also to ensure that any drones watching them didn't spot that they were in fact abandoning their settlement. Alice had bawled and pleaded when it was obvious that her father would stay. He had just held her tight and spoke to her as she cried.

'Alice, you must survive. Dr. Protima and her secret must survive. Just remember that and while you are young, you must now lead the ones who remain.'

The remaining people half-crouched, half-crawled through the narrow irrigation tunnels behind the settlement. Alice's father had them covered long ago, thinking they would provide a good place to hide or to make a quiet getaway, and now they were being put to use as Alice, her mother, sister, Dr. Protima and the others made for the neighboring forests. It was from there that Alice saw the attack unfold. Three black helicopters swept in low and took positions, hovering just meters above the settlement. Appleseed was in one of them, and Alice could hear his voice booming over a loudspeaker, offering one last chance for surrender. When there was no response, Zeus troopers began rappelling out of the helicopters. For a split second, Alice's heart had harbored hopes that her father and the other men may make it when their first volley brought down several of the Zeus troopers. But then she realized both just how cruel and how merciless Appleseed was. He had sacrificed his first men as pawns to make the defenders reveal their positions. Three more helicopters, sleek, fast gunships, swept in, raking the settlement with rockets and machine guns. A brutal, hammering assault that ended when more than half the buildings in the settlement were ablaze and all defending guns silent.

Another wave of Zeus troopers landed, but Alice saw that her father had more tricks up his sleeve. She watched through tear-filled eyes as several jury-rigged bombs, mostly cans filled with fuel, were set off, making the Zeus troopers dive for cover, and a single sniper rifle barked several times from the second floor of the building where Alice's parents had lived. Two Zeus troopers fell and didn't get up. Four troopers tried to rush the building, but two more were brought down by sniper fire. Finally a helicopter fired two rockets that destroyed the building as Alice screamed in agony.

More Zeus troopers entered the settlement, and started going door to door. When it was obvious that most of the residents had abandoned the settlement, Alice saw them signal frantically to the hovering helicopters. She knew that she could wait no longer. Her throat burned and she longed to strike out at the men who had just killed her father, but she remembered what her father had told her. Most of the combat-tested veterans had chosen to stay behind at the settlement, choosing to go down fighting so that their families may have a chance. Of the ones left, leave aside a couple of men who were good shots, Alice was perhaps the most experienced in both battle and in navigating the woods. She now had to lead them to safety. In the confusion of the hasty flight into the woods, she had lost sight of the Queen, and only hoped that she had not abandoned the humans who had sacrificed so much to keep her and her cause alive.

It was now nearly dark, and they could no longer hear the helicopters at the settlement. That could mean only one thing: that Appleseed had realized that pursuing them from the air was of no use in the dark when they were walking through a thick forest. They would have to come for them on foot. That suited Alice just fine. She, like most of the other survivors from the settlement, had learnt to live off the land and to fight on foot, in the dark, and with nothing but the weapons they could carry. She had seen the awesome firepower Zeus could bring to bear, but also had seen that its troopers relied too much on air power and heavy weapons. Now they were on Alice's turf and she would make them pay for what they had done.

She asked the group to halt and scanned them. More than half were children too young to fight, or those who were too old or sick to fight against trained troopers. Everyone at the settlement knew how to handle weapons; after The Rising that was almost an elementary education every human child had to go through if they wanted to live beyond a few years. But it was one thing to snipe at mindless Biters, and quite another thing to take on heavily armed and trained Zeus troopers. Alice picked a dozen young men and women, all of whom she had trained with and knew were good in close combat. She was the youngest of them, but nobody questioned her authority. Alice had always been acknowledged as someone with fighting skills well beyond her age, but with the role she had played in unearthing the deadly secret behind the Biters, there was even more of an aura surrounding her.

Alice asked the rest of the group to go ahead. She knew that there were some abandoned mines about five kilometers away and that was to be their resting place for the night. If they got there undetected, it would be virtually impossible for Zeus to locate them from the air, and once the sun rose, she planned to make contact with the Queen. Her hope was that she would give refuge to Alice and her fellow humans. What followed then was something Alice had not had time to plan for or think through. Alice took the dozen she had asked to stay with her and asked them to gather in a circle.

'These are not Biters. They will not come in blindly to be shot. They have better weapons than us and they know how to use them.'

'Thanks for that inspirational speech, boss,' one of the boys quipped.

Alice smiled as she replied, 'They are not Biters, but they are human. That means they will feel one thing Biters do not.'

'What's that, Alice?'
'Fear.'

Alice sat with bated breath, some thirty feet above the ground, hidden by the branches of the tree she was perched on. The others with her were similarly hidden, waiting for the Zeus troopers to appear. Two boys had been sent ahead as scouts, and when they had understood the likely route the troopers were taking through the forest, Alice had told everyone to take their positions. This was a tactic that they had often used before, born out of the simple insight that no matter how ferocious Biters could be, nobody had yet seen a Biter climb a tree. Alice could hear the troopers long before she saw their shadows in the dark.

'They move like pregnant cows,' she thought to herself as she heard their heavy footfalls and their voices. For someone who had grown up in the open countryside and learnt from an early age what it meant to move with stealth and in the darkness, Alice knew this form of warfare intimately. The Zeus troopers, used to swooping down from the air and with heavy air cover to back them up, found this totally alien to how they normally went to war. That was the fatal weakness Alice hoped to exploit.

As Alice sighted her rifle at the nearest shadow, a flicker of doubt crossed her mind. This was not like shooting Biters, whom she had regarded as lifeless, mindless zombies, but shooting men; men who would bleed, men who would scream and thrash about as they died, men who were perhaps conscripts in the Zeus force from other settlements. Then she remembered what she had witnessed at her settlement and steeled herself and opened fire.

A single shot rang out and a trooper fell, hit in the leg. He screamed aloud and his comrades stopped, watching for attackers they could not see. They had night vision optics on their scopes, but night vision was of use only when you knew what you were looking for. A flash bang grenade rolled towards the troopers and as it exploded, it blinded them, rendering their night vision useless and also illuminating them in a ghostly glow. Alice and her comrades opened fire, using carefully aimed single shots. The firing lasted for less than twenty seconds, and when it had finished, not one of the dozen Zeus troopers was standing. Alice whistled, and all of them clambered down the trees and ran towards their escape route. They would not go straight for the mines, lest they lead the troopers to the larger group headed there, but would create a diversion, moving north and then looping back when they were in the clear.

Alice ran through the trees, her heart hammering, and keenly aware of the sounds behind her. She heard several helicopters overhead, and while the helicopters would not be able to target them through the thick forest cover, it meant that Zeus had perhaps called for reinforcements. More troopers were coming after them to avenge their comrades and she thought she heard Appleseed bellowing orders. Part of her wanted to stop and seek her vengeance against him, but she knew that she would not be able to do what her father had entrusted her with by leading a suicide mission. With the element of surprise gone, they would be not much of a match for the more numerous and better equipped Zeus troopers. She had to regain the advantage of surprise, otherwise they would not live to see the next morning.

It was impossible for her to account for every man and woman in her squad in the darkness and as she spotted a good hiding spot, she slid to a stop behind a large fallen tree.

She whistled, hoping her comrades would join her, and soon enough they were sliding into position next to her. She did a quick voice count and came up three short.

'Where are Rahul, Divya and Chetan?'

She was answered a second later when she heard bursts of gunfire. A voice cried out for mercy and was silenced with a single shot. Alice blinked back tears and tried to think what to do. She knew how to fight, but had always counted on her father being there to lead everyone, to give direction. Now being accountable for the lives of so many was a responsibility she did not think she was ready for. But whether she was ready or not, she had to act because she could now hear the Zeus troopers coming closer.

'Everyone, let's move west over the irrigation canal and then we'll get to the mines.'

They moved instantly on her suggestion, running through the forest, their homemade and patched soft soles barely making a noise, in contrast to the heavy boots of the Zeus troopers now in hot pursuit behind them. Alice saw some shadows ahead of them and skidded to a stop as she saw one of them raise a rifle.

'Stop!'

Her warning was too late as a rifle barked and Alice saw the boy next to her fall. He screamed once and then was silent.

'They're in front of us!'

Alice had her group scatter for cover behind trees, but now she knew the awful truth. Zeus had not just been flying in reinforcements, but they were using the mobility of their helicopters to flank Alice and her group. Now Alice had Zeus troopers on both sides of her, closing in on her position. She raised her rifle and fired at the nearest shadow, but could not be sure if she hit anything. The Zeus troopers, with their night vision scopes, had no such disadvantages. Two bullets slammed into the tree trunk inches from her face, showering her with splinters as she screamed and took cover, bleeding from her right cheek. Gunshots were ringing out all around her and now she had totally lost control of her situation. They were no longer a cohesive unit, but just eight or nine scared individuals in the dark against a larger number of heavily armed troopers.

She heard one of her friends scream in agony, and then something snapped inside Alice. Her life had been tough enough, but at least she had known a loving family, known the comfort that came from living among people who cared about each other. She was not going to have all of that taken away in one night because of the greed and cruelty of some men. She saw a large group of Zeus troopers emerge in front of her, and she took out her last remaining flash bang grenade and rolled it towards them, closing her eyes as it exploded, temporarily blinding the Zeus troopers.

She slung her rifle across her back and took her handgun in her right hand and her knife in her left and emerged from the shadows towards the Zeus troopers, running towards them at full tilt. The first trooper she encountered was one who was still rubbing his eyes to clear them. She fired two rounds, aiming for the face, knowing that the troopers wore body armor that would fend off small arms fire. As the trooper went down, she placed her right hand on his back, vaulting over him and coming up in a crouch as she brought her knife up into another trooper's leg. As he grabbed his leg and screamed, she stood up and fired into his face. Another trooper behind her was trying to raise his rifle when one of her friends shot him.

Alice jumped into the trees, leaving the disoriented Zeus troopers behind. She saw fleeing shadows and knew that she had bought enough time for her friends to get away, but now she was alone in the dark and surrounded by enemy troopers.

She heard Appleseed shout, 'You little blond witch, come on out and I may still let you surrender. Don't make us hunt you down, because then it won't be pretty when we're finished with you.'

Alice tried to force herself to stay calm, but it felt like her breathing was so loud that it could be heard across the entire forest. She pressed herself flat against a tree, and could hear Zeus troopers move all around her. It was just a matter of time before one of them looked in her direction through his night vision scope and the game would be up. She thought of climbing up the tree she was near but froze when she heard footsteps near her. There was a Zeus trooper on the other side of the tree, and she heard him unzip his trousers as he relieved himself. She stifled an urge to laugh at the absurdity of the whole situation, and waited till he moved on.

She peered around to see if the coast was clear and then moved slowly behind another tree. It was excruciatingly slow progress, moving from one tree to another, but at least she was moving closer to where her friends would be. The one thing she hoped was that they did not try and rescue her; that would be sure suicide with the odds against them. She stepped on a branch and the cracking noise made her cringe, but when she heard no response from the troopers she moved on. And then she found herself face to face with a grinning trooper. The man was at least twice as broad as Alice and towered over her. In the dark, she saw the whites of his teeth as he grinned. It was the first time she got a close look at the troopers they were fighting and she realized that he looked very different from the brown skinned people of what had been known as India in the Old Days, or even white-skinned people like herself. This trooper had narrow, slanted eyes and spoke with a strange accent. He must have been one of the Red Guards that people spoke of.

'Hello, darling. While the others get here maybe we could have some fun.'

As he reached out to grab her, his fatal mistake was that he saw a young girl alone in a forest, not a trained killer who had shot her first Biter when she was ten years old. Alice caught his wrist in a lock, snapping it back till she heard a popping noise, and as the man gasped in pain, she broke his nose with a back-handed strike with the thick ivory handle of her knife. She was tempted to shoot him, but that would have caused too much noise, so she stepped beyond the sputtering, sobbing man and went to the next tree.

That was when she felt a searing pain in her left shoulder and a split-second later heard the boom of a gunshot. Alice was lifted off the ground by the impact and fell hard against the tree, the wind totally knocked out of her. She felt for her left shoulder and her right palm came back covered with blood. She didn't know if it was a flesh wound or if the bullet had gone inside, but either way, she knew that unless she moved fast, she would lose too much blood and be too weak to continue. As she started to get up, a bullet smacked into the tree above her head and she flattened herself, feeling for the handgun at her belt. She pulled it out and readied herself, just hoping that she got a chance to take a few of the troopers with her.

She saw approaching shadows, wearing the unmistakable bulky body armor of Zeus troopers and carrying assault rifles. They were laughing and joking, no doubt thinking that they had killed her. Just then a large shadow leaped out from behind a tree and snapped the neck of one of the troopers. As the others turned to contend with their unseen attacker, two more shadows jumped on them and beat them to the ground, smashing their heads with their bare hands. The two remaining troopers turned to run, but the large shadow grabbed them and bashed their heads together, tossing them aside like rag dolls. As the three shadows walked closer, Alice got a better look at them. The large figure was the huge Biter who wore the floppy hat. He just stood there, glaring at Alice, and then slowly extended an arm with a grunt.

Alice took it, realizing that when all had seemed lost, help had come from the most unexpected quarter.

EIGHT

ALICE OPENED HER EYES AND, barely able to speak with her parched throat, asked for water. Someone poured some cool water on her lips that she lapped up gratefully, and then lay her head down again, slipping once more into unconsciousness. She had no idea how long she had been out, and where she was, but the one thing she remembered were the dreams she had. Dreams of Appleseed burning her home, of strange slant-eyed men in black uniforms chasing her, and dreams of her father telling her that she must live.

When she finally awoke, she found her mother by her side. Her mother, always on the thin side, looked gaunt and haggard with her hair in a mess and cheeks that were stained with tears.

'Alice! Thank God you're ok.'

Alice managed to sit up and fell into her mother's arms.

'Mom, what happened?'

She learnt that she had passed out from blood loss from her wound, and had been carried back to the underground base where the Queen had led the survivors from the settlement. As she heard her mother's story, she learnt that the Queen had not abandoned them at all. Far from it: she may have saved all their lives. She had appeared in the forest and led the humans to an underground passage where they had been sheltering for the last three days, and had sent out some Biters to fetch Alice and any other survivors from the small band that had tried to hold off the Zeus troopers.

Alice got up and walked around a bit with her mother's help and saw the large underground hall where all the humans were sheltered. They were huddled together in small groups and as Alice walked in, all of them stood up. They looked filthy, had not eaten a single decent meal or taken a bath in three days, but every single one of them smiled. Many held out their hands to shake hers when she passed, and some of them hugged her. Alice's father may have appointed her to lead them, but her actions in the forest had earned her not just their leadership, but something more than that. She had earned their trust.

Alice looked towards the open door at the far end of the large hall and saw several Biters standing there. Bunny Ears was there, as was Hatter, and they all seemed to be just standing there, watching her. It was a curious dynamic; the humans knew that they owed their lives to the Biters and their Queen, and the Biters knew that Alice was somehow the key to their salvation, so they had to obey their Queen. Yet both groups seemed to almost shrink from each other. Years of mutual hatred and fear could not be undone in a few days.

The Queen emerged from behind the Biters and watched as Alice made her way towards her. Now that her true self had been revealed to all the humans, she no longer bothered wearing her glasses or gloves, but stood there as she was. Just a few days ago, the humans would have considered it impossible to be in such a confined space with Biters without the two groups bent on mutual annihilation, but they had come to realize that the world was not quite what they had been taught to believe.

The Queen looked at Alice's bandaged wounds and then at her.

'I'm glad to see you have recovered. Thank you for the sacrifices you have all made.'

Alice suddenly remembered her father and the others who had been lost and struggled to keep her composure, leaning against her mother, looking more like a frail, lost young girl than the leader the humans took her to be.

'Alice, I know you have had a very tough time, but we do need to talk. Please come to my room as soon as you can.'

A few minutes later, Alice was in front of the Queen, and the dilemma that was weighing on the Queen's mind was clear. She could easily shelter more than a hundred humans in her underground lair, but she had no way of feeding them or getting them drinking water.

'We don't need any food or water, Alice, but you do. I cannot send my folks out to get it. They won't even understand what to get.'

Alice thought back to the years of scavenging, hunting, baking homemade bread, looking for wild fruits and berries, and when they stayed in a place long enough, the occasional attempts at farming. With Zeus no doubt looking for them, there was no way such a large group could go out and look for food, so a smaller group would have to go out and forage for food and water. Alice immediately set about explaining the task, and after all they had been through together, she was not surprised when several dozen hands went up when she asked for four volunteers to scout the nearby area for food or water. She picked four of them, all young boys, all known to be fast and to have had at least some combat experience. She asked them to wait and went to the corner where her mother and sister were sitting to gather her weapons. Her mother held her hand tight.

'Alice, you must be crazy to head out in the state you're in! You've barely recovered.'

Alice looked at her mother, and gently removed her hand.

'Mom, I cannot ask any of them to head out if I'm not willing to go myself. Don't worry, I'll be careful.'

When they stepped out of the hidden entrance to the base, Alice saw that the Queen had chosen well. The entrance to the base was hidden among some old construction pipes. From even fifty meters away, nobody would guess what lay under the ground. Alice was carrying only her handgun and knife, and the boys with her were similarly armed. They planned to travel light, since the last thing they wanted to do was to get in a fight. They moved in the woods, and Alice kept her ears pricked, not just for any Zeus troopers but also for the sound of water. She knew that there was a stream nearby, and that was their best bet to get water. After just a few minutes of scouting, she heard something, and walked towards the source of the sound.

'Water!'

The boys were by her side in seconds, and they looked on with wide grins at the water flowing slowly in front of them. Three of the boys were carrying bottles tied around their waists and filled them one by one. It would hardly be enough for all the people with them, but it was a start, and Alice planned to get a larger group out to fetch more water once they knew the area was secure. Next they picked some of the nearby trees clean of berries and fruits, and when they went back, they received a heroes' welcome. The meal they shared that night was frugal by any standards, but they were all smiling, and in their eyes Alice saw the glimmer of something she had though had been lost with the ashes of their settlement: hope.

So when the Queen came to visit them, Alice was understandably in good spirits. The Queen sat down in front of her.

'We cannot keep going like this forever. Now that Zeus and their masters are onto us, sooner or later they will crush us.'

Alice was a bit surprised at this frank admission of defeat.

'You were the one who wanted to fight them.'

The Queen looked at her with her lifeless red eyes.

'Yes, but we cannot simply win in an armed conflict. That's why I so looked forward to you – a human who could help get our message and the vaccine into the right hands. They way I am, nobody would believe me.'

Alice's mother chipped in, 'You've seen what Zeus is capable of. Who could we possibly reach out to?'

'Mrs. Gladwell, of course I know many of the senior officers in Zeus are a part of the conspiracy, but do you really believe every foot soldier is? Most of them are not very different from what you were till a few days ago; scared humans from the Deadland who really believe the Biters are monsters out to exterminate them. Even at senior levels, there must be some people who also don't know the full truth. Such a conspiracy could not have involved everyone in the chain of command.'

As Alice went to sleep, she thought over the Queen's words. Was it really possible that there were men in power out there who were not part of the conspiracy? Was there hope after all?

A few days later, Alice and two others were on a scouting

mission a few kilometers away from the base. Alice was beginning to appreciate just how difficult and complicated managing logistics was. Feeding close to two hundred mouths required a lot of supplies, and they had to ensure that there were sources of food close by. She caught a glimpse of Hatter through the bush, and she knew the Queen had sent some of her Biters out to ensure that Zeus troopers were not nearby. There was still no real possibility of the humans and Biters co-operating in any organized way. The humans would likely listen to Alice if she told them that they were to work together with the Biters on their missions, but the Biters only seemed to take their orders from the Queen, and Alice did not want to risk them turning on the humans with them if they did get into a fight.

After a few minutes, Alice found a stream and asked the others to go back while she freshened up and followed them. She knelt by the water, and splashed the cool water on her face. She looked at her reflection in the water, and perhaps she was imagining it, but she looked different from what she had remembered. The old Alice always had a mischievous smile on her face, always looking to play jokes and pranks on the others in the settlement. A pixie, her father had once lovingly called her. The Alice that looked back at her had a harder face, with eyes that seemed more focused, yet much colder.

Alice got up to leave when she froze. She had just heard the voices of men talking nearby. She was in the open, with no cover and with no weapons on her other than her handgun and knife. If there was a Zeus patrol nearby, her chances of surviving a firefight were going to be slim.

She flattened herself and crawled towards a gentle rise to her left and peeked over the other side. Sitting there, less than ten feet from her, were three fully armed Zeus troopers.

They apparently had not got wind of her, since they had their helmets off, with their rifles on the ground beside them, and were eating a snack. From their looks, Alice guessed they were local boys, which was confirmed when they began speaking to each other in a mixture of Hindi and English, a combination Alice had grown up both hearing and speaking every day. One of them, who looked to be the youngest of the lot, and perhaps not much older than Alice, seemed to be troubled by something.

'Ashok, you know what all the other guys are saying, don't you?'

The older and larger boy he had just spoken to spat on the ground.

'Jeevan, how many times do I have to tell you to keep both your ears and mouth shut? Don't you get it? We have a stable job. Our families get rations and are safe. Remember what our lives were like out in the Deadland?'

The third boy, who had stayed silent till now, looked up. 'Ashok, he does have a point. We signed up not just for the food and safety, but because we thought we would get a chance to protect other people and finally get back at the Biters who had taken so much from us. Where does the attack on a human settlement figure in that?'

Now they had Alice's full attention, since she realized that they must have been speaking about the attack on her settlement. Curious to know what else the troopers might know, she let her curiosity get the better of her and crept closer, peering as far beyond the edge of the rise as she dared.

'Naveen, they said they were traitors!'

The boy called Naveen whirled around at the older boy, his voice displaying barely controlled fury.

'Traitors? Why did our local officers not tell us anything about it before? Why was that explanation given after the attack by that bald white officer? And tell me this: why did they not use any local units for it, but flew in their Chinese Red Guards?'

It suddenly struck Alice why the troopers she had encountered looked so different from any men she had seen before. She had heard about China in the context of the Old Nations and about how the Red Guards were supposed to be the real army of the hidden masters behind Zeus, but she wondered why Zeus would fly in troops from there.

'Naveen, those troops were based in Ladakh, and you know the Red Guards are all Chinese.'

'It still doesn't add up, and I don't like it.'

There was an uncomfortable silence while the boys finished their snacks, and then began packing their kit. Alice began backing up the way she had come when she felt her foot hit something. She whirled around and saw a large Zeus trooper looming over her. She tried to reach the gun tucked into her belt, but he had his gun up in a second, and Alice found herself peering down the barrel of an assault rifle.

'Guys, we have ourselves some company!'

The other troopers clambered over the rise, and Alice was now surrounded by armed Zeus troopers. She got up to her feet and addressed the young trooper she had heard speak first.

'I heard you talk about the settlement that was attacked. I'm from there.'

The big trooper who had caught her spun her around.

'Talk to me! I'm in charge here, and you are my prisoner.'

He said the last word with a leer forming on his face, and in an instant Alice knew what his intentions were. A girl her age in more innocent times before the world had gone up in flames might have been paralyzed with fear in a situation like this, but for Alice, instinct and training came first, and fear followed only later. She kicked out at the boy's groin, making solid contact as the boy doubled over in agony. Another boy tried to grab her from behind, but she caught his arm at the elbow, twisting it so he fell to his knees, and then she kneed him hard in the face. The boy fell back, his nose broken as Alice jumped over the rise, sprinting for the cover of the trees. She heard guns being cocked behind her and prepared herself for the spray of automatic weapons fire that would no doubt follow, when she heard an order bellowed with such force and authority that she found herself unconsciously slowing down and turning to see who it was.

'Hold your fire!'

She turned and saw Dewan standing there, with his rifle raised to his shoulders. For a second, she harbored hopes that he would rescue her, but she realized that his rifle was pointing straight at her.

Without taking his eyes off her, he spoke to the troopers. 'Do you morons ever think with your brains? Check the Communicator and see who she is.'

Alice was frozen in place, knowing that there was no way she could get away without being shot as one of the troopers took out a small device from his pocket and looked at it. All four troopers were now standing at attention in front of Dewan as he continued to give them a tongue lashing.

'She is a wanted terrorist, not a plaything for you idiots, and I want her alive for questioning. Now go and join the unit and I'll bring her in myself.'

Suitably chastised, the four troopers left as Dewan walked towards Alice, his gun still raised.

'Colonel...'

'Shut up!'

Alice was shocked by the reply she got from Dewan, who had been so friendly and helpful when she had last met him.

He kept his gun raised in his left hand while he took out a small device with his right hand and pointed it at Alice.

'Take a look at this.'

The screen showed a picture of Alice with a lot of words around it. On top were the words 'Wanted'. Alice would have taken too long to try and decipher all the other words so she asked Dewan what it said.

'It says that you're a dangerous terrorist wanted in the deaths of several Red Guards and suspected of collaborating with elements who are out to destabilize the peace that the Central Committee is trying to bring to the Deadland.'

Alice almost laughed at the absurdity of it all.

'Come on, Colonel, you know I'm no terrorist. Do you even know what that Appleseed did?'

Dewan came close and now Alice could see that he looked frightened.

'I know it all, which is why I've been looking for you. I know this terrorist thing is all garbage, but I don't know why this is happening. When I found out what happened to your settlement and that they were hunting you, I came down to try and get to you first.'

Alice felt a wave of relief wash over her, but she noticed that Dewan was suddenly alert.

'The rest of the squad will be here anytime. Got anywhere we can talk in private?'

Alice wondered if she should mention that her definition of private meant being in the company of two hundred people and several Biters, but thought better of it. She remembered what the Queen had said about finding someone in authority who would be willing to believe them, and Dewan seemed like her last hope.

She motioned for Dewan to follow her and they disappeared in the jungle before the first trooper got there.

Alice guided Dewan through one of the hidden entrances to the base, which had been carved out of the trunk of a tree. Dewan looked around as he entered the narrow tunnel.

'How did you guys make such an elaborate hiding place in just a few days?'

Alice did not reply, weighing in her mind when and how she should break the full reality of her situation to Dewan. She needed him to be on her side and to trust her, and she was not sure if revealing the true nature of the Biters and Zeus would be too much too soon. As they progressed down the tunnel far enough that Alice was confident they could not be heard overground, she asked Dewan to sit down.

'Colonel...'

'Just call me Amit.'

'Ok, Amit. There's a lot going on here that you need to know about. I don't know where to start. It all sounds crazy.'

Dewan laid a reassuring hand on her shoulder. He was very different from her father. He was shorter, built much broader, and had a much squarer face, but his eyes had the same kindness in them. Alice found it easy to be relaxed in his company as he spoke.

'Alice, I was a newly commissioned officer in the Indian Army. I had a girl I was going to propose to. I had a career to look ahead to. Then one day, my life and my world collapsed around me, and I found myself fighting for survival. I hid in the Deadland for months, surviving off the land, using my special forces training in a way I had never imagined before, fighting Biters and human scavengers alike, till I was picked up by a Zeus helicopter. They were the first promise of stability and safety in this crazy new world, and I signed up without a second thought. Since then, my life has had one purpose: to fight the monsters who had caused so much loss and to help the humans still in the Deadland. I never doubted anything I was doing, till now. So compared to what I have seen and been through, nothing you tell or show me can be too crazy for me to handle.'

Alice was about to begin when a shadow moved in front of her and she gasped. It was Bunny Ears, standing there looking at her, as if wondering why she was with a Zeus trooper inside the base.

'Holy shit!'

Dewan was on his feet and was about to bring his rifle up. Bunny Ears, startled by the move, had bared his teeth and was hissing when Alice grabbed Dewan's hands.

'Amit, no! Please don't shoot!'

'But, this is...'

Alice looked at him, pleading with him.

'Just believe me for a minute and come further down. You'll see for yourself everything that I've discovered and the real reason behind why Appleseed suddenly wants me and my friends dead.'

Dewan seemed to be struggling with himself for some time. All his training and experience were telling him to open fire, yet he wanted to trust Alice. When Alice let go of his hands, she saw him look at her but then quickly shift his gaze to Bunny Ears.

'Alice, if you were a terrorist and you wanted me dead, I wouldn't be alive now. So I will trust you – but not this... thing. Any sudden move and I blow his head off.'

Bunny Ears growled as Dewan looked at him defiantly. An uneasy truce having been established between them, the three of them walked down the narrow path deeper into the base. When they entered the hall where the humans were sheltering, Alice heard several weapons being raised and cocked at the sight of a Zeus trooper in uniform. Alice stepped in front of Dewan.

'Please, he's a friend. He can help us.'

Everyone listened to Alice, but if looks could kill, Dewan would have been dead within a few paces with everyone in the room looking at him with undisguised hostility and contempt. Alice took him straight to the Queen's room, and apparently having heard of the arrival of a guest, she was dressed for the occasion, wearing her dark glasses and gloves and with a shawl covering her body. One glance at her and something clicked in Dewan's head and he took out his palmtop device.

'Let me guess. I am a wanted terrorist in your system, am I not?'

He looked sheepishly at the Queen, who smiled, showing reddish teeth that caused Dewan to blanch as he began to wonder who or what he was dealing with. Alice asked him to sit and told the Queen about how he had helped her earlier, and then looked at Dewan.

'Amit, please listen to what she has to say and read the documents she has. That's all I ask of you. Just listen to it all first before you say anything.'

Dewan sat impassively as the Queen took him through her tale, complete with all the documents she had and topped off with her revealing her true nature. Alice saw that Dewan didn't seem fazed at all by everything he saw. If anything, he seemed lost in thought, almost as if his mind were somewhere else. When the Queen finished, all eyes were on Dewan, waiting to see what his reaction would be. He got up and let his breath out in an audible sigh and then buried his face in his hands. Alice was worried that he was losing it and started to walk towards him, but he held out a palm, motioning for her to stop. When he finally spoke, it was in a tone that was barely a whisper.

'When people are scared enough, they begin to accept any form of tyranny because unquestioning obedience to unknown masters is better than facing known dangers.'

Alice sensed that Dewan needed to talk, so she stepped back as Dewan continued, talking more to himself than to anyone in the room.

'In all these years, I never asked who we served. All I heard was that the Central Committee had been set up in China and was overseeing all rehabilitation efforts, but I never asked who they were. I met my senior officers once in a while, and the only order they gave was simple: exterminate the Biters and bring more humans in the Deadland into settlements regulated by the Central Committee. When settlements refused to sign up, we were somehow assigned other duties, and we saw Red Guards from China who were flown in and kept in isolated camps on our bases, but we never asked why they had to come in.'

He stopped, and then looked at Alice, and she saw the beginnings of tears in his eyes.

'I saw thousands of people flown to China to be resettled. There were always rumors that they were being taken to slave camps, but I always ignored the stories, convincing myself that these were just conspiracy theories. You know the funny thing about everything you've shown me?'

Alice watched the Colonel come to grips with himself as he continued.

'The funny thing is that I, and perhaps many other officers, guessed that there was something going on, that this mysterious Central Committee was not just doing things out of the goodness of its heart, that we were serving masters whose agendas were not always transparent. But we had seen how chaotic and fickle life was in the Deadland, with no authority or government, and we chose to close our eyes and hang on to the illusion that we were fighting a just war. But what you've showed me goes so far beyond just today's reality. This could change everything!'

The Queen had been watching Dewan and now she came closer.

'Colonel, we need your help. We know we cannot survive a war against the Central Committee forever, but we need someone in the administration to help get the truth out. Is there someone in power we could reach out to?'

Dewan shook his head. 'I don't know, and with Appleseed now so involved in the operations, I don't know whom to trust. As I said, I've never even seen anyone on the Central Committee, but you don't need to reach the top to get your message across.'

'What do you mean?'

Dewan looked at Alice as he answered her. 'We start at the bottom: with the common troops, young boys and girls from settlements like yours, who form the backbone of Zeus here. That's where we get this thing started.'

NINE

EVERAL OF THE HUMANS WERE gathered around
Dewan as he dug into his backpack and took out a flat,
sleek device.

'What it it?'

Alice's mother answered her. 'Looks a lot like a tablet
computer, but I haven't seen one in years.'

Alice had grown up without many of the technological
trappings and toys that kids had enjoyed before The Rising,
and by the time she had grown up enough to understand what
they were, the people at her settlement had lost or thrown
away their computers and cellphones. She leaned over her
mother's shoulder to see what Dewan had in his hand. The
device suddenly seemed to come to life with bright, vivid
colors appearing on its screen. She saw the Zeus logo, which
was then replaced by lots of numbers and letters and symbols.
As Dewan touched one of the pictures with a finger, a new
set of visuals and text filled the surface. To Alice, it looked
almost magical. Her mother was reading it aloud for the
benefit of everyone around.

'The Central Committee has announced the beginning
of the new harvest season, where workers are joyously
participating in planting seeds and working the fields in

preparation for a new year of prosperity. Chairman Wang has said that the Red Guards are vigorously pursuing heroic actions in the Deadland in India and America to continue their victorious charge against the Biter hordes, and in helping bring more human survivors into the fold of the People's Revolution.'

Alice could see her mother's mouth twist in disgust as she looked at Dewan.

'What is this crap? Do the Chinese control everything now?'

Dewan looked at her, surprise on his face.

'Didn't you know? Oh, I forgot, you guys have been off the grid for some time now. A few years after The Rising, when people started rebuilding, China was the only major power that was relatively untouched, and they set about taking charge under the Central Committee. They used the old Chinese Army as the beginning of the Red Guards but then contracted Zeus to help in the Deadland.'

The Queen was now right behind Dewan.

'I find it very convenient that the net outcome of The Rising was that the US and other powers were largely scattered and destroyed and China emerged as the centre of the new human civilization. I used to think that the US decision to hit China was madness on our part. Now, I'm not so sure. Perhaps it was true that the elites in the West who wanted a New World Order joined up with the Chinese to engineer this.'

Dewan sat in silence, considering it in his mind. 'Look, Dr. Protima, I was in the old Indian Army and we hardly saw China as a friend, but I'm not sure they would have done this. Why destroy the whole world and rule over the ashes?'

Alice's mother spoke up. 'Colonel, I worked in a bank in my old life, and we all remember the way the world was. Markets were melting down and the US on the verge of defaulting on its debt. There were protests throughout the world against the elite who had brought the world to such a state. China's economy was booming, but it was also the largest holder of US debt: if the US had collapsed and defaulted, China would have been ruined. Add to that growing demands for democracy in China, and the second Tinanmen Square massacre of 2012, and I don't find it hard to believe they could have engineered this. From what I see here, they seem to be fine, maybe because they prepared for it. They still have big cities, and are using slave labor from the Deadland to harvest their crops and feed their people. And every surviving human is so terrified that they are willing to live with any level of dictatorship if it means some level of safety.'

Alice's mind was reeling. Why would anyone destroy so much, and kill so many countless numbers of people, to hold on to power? She began to understand why her father had hated men who craved power and had tried so hard to keep their settlement out of the clutches of Zeus and its masters. Now, as she looked at Dewan, she began to see the first cracks appear as he perhaps for the first time began to understand the role he had unwittingly played in the whole conspiracy.

Alice sat down next to him. 'Amit, what can we do to fight this army of theirs? Could you help train some of us or maybe help us get better weapons?'

Dewan shook his head. 'No, Alice. You cannot win this war through weapons alone. What you've seen is nothing compared to the firepower they have. The Zeus troopers only have personal weapons and some air support, but the Central Committee has missiles and heavy bombers. They would flatten us without us even getting a chance to take a shot at them.'

'So what do we do?'

Dewan was up and he began pacing the room.

'Exactly as I said before, we need to get the rank and file of the Zeus troops to know the truth. Once they know what they are doing and who they are really serving, we'll get more allies in the battle.'

Alice's mother was now holding the tablet and she looked at Dewan, an idea forming in her mind.

'We are totally cut from the information networks Zeus and the Central Committee uses, but you are plugged into it. If you leave this tablet here, we could post messages that all Zeus troopers would be able to see.'

Dewan clearly didn't think that was a good idea as he shook his head vigorously.

'They would track the tablet down in a few minutes and how could...'

As he was saying something, he suddenly stopped, as if a new idea had struck him.

'What if I lost my backpack in a firefight and someone took my kit, including my tablet?'

The Queen saw where Dewan was going and chipped in, 'Could any of us use this device? We haven't been near computers for years and this is more advanced than anything we used in our time.'

A man stepped forward. 'Hey, I was really into tech and was a blogger before The Rising. I'm sure I could learn if the Colonel here showed me the basics.'

'Then we have a plan.'

Alice looked at Dewan. 'Plan? We keep the tablet here, and figure out some way of getting messages to the Zeus troopers, but what about you?'

Dewan looked at her. 'I go back to my base, pretending to have survived a ferocious firefight, and then continue being a loyal soldier to the Central Committee.'

Several people began to speak up at the same time, and the Queen had to raise her voice to hush them.

'Quiet, everyone. Let him finish.'

'But how can we be sure he won't lead them here?'

Dewan turned to face the speaker, an elderly woman who shrank back under his gaze.

'Look, you just have to trust me. I took enough of a risk wandering out alone to look for Alice. If I just wanted to follow orders, I would have arrested or killed her when I had her alone in the forest.'

Alice heard a few more people grumble, so she stood in front of Dewan and addressed the crowd.

'Everyone, on this you need to trust me. The Colonel didn't have to come down here with me, he didn't need to save me from his men in the forest, and he certainly didn't need to put himself at so much risk by trusting me. I trust him, and ask you to go along with his plan if you trust me.'

Her words carried the day, and as Alice watched everyone back down, and many of the gathered people averted their gazes when she looked at them, she was once more surprised at what she had become. She had never wanted to be a leader of any sort, and certainly would not have asked for the responsibility and burden that came with it, but now, whether she liked it or not, she realized that everyone was looking to her. She just hoped that she did not mess things up too much.

Dewan touched her gently on the shoulder. 'Thanks, Alice. You'll all be better off having someone on the inside helping you.'

After brief goodbyes, Dewan gathered his weapon but left the rest of his kit behind and slipped out into the forest. He turned once to wave at her and then Alice saw him disappear behind the trees. Her heart was pounding as she wondered if she had done the right thing by letting him go or had doomed all of them.

Dewan was sitting at his desk, typing his After Action Report for the third time. He had sent in his first draft, which had been sent back by Appleseed with more than a dozen questions. He had tried to address all of them systematically, but knew that no matter what he wrote down in a formal memo, he could not address the underlying skepticism of how an elite officer like him was caught in close combat with terrorists and managed to escape without his kit. His second draft had gone through to the Central Committee in Shanghai and had come back with more notations and questions. Dewan had half-hoped that he would not attract too much scrutiny but with the high level of anxiety, even paranoia, that Appleseed had about Alice and the escaped humans, he was not going to let Dewan off the hook so easily. Dewan noticed that Appleseed said nothing about the attack on the settlement and made no mention of the Queen. If Dewan had any doubts about what he had heard from Alice and the others, Appleseed's behavior nailed it for him.

The Messenger window on his screen beeped and he saw that he was being called for a debriefing to Appleseed's office. When he reached there a few minutes later, he was surprised to see Appleseed sitting with a Chinese general whom he had never met before. The slight man was wearing his cap even indoors, and as he stood, Dewan saw the red star emblazoned on it. Dewan saluted and the man returned his salute.

'At ease, Colonel. I am General Chen from the Central Committee. I flew down from Shanghai last night to meet you for myself.'

Dewan was instantly on guard.

'Sir, I would have been available anytime for a call. I'm sorry you had to travel so far on my account.'

Chen smiled, his thin lips pursed back, and Dewan realized that he was looking at a man who could be very dangerous.

'Colonel, you have had a number of brushes with the Biters recently, and you brought in this counter-revolutionary, this girl Alice. We have spoken to some of your men and it seems you had recaptured her when they last saw you.'

Dewan tried not to betray the fear he felt.

'Sir, I had her, but when I was bringing her in, I was ambushed by a force of her supporters and I lost her.'

Chen looked at him for several seconds before turning his back to Dewan.

'Yes, Colonel, and it seems you lost much of your kit, including your service tablet.'

'Yes, sir. One of them grabbed my backpack and pulled it off.'

Chen was picking something off the desk and when he turned to face Dewan, he was carrying a tablet in his hand. He powered it on and tapped the Browser. When it opened up, Dewan saw a new post on the Intranet Board used by Zeus. His heart skipped a beat when he saw the headline.

What is the real truth behind The Rising? Read more to find out.

'Colonel, this was posted last evening. We triangulated the location to somewhere deep in the Deadland, but of course nobody was there when a squad got there.'

When Dewan replied truthfully that he had not seen the post, Chen smiled.

'Of course you did not. It was up for only five minutes before we removed it and locked your account, from which it was posted. That won't stop whoever did it from creating new accounts and posting again, but it does make you wonder. Biters cannot use tablets, but their terrorist human collaborators can. Counter-revolutionaries like this Alice of yours.'

The last two words caught Dewan totally off guard, and he realized he was walking a razor's edge and that anything he said could land him in serious danger.

'Sir, I have devoted the last fourteen years to serving the cause we all fight for, and I want to help in any way I can.'

Chen dismissed him and told him that he could go and rejoin his unit.

'Colonel, I may take you up on that offer someday.'

Dewan reached his desk, his heart pounding. He knew his story was wafer thin, and the fact that Chen was here showed just how a serious a threat the Central Committee saw the situation as. Media and what had been recreated of the Internet was strictly regulated, and nobody had really complained, once again trading off democracy for security. But for the first time ever, that tightly controlled information flow had been breached.

A few minutes later, he went to the cafeteria to have dinner and saw several troopers there. He sat down next to a few young recruits and while they quickly shut up when he sat, he could see that they had been in the middle of an animated conversation.

'So, guys, what were you talking about?'

One of the troopers looked around, as if seeking support from his comrades, and then looked at Dewan. 'Sir, it's nothing; just some stupid rumors some of the guys had seen.'

Dewan had always been well liked by his men, not least because he was always accessible and was someone they could count on to help. Many of his men had been mere boys who had been picked up from the Deadland, and Dewan had trained them and, in many cases, saved their lives in combat.

He looked at a young trooper he knew well. 'Satish, what are these rumors?'

The young trooper seemed to be struggling with how to say what was on his mind.

'Sir, it seems someone hacked into your account and posted some stuff about The Rising last night. A few of the guys happened to read it, and have been telling all sorts of wild stories.'

Dewan had to stop himself from smiling.

'I heard some bastards hacked my account. What did they post?'

Another trooper spoke, seemingly hesitant to even say the words out loud. 'Something about The Rising having been caused by human governments and about how China was behind so much of it.'

Another trooper, now more confident since the subject had been broached, spoke up. 'I also heard that it mentioned something about what all the folks from the Deadland were doing in the colonies being set up for them. Something about them being little more than slave labor. Sir, they may all be lies for all I know, but why would someone suddenly make up such lies and post them on our boards?'

He quickly shut up when a whole squad of Red Guards came into the cafeteria and sat at an adjoining table, and they continued their meal in silence, but Dewan, despite the fear he had felt while meeting Chen, was exulting inside.

His plan was beginning to work. Now it was all up to Alice and her group to take it forward. With Chen and his Red Guards here in force, he knew they would hardly have it easy.

'Nikhil, hurry up!'

Alice was gnashing her teeth in frustration at the time Nikhil was taking to upload his latest post. She scarcely understood the technology involved in it all, but she knew that the Red Guards would know within minutes where the post had been uploaded from and would be sending troopers their way. So far, in the last week they had uploaded two posts. In both cases, they had ventured far from their base, making an overnight journey through the forests, uploaded the posts and then made their way back. Alice had no idea if anyone had even read the posts or what impact they were having, but Nikhil was sure that the Central Committee would be trying its best to delete or block the posts.

Nikhil was over fifty and quite unlike most of the other men at the settlement. He was slightly built, and wore broken glasses that were crudely held together by adhesive tape. Before The Rising, he had claimed to be a blogger, though many of the older folks said he had been a hacker. Alice didn't really know what those words meant, but she knew that he was able to use the tablet Dewan had left behind and was willing to make the dangerous journey with her through the forest.

To minimize their chances of detection, only the two of them had ventured out. While that made for better stealth, it also meant that if they ran into trouble, their chances of survival were low. Alice was armed to the teeth, with her handgun, knife and an automatic weapon that they had salvaged from a Zeus trooper. But while Nikhil carried a handgun, she was not sure he even knew how to use it properly. To make things worse, he had been sitting hunched over the tablet for the last fifteen minutes, whispering something about firewalls. The post he was uploading was one that was a detailed first person account of Appleseed's role in the destruction of their settlement, based on Alice's story. It was a risk to personally identify her, but they had reasoned that putting a face to the messages would make it more believable than them being from anonymous posters. Also, with Alice supposedly a wanted terrorist, this would help sow doubts in the minds of Zeus troopers about whom the real bad guys were.

Finally, he got up and looked at Alice with a look of triumph.

'It's done! And this time I waited to see if there were any responses so I could be sure somebody is reading our posts.'

Alice froze.

'You waited! You know they'll be coming soon. Let's get out of here.'

Nikhil persisted and handed her the tablet.

'Look at this.'

Knowing that this war was going to be fought and won as much with words as with bullets, Alice had finally got around to asking her mother to teach her to read and had been brushing up her reading skills. There was only one reply to Nikhil's post and it was short enough for it to not tax her reading skills much. A Zeus trooper had posted, 'So that's why the Red Guards are all over the place nowadays.'

Alice knew that whoever had replied to the post would likely get into a lot of trouble, but it was a small yet significant sign: their messages were getting through to the Zeus troopers and they were beginning to create some doubts in their minds. As Nikhil turned off the tablet and put it in his backpack, Alice heard the dull roar of approaching helicopters.

'Nikhil, come on! They'll be here any minute!'

The sun had barely risen and Nikhil had timed his

message to catch the attention of any Zeus trooper who was up but had some time to go before their morning drills. This was one among many details shared by Dewan which were helping them time their postings to coincide with downtimes for Zeus troopers when they were likely to be surfing on their tablets.

Alice and Nikhil were running into the trees when the first helicopter appeared over the horizon. Alice turned around and saw that there were two sleek gunships and a larger troop carrier. By the time the first Red Guards were on the ground, Alice and Nikhil were already more than a kilometer away, tearing through the forest as fast as they could run. From her previous run-in with the Red Guards, Alice knew that they would likely be trying to flank them and drive them into a trap, so instead of taking the path that led to the road which they needed to follow back to their base, they turned right, running through the forest till they came to a clearing. She could see the broken shells of old buildings. Nikhil had told her that once upon a time this had been a posh suburb and that some of the wooded areas they had run through had once been part of farmlands of the elite. That was a world that sounded totally alien to her, but she was happy for the cover the buildings would provide them. They ran into an old apartment building and rushed up the stairs. On the second floor, they stopped to see where their pursuers were, but saw no sign of them.

Alice relaxed a bit and took a look around her. For someone who had lived in the open for much of her life, it was hard to imagine living in these concrete shells – but then, their occupants never had making an instant getaway as a priority. Perhaps if they had, they would have lived longer than they did during The Rising. The apartment was obviously abandoned and as they walked from one flat to another, they found little of use or interest, since they had been picked clean over the years.

As Alice entered one flat, she saw something small lying in a corner. It was a small female figure with half burnt blonde hair.

'Nikhil, what is this?'

'Alice, that was a Barbie doll that girls used to play with.'

Alice flung the doll to one side, wondering how girls ever had enough spare time to sit and play with silly little figurines. She looked out the window and froze. There were a dozen or more Red Guards outside, their rifles at the ready, walking past the apartment. She motioned for Nikhil to get down as she continued watching the men outside. One of them was speaking into a handheld radio and as Alice looked up in the sky, she saw the faint outline of something black hovering above them. That must have been one of the drones Appleseed had mentioned, thought Alice, wondering if they had been spotted on their way into the apartment. Most of the Guards walked past and Alice was beginning to relax when one of them suddenly stopped and looked back at the apartment. Alice ducked down as he brought his rifle up to his shoulder, looked through the scope and casually fired a single round.

The bullet hit the wall just outside the window where Alice and Nikhil were sheltering, and they waited for a minute or more, hoping the Guard had moved on. Nikhil, tired of sitting on his haunches, started to get up to stretch when another bullet shattered the glass on the window. Nikhil dove to his right, and even without hearing the Red Guard's bellowed command to his men, Alice knew that the sudden movement had given them away. Alice was at the window in a split second, her rifle at the ready, and she fired at the first Red Guards approaching the apartment. Her bullets kicked up the dirt around them and she saw one of them fall before he was pulled behind cover by a comrade. Before she could find new targets, the other Guards opened fire on full automatic, shredding the window and showering her with glass. With the numbers so stacked against her, standing her ground and hoping to win the firefight was a losing cause.

She saw that Nikhil was crouched against the wall, and while his hands were gripping his gun, they were shaking uncontrollably. An idea came to her as she considered the odds against them.

'Nikhil, just point your gun out the window and fire down at them. You don't even have to aim; just stick it out and shoot once every few seconds and please don't get yourself killed.'

He offered her a wan smile, as she took her rifle and ran out of the flat and down the stairs. She could hear the pop of Nikhil's gun, immediately answered by an overwhelming volley of automatic weapon fire from the Red Guards. She rounded the corner on the corridor and climbed out an open window that had once served as a fire exit. She crouched on the narrow stairwell outside and saw the Guards, four of whom were now advancing from cover to cover while their comrades kept up a withering rate of fire at the window where Nikhil was hiding. She was almost behind the Red Guards and they had not yet spotted her. She selected single shot mode, not wanting to waste bullets, and aimed carefully at the Guards advancing on the apartment. Her first shot took a Guard in the neck, killing him instantly. Before the others had realized what had happened, another was down. By the time the Guards spotted her and their officer, a tall and thin man, screamed orders to his men, a third Guard was down.

As Alice dove back into the corridor, bullets slammed into the stairwell where she had been seconds ago. There were still nine Guards left and while she had managed to give them a nasty surprise, the odds were still very much against them. She retreated back up the stairs and found Nikhil grinning.

'Did I hit anyone?'

Despite all the stress, she smiled.

'Nikhil, you should stick to that tablet thing of yours.'

As she peered out another window, she saw that the Guards were again advancing on the apartment, and she brought her rifle up, determined not to go down without a fight. Just then, a dark figure wearing a hat rushed out from the forest and picked up the nearest Red Guard, snapping his neck and tossing his body away. Several more Biters jumped out of the bushes, and Alice saw the Red Guard officer shoot one in the head before beginning to run towards the apartment. Taken by surprise and outnumbered, the Red Guards never stood much of a chance, and two or three more were killed before Alice saw Hatter stand up to his full height and scream. The other Biters took his cue and the remaining Red Guards were not killed but bitten. The Officer who had been running towards the apartment raised his rifle, aiming straight at Hatter, who was now lunging towards him. The Red Guard Officer was about to pull the trigger when a single bullet from Alice hit him in the neck and he went down. Hatter looked up with his expressionless, red eyes and saw Alice at the window.

Alice had never been so happy to see Biters before, and as she and Nikhil came down, they saw that the four Guards who had been bitten were now twitching on the ground, as if suffering a violent fit, and then they sat up, all trace of humanity gone in their lifeless eyes, blood from the bites they had suffered streaming down their bodies. They looked at Alice and Nikhil and one of them hissed and started to move towards them, when Hatter hit him hard and then barked something to them. Alice didn't understand what he said, but it was clear that they knew who was in charge because as they ran into the forest to get back to their base, the newly converted Biters made no move to attack them. Alice turned back after a few minutes of running to see Hatter and the other Biters following them. Some distance behind them were the new converts.

Alice smiled and Nikhil asked her what she found so funny about their near brush with death.

'When the colonel talked about us turning Zeus troopers to our side, I'm guessing he didn't have this in mind.'

TEN

'THREE HUNDRED?'

Appleseed withered in the face of Chen's rhetorical questions. The one thing that Appleseed had learnt about his Chinese boss was that when he asked a question, he rarely wanted an answer. Instead, he was usually passing judgment, and in this case, Appleseed knew that the judgment being passed could be deadly for him. Appleseed had been a career military officer in the old US Army, when as a colonel based in Afghanistan he had been approached by some old mentors who had mentioned certain special projects they wanted him to help with. At the time, a million dollars in cash seemed to be worth the secrecy and subterfuge he had dealt with, and when The Rising had taken place, he actually thought that he had been chosen to be one of the elites to fight this scourge. Fifteen years later, he was not so sure anymore about who or what cause he really served. The money was no longer worth much, but he did have a wife and three kids, and he knew that if Chen ordered it, in an instant he could be reduced to being no more than yet another of the millions of slave laborers who lived and died without much fanfare in the many camps that sustained the utopian new world that the Central Committee promised to usher in. The only currency he knew and recognized that still mattered in this new world was power, and he was determined to cling on to that.

He straightened his back and faced Chen, whom he towered over.

'Yes, sir. Over the past one week, we have had more than three hundred desertions in the force.'

Appleseed saw Chen's pale face darken and his fists turn red as he clenched the chair in front on him.

'That, General, is the problem of using the occupied to manage their own territories.'

Appleseed bit his tongue. He knew how badly the Chinese Red Army had been hit by retaliatory strikes by US nuclear forces in the days following The Rising, and while the erstwhile United States was little better than the Asian Deadland Appleseed oversaw, there was continued fierce resistance from bands of American guerillas that was bleeding the Red Guards dry. He knew that Chen and his Chinese masters badly wanted to nip in the bud any possible insurrection in Asia and that they were counting on him to do it. That was the single most important source of Appleseed's power. For the past fifteen years, he had managed the Asian Deadland with an iron fist, born out of extensive experience in Afghanistan before The Rising, a fiery grounding in counter-insurgency that had helped him decimate the Biters and bring into the Central Committee's fold most of the remaining human settlements. That was, of course, till that silly girl called Alice surfaced and the whole matter threatened to spiral out of control. He felt a familiar stirring as he recalled being alone with her. In his mind, he was a soldier who was doing his duty, but there were dark moments and dark deeds that he tried hard to not consciously face, for in his hearts of hearts he enjoyed the power he held over others, the power to make them submit to his will, the power to make them beg him. He recalled all the grief this Alice had caused him and promised himself that the next time she was alone with him, she would be begging him for mercy.

Over the past two weeks, her cohorts had been bombarding the Zeus Intranet with messages, averaging more than three a day, and while Chen had flown in Information Technology specialists from Shanghai who would delete every posting within minutes, the seditious messages were slowly but surely having an impact. The hardest hit were recruits from the human settlements in the Deadland of what had once been India, and desertions had been on the rise. All attempts to track down the posters had proven to be in vain and the efforts at striking back against them had produced little by way of tangible results other than many scores of casualties.

'Eighty-five Red Guards have died in one week. Does that sound like something the Central Committee will tolerate?'

Appleseed had posed a rhetorical question to Dewan not unlike the ones being posed to him by Chen, and he was infuriated to see Dewan standing impassively in front of him.

'Goddamit, Colonel! You've been patrolling these areas for years. Don't tell me you don't know where these people can be.'

Dewan looked Appleseed straight in the eye, and waited for a few seconds before replying, as if weighing how best to phrase his reply.

'Sir, General Chen insists on flying in Red Guards straight from Tibet or mainland China who know nothing of the local people or terrain. That's why they walk into one ambush after another. If they let me and my boys get a free reign, we may actually produce better results.'

Appleseed turned on Dewan with a fury. 'Colonel, the

reason he does that is because he is not sure whether any of the local troops can be trusted. I hope I don't have to remind you of the number of desertions we've seen over the past couple of weeks.'

Dewan thought of how to reply to that, and when he did, Appleseed noticed that the colonel was not looking him in the eye.

'General, the boys are no longer sure of what the truth is. These posters from the Deadland are sending out messages that challenge the very reason we are doing what we are. I haven't really seen the Central Committee counter those with any compelling arguments other than to censor the posts and send out Red Guards against locations where the posts were supposedly uploaded.'

'Colonel, I hope you realize that such statements about the Central Committee border on treason!'

Appleseed noticed that Dewan did not flinch under the implicit threat, and an idea came to him.

'Colonel, would you say that anyone not in approved settlements can be considered at the very least a sympathizer, if not an active collaborator with the counter-revolutionaries among the humans and no more deserving of mercy than the damned Biters?'

Dewan was taken aback by Appleseed lapsing into the lingo used by Chen and his Chinese masters, and his hesitation led Appleseed to press ahead.

'I take it that this Alice and her cohorts could not move so freely in the Deadland if the remaining human settlements there did not at least implicitly support her?'

Dewan did not know where this was going and he knew that anything he said would not help his cause, so he just stayed silent as Appleseed continued.

'So, Colonel Dewan, from your response, I take it that

anyone still in the Deadland in unauthorized settlements is probably a human sympathizer of this Alice or have been subverted by the Biters and their supposed Queen. For years we have resisted taking active measures against the Biters in the Deadland because we wanted to minimize collateral damage among the human settlements there. Perhaps that equation has now changed.'

Dewan felt a chill go up his spine as he realized where this was going. Appleseed picked up his radio to call Chen.

'General Chen, I have a plan that may help us eradicate the threat we face once and for all.'

As Dewan heard Appleseed outline his plan, he was seized with panic. He had to do something to warn Alice and the others, but there was no way he could do that without compromising himself.

'It's her!'

Over the last couple of weeks, Alice had slowly got used to this kind of reception whenever she walked into a human settlement in the Deadland. While Nikhil had kept up a relentless barrage of messages aimed at the Zeus troops, Alice had never really accounted for how fast the news would spread among the settlements. Most of the deserters found their way back to their settlements, and there they shared tales of the lies they had been told, of how the Central Committee, far from being a benevolent power, represented forces that had perhaps brought upon the catastrophe of The Rising in the first place to serve their pursuit of power. Most people found it hard to think of the Biters as anything other than the monsters they had always taken them for, but once doubts were sowed about the true nature of the

Central Committee, they proved hard to undo. Add to that the heavy-handed tactics of the Red Guards and Chen, and one settlement after another had started to side with Alice.

Alice found herself facing more than three hundred people in the settlement, located just west of what had once been the suburb of Noida. Their leader, a grizzled old man, walked up to her and looked at her as if sizing her up.

'You are but a young girl, little more than child, and a foreigner at that. What makes you expect that we would side with you and risk facing the Red Guards?'

Alice looked the old man in the eye. 'I don't expect you or your people to do anything other than to hear me out. After that, you can still choose to send your young ones to serve Zeus and to slave in the Central Committee's labor camps. Or you can choose to fight.'

The old man snorted derisively. 'Fight for what? You speak very fancy words for someone so young. Do you even know what those words mean?'

Alice did not even flinch as she replied, 'I fight for the freedom that we all have as human beings. The freedom to live the way we want, the freedom to choose our leaders, the freedom my father and hundreds of others have died to protect.'

The man averted his eyes and turned to the assembled crowd.

'Let us hear her out.'

When Alice finished, twenty more young men and women had joined her ranks. She never quite realized when her struggle to ensure safety and survival for her settlement had become something more. Perhaps it was when she watched her father and his friends be killed by the Red Guards; perhaps it was when she realized the full extent of the conspiracy behind it all – but what mattered now was that whether she liked it or not, she was effectively leading an ever growing army that fought back against the Red Guards. The Biters still would not really take orders from her, but she noticed that they were always lurking in the background on the Queen's orders, waiting to wade into the battle to support her.

Alice waited on the small hill outside the settlement as Nikhil uploaded his latest message, about how more and more desertions were taking place. They had actually met a dozen deserters who had returned to their settlements, and Nikhil had used the tablet's camera to record a few of their testimonies that he was also uploading. When he finished, he looked at Alice.

'I'm almost out of juice. We need to be heading back.'

Alice realized that the small tablet in Nikhil's hand had proved to be a more devastating weapon in their struggle than any amount of firepower, and she also understood that it needed recharging. Dewan had left a charger behind, but only one of the underground shelters had an old generator which was being carefully husbanded to provide limited electricity and now also to power up the tablet. Alice and Nikhil set off at a brisk pace, jogging more than walking through the forest. Along the way, Alice spotted three men with rifles who waved to her. Even if people had not met her, almost everyone seemed to know about the blond haired girl who was fighting back.

As Alice ran faster and faster, she felt Nikhil fall behind, but she wasn't worried. There was no sign of Red Guards nearby and they had only about five kilometers to go before they could disappear underground. Running always helped clear her mind, and Alice realized just what a motley crew she was leading. There were, of course, the people from her own settlement, who she knew would follow her to the end;

then there were some from other settlements in the Deadland who had supported her but would not trust the Biters and so chose to stay in their own settlements while helping her with scouting; and finally there were those who said they wanted to help but would not bring themselves to follow a young girl, and remained uneasy allies at best. Even among the Biters, Alice had realized that while the Queen commanded the loyalty of many of them, there were small bands in the Deadland who had gone almost rabid, crazed with fear and hate, and would attack any human on sight. That made it tougher for her to sell her story of how the Biters could be worked with. It was all such a complicated mess that it made her head hurt and made her wish that she did not have to be the one to deal with it all.

'Alice, stop!'

Alice slowed down and saw Nikhil bent over, holding his knees, trying to catch his breath.

'Nikhil, the Red Guards will be at the site of our last transmission any time. We need to get underground as soon as we can.'

Nikhil closed his palms together in a theatrical show of begging for mercy. Alice laughed out loud. Nikhil was not much of a fighter, but he was fun to have around, and he was the only one who knew how to use the tablet, and that made him invaluable.

'Ok, get a drink of water and we'll be on our way.'

Nikhil took out a bottle from his backpack, and drank and when he was about to put it back, took out his tablet for one last look.

'Let me see if they've already taken down my message.'

Alice watched his expression and knew that something was very wrong.

'Nikhil, what happened?'

He called her closer and showed her the screen. There was a single message.

'To all friends in the Deadland: keep you heads down. Heavy downpour expected soon.'

The message had been uploaded from Dewan's account. Alice ground her teeth in anger and frustration.

'Why the Hell would he expose himself by posting like that? Appleseed and the others will be sure to question him.'

Nikhil turned the tablet off.

'Alice, he was trying to be as cryptic as he could, and I guess he could claim it was aimed at his men and comrades on mission in the Deadland, but he would take such a risk only if he desperately needed to get a message through to us.'

'What...'

Alice never got a chance to finish her sentence as her voice was drowned out by the drone of multiple jet engines overhead. Alice looked up see dozens of jets approaching from over the horizon. She had seen the occasional Zeus attack helicopter, but she had never seen aircraft such as this: large bombers with swept wings, flying in formation, darkening the sky like a swarm of locusts.

'Nikhil! Are they coming to bomb where we last transmitted from?'

She saw that Nikhil was staring at the approaching armada, his face frozen in fear.

'Alice, they don't need so many heavy bombers to target one location. That fleet could flatten many, many miles of land.'

'Could they get through to our underground shelters?'

Nikhil never took his eyes off the approaching aircraft as he replied, 'I don't know. Some of them seem to be hardened bomb shelters that were built before The Rising, but the rest are no more than old sewers, maintenance tunnels and underground parking lots. Those wouldn't survive a direct hit. And nobody in the open would have a chance.'

Alice thought of the hundreds of people, including her mother and sister, in one of those shelters, and of the hundreds, perhaps thousands, of human settlements overground in the Deadland.

'Nikhil, we've got to...'

Alice stopped in mid-sentence. She really didn't know what she could say that would be even remotely adequate. They couldn't really warn anyone, and there was no question of saving anyone else's lives. They were still more than a kilometer away from the underground entrance that would lead them to where the rest of their group was hidden. She stood quietly for a minute, looking back at the direction they had come from, and she could see several pillars of smoke rising in the horizon. Fires at the human settlements, where people were seeking warmth or perhaps cooking their frugal meals, and perhaps, like Alice and Nikhil, watching the approaching fleet, not knowing what was coming their way.

Alice felt Nikhil pull hard at her arm.

'Alice, they aren't that far away. All we can do is run and try and find some cover.'

Alice ran like she had never run before, and soon they could see the three large yellow leaves laid across a branch that signaled the entrance to their underground passage. Alice turned to say something to Nikhil, and saw that he was struggling to keep up. She screamed something to him, but her voice was now drowned out by the roar of the dozens of engines overhead. Alice dove through the branches and clambered on all fours through the narrow passageway, hoping that Nikhil was following. She knew that there was little cover overhead other than tree trunks and kept going faster, her palms and knees cut and scratched in a dozen places as she reached the near vertical drop that led to the hardened bomb shelter below.

She dove in as the first bombs hit and she fell to the concrete floor. As she managed to sit up and get her bearings, she felt the ground shake all around her and bits and pieces of the concrete roof chip off and fall as the bombs continued to rain down. There was no sign of Nikhil. She screamed out for him several times but heard no response. In the darkness, she felt along the walls for the unlit torch she knew would be there, and from her backpack took out the small can of fuel and flint she needed to light it. When it was lit, she saw that larger pieces of the ceiling were now falling down towards her and when one particularly large piece missed her head by inches, she hung the torch on the wall and lay down in a fetal position, with her head covered in her hands. The rumbling continued and she thought she heard a voice and she looked up to see Nikhil at the edge of the drop. He threw his backpack down and was about to jump down when there was a huge crash that lifted Alice cleanly off the ground and threw her across the corridor.

Then she saw no more.

Dewan studied the pistol in his hands, wondering just how much easier it was to take another life than to contemplate taking one's own. He had no family and not much that he could say he had to live for, yet it seemed awfully hard to put the gun to his head and pull the trigger. He had shot others, men and Biters, dozens of times without conscious thought in the years of fighting that had dominated his life, but now he could not bring himself to do the same to himself. It wasn't just fear that held him back, though that was certainly there, but a feeling of infinite sadness that came from realizing that his life had not really amounted to much after all. He had spent most of his life serving a cause that had been a lie, and when he thought he had a chance to make amends, it was all too little too late. He had seen the heavy bombers fly in from Tibet and knew that Chen's orders were as simple as they were brutal. He had ordered a saturation fire-bombing of the Deadland near Delhi, with wave upon wave of flights till nothing remained. Dewan had been unable to face his own troops in the cafeteria, local boys who had looked at him with horrified eyes. He had no answers for the questions behind those eyes. No answers as to why their friends and families had just been sentenced to a horrific death by the same Central Committee they were serving to supposedly help human survivors.

Hundreds of Red Guards had flown in the night before and all Zeus units where desertions had taken place had been disarmed and were now effectively under arrest. The Central Committee propaganda machine was in overdrive with reports about how counter-revolutionaries and terrorists had subverted some isolated units in the Deadland in North India and were currently being pacified by the heroic efforts of the Red Guards. Dewan had taken the risk of sending out his warning, but he knew it was likely to be too late. He also knew that it was too late for him. The Red Guards would be coming for him soon.

As he put the gun to his head one last time, he heard footsteps outside his door and he paused. No, if he was going to die, he would at least put what remained of his life to some use after all.

He brought up the Browser on his tablet and logged in to his official email account. He had already barricaded his door with a bulky bookshelf and he heard banging on the door as he began typing. He wrote at breakneck speed, writing of what he had learnt, of the deception behind The Rising, and then of how Chen and his masters in the Central Committee were misleading all Zeus troops. He heard shots as the Red Guards outside shredded the door with automatic weapons and began kicking it open. Dewan finished and pressed 'send' as the first Red Guard came in. Dewan flung his tablet at the man and as the Red Guard lost his balance, shot him twice. Two more Red Guards came into the room and Dewan put them down with single shots to the head. Years of hunting Biters had taught him a thing or two that were finally going to be put to some use, he thought as he picked up the first Guard's rifle and rolled behind his study desk. He saw feet gathered outside his door and fired a short burst, hearing screams as the Guards took cover. He heard something hit the floor and looked to see a black cylinder rolling towards him. As the stun grenade went off, he closed his eyes, but he had not been fast enough. When he opened his eyes, he saw little more than flashes of white and black and he stood up unsteadily, trying to gauge from the footsteps where the Guards were, and fired his rifle on full automatic, not knowing if he hit anyone. He was trying to blink away the bright lights when the first bullets struck him.

Alice opened her eyes, and the first thing she felt was the wetness on her face. For a moment she wondered where all the water had come from, but the rusty smell and the acrid taste told her that it was her own blood. She got up gingerly, and as she looked around she saw that the passageway she was in was bathed in light. She looked up to see a hole in the ground above that had been blasted open by the bombing. Several large pieces of concrete lay around her and as she felt the throbbing lump on her head from which blood still flowed, and the countless scrapes and cuts all over her body, she knew that she had been hit by her fair share or more of the debris. Still, she was alive, and that was something to be thankful for. She took a deep breath and felt her ribs hurt, and hoped that she had not broken anything inside. The dust raised by the shattered concrete made her gag with every breath and she found that the passageway leading onto the tunnels she had planned to enter had collapsed. She tried to grab handholds on the walls to climb out of the hole caused by the bombing – and then she saw Nikhil. Or rather, she saw his hand, still grabbing his tablet. The rest of him was hidden under a giant slab of concrete. Alice knelt down beside him for a few seconds, feeling his lifeless, cold hands, and then she took the tablet from his grip, putting it into hers.

'Goodbye, Nikhil.'

She climbed out and saw something that looked like the Hell that the old religions had believed in. Some humans still prayed before their idols and crosses and holy books, but Alice had never really been brought up with any particular gods to believe in. Her father had once told her that there must be a power beyond human comprehension, otherwise The Rising could never be explained, yet it was vain and stupid to create our own vision of these gods and fight over whose vision was right. The fear of Biters and human marauders hunting you down had a good way of making people band together, irrespective of the gods they once worshipped. Nevertheless, Alice now knew what the old religions had meant when they spoke of a place called Hell. All around her, the forests were on fire, vast charred swathes of ashes and burning stumps that finally did justice to the name this area had carried for years: the Deadland.

Alice ran as fast as she could, desperate to reach her mother, sister and the others. After a few minutes of running, she came upon the ruins of a small settlement. The dozen or so small tents had been almost vaporized by the bombing, and other than ashes and a few scattered limbs, there was no sign of any people. Alice gagged and threw up on the ground, blinking back tears.

How many thousands had died today? What kind of men could be capable of such evil?

The answer was right there for her to see. The same kind of men who had almost wiped out human civilization so that they could rule over the ashes. The same men who now hid behind the anonymity of the Central Committee and used the Red Guards and Zeus troopers to enforce their will, wiping out any remaining trace of resistance and ruling over their empire while the rest of humanity lived and died like animals.

Alice ran on, her mind plagued with worries for what had happened to the others, but through the agony she felt in her mind and body, one thought was crystal clear.

She would make sure Nikhil and the thousands of others who had perished today would not go unavenged.

ELEVEN

ALICE RAN THROUGH A CHARRED forest, trying hard to see through the smoke and to breathe despite the suffocating fumes all around her. Much of the ground was still burning as far as she could see. What kind of weapons had the Red Guards unleashed that had caused such damage, turning acres of land into a sea of fire? She raised her hands to her mouth, trying to stifle a gasp of horror as she saw a gaping hole where the entrance to their shelter should have been. She kept hoping that perhaps people would have had a chance to go deeper into the hardened shelters further underground, but as she ran closer she knew she was hoping against hope. People would have stayed in the larger but less secure chambers close to the surface. There was no reason for them to cram into the smaller chambers deeper underground as they had no warning of what was coming. She stopped abruptly as she saw what the hole in the ground revealed, and then she fell to her knees, crying and screaming as she saw dozens of bodies heaped upon each other, many burnt beyond recognition.

Alice didn't know how long she just sat there, afraid to go in and see the true extent of the horror inside and unwilling to confront her loss. She felt a hand on her shoulder and whirled around, ready to fight. Instead she saw the Queen standing there unsteadily, her body cut in dozens of places and her left hand a stump below the elbow.

'Alice, it's all gone. They are all gone.'

'Mom…'

The Queen shuffled away, mumbling to herself. 'All gone. All gone.'

Alice jumped into the hole, and thirty minutes later was back, sitting with her back against a tree, her mind vacant with the loss and the horror she had just endured. There had not been a single human survivor, and from what she could see, all the Biters inside had also been incinerated. She took the pistol from her belt and toyed with it. A single pull of the trigger was all it would take, and she could end it all. What was the point of a life where she had lost every single person and thing she had taken to be her own in just a few days?

She felt someone standing next to her, and she looked up to see the Queen there. There was no emotion on her face, but she seemed to be looking into the distance as she asked Alice to put the gun away.

'Alice, the prophecy still lives.'

Alice saw that she was holding onto the book she treasured so much in her remaining hand. Alice grabbed the charred book and threw it away, turning on the Queen with a fury.

'Damn you and damn your stupid prophecy! Look around us: everything's gone. Everything!'

Alice walked away and sat down against a tree, sobbing. From the corner of her eyes, she saw the Queen get up and walk towards the book. She picked it up and then Alice saw her expression change as her lips curled back, revealing her jagged teeth, and like a cornered wild animal she hissed and spat at someone approaching from Alice's right. Alice looked up and saw more than a dozen fully armed Zeus troopers standing there, automatic weapons in their hands. Instinctively Alice felt for the gun at her belt and even before her hand reached the gun, she knew that she would never have enough time.

A young trooper stepped ahead of the others.

'You must be Alice.'

Alice still had her hand on the gun, weighing in her mind whether she should just try and take at least one of the Zeus troopers with her instead of being taken alive. The trooper must have sensed what was on her mind so he put his rifle on the ground.

'Relax. We're not here to kill you or arrest you.'

Alice kept her hand on the gun but now took a closer look at the troopers. They looked like they had just come out of a battle; many had cuts and scrapes from running through the forest, and at least one had a bloody bandage around his head. The trooper extended a hand, and as Alice got a closer look at him, she saw that he must have been very young, and looked like a local boy; certainly not one of the dreaded Red Guards.

'Alice, my name is Satish. I was from a settlement near the old city of Agra. All of us were drafted into Zeus from settlements in the Deadland.'

He turned to see the Queen, who was still on edge, and Alice could see his eyes widen, but he made no threatening move.

'Dr. Protima, I presume.'

The Queen stopped hissing, but still stood rigidly, her book clutched to her chest with her one remaining arm.

'Satish, how do you know who we are?'

The trooper smiled. 'A blond girl and a half-Biter are not exactly a common sight in these parts. Plus, Colonel Dewan had given all the details of who you were and what role you'd played so far.'

At the mention of Dewan's name, Alice sat bolt upright.

'The Colonel. Amit. Is he okay?'

Satish motioned for the other troopers to fan out.

'Guys, keep a watch while I fill them in on what's going on.'

He sat down in front of Alice and took out a tablet from his backpack. Alice saw that the Queen, while not feeling at ease enough to join them, had come closer to listen to what he had to say.

He told them about how initially Dewan had pretended that someone had just hacked into his account to post the first messages, and then when messages started being posted from other accounts created by Nikhil, he never showed any signs of support in public. However, when the Red Guards were brought into the Deadland in ever increasing numbers and their tactics kept getting increasingly brutal, his men had sensed a shift in his mood. When troopers began deserting, he stayed at his post, but on more than one occasion he saw troopers slip out but didn't raise the alarm.

'But none of us knew just how deeply he supported your cause till in his last moments; he posted this. We all saw his last warning when he learnt of the air raids, but it was all too late to warn anyone in the Deadland. The Reds have deleted his post, but I saved a copy to my tablet.'

Satish held his tablet up and both Alice and the Queen skimmed it. Dewan had laid out everything he had learnt. Coming from anonymous posters, such messages could always have been dismissed and countered by official propaganda. Coming from a veteran officer in Zeus, it would have been explosive, and with the devastation the air raids had unleashed on the Deadland, there was now more or less open mutiny among the local Zeus troopers.

'Is that why you deserted? What happened to the colonel?'

Satish looked at Alice and she noticed that he was quite terrified. 'Red Guards were hunting down all local troopers. We managed to get out just in time to save our lives. I'm not sure if the colonel made it, but I heard that they sent several units to attack his quarters.'

Alice looked at the Queen.

'They've now declared war on their own troopers! That's crazy. Why would they do that?'

The Queen was studying the tablet as she replied, 'Alice, troopers like Satish have always been expendable. If what Dewan wrote about the ongoing insurgencies in other parts of the world like America is true, then using local troopers under Zeus just helped them wipe out the remaining Biters and ensure human settlements continued to provide labor while their main forces were being used to suppress resistance in what was the United States.'

Alice was looking off into the distance and the Queen asked what was on her mind.

'I'm thinking of how we could fight this war.'

The next week went by in a blur. Alice, the Queen and the Zeus troopers spent much of it in hiding from the Red Guards who had been airdropped across the Deadland to mop up any survivors. With much of the foliage burnt out and a lot of the underground passages and tunnels exposed by the bombing, they were forced to use a different tactic, and instead of moving deeper into the Deadland, they moved into the heart of what had once been the city of Delhi. There they sought refuge among the ruins of the buildings that had once been the landmarks of the Indian capital. Almost all the buildings bore signs of damage, the result of the many waves of devastation Delhi, like many other cities, had suffered. The ravages of The Rising, the nuclear bursts that came soon after, and then years of warfare that had followed till the remaining human survivors had left the city to seek refuge in the Deadland had all taken their toll on the city. Now what had once been the bustling, overcrowded city of Delhi looked deserted, but Alice knew better than that. The Queen had told her that several bands of Biters were likely hidden in the city, usually emerging at night.

Alice saw a tall building which had half of its top cleaved off, as if a giant unseen hand had taken an axe and chopped it off. The Queen muttered, 'Well, I guess we'll have 5 Star accommodation tonight. Welcome to what's left of the Taj Hotel.'

Satish, as young and inexperienced as he was, had become the de facto leader of the Zeus troopers and he told three of them to take up positions near the lobby to watch for any attackers while the others went deeper into the hotel. Alice had never been in a hotel before, though she had heard stories of the nice hotels her parents had been to when they had gone on holidays before The Rising. Imagine that! Someone to bring you food and drink whenever you wanted, and a warm, cozy bed to sleep in instead of a dirty old sleeping bag. Alice wanted to go upstairs and look at the rooms but Satish stopped her.

'The stairs looks pretty unstable and I don't want us to be stuck in here if there's any trouble.'

So they lay down in what had once been the lobby and Alice was about to sleep when one of the sentries spoke in a hoarse whisper.

'Folks, I see multiple shadows approaching!'

All around her, Alice heard the sounds of guns being loaded and cocked. She had only her pistol with her, having lost her rifle in the bombing, but she quickly rushed to a window to see what was happening. As she looked around her in the darkness, she realized that the Zeus troopers may have been lavishly equipped with their night vision scopes and rifles, but most of these boys had never seen much combat before. Satish was hurrying to get them into position and she saw them fumble their way in the dark. With an army like this, Alice realized their war was off to a pretty bad start.

Satish crawled up next to her, and she saw that he was carrying a spare assault rifle, which he handed to her with a smile.

'I think you can use this better than most of these kids.'

Alice took the rifle in her hands and flipped on the scope and looked through it. In the ghostly green light of the night vision scope, she saw a large mob appearing over the driveway that led to the hotel lobby. She switched off the scope, knowing that they needed to preserve the precious batteries of the night vision sights till they found refuge someplace with a generator which they could jury-rig to recharge them.

What she had just seen did not make any sense. The figures were not moving like Biters, but like humans. However, there was no way such a large group of Red Guards would just amble up to them in the open, where they were sitting ducks for the defenders.

'What do you make of it? Should we fire?'

Alice shook her head. 'No, Satish. I don't think they mean to attack us. They probably outnumber us three to one or more, but walking in the open like that means we could pick them all off with probably little or no losses. I think they're trying to signal that they're friendly.'

'Friendly? Who could they be?'

As if by way of reply, a male voice spoke up outside.

'Which one of you is Alice?'

Satish was about to rest a restraining hand on Alice's arm, but she replied, 'Who is asking?'

'Why does that matter?'

Alice sighted her rifle on the man who had been speaking and saw him through her night vision scope. He was heavily bearded, wearing a cap and carrying at least two rifles slung across his back, but his hands were held up in front of him. She spoke up again.

'It matters because it determines whether I greet you with a smile or a bullet through that silly cap of yours.'

She heard several chuckles outside and the man answered, his voice now much softer, 'We are friends. We come to join you.'

Satish and the troopers covered her while Alice stepped out. She still had her rifle at her shoulder but she lowered it when she saw the man smile and motion for all those with him to put their weapons down on the ground. There must have been over thirty of them: men, women and some children. Every one of them was carrying at least two guns, which Alice noted seemed to be all weapons taken from Zeus troopers or Red Guards. The man stepped forward, extending a hand that Alice shook.

'Alice, we have heard so much about you. My name is Arjun, and we would like to join your group.'

For a minute Alice was too surprised to reply. She had never really consciously thought that she was leading anyone or anything. They had just been so focused on staying alive for the last few days that she had not had much time to think of anything beyond immediate survival. Arjun coughed softly, which snapped her back to reality. To her surprise, he seemed to be almost pleading.

'Look, we may not seem like much, but we can all fight. Give us a chance.'

They all walked in and sat around the lobby, with the newcomers looking at the armed Zeus troopers with some initial suspicion. Satish broke the ice by offering his hand to Arjun.

'Arjun, we're all local boys and all on the same team. We've been trying to escape the Red Guards for the last one week and finally decided the Ruins may be a better bet than the Deadland, or what's left of it.'

Arjun sighed and sat back. 'I know; we've been tracking you since you entered the Ruins.'

Alice spoke up, the surprise in her voice evident. 'Tracking us? But we...'

Arjun smiled, his eyes creased with years of worry, and making him look much older than his forty years.

'When The Rising happened, we decided to stay and protect our homes instead of escaping out of the city as many did. The first few years we lived like rats; then we began to fight back, against human looters and the Biters alike. You never saw us, but we saw you.'

He turned to Satish. 'Zeus never came in here much. It's easier to pick off targets from the air but that's of no use in a built up area like this. We'd meet and trade with folks in the Deadland but when we learnt how Zeus was taking over, we decided to stay here and remain free.'

Alice had always taken for granted that only Biters remained in the ruins of the old city, but as she was learning, there was much more to the world than she had ever imagined.

She asked the question that had been on her mind ever since Arjun's group had shown up. 'How did you know about me?'

Now it was Arjun's turn to be surprised.

'Everyone knows about you! Many more troopers like Satish and his friends have been through the Deadland and the Ruins. They all have stories from what they read and heard, and some of them passed these papers out. Word spreads fast. We all lost everything in The Rising, and now that we know who was behind all the misery we faced, we want to help fight back.'

Alice saw the paper in Arjun's hand and saw that it had Dewan's last email printed on it. Even in death, the Colonel had more than done his duty.

'It's going to blow!'

Alice hid her head in her hands as the Improvised Explosive Device went off with an ear-splitting boom. When she peered back around the corner, she saw the results of the first ever IED she had rigged. Half of the target building was blown off and smoke and dust covered the whole area.

'Amazing what you can accomplish with a humble gas cylinder, isn't it?'

She turned to see Arjun standing there, grinning. Over the last two weeks, more human survivors in the Ruins had sought them out as well as close to a hundred more Zeus deserters. While Alice had naively believed they would all stay together, Arjun had told her to scatter them across the Ruins, to be kept in touch via a system of messengers. Satish and the other Zeus troopers were heavily armed, and Alice was skilled well beyond her years when it came to combat, but when it came to fighting in a congested, built-up environment like the Ruins, Arjun was the resident expert. His people called him General, but he had once sheepishly admitted to Alice that he had no military experience, but had been a salesman before The Rising. When he lost his young family in the chaos, he fought to survive and there his mastery of his former sales routes served him well.

With more than three hundred people now in her force, Alice had asked aloud how they should plan their campaign. Bitter at all she had lost, she had been tempted to lash out, but Satish and Arjun had convinced her otherwise.

'Alice, the Red Guards will smash us if we challenge them in the open. We need to lure them into the Ruins and bleed them.'

The Queen had been quiet and withdrawn for much of this time, and Alice wondered if it were because she had been so used to being among Biters that she found it hard to adjust to human company.

That night, the Queen came to Alice as she was about to go to sleep.

'Alice, I want you to keep something.'

She thrust the red vial that contained the vaccine into Alice's palms. When Alice protested, the Queen insisted she keep it.

'Alice, I had foolishly thought that we could find some honest men in power who would help us. It looks like we are condemned to a life of war now, but I don't want to give up hope. Keep it with you and if there is someone we can trust, hand it over.'

Alice woke the next morning to find the Queen gone. Nobody had seen her slip out during the night, and when Alice mentioned it to Arjun, his face darkened.

'Are you sure you can trust her?'

Alice was shocked at his reaction. She had been genuinely worried about the Queen being on her own in the Ruins.

'Alice, there are still bands of Biters in the Ruins, and there are areas we never go into. She seemed sane enough and I know that she and her followers helped you, but the Biters in the Ruins are crazed and would rip our throats out any chance they got.'

'She is not going to betray us.'

Alice said those words and walked away, hoping that her faith in the Queen was well placed. They did not get much of a chance to talk about it further because they soon got busy in planning their first operation.

As Alice watched the men and women move about their drills, she saw just how far they had come. Now it was impossible to tell apart someone who had been a Zeus trooper living in the relative luxury of their barracks and someone who had spent years hiding and fighting as a `Ruins Rat', as they had come to be called. The troopers had swapped their uniforms for civilian clothes, and as Alice noted, if nothing else they all smelt alike, since bathing was a luxury to be enjoyed once in a few days in the Ruins.

'Where do you want the first squad to go?'

Arjun, Satish, a woman called Sheila who led one of the groups of Rats, and Alice were huddled around a hand-drawn map showing the Ruins, the Deadland and a Forward Base just ten kilometers from the city center where a large detachment of Red Guards had set up. It took a second for Alice to realize that the question had been directed to her. She struggled to answer and then Arjun gently nudged her along.

'Maybe we could do it as you said last night. Okay?'

When the others had dispersed, Alice called Arjun aside.

'Arjun, I don't know much about leading so many people. I don't know what to do.'

Arjun smiled. 'Alice, whether you like it or not, everyone here expects you to lead them. They've all heard the stories and read the posts. Most of those are probably exaggerated, but there you have it.'

Alice started to protest. 'Look, all I want is to fight back for what happened to my own. That's all. If others want to join me, then we can work together, but I'm not so sure I like leading so many people and being responsible for them.'

Arjun looked at her, and perhaps realizing that he was talking to someone who would be not much older than the daughter he had lost in The Rising, softened his voice.

'Alice, you are more than just a leader for them. These people, me, all of us, have spent the last few years without any hope, just scratching for survival from one day to the next. You've given them something they had lost. Hope.'

Alice started to say something, but Arjun interrupted her. 'You're the one who lived among the Biters and uncovered their truth. You're the one who fought Red Guards all alone to save your people. You're the one who convinced a Zeus officer to change sides. You're the one who led hundreds of troopers to desert. And yes, you're the cause of the Deadland being firebombed. So you are already responsible for a lot, whether you like it or not.'

Alice sat down as it all sank in. How many thousands had died because of her one silly decision to jump into the hole after the Biter that had triggered all of this? She wished she could just undo everything. Life had never been easy, but it had been a damn sight better than what she had to deal with now, and as she looked at the dozens of men and women gathered around their camp, she wondered whether she was just going to lead all of them to their deaths as well.

She closed her eyes and her father's face flashed before her and she remembered his last words to her. He had somehow believed she could bear this burden of leading others. He had believed that she was more than just another young girl whose fate was in others' hands. If nothing else, she had to prove him right, to make his sacrifice mean something. He had given his life so that she could live, and had believed that by living, she could make a difference and make things better. She turned to Arjun, a new determination in her eyes.

'Without heavy weapons we have no hope of getting through their base defenses, so we need to get them out of their base.'

`Why would they come out of their base?'

'They want me. I will offer myself up as bait.'

Three days later, two vans sped out of the Ruins towards the Red Guards' Forward Base, which housed several dozen Red Guards who had been placed there as a forward patrol and were supplied daily by helicopter. What made it less than an easy target were the two remotely controlled Gatling guns mounted on its walls. Alice was in the second van, and just thirty minutes earlier, Satish had sent a message on his tablet saying that he and his men wanted to rejoin Zeus. They had managed to capture Alice and wanted a trade: Alice for their guaranteed safety. It was a gamble. There was always a chance that Appleseed and his masters would just kill Alice when they had the chance, but Alice knew that even more than her life, they craved the secrets she knew about the Biters' hidden bases, and also the Queen and her vaccine.

They were sure that the Red Guards already had drones overhead, so they did not risk going too much into the open but stopped on the outskirts of the Ruins, roughly in the area where once a sprawling high-end complex had stood, housing guests and athletes for the Commonwealth Games held in Delhi some years before The Rising. The dried up Yamuna river was nearby, and on Alice's instructions and unseen by any drones, more than three dozen fighters had crept through underground passages once used by the Queen's Biters.

They had timed it so that the Red Guards would not

have time to bring in too many reinforcements, but they could never be sure, so Alice felt her hands shake a bit as she got out of the van. She felt totally exposed as Satish and his men walked her into the open. They had all put on their Zeus uniforms and were fully armed while she had her hands loosely bound behind her. She could just about make out the Red Guards' base, which had been set up inside what had once been a large temple. She could see the two round turrets on top of the walls and she struggled to control her panic as she saw a black helicopter rise from within the complex and fly towards them. The helicopter came to a hover some distance away and she could see the large red star painted on its side. The door slid open and she saw several Red Guards inside with their rifles pointed downwards.

A voice called out over a loudspeaker, 'Send the girl forward alone and lay down your weapons. Other Red Guards are on their way to take you to our base. You have nothing to fear.'

Alice was pushed forward and she walked, her face downcast, towards the waiting helicopter, wondering if the bullet that would kill her was on the way.

TWELVE

ALICE SAW THE HELICOPTER COME lower till it was only a few dozen feet above the ground. The rotor wash was so strong it felt like it would blow her away and she had to keep her eyes half closed since she could not bring her hands up to shield them against the swirling wind and dust. She heard a dull roar in the distance and looked to her right to see two armored personnel carriers emerge from the Red Guards' base and speed towards her location. The helicopter came even lower and landed on the road only a few meters away from Alice. She watched three Red Guards disembark, their rifles pointed at the Zeus troopers behind her. As she turned, she saw that Satish and the others had put their hands behind their heads and their rifles were on the ground in front of them. Apparently satisfied that they posed no immediate threat, a Red Guard officer emerged from the helicopter and pointed towards Alice.

'Come here!'

Alice walked slowly towards the helicopter, wondering if she would survive long enough to get a shot at the revenge she so badly wanted. As she saw the smirk on the Chinese officer's face, she had to struggle to contain the fury she felt inside. So many thousands of innocent men, women and children had been killed so that men like this could retain the power they so craved.

The officer turned to Satish and shouted, 'We'll take her with us. My men are on the way in the APCs to take you in.'

Alice was sure that if the APCs did get close enough, their orders were to slaughter the Zeus deserters, but her whole plan hinged on them never getting close enough in the first place. They had not really planned on there being a helicopter at the scene, but now as Alice walked closer, she smiled. It was unplanned, but it could be a bonus. They had planned on bloodying the nose of the Red Guards enough to provoke them to try and enter the Ruins. But if they managed to take a helicopter and an officer, it would certainly add more insult to the injury. Of course, to do any of that Alice had to improvise a bit and hope that she stayed alive long enough to cause any damage.

She was now just five feet or so away from the helicopter and she stopped, as if weighing her decision. The Red Guard officer was now cajoling her to come closer, an absurd gesture since Alice wondered why he'd think anyone would willingly step towards torture and near certain death. When she did not budge, he began to lose his patience and asked one of his men to go get her. The Red Guard started walking towards her and Alice looked right, hoping that Arjun and his Rats would not let her down. She watched the two APCs now barely five hundred meters away and closing in fast, when the first APC was obscured by a giant cloud of smoke. A split second later, she heard the blast of the IED. She knew Arjun had triggered it prematurely since he wanted to create a distraction and give her a chance at getting away. He and his Rats were in tunnels around the road and even before the smoke from the explosion had cleared, she heard the sound of rifles firing as they attacked the APCs.

The Red Guard was now just a couple of feet from her and he had stopped to look at the explosion. He jerked his head around to look at Alice, but he was too late. Alice had slipped her hands out of the loose ropes binding them behind her, and now had a knife in her right hand and a pistol in her left. She jumped high and brought her knife down on the Red Guard's neck. As he went down, she didn't try and dislodge her knife, but left it there, rolling on the ground and coming up in a crouch, the handgun in both hands. She fired four or five rounds at the two Red Guards outside the helicopter and saw at least one fall, before she saw the officer bring up his own sidearm. She rolled under the helicopter as one of the Red Guards fired, the bullets kicking up the dust around her. She felt something hit her shoulder but kept going as the officer screamed.

'Stop, you idiot! You'll hit the helicopter.'

She came up on the other side of the helicopter and saw the officer turn to face her. He was way too late. She fired through the open helicopter cabin and put two rounds in his chest and clambered into the helicopter as she saw Satish and his men firing and the Red Guard outside fall to the ground. She peered into the cockpit and saw the pilot reaching for a pistol at his side.

'Not a good idea.'

He put his hands up and she dragged him outside, where his hands were tied by Satish's men. Alice saw that a fierce firefight was still raging on the road. The first APC was in flames, but the second one seemed undamaged and was backing away towards the base as rifle rounds pinged off it.

'Let's get out of here as soon as we can!'

Alice knew that when news spread that a helicopter had been lost, the Red Guards would be back in force. She looked at Satish.

'Any of you guys know how to fly this thing?'

Satish shook his head and smiled. It was a tempting thought, but even if none of them could fly the helicopter, it still was a treasure trove for them. Within fifteen minutes, they crawled back through the tunnels, bringing with them the Red Guard pilot, weapons and communication equipment taken from the fallen Red Guards, and most exciting for all of them, two RPG launchers they found in the helicopter, together with eight rockets.

Not only had they dealt a serious blow to the Red Guards' pride, but they had in one stroke suddenly exponentially increased the firepower of their arsenal.

That night was one of open celebration, and one of slightly more hidden anxiety. Many of the men and women were drinking and singing, and Alice wondered where all the alcohol had materialized from. Arjun was sitting next to her, looking quite grim.

'Don't ask. People still scavenge and find stuff and some of the more adventurous ones make their own hooch. I wouldn't drink it if I wanted to be sure I'd still be walking the next day. Alice, they have tasted their first real victory so they are celebrating, but we need to think ahead.'

Alice had considered how the Red Guards would retaliate and she was well aware of the devastation they had wreaked in the Deadland, so she looked at Arjun. 'Will they just bomb the Ruins like they did the Deadland?'

Satish had come up to join them and he replied, 'No; it's not as easy to bomb targets in an urban environment like this. Delhi was a huge city and even if most buildings are no longer standing, there are just too many places to hide for them to be sure they'll hit anything or anyone with an air strike.'

Arjun was still looking worried so Satish asked him what

was on his mind.

'You and Alice are both too young to remember what happened after The Rising. I saw the Great Fires and what nuclear weapons did to our world. Why wouldn't the Red Guards just drop a nuke on the Ruins and finish us all?'

A chill went up Alice's spine. She had only heard stories of what those terrible weapons had done to whole cities in the madness that had followed The Rising. Having seen what supposedly `ordinary' bombs had done to the Deadland, she wondered what horrors nuclear weapons could unleash if they were indeed used. She noticed that Satish had a broad smile, something she could not fathom given the grim conversation they were having.

'Satish, what's got you in such a good mood?'

'Alice, our Chinese friend there is talking, and he has a lot to say about the way the world is now and what's on the Central Committee's mind. There's one big reason they won't risk nuking us, and it's the same big reason they're still trying to get human settlements under their control.'

When Alice looked at him with a raised eyebrow, he simply replied, 'Food.'

The Red Guard pilot was in a darkened basement and when Arjun stepped in with the torch in his hand, the pilot shielded his eyes. Alice and Satish followed and sat down around the pilot. He was still in uniform and Alice could see that he was bleeding from a cut on his lip. She spun towards Arjun.

'Who hit him?'

He put his hands up defensively.

'One of the guys got overenthusiastic and I reminded

them gently how you wanted prisoners treated.'

Alice grinned. Arjun's gentle persuasion would likely have included a solid blow to the gut. Satish was talking to the pilot in a foreign language and turned to Alice to explain.

'We all had to learn a bit of Mandarin to be able to communicate with Red Guard officers, but he can speak passable English.'

The pilot now took a closer look at Alice and flinched.

'The Yellow Haired Witch.'

Alice was shocked. She was aware that the Red Guards knew of her and were hunting her, but she had never imagined that they would have such a name for her.

'The name is Alice, Colonel Li. Now tell me what you know.'

An hour later, Arjun, Satish and Alice were sitting outside. For some minutes, none of them spoke as they were all digesting what they had learnt. It turned out that the pilot they had captured was much more valuable than they had imagined. Commander Jiang Li was not only a highly decorated Red Guard pilot, but was the son of Comrade Jemin Li, one of the most senior members of the Central Committee in Shanghai. As a Red Guard pilot of his rank, he would probably not have had much information beyond immediate tactical information on bases and weapons, which Alice would have taken to be very valuable in and of themselves. But being the son of such an important person meant that Commander Li was a treasure trove of information about what was happening in the outside world.

It turned out that most of the world had been utterly devastated by The Rising and the chaos that followed. What had been China's larger cities remained largely intact as many of those in bigger cities had been put in hardened shelters, but the countryside and smaller towns had been ravaged both by The Rising and retaliatory American strikes. It had been a desperate plan, one which Commander Li's father had been privy to, but with deep worldwide recession, China's economy tottering behind the US defaulting on debt, two years of famines, and growing calls for reform and democracy in China, some of those in power had taken a last gamble. What the planners behind the whole operation had never bargained for was the way the virus mutated and the way the Biters spread out of control. That together with the smaller tit for tat nuclear exchanges in Asia and the Middle East meant that while the Central Committee in China was the one relatively organized political force to remain standing, it ruled over a planet that was little more than a pile of ashes.

And also it now had more than two hundred million mouths to feed in China. In the first few years, they had been content to follow the Central Committee unquestioningly, driven by their terror at what lay beyond the iron grip of the Committee and its Red Guards. However, over time, as food shortages set in, the Central Committee had to seek out remaining fertile lands and people to work those fields. Only two major food baskets of the world remained: what had been the heartlands of the US and India. The Americans never gave up, and ever since the first Red Guards landed, had been waging a terrible guerilla war that was bleeding the Red Guards dry. Then they turned to the Deadland of North India, subcontracting Zeus to bring human settlements under their control as a source of labor for farms in India and China.

Alice had grown up seeing little beyond the immediate concerns of her family and settlement and being worried about little more than her immediate survival. It was a bit hard at first for her to grasp the true scale of the struggle they were a part of. But a life spent surviving meant that her instincts were razor sharp and she looked at both Satish and Arjun.

'First, if this Li is the son of such an important man, they will not hit us from the air. They will try and negotiate or come on the ground. We need to be ready.'

Arjun nodded, a slight smile on his face as he realized that the young girl everyone saw as their leader was taking charge.

'Second, if food and people to work the farms is what is so critical to them, we need to hit them where it hurts. No food will mean their own people will start turning against the Central Committee.'

She saw Satish hesitate, so she continued, 'Yes, I know it's harsh and some people may starve, but we cannot be soft. Finally, we need to find some way of coordinating with the Americans if we can.'

She had not told any of the others about the vial of the vaccine she carried, but while much of India had been reduced to the Deadland, she hoped that the Americans might still have people and facilities available where they could put the vaccine to some use. She had no idea of how they could contact the Americans or how they could be of any use to each other from half way across the world, but the knowledge that other people were waging the same war against the same enemy gave her hope and made her own effort feel less lonely.

Just two days later, the first strike in Alice's plan was put into motion.

'Queen of Hearts, I am at the dinner table.'

Alice clicked her mike once by way of acknowledgement and then looking at the airfield spread out in front of her.

'King of Hearts, is the Knave in position?'

She heard a click from Arjun affirming that Satish and his men were also ready. Once Arjun had heard of the book that the Queen carried with her and the prophecy associated with it, he had suggested the code names. That had brought about much laughter among the older folks there, though Alice, never having read the book, really didn't know where the names came from.

They were about fifty kilometers from their base in the Ruins, near what had once been the international airport at Delhi. It was now a small, barely serviceable airfield, but it was the key lifeline through which local settlers were sent to farms in China, and also produce grown in farms around the region were sent to storage depots the Central Committee controlled. Alice could see three large transport aircraft and two helicopters there through her binoculars. There were several guard towers, at least two of which had remotely controlled gun turrets, and she could see many armed Red Guards walking along the airfield perimeter.

It was clearly too heavily defended to attack in a frontal assault, but that was not Alice's intent. The heist from the Red Guards' helicopter had proved to be quite valuable, and together with what the Zeus deserters had bought with them, they now not only had far superior firepower but also many more tactical radios to help in their communication. Alice was sure their transmissions were being intercepted, which was why they were using the code names Arjun had thought up.

'The Knave sees some tarts on the table.'

That meant that Satish and his men had seen the convoy approaching them from their position about five kilometers away. They were dug in below the ruins of what had once been crisscrossing flyovers that had provided easy access to the airport from the city. With a combination of the rage among the remaining human settlements in the Deadland after the air raids, and the increasing desertions among Zeus troopers, the intelligence they had on Red Guard movements had increased exponentially. So today, Alice knew that three APCs would be escorting a convoy of trucks packed with settlers to be flown to labor camps in China. Her intent was not to hurt the settlers but to take out the APCs and free the settlers. That was the job that fell to Satish and his crew. She, Arjun and a dozen others were to wreak some havoc at the airfield.

Satish's next transmission came ten minutes later. It was simple and terse.

'The Knave of Hearts, he stole some tarts.'

Alice smiled. That meant his part of the mission had been accomplished. Now she would have to put into motion her own plan. Word of the raid must have gotten to the airfield because she saw several Red Guards clamber onto APCs and two helicopter gunships begin to take off.

Alice and the others had made their way to their positions two days ago, traveling largely underground, through old sewers, and often lying still in the filth for hours when Red Guard patrols flew overhead. It had been a hard journey, but now it was all going to pay off.

As the helicopters approached their position, Alice spoke into her radio. 'King of Hearts, beat them sore.'

She saw two smoke trails emerge from the ground across the road from her as RPGs snaked out towards the approaching helicopters. One missed its mark, but the other hit the lead helicopter just behind the cockpit. The helicopter seemed to shudder in mid-flight and then began to spin out of control as it crashed to the ground. The second helicopter began to turn towards this sudden threat when Alice screamed at her men to fire. Two more rockets flew towards the helicopter and Alice shouted in triumph as they both struck home. There was a fireball and the helicopter seemed to break into two as it fell. As Alice saw four APCs speed out of the airport gates, she was tempted to wreak some more damage, but she knew that standing and fighting in the open would mean heavy casualties. So they retreated back to their underground tunnels and began the journey back to the Ruins.

When Alice got back, the first thing she did was to sleep, trying to make up for the three days she had just been through with barely any rest. When she awoke, Satish told her that they had managed to destroy the APCs accompanying the convoy and liberate more than three hundred settlers. The men and women, all angry at the casualties they knew the air raids had caused at other settlements and at being taken away from their families, were keen to join in the struggle against the Red Guards.

When Alice walked out of her room she saw a sight she was not at all prepared for.

More than five hundred people were gathered among the ruins of buildings that had once been a posh apartment complex. It was almost sunset so a few torches had been lit. She was about to ask Arjun whether it was smart for so many of them to be in the open when a huge roar welcomed her. A man walked up to her.

'My name is Swapnil, and I led our settlement near Mehrauli. Thank you for rescuing us. Some of us would want to go back to our families, but I and many others will fight for you in your army. Just tell us what you need.'

As Alice looked around her, she considered what the man had said. Did she indeed now have an army? To think that so many people depended on her and looked to her for direction was a scary thought, but at the same time she felt an intense surge of pride. If only her father could have seen her now. He had lived and died so that his people could continue to live free, and now she was finally in a position to not just avenge his death but to try and fight for what he had believed in.

The celebrations were short-lived because having so many people in the open was an invitation for an air strike. Alice was sure that the Red Guards would be furious at the loss of three helicopters in just a few days and a threat to what they had taken to be an assured source of supply for their labor camps would cause them to lash out. Add to that the fact that the son of a senior Central Committee official was a prisoner in the Ruins, and she was sure that they would take some action, and soon.

She did not have to wait long. She was in a second floor room in what had once been an apartment when she heard the dull roar of approaching helicopters. She had lookouts on the nearby rooftops and soon enough she saw RPGs reach out towards the helicopters. In the darkness it was hard to see how close they came, but without any signs of explosions, they seemed to have missed. Explosions rocked one of the rooftops as missiles fired in retaliation found their mark, and Alice wondered which of her comrades she had just lost.

'King of Hearts, Knave of Hearts. Time to go down the Rabbit Hole.'

Their plan was simple. It would be suicide to engage helicopter gunships with just RPGs and small arms. So, with the initial volley of RPGs they had got the Red Guards interested, but now they would hunker down and wait for the Red Guards to make the next move. The whole plan was to get them on the ground where they could be fought on more even terms.

Alice watched at least a half dozen helicopters hover near

the ground as black figures slithered down ropes. Part of her pitied the Red Guards, who were probably ordinary soldiers being forced into an impossible mission because the son of an important man was at stake. But she reasoned that they were doing their job, and she would do hers. Through the night vision scope on her rifle she watched the Red Guards sweep from one building to another. Commander Li was in the same building as her, sitting in the basement parking lot with four men guarding him. He did not have much more by way of intelligence to offer up, but he was a valuable bargaining chip and their best bet that the Red Guards would not just level the entire neighborhood with air strikes.

She watched a four man team of the Red Guards approach the building in front of her, across a small park where perhaps years ago, children would have played. Even today, a slide remained as a memorial to those simpler, happier days. Under that slide was what appeared to be a garbage bin. Inside it was an IED that Alice had rigged. As the Red Guards passed by the slide, she connected the two wires in front of her. The IED went off with a huge explosion that was deafening in the quiet of the night. When she put her scope back to her eyes, she saw all four Red Guards down. The others were now scrambling for cover, and one or two had fired, likely panicking and firing at shadows. Their muzzle flashes gave them away and they were met with a withering volley of rifle and RPG fire from men and women hidden in the Ruins around them. Alice saw a Red Guard run across the park, perhaps separated from his squad in the chaos. She took careful aim and fired a single round, bringing him down with a shot to the leg. As he scrambled on all fours, two shadows emerged from the darkness and took him away. The helicopters were buzzing overhead like angry hornets, but with the Red Guards mixed up in close combat, there was little they could do. One of them tried to come lower, but a near miss from an RPG sent it back up.

The firing went on for about twenty minutes and then there was silence. As per her plan, nobody cheered, and nobody went out to celebrate. In stark contrast to the deafening crescendo of gunfire and explosions that had rocked the complex just minutes ago, there was now no sound to be heard other than the helicopters overhead. Alice wondered if they would have called for reinforcements, but when and if they arrived they would find an abandoned apartment complex with nothing there but the bodies of a dozen or so Red Guards and multiple booby traps to make life interesting for any Red Guard who landed.

Alice and everyone with her, including eight Red Guards who had been captured alive, were already on their way through the Ruins and its underground tunnels to another hideout.

The deadly game of cat and mouse that was to be played in the Ruins had begun in earnest.

THIRTEEN

TWO MORE WEEKS PASSED, WHERE not a single day went by without a raid by Red Guards. After their initial heavy losses in the house-to-house fighting in the Ruins, the Red Guards were increasingly using drones and air strikes. While that meant fewer Red Guard losses, it also meant that casualties on the side of Alice and her teams were also lower, because it was easy to hide in the Ruins or in the warren of underground tunnels and sewers. Alice realized early that they did not have the numbers or firepower to engage the Red Guards in open combat, so they would hide in the Ruins and use IEDs and ambushes to extract as heavy a toll as possible. Alice's army had also been bolstered by increasing defections among Zeus troopers, and while in absolute the numbers may have been low, the experience some of the recent defectors brought with them helped increase their capabilities and knowledge exponentially. Some of them were senior officers who had been lieutenants or majors in the Indian Army before The Rising, and they began a series of classroom trainings. Alice was fascinated by what she learnt. Her knowledge of combat had been forged in the Deadland, where the best schooling was learning to survive every day. But now she learnt of past battles in the

Old World, of how insurgents in countries held off mighty armies with air power using low-tech IEDs and ambushes. She learnt of counter-insurgency and quickly grasped how much the Red Guards had bungled in alienating the local people. That was something she immediately set about capitalizing on.

Often in the darkness of night, she and a small group would travel into the Deadland and meet with settlements, telling them of the struggle that was being waged and asking them for their support. Alice had thought that telling them about how evil the Red Guards were and the conspiracy behind The Rising would be enough to get the settlements on her side, but it wasn't always so easy.

One evening, Arjun sat down next to her.

'Alice, only a few people will fight out of a desire for revenge. Maybe some people like you who have directly lost family and friends to the Red Guards. But others want safety for their families, and they won't be motivated only by wanting to destroy something, but the promise of something that is a better life.'

Alice had never thought of it that way.

'Arjun, how do you know so much about this?'

He smiled. 'Remember, I was a salesman. My job was selling things to people which they often didn't want, and the key is that we need to make them want something they may not even have considered before.'

'What would they want?'

Arjun took out a faded photograph. It showed a city street with cars and people walking around.

'Most of the leaders of the settlements were young men and women before The Rising. They remember how life was before, and if you ask all of them, including me, what they would most want, they would say that they want the safety and stability that they once had. Especially in places like India and the US, which were democracies, people would want to be able to choose their future instead of having someone sitting in Shanghai deciding it for them.'

Democracy. Alice had never seen what the Old World had been like, but her father had often talked about the ideals he had believed in, and things he had tried so hard to bring to life in their own settlement. A system where people did not rule because they were stronger or better armed, but where people chose those who would guide them, and decisions were taken by voting on them. She knew that the heavy-handed tactics of Zeus had rankled among a lot of the settlements but they had been happy to trade freedom for safety. Could she really offer them an alternative? The tactics of the Red Guards and defections among Zeus troopers had certainly made them question what they were actually signing up for when they accepted the supposed safety of operating under the Red Guard's umbrella, especially when Commander Li had revealed the inhuman conditions in the labor camps where people from the settlements were taken. But what kind of life could she offer in the desolation of the Deadland or the Ruins?

Arjun must have read her mind. 'Alice, there are now more than five hundred of us. All of us living in the Ruins. Families, people who till a day ago were strangers, all living together. Think about what we've started here.'

The next day saw several Red Guard sorties over the Ruins. Jets and helicopters seemed to be dropping bombs and firing rockets, but they were nowhere near Alice and her troops. Alice thought they must have been acting on faulty intelligence and the misguided air raid of the Red Guards was the subject of many a joke over lunch.

Alice was leading a patrol in the Ruins the next night

with two of Satish's men, when a threat that she had almost forgotten about presented itself. One of the young Zeus troopers ahead suddenly screamed and Alice was instantly on guard, bringing up her night vision scope to her eyes. She saw three shapes emerge from behind the building in front of her. From the way they moved, there was no doubt that they were Biters. The trooper was lying at their feet, his neck bent at an impossible angle. She heard a sound to her left and turned to see three more Biters emerge. Alice hesitated for only a minute, as she thought of the Queen and the Biters who had helped her, before squeezing the trigger on her rifle, sending the first Biter down with a bullet to the head. The others charged at her and she shot another before she ordered the trooper with her to retreat. In such close quarters, and not knowing how many other Biters were around, standing and fighting would be suicidal. She ran through the darkness, more than once swerving away from what she thought was a Biter lurking in the shadows but turned out to be a pipe or a broken piece of furniture.

'Vivek, you with me?'

She got no reply from the trooper and just hoped that he was okay.

A Biter suddenly appeared in front of her, and without breaking her stride she hit him on the face with the butt of her rifle, and as he went down, fired a round into his head. Knowing that she was probably too far from her base to be able to make it in the darkness while she was surrounded by Biters, she made for the nearest intact building and clambered up the stairs to the second floor. She huddled against the wall, her rifle trained at the stairs. She had two fragmentation grenades with her, so if the Biters did try and attack in force, she would give them a nice surprise.

She saw a Biter appear in the doorway and a single round

to the head put him down. Two more followed and she fired again, missing twice but then compensating with two more head shots that put them down. She retreated further up the stairs and hoped she had not drawn too much attention to herself.

When no more Biters presented themselves for a few seconds, she breathed a bit easy and looked out the window through her scope. She saw the flag that Arjun had put up, partially hidden behind an old lamppost. She thanked the Red Guards for their high technology scopes since it told her precisely that their base was two thousand meters away. She didn't know if she wanted to risk trying to walk alone in the darkness with an unknown number of Biters around, so she took out her tactical radio to call Arjun for assistance. That was when several gunshots shattered the silence of the night. There were a few scattered single shots but then someone began firing on full automatic. The gunshots were coming from the direction of their base, and as Alice looked through her scope, she could see several muzzle flashes. Sweeping her scope around, she saw several dark shadows shuffling towards the base and she knew what the Red Guards had done. They did not have to land and fight house to house after all. They had stirred up the Biters by bombing them, and now the Biters were streaming towards the areas where the humans were based. Alice gripped her rifle and prepared to rush to her friends' aid.

The Red Guards had just opened a new, deadly front in the war in the Ruins.

When Alice reached her base, she saw several Biters lying on the ground, their heads shattered by direct hits. However, when she got closer she noted with dismay that many of her team were also dead. The Biters had taken them totally by surprise. Used to days of airborne attacks by the Red Guards, they had never really anticipated a ground attack by Biters. She saw Arjun point his pistol at a writhing man on the ground and shoot him in the head. Better dead than undead was a fine slogan, but from the pain in Arjun's face, she knew how tough it was to have to shoot a friend.

She saw Satish running, his rifle in hand, screaming to his men.

'Get snipers on the roofs now. Watch for any stragglers!'

He stopped in front of Alice.

'They caught us with our pants down, Alice.'

Alice looked at the devastation around her and asked how bad their losses were.

'As best as I can tell, we lost eight or nine people. Also, we cannot stay here any longer. If the Biters are being driven from their hiding places and coming into our areas, we need to find a place that can be more easily fortified and defended.'

'But that makes us a more visible target for air strikes, right?'

Arjun gave a wan smile, showing that he knew well the kind of dilemma the Red Guards had placed them in.

The next morning was a dark one, where they buried their dead, which in itself was a tough decision for many of the Hindus among them. Funeral pyres would have been a beacon for air strikes to home in on. Then they began the search for a new stronghold.

After more than an hour of walking through the Ruins, Alice clicked twice on her radio. To avoid attracting attention, they had spread out into five separate smaller groups, and now gradually they would converge where Alice was.

'This is such a visible target, Alice. Are you sure we

should be here?'

Alice smiled at Arjun. 'Take a look around. There are so many underground parking lots and rooms that nobody could really take us out from the air. With our friend Li and the other prisoners, I doubt they'd use any heavier weapons. Also, its walls mean that we can set up defenses against any Biters or Red Guards coming from outside.'

They were inside what had once been a large sports stadium. The bleachers around the stadium were all long devastated but the huge sloping roof was still largely intact and hid the giant field and rooms below.

One of the former Zeus officers walked up and whistled.

'Good idea, Alice. This is a perfect headquarters for us, but as more and more people join us, I'd like to see them set up homes in the adjoining buildings. These were once built to house thousands of athletes during some big events. Take a look. Many of them are still livable, and being close to the stadium means that we can still create a safety net for each other, but they also get some space for themselves and their families.'

'Makes a lot of sense.'

Within a week, the stadium started becoming the focal point for what was essentially the beginning of the resettlement of the Ruins that had once been Delhi. Word spread and people began walking in, at first in small groups, and then entire settlements from the Deadland. Alice was suddenly seized with all the administrative challenges that came with taking care of more than a thousand people who essentially depended on her. Luckily, there were enough people around with skills from the Old World who could help. A former accountant took charge of maintaining inventories of food and supplies. Satish took charge of base security, which consisted of ensuring security for the stadium and for all the families now settling around it. Several of the settlers jury-rigged generators powered with fuel that could still be easily scavenged in the Ruins, and now the main eating and meeting rooms in the stadium had electricity, and there was already talk of extending that to all the apartments occupied by families.

Arjun and his Rats took charge of what he called forward security, which meant venturing deeper into the Ruins to look for supplies and also find other humans. Within days, their community numbered in the thousands, and Alice's legend seemed to only grow in the telling. One day, Alice confided to Arjun that she felt bad that a lot of the things people believed about her were not true. For example, she most certainly had not destroyed an APC single-handedly. Arjun smiled and told her that her legend was one of the glues that was binding everyone together, and if it could help achieve such a wonderful thing, it was perhaps best left alone.

In the daily meetings that Alice called where people could talk about issues and ideas to make their lives better, an old lady asked her a question that perplexed her.

'Alice, what should we call this little town of ours?'

It was then that Alice remembered the charred book that the Queen had carried with her and how much it had meant to her. She had heard nothing of the Queen since she had slipped away, and thought it may be a fitting way to remember her, so she said that their community be called Wonderland.

There was raucous laughter, especially among many of the old folks who knew the fairy tale. It was hardly an uneventful period. Red Guard sorties continued daily, and every once in a while a helicopter pilot would fire a rocket or two, but given the thick stadium roof and their dug in positions, these caused little damage. Air raids also started to lessen when the Red Guard pilots realized that some defecting Zeus troopers had taken with them man portable anti-aircraft missiles looted from armories. These had been positioned in the tallest buildings around the area and while Alice knew that they did not have enough if the Red Guards mounted a large scale attack, she also knew that the cost of any such attack would be prohibitive. So an uneasy peace came to exist between them and the Red Guards, and at least for the short term, Wonderland knew some measure of security from attacks by the Red Guards.

The Red Guards, however, continued their raids on the areas where Biters were said to be, and much like hunters driving wild animals, they continued driving Biters towards the stadium. The difference was that, now, in a clearly fortified position with lots of adjoining buildings that provided a perfect location for snipers and overlapping fields of fire, the occasional hordes of Biters that appeared were dealt with at long range, well before they could cause any damage. While Alice felt a bit bad about taking out what she knew were not really evil monsters but perhaps something closer to rabid animals, the safety of those who depended on her was the most important thing on her mind.

When she felt that they were settled in their new base, she began to set two plans in motion. The first was a renewed campaign against the supply lines of the Red Guards. Arjun volunteered to lead that effort, and there was no shortage of volunteers from the settlements in the Deadland who were eager to take revenge against the Red Guards.

The second was a more challenging endeavor: that of establishing communication with the outside world. One of the deserting Zeus officers had brought along a shortwave radio and they set up a communications centre in what had been once been the broadcast room in the stadium. Alice sat there and listened to what seemed to be an endless hiss of static before she gave up.

They had much more success with what one of the former Zeus officers called Information Warfare. They used the many tablets they had brought with them and the tablets captured from the Red Guards to bombard the Red Guard and Zeus Intranets with messages of their ongoing struggle. Within a week, the Zeus Intranet was down, a sure sign that the Red Guards had lost almost all command and control over what had once been their primary instrument for maintaining control in the Deadland of India. Zeus deserters spoke of open mutiny and warfare and of whole units of deserting Zeus troopers being slaughtered in air strikes by the Red Guards. However, that also meant that more and more Red Guards were streaming into the Deadlands, and they were bringing with them heavier weaponry.

Then one day, Alice walked into the communications room and was told that they had a very unexpected and surprising message. It was a message from the Central Committee.

That night, as they all gathered in the underground parking lot of the stadium, the tension and excitement in the air was palpable. There were a couple of lamps powered by their generator that threw off ghostly shadows on the wall lending the proceedings an even more eerie air.

'Alice, it could all be a trick.'

Arjun had said the words quietly, and Alice was thankful that he was not openly challenging her, but she also knew that he was saying what was on the minds of many of those gathered before her. Alice turned to the crowd assembled in front of her.

'Everyone, we received a message from the Central

Committee earlier today.'

Everyone had been speculating all day what the special announcement was, and now that it was out in the open, all conversation died down, all eyes trained on Alice as she continued.

'They are proposing a ceasefire.'

Several people in the audience applauded, and that told Alice a lot. After years of fighting for survival, they had begun to find a sense of safety and community in Wonderland. A ceasefire would mean that they could at least continue the process of rebuilding their lives and expanding their community without fear of attack.

Alice held up her hand and everyone was quiet again.

'Their terms are that we release Commander Li and all the dozen other Red Guards we hold prisoner and that we cease all attacks on their supply lines. In return, they commit to not launch any attacks on our base here in Wonderland.'

She heard several in the crowd mutter about how the Central Committee could not be trusted and she realized that just as with her and Arjun, opinion was divided.

Alice spoke more loudly and the voices in the crowd died down. 'I know as well as all of you of what we have lost to the Red Guards and their masters. So I have no desire to surrender to them or leave ourselves vulnerable. But there is something more than fighting to survive, there has to be. I was born in the Deadland and knew a life where all I had to look forward to was living one more day, but many of you remember a life before The Rising, a life where there was more to look forward to.'

She knew she had struck a chord and felt all eyes in the crowd on her as she continued.

'Many of you follow me, and I'm not sure I deserve all that trust, but I do know I've seen and felt something different in the last few weeks. We are now no longer just a band of fighters in hiding. We are more than that: we are starting to create a community. A community where we have laws, security, where children don't have to grow up afraid of the dark as I was. A friend once told me that we needed something more than just a common enemy to stick together, and I think we're beginning to find it: a place called home, a place we can run the way we want. A place we all call Wonderland.'

Several in the crowd shouted in approval and when she looked at Arjun, he was smiling.

'I don't like or trust the Red Guards any more than you, but it's clear that we don't have the firepower or numbers to really take the battle to them, and they know they can't wipe us out without drastic measures like nuclear weapons, and that would risk the very fertile lands they rely on to feed their people. So I will agree to stop attacks on their supply routes in return for a temporary ceasefire, and I will let our prisoners return.'

Several in the crowd began to mutter angrily, when Alice raised a hand to silence them. 'Only those prisoners will return who want to. Others will remain with us as our guests, and over time, a part of our community.'

She motioned to her left and Commander Li walked onto the raised platform, eliciting many gasps of surprise. He spoke in halting English, but what he said electrified everyone.

'I was a pilot in the Red Guards, and I believed we were fighting to protect our people from the monsters you call Biters and to help secure areas to feed our people. I've spent enough time here and seen enough documents that make me question that. So I and three of my comrades have chosen to stay here. I know this war cannot be fought to victory by either side, but with the influence my father has and through my words, I hope I can help bring some sort of a workable peace.'

Arjun was looking at Alice in surprise. While he had been out raiding, she had been at work, talking to Li and trying to convince him of all that she herself had discovered not too long ago. Alice knew there was a risk that the Central Committee would denounce Li as a traitor and they would lose the leverage they had, but she was counting on the fact that they would choose to believe that he was being kept prisoner as a pawn for further negotiations.

Alice concluded by saying that they vote on it. This was her first real experience of what people called democracy, and she was nervous that the idea would split the group. Instead, she saw a near unanimous acceptance of the proposal.

Alice walked away with slightly conflicted feelings. On the one hand, part of her felt that her vengeance for the deaths of her family and friends was incomplete, and wanted to continue the battle. On the other hand, she now felt responsible for the thousands of people who depended on her, and didn't want to throw away their lives for her personal vengeance.

Arjun walked up to her. 'Alice, you did a very brave thing. When I first met you, you were an angry young girl looking for revenge. Today, you are a young woman whom I'd be led by any day.'

The next day was spent preparing for the swap. Eight Red Guard prisoners were to be escorted by Alice, Arjun and close to fifty heavily armed men. Four of them were carrying man-portable SAMs and would be traveling in jeeps and taking up position slightly behind the group in case of any surprise air attacks. The meeting point was deeper in the Deadland, close to where the malls and offices had been in the suburb called Noida. As they passed the area, Alice saw the shattered remains of a giant statue that she had been told had once been a statue of the Hindu god Shiva. It was fitting that it lay in ruins along with the Old World it represented.

'Alice, you should not have come.'

It was not the first time Arjun had suggested it, but she was not going to send so many of her people into harm's way without being there to share the risks with them. And if this decision was going to mean that the people of Wonderland could enjoy at least a few days of peace, then it was worth it. As they reached the rendezvous point, near the ruins of what had once supposedly been one of the largest shopping malls in the city, Alice gawked at it for a few seconds, imagining what it must have been like to walk into a building and buy whatever you wanted – food, clothes, games – and walk out, without worrying about Biters or Red Guards.

She heard the helicopter before she saw it, and looked up to see a large transport helicopter approaching. As it came closer, she heard some of the men cocking their guns, and she whispered for them to not make any threatening moves. While she was trying to appear calm and composed, she was constantly fidgeting with the necklace she was wearing. Not knowing what else to do with the vial the Queen had given her, and also wanting to keep it safe, she had looped a chain through it and had been wearing it ever since the Queen disappeared.

She saw the helicopter land a few meters away and a single officer got out and began walking towards her. She had to admire his courage for walking towards more than fifty heavily armed enemies all alone and seemingly unarmed. There were two snipers inside the helicopter but they made no move to get out of the helicopter or even to sight their weapons.

The officer now was close enough for her to hear and he

stopped, speaking in impeccable English, and smiling slightly.

'So, you must be this Alice who has caused us so much trouble. I am General Chen of the Red Guards, and I have come to take possession of my men. Please have them walk towards me and then we will leave and fully honor the agreement we have made.'

Alice motioned to Arjun, who nudged the Red Guard prisoners forward, and they began walking towards Chen. It was then that she noticed something odd. Chen had taken out a thin mask and was putting it on his face. She saw the two Red Guards in the helicopter lean out and fire something in the air. As she watched the small projectiles loop up in the air and fall towards them, she screamed to Arjun and the others to take cover.

She had her rifle up and was firing at the helicopter when the first projectile struck somewhere behind her. She saw one of the Red Guards twitch and fall as her bullets hit home, and then she instinctively dove for cover as she heard an explosion behind her. When she looked back, she saw that it was not a grenade as she had feared. Instead, there was a greenish haze that was enveloping Arjun and the others, who were grabbing their necks and falling to the ground. Arjun tried to raise his rifle, but he seemed to gag and then fall to his knees. The wind was carrying the gas further away, and then she saw the men with the SAMs fall in their jeeps. She felt a burning sensation in her throat and started coughing violently, as if she were choking on something. Then she felt a boot on the small of her back. It was Chen.

'This one I want alive.'

Two masked Red Guards pulled her up and one of them put a mask on her face. If she had any notions of fighting back, they dissipated when one of them injected her with something that made her muscles go limp. She could see

Chen standing there in front of her, and he pointed to the sky. When she looked up, she saw waves of heavy bombers headed south. Towards Wonderland. When she tried to struggle against the men holding her, one of them hit her in the head, knocking her out.

Her last thought was that, yet again, she was going to fail those who had depended on her.

FOURTEEN

WHEN ALICE OPENED HER EYES, they were watering and her mouth was dry. She tried to bring her hands up but found that she could not move them. As she moved her head to look around, she found that she was lying on a bed and her hands and legs were tied down by thick belts. She was in a room where there was no other furniture other than a single metal chair, and there were no windows, only a single door. When the door swung open, she saw a familiar shape walk in.

It was Appleseed.

Then the memory of what had happened kicked in, and she thrashed about on the bed, trying to free herself, trying to get at the men who had caused her so much loss. Appleseed calmly sat down on the chair next to her.

'Alice, it's no use. You should just relax.'

'What happened to Wonder...the people with me?'

Appleseed smiled. 'It's a miracle what two dozen heavy bombers, each carrying ten thousand pounds of fuel air explosives, can do. I overflew the site of your so called Wonderland in a helicopter soon afterwards. Let's just say most, if not all, of your friends are burning in Hell, as they should.'

Alice felt hot tears streaming down her face. 'But Commander Li and the others...'

Appleseed cut her off. 'Do you really think we would negotiate with you for one man, no matter whose son he might be? The Central Committee ordered the raid after Commander Li's father himself denounced him as a counter-revolutionary. The old man was forced to do it when the Central Committee figured they had a plan to kill or capture you. Now I hope you understand the kind of men I serve, and the kind of men you chose to pick a fight with.'

Alice cried silently at the loss of so many innocent lives, and then spat at Appleseed, who flinched as the spittle hit his face.

'All we wanted to do was to be left alone. That's all any of us ever wanted.'

Appleseed wiped his face clean, but to Alice's surprise, there was no anger in his voice. 'Alice, don't you get it? It doesn't matter what you want or what your father wanted. If there's one thing you should learn from all this, it's that the world has always been ruled by a few powerful men. Men who brought about The Rising, men who make up the Central Committee, and don't for a moment think they're all Chinese. You'll be surprised who from the Old World is there: billionaire businessmen, bankers, Presidents, arms brokers – all part of one brotherhood that was planning for a day when the world would not have enough resources to support its population and when the masses would start turning against the power they held. We are just tools to get their work done. The sooner you reconcile to that, the longer your life will be.'

Alice wondered why he was confiding in her and what his masters wanted with her. Appleseed saw the question in her eyes.

'You are different. You became a visible symbol of opposition to them, and that started making other people think that there is a way to live in safety outside of the Central Committee's New World Order. It started giving people dangerous ideas about who and what the Biters may be, and whether they could actually be cured or assimilated. You were a public threat, and they will make a public spectacle of you. Tomorrow you are to be flown to Shanghai to be executed, and that execution will be broadcast live to all settlements in the New World.'

The prospect of death did not scare Alice as much as she had thought it might. Instead, what scared her the most was the emptiness she felt inside. She literally had nothing or nobody to live for anymore. She had failed those who had put their faith in her, believing naively that they could make a fresh start in a world where the only thing that mattered was power and everyone was but a puppet dancing to strings that were in the hands of the men who commanded Appleseed and Chen. She had never felt so bereft of hope before in her life, and cried for everything she had lost.

Appleseed walked over to her, resting his hand on her stomach. Something about his touch made her look at him.

'Get your hands off me!'

Appleseed smiled and leaned closer.

'I don't think you are in much of a position to tell me what to do. Do you realize just how much you have cost me? I lost my best men, and the army I once commanded is now hunted down by the Red Guards. I survived only because of my loyalty and because I personally helped track down and eliminate deserters.'

His hand was now moving up her body and Alice struggled against the belts holding her down in vain as his hand came to a stop just below her chest and he leaned down closer towards her face.

'Once, I would have been tempted with a young girl as attractive as you lying in front of me. I often wished that I could punish you for all you have done by making you beg and scream for mercy as I forced myself on you.'

Alice lay still, listening to Appleseed. She had already made up her mind. If he did try to rape her, he would have to undo at least one of the belts holding her legs together. Even with just one leg free, she would try and cause enough damage for him to be angry enough to end it all. She had heard the slogan better dead than undead many times in training, but she knew that sometimes, there were things worse than being undead, and being at the mercy of a brute like Appleseed was one of them.

Appleseed paused. 'Now that you're in front of me, I just want to blow your brains out. Too bad I have to leave that pleasure to the folks in Shanghai. But at least I won't be deprived of all pleasure.'

Appleseed began loosening his belt when suddenly several shots rang out. Someone was firing on full automatic. The door burst open and a Red Guard walked in. When he saw Appleseed with his belt open, he paused till the general barked at him.

'Which idiot is firing outside?'

The Red Guard was ashen-faced as he replied, and Alice could see the fear in his eyes. 'Sir, we're under attack.'

Appleseed was irritated at having been interrupted and waved his hand to dismiss the Red Guard. 'An attack? We wiped most of those fools out in the Ruins two days ago. If it's a rabble of some insurgents, tell the men to get the choppers in the air and send out a squad of Guards. I'll be with you shortly.'

Appleseed had turned to face Alice again when she saw

the Red Guard hesitate as he spoke again. 'Sir, we need you at the Command Centre. We've never seen such an attack before.'

Appleseed turned on him in fury. 'What the hell is wrong with you? Don't you understand a simple order? Ok, tell me, who is attacking us?'

Alice saw the Red Guard's eyes widen and he spoke in what was barely a whisper. 'Sir, we're under attack by an army of Biters. Thousands and thousands of them.'

Alice watched the look of surprise on Appleseed's face as more shots rang out outside. She could see him hesitate for a moment before his face hardened.

'Thousands, my foot! Must be a band of Biters that has wandered our way. Come with me!'

As he went out of the room, Alice's relief at being spared was quickly replaced by anxiety about what was happening outside. She heard more gunshots and then she heard something that chilled her. It sounded like thousands of animals baying and roaring together, creating a bizarre symphony. She didn't know if there were actually thousands of Biters outside or not, but she had never heard so many of them together, and screaming with such ferocity that they could be heard above the din of gunfire. She then heard the buzz of helicopters taking off, and then loud explosions as what she presumed were rockets streaked into the approaching Biters. She had grown up thinking of Biters as mindless monsters, but had also seen them at close quarters as more like frightened, infected animals. She wondered what could be making them walk into a slaughter with the firepower that Appleseed and the Red Guards would have arrayed against them.

Then the room seemed to shake and Alice saw several bricks fall off the wall. Another loud explosion and the bed fell over on its side. Alice cried out as her head hit the floor and wondered why the Red Guards were firing on their own base. Another explosion shook the base and she felt the belt holding one of her hands snap open as the bed shook from the impact. Alice quickly undid the other belts and then stepped towards the open door. The corridor outside did not seem to be guarded and so she walked down it and then peered around the corner, where she saw what appeared to be a Command Centre with many display screens and a large window. It was from here that Appleseed and his staff seemed to be directing the battle. There were at least twenty staffers with Appleseed and they all seemed to be focusing out the window, so nobody saw her behind them.

When Alice looked out the window, she froze at the sight. There was a small courtyard with a helipad to one side, and then a high perimeter wall ringed by automatic gun turrets and guard towers. Outside the wall, as far as she could see, was a sea of approaching Biters. The Red Guard had been right: there must have been thousands of them, and while they were steadily being mowed down by fire from the turrets and rockets from two hovering helicopters, with their sheer weight of numbers they kept closing in.

Appleseed was screaming to his men. 'Morons! Biters don't fire RPGs. There are people mixed in among them.'

Alice saw several smoke trails from the mob of Biters outside and realized what had hit the building, freeing her in the process. Several RPGs reached out towards the perimeter wall and a guard tower was obliterated. A cheer went up from the mob outside, and Alice heard a few human voices mixed among the howls of the Biters. Part of her wondered how this army had been assembled and who was leading it, but for now she was transfixed by the battle unfolding before her. Appleseed was screaming at his men to pick off the humans in the army outside since they presented the biggest threat with the RPGs they were carrying, but what was obvious to Alice was that this battle was already lost for Appleseed and his men. There were just too many Biters approaching to be taken out by two helicopters and the handful of Red Guards she saw, and clearly Appleseed's men had never anticipated that there would be humans with firearms mixed in among them.

Appleseed was screaming as to why nobody had told him earlier when one of his subordinates blurted out, 'Sir, we saw only a dozen Biters and we thought our patrol outside could handle them. Then they started streaming out of holes in the ground.'

'Have you called in for air support?'

'Sir, they say close air fighters are airborne, but won't get here for at least another fifteen minutes.'

As Appleseed screamed out his rage, Alice looked outside and saw a jeep appear over the horizon, speeding towards the base. In the glow created by exploding rockets she saw a figure standing in the jeep, grey hair flowing behind her, holding aloft a book in one hand.

It was the Queen.

Appleseed had seen the jeep as well and shouted to his men, 'That bitch is leading them! She's that freak they think is their Queen. Take her out first.'

As one of his men moved to the radio to relay his orders, Alice moved into the room. She had no weapons with her, but saw a small fire extinguisher behind her on the wall. She picked it up and threw it at the Red Guard who was about to order an attack on the jeep. The extinguisher hit him on the back and he fell from his chair.

Appleseed turned to see what had happened and glared in unadulterated fury as he saw Alice. He reached for the gun at his waist when Alice leapt forward, grabbing the fallen Red Guard's pistol and coming up in a roll behind the console next to Appleseed. He fired two rounds that destroyed a monitor, showering Alice with bits of glass and plastic. Alice saw two Red Guards get up from their chairs and move towards her. Both were reaching for their pistols, but they were communications officers who had never seen close combat before and were just too slow. Alice squeezed off three rounds in quick succession, felling one of them and sending the other diving for cover.

She heard some of the men scream, the despair in their voices clear.

'Sir, they shot down a chopper!'

'The Biters are at the wall!'

The room was suddenly plunged into darkness, and Alice heard Appleseed shout to his men, 'Finish her and join me for extraction.'

And then Alice was left in a dark room, facing more than a dozen Red Guards, armed with only a pistol that had eight rounds left in it.

Alice heard the Guards fumbling in the dark, shouting to each other in Chinese. She thanked her stars that these were not combat troops and also that they did not seem to have automatic rifles. Even if one of them began spraying with a rifle, life would get very interesting for her. Alice tore a piece of cloth from her shirt and wrapped it around her right hand, grabbing a broken shard of glass. In her left hand was the pistol. The Guards were moving around noisily, perhaps confident that they had her cornered. She stayed glued to where she was sitting, trying not to make any noise. When she sensed movement to her right, she swung her right hand out, feeling the glass bite into something soft. The Guard howled in pain as Alice swept his feet from under him and brought down the glass shard on his body, feeling his blood spurt onto her hands. She then rolled over behind another desk. The explosions outside were bathing the room in occasional flashes of light, and Alice saw two Guards illuminated briefly and fired at them four times. Moving and in near total darkness, she wasn't sure if she put them down, but the shouts of pain she heard told her than she must have scored at least one hit.

Four rounds left.

Alice knew that she could not hope to kill or incapacitate all her opponents. It would be a matter of time before their numbers worked in their favor, so she consciously crawled towards the thin sliver of light showing from the door through which Appleseed had fled. In the darkness, she felt something bump into her, and without looking, she fired two rounds and heard a man scream. Her muzzle flash had attracted attention and she felt a bullet whistle past her face. She rolled on the ground, firing twice at the muzzle flash of the Guard who had fired at her. She didn't know if she hit him or he was just diving for cover, but she heard the sound of a body hitting the deck.

No bullets left.

The door was now barely ten feet away and Alice got up in a crouch, ready to make a run for it, when several bullets pinged off the floor near her. She sat down behind an overturned table as she heard the continuing sounds of the battle outside. The difference was that she could no longer hear the helicopters and the gun turrets were silent. The only sounds were the howling of the Biters, rifles firing on full automatic, and the occasional thump of an RPG round hitting home. That would mean the wall must have been breached. She took her pistol and hurled it towards a corner of the room, and as it landed, several of the Guards opened fire at it. That gave Alice the window of opportunity she needed, and she sprinted out the door, closing it as she felt bullets impact into it from the other side. She locked the door, and while she knew that the Guards would probably break it down soon enough, at least she would buy herself some time.

She was in a corridor that was illuminated by only a handful of small lights along the ceiling. She couldn't see any doors or windows along the corridor other than a single door at its end. As she heard the Red Guards start to try and break down the door behind her, she ran down the corridor. When she reached the door, she found it unlocked and found a single Red Guard standing on the other side. He turned around, surprised to see anyone inside other than fellow Red Guards. He had an assault rifle in his hand, but before he could bring it up, Alice grabbed the rifle with both hands and brought it up, smashing the butt in the man's face. As he staggered back, Alice reached into the holster on his belt and took out his pistol. By the time the man had recovered enough to charge at her, she fired two rounds at point blank range. The Red Guard went down and did not get up. As eager as she was to go after Appleseed, she realized that blundering on ahead unarmed was going to be sure suicide. So she took a minute to take the Red Guard's rifle, pistol and the belt that held his spare clips. Then she set down the dark corridor. The first thing she noticed were the growling noises coming from both sides.

She picked up a lamp from the wall and shone it around, and saw a row of cells lining the corridor. From several of the cells came moaning or growling sounds, and the whole place had a foul stench. Alice figured this was a prison where Appleseed and the Red Guards kept prisoners, and she approached one of the cells, trying to see who was inside.

'Hello, is someone inside?'

A yellowed hand grabbed the bars and a decayed, torn face smashed up against them. Alice was so stunned she fell back as the Biter began beating his head against the bars. The lamp in her hand shattered against the ground, and the room was enveloped in darkness. Biters in several other cells along the corridor began screaming as Alice grabbed her weapons and ran down the corridor, trying to get away as fast as possible. She couldn't figure out why anyone would keep Biters in cells like these, but knowing Appleseed and his masters, she knew that they must not have been up to any good.

She saw a stairwell at the end of the corridor and climbed up, opening a small door to the outside. When she stepped out, she found herself on a narrow ledge near the rooftop. She could see Appleseed with two Red Guards on the roof and she heard him shout to one of his men.

'Get on the radio again and ask how far that chopper is.'

Alice leaned over and saw that the battle outside was all but over. Biters were now streaming into the courtyard and mixed with them were men carrying assault rifles and RPGs. She could not be sure in the darkness, but she thought she spotted Satish and a few of his men. As Alice saw them she hoped that more of her friends from Wonderland had survived.

There were still a few pockets of resistance as she saw Red Guards firing from windows, but it was a losing battle given the sheer numbers of Biters who were now rampaging inside, and the firepower their human comrades were bringing to bear.

The jeep carrying the Queen was also now entering the courtyard and Alice saw her look up straight at her. Next to the Queen was Bunny Ears.

'Alice!'

The Queen had shouted out to her, obviously relieved at seeing her alive and well, but in doing so she had attracted Appleseed's attention. Alice ducked as a bullet slammed into the bricks behind her and dove onto the rooftop, taking cover behind a water tank. Appleseed was on the other side of the roof and he and his men were now crouched behind a large satellite dish. Both Red Guards had rifles and seemed to know how to use them. Every time Alice tried to lean around the corner of the tank to take a shot, they would lay down a withering fire that had her ducking for cover. She heard a voice that she recognized scream above the din of gunfire and howling.

'Save Alice. She must live!'

It was the Queen.

Alice watched as two black clad men climbed onto the roof, but the Red Guards were in a great defensive position, covered by the large satellite dishes and boxes near them. Both Zeus troopers went down under a steady volley of fire. However, that gave Alice time to take aim and fire a quick burst at the two Red Guards, sending them scampering for cover. She leaned out and saw several Biters try and climb up to the roof. Many of them fell in trying to climb the stairs, and even when one or two actually made it close to the roof, the Red Guards picked them off one by one with carefully aimed head shots. When two Biters actually seemed to be about to make it to the top, one of the Red Guards tossed a grenade that obliterated them.

Alice heard a helicopter approach, and that galvanized her into action. After all he had done, Appleseed could not be allowed to escape. She leaned out and saw that both Red Guards were now frantically firing at the mass of Biters. While the Biters were having trouble climbing the ladders, two black-clad men were now almost at the roof, and firing at the Red Guards. While both men went down to another grenade rolled at them, they had distracted the Red Guards long enough to not notice the new danger they faced.

A large truck had been driven up along the roof, and Biters were launching themselves off its top at the roof. Several fell short, but many made it, and all the while the Queen kept screaming.

'The prophecy must be fulfilled! Alice must live!'

The two Red Guards were now beginning to falter as they realized that there was no way they could hold back the flood of Biters, and they were steadily backing up behind the satellite dishes. Alice caught a glimpse of Appleseed, firing his pistol at the approaching Biters.

Even as Biters fell, more climbed over them, trying to get to the Red Guards. Alice saw that she had a clear shot and fired a burst that caught one of the Red Guards in the shoulder. He fell, screaming in agony, and his comrade now panicked, knowing there was no way he could hold his position alone. That split second of indecision cost them dearly as the Biters were on them, clawing and biting as they screamed for mercy, till they spoke no more.

Appleseed raced across the roof with a speed that belied his bulk, throwing two grenades that scattered the Biters in his path and firing with his pistol as he ran back towards the building. Alice fired but missed as her aim was thrown off by an exploding grenade, and saw Appleseed climb back through the door she had used to get to the rooftop. Thinking that Appleseed probably had another escape route planned, she followed him inside. As soon as she had stepped into the darkness, she felt a burning pain in her right thigh as Appleseed plunged a knife into her. He pulled the knife out and then pushed her backwards, sending her falling ten feet to the floor below. Alice landed hard, the wind totally knocked out of her as Appleseed climbed down the stairs. He kicked her pistol away when she tried to reach for it and stood over her.

'You bitch, I should have just gutted you when I had the chance. But it's never too late to set things right.'

He brought his hand up to stab her. Alice saw his shadow move and brought her left leg up in a kick that hit him in the groin, sending him back, doubling over with pain. She could hear him groaning and swearing as she got up and tried to get her bearings. There was moonlight coming in the through the open door above, and as her eyes adjusted, she saw him circling back for another strike. As he lunged towards her, she was ready for him. She grabbed his wrist and turned, using his weight and momentum against him. Appleseed went crashing to the ground as Alice followed through with a kick aimed at his head. Appleseed blocked the kick and twisted her ankle, sending her down again. He got up, rubbing his sore hand and swearing.

'You think you're so tough. I can crush you with my bare hands.'

All of Alice's training came back to her and she made a conscious effort to relax and still her mind. Fight angry and you will make mistakes, and a single mistake can be fatal. That was one of the lessons her instructors had drilled into her, especially given her usually impulsive nature. But now those lessons learnt in classes, and more importantly in several life and death battles in the Deadland, saved her life. Appleseed feinted with his right hand and brought his left up in a punch aimed at her throat. Alice saw him telegraph the blow with the slight roll of his left shoulder and she stepped inside his blow, blocking his arm with her right forearm and then using her head to butt him in the nose. As he groaned and stumbled back, she followed with a punch to the solar plexus and then another to Appleseed's already damaged nose. She heard a crunching noise and was sure she broke his nose when he screamed in agony. Appleseed fell back, but in doing so, pushed Alice hard, sending her bouncing off a wall and to the ground.

To her surprise, instead of attacking again, Appleseed ran towards the far door. Alice was on her feet, but with her twisted ankle was not able to move fast enough to catch him before he reached the door. He turned on a small table lamp and she saw his bloodied face as he glared at her.

'Now rot in Hell with the Biters you love so much.'

He reached over to the wall and pulled a switch. Alice heard a creaking noise as all the cell doors swung open and Appleseed disappeared behind the door. Alice would have followed him except for the fact that now she saw Biters emerge from four of the cells. They all wore collars and were filthy and bloodied. One of them, a large man with one ear missing, snarled at her and lunged. Alice rolled out of the way and grabbed the pistol on the ground, coming up in a crouch and drilling him with three rounds, two to the chest and one to the head that dropped him. The other three Biters now charged at her, screaming and howling. She shot one more in the head before she realized that that they were too close for her to get another shot. She ducked under one's outstretched hands and kicked out at the other, sending him down. She rolled across the corridor, hoping to put some distance between them and get another shot, when another figure jumped into the fray.

It was the Queen. She was carrying a large axe and brought it down on one of the Biter's necks, and as he stumbled forward, she brought the axe down again on his skull. The last remaining Biter spat at her and lunged forward, swatting her against the wall as Alice fired, hitting the Biter in the leg. The Biter fell down, and Alice rushed to help the Queen.

'Are you okay?'

The Queen smiled, a strange expression given her lifeless eyes. 'Alice, am I glad to see you alive. The prophecy...'

Before she could complete her sentence, the Biter on the ground jumped at Alice and sank his teeth into her leg. She screamed in agony and on reflex shot him in the head. She grabbed her bleeding leg and stared at the Queen in horror.

'Help me!'

The Queen seemed to flounder and then saw the vial around Alice's neck.

'We must use the vaccine now!'

The Queen wrenched the vial from Alice's neck and took out the syringe, pressing the needle deep into Alice's calf, but was able to inject only half the contents before Alice spasmed and the needle came out, spraying some of the precious liquid on the floor. Alice felt a burning sensation spread from her legs to her entire body. Her hands were shaking and her vision was blurring. She tried to say something but it felt like there was a giant lump in her throat. The Queen lay Alice on her lap and took the vial and opened it, pouring the remaining contents down Alice's throat.

'Alice, my child. You cannot die or become just another Biter. The prophecy needs you to live, to bring an end to all this suffering.'

Alice felt the liquid flow down her throat and it felt as

if her entire body were on fire. She saw the Queen glance up and then she pushed something into Alice's hand. Before Alice could say anything, she saw the Queen's head disappear in a spray of blood. As the Queen's body fell, she dropped Alice to the ground. Alice's head hit the ground hard and through the red mist that clouded her vision she saw someone approaching, a pistol in his hand. Alice screamed as her body spasmed time and again, and then went still.

Appleseed had come back into the room, looking for the key card that he must have dropped in his struggle with Alice. He had only one hope now: to hide in the small panic room near the Command Center and hope that he was not discovered till Red Guard reinforcements arrived. When he entered the room, he saw that all the Biters were down but also noted with satisfaction that Alice was down as well. He had spotted the Biter Queen near Alice and had taken her head off with a single shot.

As he came closer, in the dim light he saw Alice's leg twitching and he put a bullet into it. Her leg jerked once and was then moved no more.

Appleseed screamed at nobody in particular, 'I got you all, didn't I?'

He took out a small flashlight and began to search among the mangled bodies littering the floor for his key card. He could now hear footsteps on the roof, and he knew he had very limited time. His foot hit something and he looked down to see a charred book clutched in Alice's hand. He stopped, wondering why anyone would be carrying an old children's fairy tale into a battle.

'All that's left of your damn Wonderland is ashes.'

He began to move on when he felt a cold, clammy hand grip his feet. Appleseed froze with fear. One of the Biters was not yet destroyed. He spun around to face the threat when the door above him swing open and Satish and two other men ran in, rifles at the ready. Satish saw Appleseed and fired, grazing him on the shoulder. Appleseed fell to the ground, and his flashlight and pistol both fell from his hands. He clambered to his feet again, trying to find his weapon, when cold hands gripped his wrist and twisted it till he screamed in agony as his bones snapped. He managed to free his hand and saw his pistol lying nearby, but before he could grab it he saw a hand reaching for it and raising it towards him in the darkness. Bullet after bullet tore into Appleseed as he fell, not knowing who or what had killed him.

EPILOGUE

SIX MONTHS LATER

'Comrade General, are you sure you want us to land at the forward base?'

Chen glared at the pilot next to him. 'Comrade Colonel, do I take it that your revolutionary fervor is waning in the face of the enemy?'

The pilot blanched and looked away, taking the helicopter into a slight turn as they approached the base near the Deadland. He knew that for all that had changed in the last six months, a mere insinuation from someone like Chen could send him and his family to a labor camp for indoctrination. That, he knew, was a death sentence in all but name.

Chen looked down at the parked APCs and the Red Guards milling about the base and wondered just how long they could keep any meaningful presence in the Deadland. Expressing such thoughts in front of his masters in the Central Committee would be unthinkable, but as a professional military man, he knew the momentum was against them. While he knew his career, and indeed his life, depended on unquestioning obedience to his masters, he also knew that when political masters refused to see battlefield realities, it usually meant that defeat was around the corner. It had begun with the events in the Deadland, revolving around that damned Biter Queen and the girl called Alice. The rout of the Red Guard base and Appleseed's death was a minor tactical reverse, but the larger strategic ramifications of those events had been great. The large scale defections among Zeus had meant that the Central Committee had deemed that only frontline Red Guard units be used in the Deadland. That in turn had meant fewer troops for the continuing war in the Americas, where the enemy was making steady progress in its brutal insurgency campaign. But that was a military campaign – one Chen knew how to wage. What had happened in the Deadland was different, and more dangerous. An idea had been born: the idea that humans and Biters could somehow co-exist and that the Central Committee and its masters were behind the catastrophe that had been The Rising. The idea that it was possible to start to recreate civilization without the control of the Central Committee and its Red Guards. That idea had taken root throughout the Deadland and had begun to seep into the cities of the Mainland. That, Chen mused with a bitter smile, had perhaps less to do with ideology and more to do with the choking off of slave labor from the Deadland. When the citizens of Shanghai and Guangzhou were called on to work the farms, they realized the utopia the Central Committee had promised was not quite the same without slave labor from the Deadland to lubricate the wheels of their utopian society. A nascent campaign of resistance had begun, and many of the dangerous messages which had preceded The Rising – calls for freedom, democracy and accountability – were once again whispered in the Mainland.

The helicopter landed and Chen stepped out, saluting the Red Guards outside who stood at attention. He singled out the commanding officer, a burly officer whose eyes seemed to be constantly scanning the horizon. Chen had read his dossier. The major had never been in combat before, but had been a rising star back in Shanghai due to his political connections. The mere fact that officers like him were being shipped out to the Deadland to make up for losses among frontline troops was a clear sign of how the war was going.

'Comrade Major Liang, how is the war progressing?'

The major snapped to attention, but Chen noticed that he seemed to be on edge.

'Sir, we are carrying on our struggle to liberate the citizens of the Deadland from the tyranny of fear that the Biters impose and the counter-revolutionary ideas of the terrorists.'

Chen smirked. The young officer no doubt had excelled in his political education back in Shanghai. He just wondered how long he would last out here. As Chen sat in the Command Center and was subjected to a briefing containing what he had little doubt were largely fictional figures of losses the unit had inflicted on the enemy, his mind began to wander. He had no wish to be out here, but the Central Committee had decreed that senior officers needed to visit forward bases to bolster morale and no doubt provide photo-ops which would reassure the people back home that things were under control.

He was snapped back to reality when they heard a sentry cry out on the radio.

'Multiple contacts coming in fast.'

Liang was instantly at his command screen, where live video from a circling unmanned drone overhead was being streamed. The looting of man-portable SAMs from overrun Red Guard armories and experienced Zeus operators to use them had meant that several drones had been lost in the last few months. As a result, drones were being used for largely static defense, hovering close to bases like this one. Still, it was better than getting no warning at all. Chen peered over Liang's shoulder and saw six jeeps kicking up dust as they approached the base.

Something didn't seem right to Chen. From all he had heard, the enemy was not so stupid as to walk into overwhelming firepower.

Liang barked into his radio, 'Get the two gunships in the air. I want them obliterated before they get within RPG range.'

Another display showed the footage from both helicopter gunships as they took off and turned towards the approaching vehicles. The radio crackled with another transmission from the drone operator.

'Sir, I have three more jeeps coming in from the opposite direction.'

Chen had a sinking feeling in his gut. They had two gunships at their base and should theoretically be able to deal with such a threat, but he had heard of too many bases being overrun. Part of him told him to get to his chopper and get out, but he could not abandon his troops when they were under attack.

He heard Liang speak in little more than a whisper.

'It's the witch. She rides with them.'

Chen's attention snapped to the display and he saw a close up of one of the jeeps, and standing there was a young woman with her fair hair streaming behind her, her eyes covered by dark glasses. The other jeeps seemed to have only a driver, with the cab behind covered in what appeared to be canvas.

'Sir, she cannot be killed. I have heard so many comrades…'

Chen shut Liang up viciously. 'Comrade Major, you are the ranking officer in charge of this base. Weakness and superstitious babbling will not help your men. Decisive action will.'

Even as Chen said the words, he had to admit that he too felt a stab of irrational fear. It was one thing to fight men who could be killed and to hunt mindless Biters, but it was quite another to fight an enemy who supposedly could not be killed but could fight like the best trained soldier and handle the most sophisticated weaponry. This witch had been leading the enemy to victory after victory and now she seemed to be bearing down on him. Liang was so focused on the jeep carrying the witch that he paid little attention to the three jeeps that the drone had picked up.

'Pilots, fire at will and aim at the third jeep from the left. That's where their leader is'

The drone operator screamed out, 'Sir, those three new jeeps are firing SAMs—'

His transmission was cut short as the screen relaying footage from the drone was filled with static. A second later he heard calls for help from the two gunship pilots who reported multiple SAM trails headed towards them. Chen watched in impotent fury as the gunships tried to evade the incoming missiles, and then their display screens were also replaced by static. Liang seemed to be on the verge of panic, having just lost the edge in firepower he had. In his panic and anger, Chen snapped, all trace of civility gone.

'You idiot! Stop staring at those screens. We still have our eyes and our weapons. Come on to the deck and get binoculars.'

Chen walked outside and saw through his binoculars that the jeeps had stopped and all of them had their canvas covers removed, revealing multi-barrel rocket launchers of the sort that were carried underwing by Red Guard helicopter gunships. Chen's lips tightened.

'So that's why they've been reported to be so interested in

picking dry the wreckage of the choppers we lose.'

He had no time to admire the ingenuity of the enemy as one of the jeeps fired. He saw a flash of light and six rockets streaked towards the base. It was an inaccurate weapon, but at such close range they did not need pinpoint accuracy. Three rockets exploded short of their target, but three arched into the base, exploding in the grounds outside, sending Red Guards scampering for cover. Chen looked down and saw several men lying bloodied after the strike.

Liang was screaming at his men to open fire with the Gatling gun emplacements. Chen shouted at him to shut up.

'Liang, they are out of range. They have clearly thought this through better than you.'

Liang blanched as Chen walked back into the command center, trying to salvage the situation the best he could.

'Order everyone into the underground shelters. They can fire all the rockets they want, but they can't get us there. If they try and close in after that, we still have a fighting chance since they only seem to have a handful of men and we have more than two hundred fully armed soldiers here. Liang, get on the radio and call in an air strike.'

Chen knew that any air strike would be at least fifteen minutes away, but he wanted the men to feel that the initiative still lay with them. That was when one of the guards on the perimeter wall wailed on the radio, the fear in his voice apparent. The words he said robbed Chen of all the fight he had left in him.

'Sir, Biters are coming in from all sides. Hundreds of them just popped up from tunnels! What do we do?'

Chen went back to the deck and froze at what he saw. As

far as the eye could see, there were Biters walking towards their base. Each wall had a remotely controlled gun turret and he shouted for one of them to open fire. He heard the familiar buzzing sound as the gun turret fired, cutting through the front ranks of the approaching Biters like a scythe, tearing limbs and bodies. He could see some of the undead monsters still trying to crawl towards the base as the others behind them stepped over them and continued approaching. Just then, two more of the jeeps fired rockets. This time, their aim was better, and most of the rockets slammed into the base. One tore a gaping hole in the front wall, destroying the gun turret, while others hit the inside of the base, and Chen dove for cover as the helicopter he had come in exploded in a giant fireball.

He crawled back inside, feeling the skin on his arm burn from a near miss from shrapnel. Liang was staring at him open-mouthed.

'Sir, they are on the radio.'

Chen heard a female voice on the radio.

'Red Guards, surrender and I guarantee that you will be left alive. Fight us and you will be destroyed without mercy.'

Chen had heard enough stories about other bases that had received similar messages. Some had fought till the end, but others had surrendered to be looted of all their weapons and equipment. The survivors brought back tales of horror that spread further fear and discontent in the Mainland, and uncomfortable questions about the nature of the enemy and the war they were really fighting. The Central Committee had initially reacted the only way it knew how: to sentence the officers and troops to long stints in labor camps to build back their 'revolutionary fervor'. But that had only further sucked dry the supply of battle-hardened troops. Which is why fools like Liang were now here.

Liang seemed to be on the verge of total panic and grabbed at the holster on his belt.

'Sir, we cannot let those monsters take us!'

Chen sighed. It would sound brave to talk of fighting to the end, but then he saw the frightened faces around him. Young men, many with families back in the Mainland, fighting a war that now had no clear agenda, far away from home, against an enemy whom they had been misled about. General Chen had always been a good Party Man but he could not let these young men be slaughtered for no purpose. He would surrender and take accountability for it, and plead that the soldiers had wanted to fight, but he had overridden them. He knew that he would not survive long in a labor camp, but perhaps it was time he finally did his true duty as an officer: to his men, not to his masters back in the Central Committee.

He grabbed the mike from Liang and spoke, noting the horror in the major's face. 'I agree, but we will surrender to humans. Ask those monsters to hold back.'

He asked all his men to put their weapons away, and then walked to the deck. He saw that the Biters had indeed stopped and wondered how this witch exercised such control over what were surely mindless brutes and monsters. The jeeps closed in on the base, and he saw black-clad men disembark from them and enter the base, assault rifles at the ready. The witch was among them, her blond hair marking her out from all the others. The black clad men fanned out across the base and gathered the Red Guards outside in a group, herding them into a room where they were locked. Others began to climb to the Command Center.

Chen turned to see the door open and four heavily armed men walk inside. They were all locals, and wore old Zeus uniforms. One of them looked at Chen and whistled.

'I never thought we'd have a general here as our guest. Everyone, get down on your knees and put your hands behind your head.'

Chen nodded to his men and they all complied. He noted that he could not see Liang and wondered where the fool was. Then he looked up and saw the witch enter, flanked by two men wielding shotguns. She seemed little more than a girl, dressed all in black and with her mouth covered by a mask and her eyes obscured by dark sunglasses. She was armed to the teeth, with a shotgun and sniper rifle slung across her back and a pistol and knife at her belt. Tied at her belt was a book. When Chen took a closer look, he noticed that it seemed to be some old children's book. She may not have looked physically imposing, but her very sight made several of the Red Guards break out into sobs of terror, crying for mercy.

She walked towards Chen and motioned for him to stand up.

'General, my men will be clearing out all your weapons and communications equipment. We will leave enough food to last you a day and then leave. I'm sure your reinforcements will be here soon enough.'

She came closer, and Chen found himself involuntarily shrinking back.

'When you get back, do one thing for me. Tell your masters that the Deadland is now free, and we don't want any Red Guards here. Not a single settler will go to your camps and we will continue rebuilding society the way we want.'

Chen saw a blur of movement from the corner of his eye, and the girl saw his reaction, turning just in time to see Liang emerge from a closet, carrying a pistol. He fired a shot at point blank range before two of the black-clad men shredded him with shotgun blasts. Chen watched the girl stagger to the ground and then gasped in horror as she got up, calmly picking at a hole in her torso. There was barely a thin trickle of blood, and a shot that should have killed her did not even seem to faze her. She turned to Chen, pointing at what remained of Liang.

'Tell your other men not to be so stupid. I don't want any unnecessary bloodshed.'

Chen stammered out the words that were paramount on his mind. 'What...what are you?'

The girl came closer and said in almost a whisper, 'You should remember me, General Chen, and you should have killed me when you had the chance all those months ago.'

Then she removed her glasses and mask and Chen gasped as he looked into her lifeless yellow eyes and skin that was peeling off in patches from her face.

She said her last words to Chen and disappeared with her men.

'My name is Alice Gladwell. They call me the Queen of Wonderland.'

THROUGH THE KILLING GLASS:

ALICE IN DEADLAND BOOK II

ONE

WHAT ALICE REGRETTED THE MOST about not being fully human was the fact that she could no longer cry. cry. More than a year had passed since Alice set in motion events that had changed her life and that of everyone in the Deadland by following a Biter with bunny ears down a hole in the ground. Events that had led to the creation of a new settlement, a settlement unlike any the world had seen since The Rising. What had followed had been the re-settlement of the city of Delhi by thousands of humans who had streamed in from the Deadland to live together in a community. A community that had laws, security and houses for people to live in. A community where every night was not spent in dread of marauding Biters or raids by the Red Guards. A community that was now known simply as Wonderland.

The cost of this victory had been high. Thousands had perished in the Deadland during the struggle against the Red Guards, and hundreds more in the air raids that had been unleashed when Alice had been captured. Alice's personal costs had been high, too. She had lost her entire family, and her identity. No longer was she the mercurial fifteen year-old girl her father had doted upon. She was now the Queen of

Wonderland, whom people looked at with awe and fear. But being part-Biter, she could never taste food again; she now simply had no need for it. She could never dream of her family again, for Biters could not dream, and while she often thought back to all she had lost, she could not cry to lessen that pain, for Biters shed no tears.

To her enemies, Alice was a formidable adversary, with the training and battle-tested instincts of the most elite human soldier, but also with the inexhaustible stamina and immunity to all forms of damage short of a direct head shot that her Biter half gave her. To her human followers, she was a messiah who had rescued them from the Deadland to give them hope that they could live again like civilized people. To the Biters who followed her, she was the leader of the pack, to be followed with animal instinct and devotion.

But to herself, she was still Alice Gladwell, daughter and sister to her murdered family. . She had taken her vengeance against the Red Guards, and what had begun as a mission of personal vendetta had led to something much bigger. Alice had never fashioned herself as a leader, but now she knew more than ten thousand humans in Wonderland depended on her. Whether or not she wanted this burden of leadership, it was now hers, and she was determined not to let down those who counted on her.

Much of her own young life had been spent forged in battle, and her education had consisted of little more than learning to fight and to survive in the Deadland, but today Alice was going to do something she had never done before. She was going to inaugurate the first school in Wonderland.

There was a hush among the gathered thousands as she stepped onto the makeshift podium. Arjun, her confidante and trusted advisor, had chosen the location with his usual sense of humor. The school was to be located in what had once been the Delhi Zoo.

'People of Wonderland, thank you for coming. I myself had little education beyond learning to survive in the Deadland, but now our children will learn what people did before The Rising, and one day they will revive our world the way it was.'

There was thunderous applause, but when Alice stepped off the podium, she felt a bit hollow inside. She knew nothing of what life had been like before The Rising, and while she was proud of what they had achieved together, she wondered if she was really needed in Wonderland anymore. She knew nothing of managing a city, with its squabbles over water and romantic affairs. She itched for the camaraderie she had known in the settlement where everyone knew each other, not the anonymity of urban life, where people huddled in their apartments in the center of what had once been posh government colonies in Delhi.

She saw a young couple holding hands, and she looked away. That was another experience she was never to have. She was young enough and human enough to regret never being able to be loved, but she was Biter enough to never feel such emotions. Besides, her appearance did enough to seal that deal.

As she walked back to her room in what had once been the Red Fort in the heart of Delhi, Arjun caught up with her.

'Alice, we've sent out patrols north of Wonderland again this week, but people are beginning to complain about the patrols. They say that we haven't seen Red Guards for months.'

Alice turned towards Arjun and she noted with dismay how even he flinched at her sight. Her impish smile and twinkling eyes were long gone, replaced by a vacant, yellowed gaze and skin that seemed to be rotting, giving off a foul stench. She turned away, trying not to see the expression on his face.

'Arjun, people grow fat and happy. They forget that this safety was won with blood, and that the war still rages outside of their apartments, and any day it may visit us again.'

Arjun was with Alice – she knew that – but she also knew the pressure he faced. It was no longer popular to talk about the war. After their crippling losses in battle, the Red Guards had effectively ceded control of what had been the Deadland in North India. Occasionally a jet would be spotted high in the skies, but even they did not come lower, knowing that Wonderland's defenses bristled with hand held Surface to Air missiles wielded by experienced troopers who had once served Zeus, the mercenary arm that had done the Central Committee's bidding before they had mutinied and the Red Guards had been called in from the mainland in China.

At times like this, Alice got on her bicycle and rode alone, crossing the dried up Yamuna river to the forested area that had now been reserved for Biters. Someone had said it was like an animal reserve from before The Rising, and strangely Alice had felt herself bristle at that comment. The Biters were kept confined in a wooded area ringed by electrified fences with tunnels that allowed them to go out to the Deadland. Was the Biter part of her so strong now that she identified herself more with them than with humans? She drove with the wind blowing her flowing blond hair behind her. That was the one part of her body that had not changed when she had been transformed into the hybrid she had become.

By now, the sun was setting and darkness settling over the forests, and she saw a couple of familiar shapes. Closest to her was a Biter wearing bunny ears, with a shuffling gait and a left hand that been taken off below the elbow by a Red Guard grenade. The second was a hulking Biter wearing a hat. If Alice was the leader of the pack, then Bunny Ears and Hatter were her enforcers. After being transformed, she realized that while the Biters could not really communicate in any human language, they did communicate like animals, and had a strong pack mentality. Bringing an end to the war in the Deadland meant not just fighting the Red Guards to a bloody standstill but also ensuring that Biters and humans could at least co-exist, if not actively work together. Doing that had meant establishing herself as the leader of the pack. Now she commanded an army of thousands of Biters who emerged from the dark forest, kneeling before her.

Alice held an old, charred book in her left hand. It was the last book left in the Deadland and she had first encountered it in the underground base of the Biters in the possession of the Biter Queen. Its title was Alice in Wonderland. The Queen had believed that the book held a prophecy for healing the world, and that Alice was destined to carry out the prophecy it contained. Now that Alice had brushed up on her reading skills, she understood the coincidences leading to the Queen's belief in the 'prophecy' and Alice's part in it. Alice did not know if there was any truth to the supposed prophecy, but she did know two things. One, until someone actually sat down and wrote another book, this was indeed perhaps the last book in the Deadland, and that in itself made it a precious thing to protect, and second, that the Biters held it in an almost religious awe. That was the reason why she carried it with her every time she came to them.

Alice had come to realize that loyalty from Biters was never a given, since they were as impulsive and as aggressive as rabid animals, and when one or two of the newcomers shuffled towards her, Hatter stepped in front of them and swatted them away. Before, Alice had been disgusted by their fetid smell of rot. Now it barely bothered her.

She sat down by a tree, looking at the night sky. But now more than stars illuminated what had once been the Deadland: lights from several apartments flickered in the dark.

'They grow complacent. They light up the settlement to be the easiest target for miles.'

She had just whispered to herself but Bunny Ears came and sat down next to her, awaiting her orders. While the Biters communicated in grunts and screeches, they seemed to understand human language to some extent. Perhaps some part of their brains still functioned despite the virus that had reduced them to this condition.

'Don't worry, Bunny Ears. Nothing I can't handle.'

She waved him away when the tactical radio strapped to her side came to life.

'White Queen, this is White Rook. Please come to the Looking Glass immediately.'

Alice got up and sped away towards the nearby temple that served as their communication center, their only real window to what was happening in the outside world. Satish – or White Rook – had named this place Looking Glass. Before he defected, Satish had been a Zeus warrior, and over time he had effectively become the head of the armed forces of Wonderland.

For months they had tried to get in touch with the ongoing resistance in what had been the United States, but without much success. Other than that, they used captured computers and handheld tablets to monitor what the Central Committee and its minions were up to. There was no news other than what the Central Committee allowed to be transmitted, but at least it gave them some idea of what was happening outside their settlement. Looking Glass had been initially located in the heart of the city, but then people had asked for it to be moved to the outskirts, since they did not really want to hear the bad news from the outside world. That was another sign that people had grown complacent, and forgotten the struggle that had won them this peace.

Alice wondered what Satish had learnt that required her to be in the Looking Glass at this time of night.

'The fools want to create political parties and have an election.'

Alice could sense the disdain in Satish's voice. She knew that with relative peace, people in Wonderland had been quick to lapse into the jockeying for power that was perhaps inherent to man. It was a shame that it required something like The Rising and being hunted by Biters for men to realize that petty tokens of power and prestige were not what really mattered.

'That bastard Arun is riling everyone up, telling them we need true democracy and that they no longer need you.'

Alice tried not to get involved in the politics of men like Arun, who had been a politician before The Rising. She had continued to run Wonderland the way it had been, by a small committee of elders, and with every big decision being put to a vote.

'Satish, they will talk because they have nothing better to do. I don't think it means anything.'

Satish turned towards Alice. With all they had been through together, he saw beyond the decayed skin and yellow eyes. He still saw the incredibly brave yet naïve young girl who had done so much for everyone in the Deadland.

'Alice, you don't know how men like them work. They are no better than the leeches in the Central Committee in

Shanghai. Give them half a chance and they will become tyrants in their own right.'

It was an old argument. Both Arjun and Satish hated how all they had fought for was being lost, and people were lapsing into petty politicking. A few months of security, one which they and their friends had shed blood to win, had led men like Arun to proclaim that they no longer had a war to fight, and they needed to create a more peaceful, democratic society. One where people like Alice and Satish did not need to have such a prominent role, and of course one where, conveniently enough, politicians occupied the highest rungs of the ladder.

'Satish, I'm sure you didn't call me here at this time to bitch about Arun.'

Satish slapped himself on the forehead in exaggerated apology.

'No, no, of course not. Come on, we have some exciting news. For the first time, we actually may see something of value though our Looking Glass.'

Alice followed him to a console in front of which an elderly man was sitting, hunched over a computer terminal and with headphones around his ears.

'Danish, have you got anything yet?'

Danish raised one hand as he focused on tuning the radio in front of him. Danish had been a Communications Officer in the Indian Army before The Rising, and now he was in charge of running the Looking Glass in their continuing endeavor to learn about what was happening outside Wonderland, and also to try and make contact with others like themselves.

'We've finally made contact! Check this.'

Alice peered over his shoulder to see a single message displayed on the computer screen.

'We are your brothers in arms, fighting for the independence of the United States of America. We have heard much of you and your Queen. Listen for us in a day's time.'

Danish was visibly excited, his old, wrinkled eyes twinkling as he spoke.

'They managed to get an old server up and put up this page. This is the first Internet posting in sixteen years, and looks like the Central Committee hasn't seen it yet.'

Alice had been born after The Rising, when people were more bothered about escaping from hordes of Biters than surfing the Internet, but she had seen how powerful information could be in their own struggle against the Central Committee. With tablets brought over by defecting Zeus officers, they had managed to hack into the Central Committee's Intranet. Since then they had been posting messages that led to further defections among Zeus and also started creating discontent among the masses in mainland China, who had begun to question the true nature of the war they had been sold.

Before Alice could say anything, Danish hushed her, putting on his headphones, and then passed them on to her.

'Alice, they want to talk to you.'

Alice put on the headphones and heard the crackle of static. Then there was the deep voice of a man.

'Alice, this is General Konrath of the Free American Army based out of Forth Worth, Texas. We have been fighting our own war against the same enemy you face, and we are all proud to call you a fellow American.'

Alice's father had been with the American Embassy in New Delhi before The Rising, but she had been born in a world where the countries of the old world were little more than memories. Still, it was good to make contact with people from outside the Deadland where she had been born. It made their struggle feel less lonely.

'General, we have had a few months of relative quiet in Wonderland, and the Red Guards don't really come here anymore. How are things in the United States?'

There came a pause before the general's reply.

'Alice, we are facing brutal house to house fighting against the Red Guards and the still loyal Zeus mercenaries. Our bigger problem is that we're fighting them and also fighting against the damned Biters.'

Another pause, before he added, 'You know what I mean, Alice.'

'General, there's no need to apologize. I lived in fear of Biters for the first fifteen years of my life as well.'

'Alice, I wish we had someone like you to bring peace with the Biters. But for now, we need your help. Two of our people have escaped from a labor camp of the Reds and are making their way to the plains. They have nowhere else to go, so they are trying to escape to your city. Help them if you can.'

Static muffled the connection, and then the line was terminated. Alice felt Satish exhale loudly beside her. She knew that they were being asked to re-enter a fight that many in Wonderland believed was over.

'Alice, what do you plan to do?'

Alice answered without a pause. 'Satish, I lost my entire family so we could live free. I will not allow others seeking their freedom to be hunted down when I can help them.'

Satish just sniggered.

'Satish, what are you thinking?'

Satish grinned. 'I'm thinking that fat old Arun will have a heart attack if he knows about this.'

'He doesn't have to know, does he? Well, we don't even know that they'll make it anywhere close to Wonderland.'

Danish coughed to get their attention. He had one of his tactical radios held to his ear.

'Folks, something's up. One of the advance recon parties saw a convoy of Red Guards a hundred kilometers to the north east, on the old National Highway 8. They report two trucks and some jeeps.'

'Satish, I'm getting my kit. You get some men ready and join me.'

Five minutes later, Alice was outside near her bike. Her kit consisted of a handgun in a holster strapped to her left thigh, a serrated combat knife on her right thigh, an extra handgun on an ankle holster, and an assault rifle across her back. Satish was there with three of his men, getting into their jeep.

'Alice, are you sure you want to go along? This could be a trap for all we know.'

'I'm all dressed up for the party. I cannot back out now, can I?'

As she started off on her bicycle, Satish felt a lump in his throat. The thin girl he had first met in the Deadland had become a true warrior queen, and while she looked fearsome, he still remembered the crying girl he had met in the forests of the Deadland. A girl who had just lost her family to the Red Guards. He had nearly lost her once before, to a Red Guard trap. There was no way he was going to let her down again. He checked his own assault rifle and shouted to the driver.

'What are you waiting for? Let's go!'

By the time they started, Alice was well on her way, blond hair billowing behind her. Just a couple of years ago she would have felt fear at the prospect of such imminent danger. Now she welcomed it like an old friend. Far from the petty politicking of Wonderland, now it would be the way it had been, the way she had always liked it.

Alice saw that there were at least two dozen Red Guards, all wearing night vision goggles and armed with assault rifles. Their trucks were parked on the road behind them. She had left her bike a kilometer behind, tracking them the rest of the way on foot. They may have had night vision goggles and the latest equipment, but with the frontline ranks thinned by months of vicious combat, she knew from the Central Committee's Intranet that young men with no combat experience were being drafted and sent on combat missions. In contrast, she had spent her entire life training and fighting in circumstances like this. Also, one added benefit of her current state was that like Biters, she felt no fatigue. She could keep running and fighting all night long if she needed to.

Satish and his men were nearby, but for now she was alone. She saw the Red Guard officer raise his hand and shout a command in Mandarin. The Red Guards started to get back in their trucks. It seemed that they had achieved whatever they had set out to do. Alice wasn't sure what they had been up to, but she did not like it one bit. It certainly wasn't recon; they wouldn't need two large trucks and so many men for that. There was only one way to find out, and also to send a message to their masters that the Red Guards were not welcome here any more.

She raised her assault rifle to her shoulder and aimed at the officer through the night vision scope. The crosshairs were on his forehead when she shouted her warning.

'Red Guards! You are in our territory. Lay down your weapons and surrender and we will send you back unharmed.'

The Red Guards froze. Some of them muttered something she knew very well: 'Nu wu.'

'Witch' in Mandarin. Alice had come to be known among the Red Guards as the Yellow Witch, and she hoped that the fear her reputation generated would lead them to surrender. She certainly had no wish to slaughter green conscripts.

But that was not to be the case tonight. Whether driven by fear or perhaps to act brave in front of his men, the officer took out his handgun and fired in Alice's direction. That was the last mistake he made before a single round shattered his head. The Red Guards scattered, several of them firing wildly despite the fact that they were wearing night vision goggles. Alice had her rifle on single-shot mode and was now moving in an arc around the Red Guards, picking them off one by one. Several other rifles barked and she saw three Red Guards spin and fall.

Satish and his men had joined the battle.

Sandwiched between Alice and Satish's men, the remaining Red Guards gave into wild panic and rushed towards her. Alice put her rifle down and rose to meet them, handgun in one hand and knife in the other. The first Red Guard was but feet away when she put him down with two shots. The one behind him was about to bring his rifle up to fire when Alice dove towards him, rolling on the ground and coming up in a crouch near his feet. She fired thrice, feeling more then seeing him fall as she pivoted to meet the next threat. The Red Guard she faced was terrified out of his mind and screaming incoherently, but with a rifle in his hands he was still a threat to be dealt with.

Realizing he could never get a shot off in time, he swung the rifle like a club at Alice's head. She rolled under the blow and passed the man, stabbing him twice in quick succession, getting up behind him as he fell to the ground. Another Red

Guard was behind her and stabbed her with a knife in the chest. But Alice felt little more than a prick, and the man staggered back in horror as she calmly extracted the knife.

He stammered in broken English, 'Yellow Witch! Please let me go.'

Alice tossed the knife aside as she heard Satish and his men mop up the remaining resistance. The Red Guard in front of her was little more than a boy, perhaps not much older than herself. She drew closer to him and saw that he was shaking in fear.

'Go back and tell your officers that Red Guards are no longer welcome in our land.'

The man ran without hesitation and never looked back.

Satish and his men were gathering the captured weapons and equipment. So many night vision goggles and extra ammunition were always welcome but Alice had her eyes on something else.

'Satish, those trucks would make for nice school buses.'

He smiled and then stopped on seeing the wound in Alice's chest. She caught his gaze. The wound was a couple of inches wide and there was some blood on its edges. Alice shrugged.

'It looks far worse than it feels. I'm more worried about ruining a perfectly good shirt.'

Satish grinned and continued as Alice went back to gather her rifle. Short of a direct shot to the head, Alice could not die, and she had taken more than her share of gunshots and knife wounds in the months of fierce fighting that had followed her transformation. As a result her body was crisscrossed with bloody wounds. While ordinary Biters were oblivious to these and walked about with their wounds plainly visible, Alice still retained enough of her old self to not want to be seen as she really was. So she insisted on wearing black turtleneck sweatshirts, jeans, gloves and boots at all times. It had become a trademark of hers, but nobody really knew the solitary pain behind the look.

They drove back as the sun rose over the horizon, and after changing her bloody clothes Alice went to the Council meeting that had been called that morning. She hoped that her present of two new school buses would help mollify Arun and his friends.

When she walked into the room, she saw that all the dozen members of the Council were there

The dozen council members were already present when Alice arrived, including Arjun and Satish. Arun was in a corner, mumbling something to two of his friends, and when she entered the room, he rose to address her.

'Good of you join us, our Queen.'

Alice saw murder in Arjun's eyes and she gently tapped him on the shoulder as she passed him. She had no idea why Arun was so riled up this morning, but the last thing she wanted to do was to take the bait and say anything she might regret. She sat down and the meeting began.

As Wonderland had begun to take shape, Alice had gained a new appreciation for all the complexities her father had to deal with as one of the leaders of their settlement in the Deadland. Fights over food supplies, disputes over who took how much of the communal pool of clean drinking water, cases of adultery and of people getting into fights after having too much to drink – all the problems that ironically came with humans becoming more civilized and living in more settled communities. Today was no different, and they talked about the banalities of running the community for some time. Alice noticed that Arun seemed on edge, as if he was dying to say something.

Throughout, Arun seemed to be on edge. Alice tried to

work out what it could be – and then, when the discussion turned to security, she realized what it was..

As the head of security within Wonderland, Arjun first rose to give his update. 'Folks, no real crime to report since last week, unless you count the Chopra kid getting drunk and taking a leak in front of Arun's house as an offense.'

Everyone laughed, and Alice was once again grateful as to how the salesman turned guerilla leader turned security chief seemed to have a natural talent for defusing tension. But things took a turn for the worst when Satish rose to give his update on external security.

'Thankfully, not much excitement to report outside either. The Red Guards have been relatively quiet in our neighborhood. Intranet reports show that the Central Committee is dealing with enough unrest in China and a very tough war in America to pay us much attention. We do have some big news to report, though.'

Everyone seemed to sit up as he continued, 'We made contact with the Americans last night.'

There was a palpable buzz in the room as Satish outlined what had been said, but before he could talk about the incident involving the Red Guards, Arun stood up.

'Alice, the Red Guards no longer bother us and we enjoy a peace we have not known for years. Why did you then provoke war with your ambush last night?'

Alice was not entirely surprised. Many of Satish's men had taken up wives in the settlement and word would have spread.

'We did not ambush anyone. There was a large force of Red Guards well within our territory, and we gave them a chance to surrender. When they fired, we had to defend ourselves.'

Arun glared at her, his jowls almost shaking as he contained his anger. He had been a politician before The

Rising, and Alice knew that in Wonderland, he finally saw his chance at gaining that kind of power again. The problem was that she came in his way. He knew that many people in Wonderland would unquestioningly follow the young girl who had brought them together and lost so much on their behalf rather than trust him – once a career politician, and a man who had joined them only after the worst of the fighting was over.

Alice adopted a more conciliatory tone. 'Arun, we got two buses I thought the school could use. Moreover, whatever the Red Guards were up to, they would have got the message that they cannot come here anymore.'

The subject dropped, but Arun moved onto something else to needle Alice.

'What news of those Biters?'

Alice's eyes narrowed at the contempt in his tone.

'They are well within the area we had decided to give to them, and I have people in charge who I can trust.'

'People indeed.'

Several other sniggers whispered through the room.

Alice's voice took on a new edge. 'You all seem to have forgotten that we would never have defeated the Red Guards without the thousands of Biters who died acting as our foot soldiers.'

'They owe us no loyalty or love, Alice. They are animals that follow only you. I want our children to grow up without their shadow, to grow up like civilized people did before The Rising.'

Satish stepped in on Alice's behalf. 'Arun, the Biters cause us no problems now. Just let it be and let's move on.'

Just then, the door swung open and two people walked in. Alice recognized them as two of Arjun's men who had been assigned to do the rounds of Wonderland during the daytime. They both looked ashen-faced and their hands and clothes were covered with blood.

Alice had left her other weapons in her room, but still had her handgun. Instinctively she gripped it, ready for action.

'What happened? Did the Red Guards attack?'

One of the men looked at Alice, a snarl of hatred forming on his face.

'It was the damn Biters. They slaughtered our kids!'

TWO

ALICE RACED OUT OF THE building and rode her bike as fast as she could towards the area where the incident had taken place. Ten children of between eight and ten years of age had been taken for a trip by their teacher. Their first day at the new school was to have been a special treat, a visit to the old airport where they were to learn of how the city had been once, how the Red Guards had used the airport to fly out settlers from the Deadland to work in labor camps, and also learn about the famous battles waged there against the Red Guards.

As Alice dismounted, she saw the pick-up truck that had carried them there on the side of the road. She could not see any bodies yet, but the stench of death was unmistakable in the air. Some people had already arrived, most of them parents of the kids who had gone on the trip. One of the mothers, a recent entrant to Wonderland whom Alice did not know well, lunged at her.

'You monster! See what your people have done.'

Her husband held her back as she continued screaming.

Laying eyes on the bodies, Alice cursed that she could not cry. Biters did not shed tears, but her heart broke and she fell to her knees as she saw the torn bodies strewn across the field beside the road. The teacher, a young man called Gaurav, had tried to protect the children, and from the looks of it had gone down fighting. His right hand still gripped the pistol he carried – but that was about the only intact part of his body. The rest of him had been torn to ribbons. Even with the relative peace they enjoyed, no adult went about unarmed, yet nobody had thought that an innocent school trip would have required more protection or heavier firepower.

Satish and Arjun caught up and jumped out of their jeep to run to the scene of the carnage. Both had seen brutal combat up close, but the slaughter of innocent children was too much even for them. Arjun had tears streaming down his face and he put his hand on Alice's shoulder.

'Alice, we need to get you out of here now.'

Alice looked up. 'I have to be here. These are my people. These are the same people I promised I would keep safe. These...'

Her words dwindled to silence as Arun had come up to join them. He knelt and retched at the sight before him. He looked at Alice, his face pale.

'What have your Biters done? What have you brought upon us?'

Alice was too stunned to reply. She had sacrificed everything: her family, and ultimately her humanity, so that the people who depended on her could live in safety. So that she could fulfill her father's last wish that she not let her people down and lead them to a better life. She lived a tortured existence where she could feel some human emotions but never act on them. And now, in one fell swoop, the same people she had done nothing but help, asking for nothing in return, were casting her off.

She felt strong arms grip her and Arjun guided her away. She noticed that Satish had his assault rifle in his hands.

She was about to ask him if that was necessary when she saw several of the men around Arun with their guns drawn. Arjun bundled her into his jeep and Satish joined them as they drove off. Alice just sat there, her shaking hands the only sign of the turmoil she felt inside. What had just happened?

When she asked Satish where they were going, he replied grimly, 'The Looking Glass. If there's trouble, we can at least defend ourselves there.'

The drive was taken in silence. When they arrived, they saw Danish standing at the entrance, a shotgun in hand. It was the first time Alice had seen him with a gun.

The Looking Glass was in a temple complex, with the main communications room in what had once been the glass-fronted office. When he had set it up, Satish had been clear it needed to be defensible against Red Guard assaults, so there were two hardened positions on the roof from where his men could fire man-portable ground to air missiles. Those would be of no use today, but there was one remotely controlled gun turret that they had captured from a Red Guard base. That had been installed on an elevated position on the roof, offering 360-degree coverage. As Alice entered the Looking Glass, she shuddered at what things had come to. She would never have imagined using these defenses against her own people, and hoped it never came to that.

Inside, Alice sat in silence, trying to understand what she had seen. Arjun looked at her and shook his head sadly. Danish was sitting quietly in a corner. Gaurav had been a good friend of his, and he looked devastated.

'Arjun, it could not have been one of the Biters around Wonderland!'

'Alice, Biters did kill those kids. No man could have torn them apart like that. While it's possible that a band of outside Biters crept in, there's no way we can prove anything.'

Danish spoke up, having got a message from one of his men in the city. 'There's a mob headed our way. This could get ugly.'

'Alice, there are people who love you and would die for you, but with so many deaths, people are losing their minds. Let Arjun and me try and cool things down. The Looking Glass is set up to be defended, so if it comes to a fight, we can make a stand here.'

'Make a stand? Mobs? God, Satish, listen to yourself. This is our own Wonderland, our home.'

Arjun spoke up for the first time. 'Satish is right. Human mobs are every bit as dangerous as a Biter horde. They won't think; they won't ask questions. We need to get some sense into people's heads before anyone gets to you.'

Taking Danish into a corner, Arjun said, 'You can go if you want. You don't have to stay.'

Danish sat down at his console. 'I lost my family in The Rising, and then lived like a rat for years. The only purpose I have in my life now is helping us stay in touch with the world through the Looking Glass, and the only family I have is the people of Wonderland. Both of those I owe to Alice. I will not desert her now. You thugs do what you need to do; I need to keep the Looking Glass running.'

Satish used the radio to get in touch with his teams. Most of his men were part of his original unit at Zeus and had fought side by side with Alice since they first met up. They were fiercely loyal to her and he knew they would fight for her if it came to it.

'White Rook One, this is White Rook. Get to the Looking Glass to reinforce positions.'

Alice touched his arm, shaking her head.

'No, Satish. I will not have our people turn on each other because of me. Tell your men to stay away and not get involved in the fight.'

Alice looked at the feed from the camera mounted on top of the Looking Glass. A mob of at least a hundred men was approaching, among their numbers some of the fathers to the dead children. All of them were armed, and one or two carried half-full bottles of alcohol. Arun was with them, and while he was not egging them on, he was not doing anything to try and stop them either.

'He wants to be a leader, and is now no more than a common rabble-rouser. He should be the one talking some sense into the younger ones. Instead, he leads them.'

Without even waiting for Alice to suggest it, Satish had moved the joystick controlling the gun turret, swiveling it until it was aimed at the approaching mob.

'They won't last more than ten seconds if I let go on full auto.'

The mob stopped, knowing they would be seriously outmatched if it came to a fight. The only way for someone to take the Looking Glass was with heavy anti-tank weapons or RPGs, and the only ones with such weapons in Wonderland were Satish's forward recon teams.

Alice touched Satish's arm and she felt him flinch at the contact, once more aware of how different she was now. Her touch had none of the warmth it once held. It was now as cold as a corpse.

'No, Satish. There will be no more killing here today.'

'Bring the Biter bitch out!'

Satish stepped out, his rifle at his shoulder.

'Which son of a whore said that? Step forward if you're man enough to back those words up!'

No answer came. Satish turned furiously to Arun.

'These men look up to you. Ask them to go back home. We can all talk when people cool down.'

`Cool down? My son was torn apart by her kind, and you ask me to cool down? We should have destroyed the Biters, but we had to tolerate their presence because of her.'

Satish turned on the man who had just spoken and looked him in the eye.

'Jai, you do remember that I took a bullet to save your family when the Red Guards came? I also share your grief and want to punish those responsible, but don't turn on Alice or rush to conclusions.'

Arjun was now outside, with Alice beside him. The big man strode forward, and while he had his gun holstered, Alice saw several of the men lower their guns as he approached. Satish had been an invaluable soldier in their struggle, but he was a relative newcomer. In contrast, Arjun had been leading his band of `Ruin Rats' for years, helping them survive against Biters and Zeus troopers alike. Many of the men in the crowd had been part of his original crew, and looked away as he addressed them.

'Jai, Ritesh, Ankush...all of you were my brothers. Brothers who bled and fought with me.'

Alice saw some of the men sheepishly put away their weapons as Arjun continued.

'But today you insult that bond by turning on a girl who has perhaps sacrificed more than all of us. Give her a chance, that's all I ask of you.'

Alice now stepped forward. She had left all her weapons inside the Looking Glass.

'I did not choose to be this way. I too want to play with my sister and eat meals with my parents. I too want to go to school and learn something other than killing people. But I have no regrets, for in all that loss we had created a bigger family than I ever had. A family called Wonderland. I promise to personally bring to justice those who have done this to your families and children, but please trust me at least this much. For all we've been through together, please give me this much trust, and let me find out who was behind this. If it was one of the Biters in Wonderland, I promise you I will spare none of them.'

Whether it was the impact of her words, Arjun's cajoling, or the simple fact that through the entire exchange the gun turret had been trained on the group, they grudgingly dispersed, leaving only Arun. He walked up to Alice and she half expected him to say something sarcastic or provocative. Instead, he looked genuinely shell-shocked.

'Alice, I know we've had our differences. I know that in the last few months people have been questioning why we still live in a state of war when there is no war to be fought, and I know that yet others question why we keep the Biters close at hand. But I'm willing to forget all of that if you help us find out who was responsible for this massacre.'

Alice looked at him, trying to gauge whether he was sincere or he just wanted to maintain the status quo since that best served his political agenda. She was perhaps too young to judge and took him at face value.

'Arun, we have known some measure of peace, but the world outside is still at war. I know we situated Looking Glass outside the center of Wonderland because you thought people would get alarmed at all the bad news. The reality is we cannot pretend away the fact that the world is still bleeding, and today some of that blood seeped into Wonderland.'

Arun looked away sheepishly as Arjun took up where Alice had left off.

'Arun, you and others had voted to reduce patrols and cancel regular combat training. We cannot pretend this is the Delhi the way it was before the Rising. We know peace now, but that might change at any moment. Let us get to the bottom of today's killing, but you as an elder need to help people understand that things are much more dangerous outside Wonderland than they may want to believe.'

Suitably chastised, Arun went back, and then Alice mounted her bike.

'Alice, do you want me to come?'

Alice refused Satish's offer. This was something she had to do alone. Maintaining her composure had been necessary in front of the bereaved families, but now she was gripped with fury. Whoever had killed those children would pay dearly.

The groaning Biter went down on his back, his hand cracking in several places as Alice twisted it and threw him over her shoulder. Before he had been turned, he had been a slight old man, but there was no sympathy or pity in Alice's eyes as she kicked him, dislocating his chin. That did nothing to improve his face, which already had skin peeling off in several places and an ear missing from a gunshot.

'What lunacy made you let outsiders into Wonderland?'

She was not sure how much he understood, but she was so angry she really did not care. The Biter was now on his knees, snarling, all obedience to Alice gone. His teeth were bared, jagged and covered with dried blood. He snapped as she came closer but she easily weaved out of the way. In the time she had spent with the Biters, she knew that they would only obey a leader who spoke from a position of strength. With Dr. Protima, their first Queen, who had first opened Alice's eyes to the true nature of the Biters and the conspiracy behind The Rising, that authority had come from her ability to speak and reason like a human and her possession of the tattered copy of Alice in Wonderland that the Biters had come to revere as their holy relic. For Alice, that authority was backed up by her combat skills honed in years of fighting to survive in the Deadland.

The Biter lunged at her again, and this time Alice caught his right hand, snapping it back and then bringing the heel of her own right hand snapping against his nose. The blow would have killed a grown man, but Biters did not die so easily. The Biter fell back and struggled to get back up, his face mangled and bloody, when Alice took out her combat knife and stabbed him through the head. He did not get back up again.

Alice had come to the Biters' reserve and told Hatter and Bunny Ears about what had happened. They knew the potential implications and she sensed their panic, and within minutes they had brought the old Biter in front of her. He had screeched and groaned as if pleading for mercy, but the hand gestures Hatter made were clear enough. This Biter had let in a band of outsiders in return for a thick bunch of ganja leaves that some of the Biters favored. Pleading had soon given away to a desperate attempt to escape as the Biter, like a cornered animal, had turned on Alice. That had been his last mistake.

As the adrenaline wore off, Alice tried to calm herself down and looked at Hatter and Bunny Ears. Hatter looked imposing, standing well over six feet tall and built like a tank. The hat he guarded with such pride still stood atop his head. He had suffered more than his share of wounds over the years: at least six bullet holes pocked were visible on his chest and bites too numerous to count crisscrossed his body. His eyes were dilated and red, and his yellowed face was covered with dried blood. Just a year ago, Alice would have run in terror at such a sight. Today he seemed to be cowering before her.

'Hatter, what the hell happened? I told you to make sure everyone stays here and does not wander.'

Bunny Ears had his head down, like a pet that had just been disciplined. His face was still contorted in what at first glance appeared to be a lopsided grin, but Alice figured out later had been the result of a gash drawn across his face by Biter nails when he had been bitten and turned.

'You do know what people will want to do, don't you? They will start hunting you down again!'

At this, Hatter looked at her and a low growl came from the back of his throat. Alice sighed.

'Yes, and you will fight, won't you? And then we'll be back where we were. Tearing ourselves apart while the Red Guards and their masters rule over us.'

Not wanting to face any of the affected families, Alice did not go back to the city center but instead went back to the Looking Glass. Danish was there, as usual, playing with his computers and radio equipment.

'Danish, anything new?'

He tapped on the monitor in front of him. 'The Americans posted again.'

Alice leaned over and read the message.

Free American forces under Colonel Barnett swept aside Red Guards at New Orleans, and are linking with other forces to press the offensive to liberate the city. If you are anywhere near, find safety or join the fight.

'They seem to have their communications working again,' she said, 'How did they manage that?'

'America was much more developed thant India, and I suspect their Armed Forces and government would have had secure and protected networks and servers. They were ready to survive a nuclear apocalypse with Russia at one time, so something must have survived. Also, in India hardly anyone other than the Police and Armed Forces had guns since public gun ownership was limited. In the US, lots of people had their own guns, so it was easier to fight back when they needed to. I think it just took time for them to regroup and get over the shock of the Biters to start organizing. Plus, I was on the radio with them earlier today. They think we helped a lot.'

'How did we help?'

'Our postings and messages first started causing dissension in Zeus. Before The Rising, Zeus was an American Private Military Contractor, so most of their senior officers were American, especially ex-military folks. When the news started coming out that the whole mess had been orchestrated by elements in China and some American elites, many of them revolted. We're much closer to China, so significant Red Guard reinforcements came faster. In America, that took more time, and by then the Zeus deserters and local settlers had made a lot of headway.'

Alice had to ask the next question given what she had been through over the day.

'Danish, what about the Biters in America?'

Danish tuttelooked awayd.

'Well, they hear that it's more like a disease, that they can be lived with – they hear about you. But they're not buying it. I can't blame them. Remember how things were here before you got here? They hunt down Biters and burn them. They call it a Biter Barbeque. Not pretty.'

That night was anxious for Alice, spent wondering how she could possibly keep things from exploding. The next morning, she did what she thought was the right thing to do. She went to visit each of the families who had lost children in the attack. She told them about what had happened in the Biter Reservation and promised them that she would not allow such a thing to happen again.

Then she called Arjun and Satish for a meeting in her room.

'Guys, there is no way such a thing can take place ever again. I've told Hatter and Bunny Ears, but you know that discipline is too much to expect from every Biter out there. So we need to help.'

'What do you have in mind?'

'Arjun, we need more security patrols inside Wonderland to watch the borders from the inside.'

Arjun sadly shook his head. 'It's not as simple as that now we number so many. Now we'd need it voted in the Council, and you know how Arun and his friends feel.'

'Come on, they would think differently after the attack, wouldn't they?'

Arjun looked at Alice grimly. He realized that for all her combat skills she was but a child, and unschooled in the murky world of politics that Arun had mastered.

'Alice, Arun was very nice to you when he last met you, but he's been telling anyone who'll listen that he doesn't believe the story about it being Biters from the outside. He says he's sure it was Biters from the Reservation. He won't vote to increase patrols; he'd much rather put the blame on you for being too soft on the Biters.'

Alice gritted her teeth. 'So what does he want to do?'

'He hasn't said it out loud as such, but he thinks we should move the Biters far away, and of course, he'd rather he run this place all by himself as leader instead of a Council where you have such a large say given your past. That's why he keeps asking for elections for a single leader.'

Satish broke his silence. 'I can help.'

Both Arjun and Alice looked at him as he elaborated.

'I could have two of my recon teams come in closer to the

city centre.'

Arjun spotted the obvious problem in the suggestion. 'We send the deep recon boys out to watch for Red Guard incursions and wild bands of Biters to intercept them before they get close. Your move would leave us exposed.'

'Yes, but only till the situation stabilizes.'

Alice shook her head. 'Word will get out. Some of those boys will speak to their wives in the city. Others will talk too much over a drink. Arun and his friends will throw a fit and accuse us of overriding them.'

Just then, Alice's tactical radio crackled to life.

'White Queen, this is Looking Glass.'

It was Danish.

'Looking Glass, what do you have to report?'

'One of our recon teams called in and said that they found fresh footprints, many of them, leading into the city. I don't know how they evaded our patrols, but they say the footprints must be of Biters by the way they seem to have moved. Then Rahul down at the farms just called on his radio, saying he saw what seemed to be a group of Biters down the road.'

The words sent a chill down Alice's spine. Satish and Arjun had both heard the transmission and they knew what the implications of another Biter attack would be. Without a word being said between them, they gathered their weapons. Alice was the first out the door, and roared down the road on Danish's bike, with Satish and Arjun following closely behind in a jeep. There was no time to call for reinforcements. They would have to handle this themselves.

Alice remembered the bodies of the children and vowed to make these Biters pay dearly for what they had done.

Alice cursed as her first burst went wide, and the Biters in front of her scattered behind the bushes overlooking the farmlands north of the city center where the Biters had been reported. Alice had let her anger get the better of her and fired even before her bike had come to a complete halt. Firing her assault rifle one-handed and on the move was something her trainers growing upback at her settlement would have frowned upon, but then they had also always advised her never to fight angry.

Stilling her mind she slipped off the bike, selecting single-shot mode on her assault rifle. Spraying rounds was hardly a smart tactic when all that mattered was putting one round into a Biter's head.

There.

She saw a Biter round the corner and she aimed and put a round into his chest. The Biter staggered back and bared his teeth at her when another round drilled him through the head. Another Biter was coming up just behind her to the right and Alice swiveled towards him, firing at him. One shot, one kill. By now Arjun and Satish had joined the battle and were firing away. Alice saw Arjun kick a large Biter down and step on his chest before shredding the Biter's head with automatic fire. Clearly she was not the only one who was fighting angry today – but given the scene of the slaughtered children, it was no surpriseno wonder.

That momentary distraction almost cost her dearly. A gnarled, bloody hand swept at her face, scratching her just below the eyes. She turned towards the Biter, looking at her with red eyes, his skin coming off in bloody patches. She brought her rifle around in an arc, shattering his jaw. Then she kicked his feet from under him and shot him twice in the head.

The shooting had stopped.

'Did we get them all?'

Satish was not about to let his guard down and swept the area, his rifle raised. Arjun kicked one of the Biters to make sure he was gone. It twitched, so he fired into the back of its head.

'I think we got all the bastards now.'

The three of them looked at each other for some time, mixed emotions coursing through all of them. They had not been in such an intense fight this far inside Wonderland for many months, and certainly they had all thought that the days of defending against Biter hordes was over. However, along with that concern came a sense of catharsis. They had avenged the deaths of the children, and while nothing would bring the kids back, this would hopefully start bridging some of the rifts that had been created between Alice and the settlers who seemed to favor Arun.

Satish and Arjun took a break, taking out their water bottles. They were about to go back to their jeep when Alice noticed something.

'Guys, something is not right here.'

They stopped and looked where she was pointing.

'Check out their faces and bodies. They are decomposed like Biters, but they don't have too many visible wounds other than the rounds we put in them. Normally they're covered with unhealing wounds from their conversion. These guys are barely scratched.'

Satish peeled off the clothes of a Biter at his feet with his knife and stepped back, shocked.

'Shit, this one has a totally clean body.'

Arjun was still taking it all in.

'Maybe they got infected recently. Maybe that's why

there aren't too many wounds.'

Alice wasn't satisfied.

'Could a dozen of them be infected at the same time? All of them without a single visible bite or scratch mark?'

Just then Satish heard a message coming over his radio in the jeep. He ran to it and picked up the mike. As he spoke, Alice saw the color leave his face.

'Satish, what happened?'

He looked her, a fear in his eyes that Alice had never seen before, even in the thick of combat against the Red Guards.

'Alice, come on. We need to get you to the Looking Glass. That's the only safe place I can think of now till things cool down.'

'What happened?'

Satish looked at her, his eyes filling with tears. 'This was a decoy. Another group of Biters got into the city. They got to some apartments before some of the men stopped them. They're saying more than twenty of us are dead, most of them women and children. Some of the Biters got away, but they killed eight of them. From what Danish said, they seem to be the same sort as the ones we killed.'

Alice held onto the side of the jeep for support, trying to comprehend what was happening.

'Biters don't use tactics like these. I don't understand what is going on.'

Satish grabbed her hand and pushed her towards the jeep. 'We'll figure all that out later. Now we need to get you to safety.'

'Safety? Satish, this is my home. We started this place together. I am not going to hide in my own home.'

As soon as she finished her sentence, a bullet whizzed past her, missing her head by inches. Driven by instinct and training, Alice rolled to her right, bringing up her handgun in a two-handed grip, aiming at where the shot had come from. The shooter was a young boy, perhaps no more than twelve years old, carrying a rifle that was too heavy for him. He was crying and had blood covering his shirt.

'Your Biters killed my brother!'

Alice lowered her handgun, too shocked to react, when Arjun snatched the gun away from the boy. Satish was still on the radio and Danish spoke with renewed urgency.

'Don't bring the White Queen here. My men report that a large mob is headed here, and another group is on its way to the Biter Reservation. They're saying that it's time to wipe out the Biters.'

Satish put the radio down.

'A war with the Biters will destroy Wonderland, and everything we've created.'

THREE

'HATTER, I KNOW YOU DID not do this, but we don't have time to prove or explain anything!'

As soon as they had got the news, Alice and Satish had rushed to the Biter Reservation on Danish's bike, while Arjun had headed to the Looking Glass, both to try and pacify the people headed there and also to keep Danish safe. Danish was not as closely associated with Alice as Satish was, but neither did he have any qualms about making his distaste for Arun known publicly. Alice had gathered the Biters and told them what had happened and their reaction was clearclear. Even without human language, their surprise and indignation was clearapparent.

Hatter reared up to his full height, roaring in frustration. Alice reached out, touching the rough, bloodied skin on his hand.

'If you fight the humans today then all will be lost. We will be back to what our lives had been like in the Deadland, fighting and slaughtering each other, and then the Red Guards and their masters would have won. Do you understand what I am asking you to do?'

Hatter had put his head down, but refused to acknowledge what Alice had just asked. Bunny Ears, however, stood next to him and emitted a low keening sound. Alice knew that he was sad, much like a pet being asked to go away, but that he would listen to her. Alice just wanted them to get out of sight while she tried to figure out where the attacking Biters had come from, and also try and cool things down with people in Wonderland.

Within minutes, there was no sign of the Biters. They had disappeared down the warren of underground tunnels and bomb shelters where Alice had first encountered them. Arun and his closest supporters were relative newcomers and would have no idea of the full extent of the tunnel network. The ones who had some idea of where the tunnels opened were the recon teams that worked for Satish, and they would not betray him or Alice.

'Satish, come on! Let's get to the Looking Glass.'

As she started her the bike, they got their first glimpse of the approaching mob. There were more than a hundred men on foot, some carrying lit torches, and all of them armed. As they saw Alice speed away, a couple of them fired, sending dust and gravel flying all around her as Alice rode away. The fact that they had opened fire without even giving her a chance to explain meant that things had totally gone out of control. She also knew that sending the Biters into hiding would only make her and the Biters look even guiltier, but that was a better option than the bloodbath that would have followed otherwise.

When they approached the Looking Glass, Alice knew that something was wrong. Arjun had driven in Satish's jeep, and now it was lying on the side of the road, pockmarked with bullet holes and with its windshield shattered. Anxious about her friend, Alice jumped off the bike and was about to run to the Looking Glass when Satish grabbed her hand.

'This could be an ambush. Let's not rush into it.'

Both of them unslung their assault rifles and approached the temple complex.

Alice said, 'I saw some movement near the doorway.'

Satish knelt down, looking through his scope. 'There's someone hiding there.'

Alice crept along the far wall while Satish hid behind the jeep, covering the doorway. Alice did not want to harm any of the people of Wonderland– after all, they were like family. But if any of them had hurt Arjun, there would be hell to pay.

Alice was now just feet away from the doorway and she dove in front of it, coming up with her rifle raised. She saw Arjun sitting huddled against the door. He had his rifle in his hands, but there was a small pool of blood forming under him, and he was struggling to keep his eyes open.

'Arjun, no!'

Hearing Alice's anguished shout, Satish ran over and they took Arjun inside the complex. Danish was there, his hands and face cut. Some of the glass surrounding the communications room had been shattered and there were three bodies lying among the bloodied glass fragments. The men wore filthy, dust-covered clothes of the sort that Alice had not seen since her people formed Wonderland.

Satish was tending to Arjun's wounds while Danish filled them in on what had happened.

'They heard that you were headed to the Reservation so most of them went there. That bastard Humpy Dumpty ordered the mob to go there. I heard him myself on the radio.'

Humpty Dumpty was Danish's preferred term for Arun, in reference to his weight and nearly bald head.

'Arjun and I were here when these three bastards came to kill us. These were not our people, Alice. They are stragglers from the Deadland someone must have hired to do their dirty work. I bet some of them are mixed in with the mobs, riling them up. Arjun took them all out, but they managed to shoot him.'

Alice took it in, but her mind refused to believe it. There were still people out in the Deadlands, mostly small groups of bandits who had terrorized the settlements before Wonderland had been formed. Alice had steadfastly refused to let any of them into Wonderland. Alice knew they would have hated her for that decision, but to think that someone from inside Wonderland had let them in to kill her was too much to believe. Satish would have seen her doubt.

'Alice, you are still too young to know how messed up people can be when they want power. I don't have any trouble believing Arun could have done this. I say we get my boys and bust him.'

'No. No.'

Everyone started at Arjun's words. He struggled to sit. Satish had bandaged the wound on his thigh, but he was clearly weak from the loss of blood.

'No, Satish. That would mean civil war, and ordinary folks would believe that Alice and our Biters were guilty of the attacks and side with Arun. We would destroy Wonderland.'

'What, then?'

'Look, these three goons here are obviously Deadlander bandits and even if Arun hired them, he would never own up to it publicly. But people are baying for blood and I can't blame them. So many families have lost people in the last two days that they aren't thinking straight.'

'So what do we do, Arjun?'

'Alice, you need to find out who's behind this. Those Biters were inserted here for these attacks, and someone human, someone very smart, thought it all up. But you can't do that from the inside. You need to get back to the Deadland and find out what's going on.'

'What about you?'

'Hey, I'll just say these bandits hurt me, which is true enough, and that I've got no idea where you are. Remember, I used to sell useless vacuum cleaners for a living to people who didn't need them. I can sell Arun any story I want.'

Arjun smiled as he said the words, but there was a pained grimace to its edgesapparent on his face. Alice took a look around, weighing the decision before her.

'Danish, radio the folks in town, telling them bandits attacked the Looking Glass, and ask for medical help. Tell nobody we were here.'

Danish looked at her, grim determination on his face.

'Alice, you can trust me. Here, take this so you can know what's going on inside and I can tell you what Humpty Dumpty is up to.'

Alice gratefully took the portable radio set he had given her and put it in her backpack. She was about to leave when Satish joined her.

'I'm coming with you.'

'Satish, you don't have to...'

He never let her finish. 'We've fought too many battles together for me to let you go alone on this one.'

And so Alice and Satish walked out through the shattered glass facade of the Looking Glass, the bloodied glass fragments crunching under their feet as they set out for their trip back into the Deadland.

General Chen watched the black helicopter glide in and land in a far corner of the airfield. It was always cold in Ladakh, where he was based, but he felt a chill go through him that had nothing to do with the temperature. After he had surrendered a forward base to Alice and her forces, he had been stripped of his command of the Red Guard forces in the Deadland, and had been sent to an indoctrination camp near Guangzhou. The Central Committee propaganda machine called these camps 'holiday camps for tired veterans to recuperate and regain their revolutionary fervor'. In reality, it was a torture camp where veterans who had become politically inconvenient or had started asking uncomfortable questions were shipped out. Like the purges of all dictators in the past, those who were perhaps most capable of defending the regime were punished, because the best soldiers are also those who dare to think. Chen had made that mistake when he surrendered his base to Alice to prevent his men from being slaughtered. He had been an officer in the Chinese Red Army before The Rising, and with the nuclear and biological weapon exchanges with the Americans and the chaos enveloping the world in the days that followed, he had devoted himself to defending his people against the Biters. It had been a clear-cut mission, one where he had little doubt as to whether he was doing the right thing or not. That was until he learnt of this girl called Alice and the stories she was spreading. He had dismissed them as propaganda, and had captured her once, intending to send her to the mainland for execution. But something had changed when he had looked at her during her attack on the Red Guard base he had been inspecting close to a year ago. He had seen the Biters following her, had seen that she was not quite human, yet not Biter either. That had planted the seeds of doubt in his mind, and he had confided to a brother officer back in Shanghai. He had raised questions about whether what the Central Committee had been telling the people about the true nature of the Biters and the war in the Deadland was entirely true. That more than his battlefield surrender had been his undoing. Chen's only relief was that his wife had been spared the horrors of the camp.

He had been rehabilitated just six months later and reinstated with all honors, to be sent to the new base at Ladakh where the Red Guards kept a watch on the community called Wonderland. It had been nothing more than glorified sentry duty and he had begun to wonder why he had been spared. Then the stealthy black helicopter he had just seen land had arrived and started going out on sorties to the Deadland. Its crew and passengers had been flown in from Shanghai and even though he was the base commander, Chen had not been allowed any access to them. They stayed in their own quarters behind a walled complex, and did not report to him.

He wondered what the old men in the Central Committee were up to now, but knew that whatever it was, the cost in blood would be paid by the young conscripts he was now supposed to lead.

The dust was swirling around her and Alice had the hood on her sweatshirt pulled up around her face. She had grown up in the Deadland, but just a few months of living in the relative comfort of Wonderland told her just how brutal and uncompromising life in the Deadland could be in comparison. When she had lived there with her family in their settlement, conventional wisdom was that no human could survive in the Deadland unless they were in a large, organized group. The Deadland was teeming with predators, Biter and human alike, and now Satish and Alice would have to contend with them on their own if they were to try and solve the mystery of the Biter attacks. Alice knew that Bunny Ears, Hatter and her other Biters would be close at hand through their network of hidden underground tunnels, but there was no way for her to contact them, and depending on them to show up when she needed help was hardly a good survival strategy.

'Alice, my boys told me that this was the only sector they did not patrol yesterday. If the attackers came into Wonderland from the outside, then it must have been through here.'

It was now getting dark, and Satish suggested that they rest. Alice was not going to get tired from walking, and Satish was a professional soldier who could keep going for some hours yet. However, they did not want to take the chance of bumping into unwelcome company in the darkness.

Alice hid the bike in the bushes and then called out, 'Up the trees.'

Satish looked at Alice incredulously.

'Come on, are you serious? Do we have to hang from branches like Tarzan?'

That puzzled Alice; she came from a time after cartoons had ceased to exist, and she had no idea who or what Tarzan was.

. She passed over it.

'No, because Biters cannot climb trees, and we'll see bandits while they're far away.'

Satish grunted at the wisdom and clambered up a tree. Taking the adjoining tree, Alice whispered, 'Take a nap. I'll keep watch.'

About two hours later, Alice heard a rustling noise nearby. She raised her rifle, looking through the night vision scope to see three men walking towards them. They were armed, though it looked like they carried a motley collection of homemade pistols and an antique looking shotgun; the hallmarks of Deadland bandits. But despite the nature of the weapons, they were no less dangerousAlice knew that men such as these could be deadly.

As the men sat down and proceeded to take some food out, Alice relaxed. They had no idea Alice and Satish were sitting just a few feet above them, and they would soon hopefully be on their way.

Then she saw something that made her take a closer look. One of the bandits was taking something out of a bag. Only it was not just any bag. It was a child's bag, cobbled together from old clothes, patched together by a loving mother, embellished with cartoon characters that the child must have heard of in tales told by the adults who had experienced them on screen and in books before The Rising. There was only one place in the Deadland where such a bag could be found now: in Wonderland. And it was likely that this had been made as a school bag for a child who had been murdered just two days ago.

Something snapped inside Alice, and she took a signal flare from her backpack and threw it to the ground, blinding the three men. Before they could gather their wits, Alice was in front of them, her rifle pointed at them.

'Where did you get that bag?'

One of them men made the fatal mistake of thinking they were faced with a mere girl, and he brought up his pistol. Alice snapped off a three round burst, hitting him in the chest and slamming him against the tree behind him. The noise had awakened Satish and he whistled to let the men below him know that he was just above them. The hood had fallen from around Alice's head and now the remaining men saw her face in the fading glow of the flare.

'The Quee—'

A bullet crashed just inches from his foot, cutting his sentence short.

'I asked you a simple question. Where did you get that bag?'

The men were now shrinking back in fear. Before The Rising they had been convicts on death row, and both men were well accustomed to violence and crime; talents that had served them well in the Deadland. But for all that, they knew that they were no match for this half-Biter girl who could not be killed. They had heard tales of her and what she had done to the Red Guards, and they had given her settlement at Wonderland a wide berth, only now to be faced with her in the middle of the Deadland.

One of them gathered up the courage to speak. 'We saw a group of Biters in the Deadland a day ago. One of them dropped this.'

Alice thought back to the strange Biters she had seen at the scene of the latest attack.

'Where were these Biters going? Were they going towards the Reservation?'

The man who had spoken now looked at her curiously.

'No, that was the weird thing. We thought all the Biters around here followed you, but not these. These ones were different.?'

Satish had now climbed down, but he kept his gun pointed at the two men.

'Why do you think these Biters were different?'

'They were picked up by a black helicopter.'

The next morning, Alice and Satish had the two bandits lead them to the location where they had seen the helicopter take off. Satish took a look around the area.

'Alice, if they come back, this is where they will come. They've flattened the ground to create some sort of a landing pad, and they've sandbagged those two hills to create guard towers.'

Satish got on his radio to call his recon teams. They checked in one by one, but not one of them had seen or heard a helicopter approach the area. Then again, if a black helicopter had flown in low at night, following the Red Guards' guidance on patrol avoidance, it was possible to pull off such an attack. Why and how someone would bring Biters in to launch such attacks was, however, beyond Satish.

Alice kicked the dust at her feet, thinking of the dead children back at Wonderland.

'Then we will wait here, and when they come back, we will kill them all.'

'It's an attack helicopter.'

Alice heard Satish's warning and looked up to see the black, predatory shape hover in the distance. They had been waiting for close to a day, and were about to give up hope and try their luck elsewhere. A makeshift bunker near the landing zone had been their regufe. They had been expecting a troop carrier, of the sort the bandit had described, and with the advantage of surprise, Alice was fairly confident that she and Satish could have handled whoever was being flown in on these deadly missions into Wonderland. However, they most certainly did not have the firepower to deal with an attack helicopter.

'How far away are your boys?'

Satish grinned. 'One of them has that chopper in his sights right now. If we order it, a SAM will be going up that chopper's tailpipe. Should we fire?'

Alice shook her head emphatically. 'No. If we show our hand now, they will not go through with their landing. Let's wait.'

But it soon became apparent this helicopter did not mean to land. It swept over the area several times, and then one of Satish's teams radioed in.

'White Rook, I can see two Red Guard APCs and two jeeps filled with Red Guards coming. Still four kilometers from your location, but they are closing in fast. Wait, they just stopped, and it looks like an officer is scanning the area with binoculars.'

Alice asked, 'What's going on?'

Satish responded, 'They seem to be on a search mission more than an attack. I have no idea what or who they might be looking for. Coming this close to Wonderland on land is a big risk for them to take, especially in broad daylight, so it must be someone important.'

Alice thought back to what she had heard in the Looking Glass. 'Could it be those Americans who had supposedly escaped?'

Satish had his own binoculars trained on the horizon and replied without shifting his gaze. 'I don't see how two escaped prisoners would warrant such a search attempt.'

Then he froze.

'Alice, look, there! At two o'clock, maybe a kilometer out, near that large Banyan tree.'

Alice had her rifle up at her shoulder and looked through the scope. It was a sunny day and there was excellent visibility, but she did not notice what Satish had seen until he pointed it out again. During her own training in the Deadland, her instructors had taught her the art of escape and evasion, but she had never really been trained to look for a concealed enemy, simply because Biter hordes were not exactly proponents of stealth and concealment. However, in the house to house fighting against the Red Guards that had followed, it had become a critical skill, one she had learnt from Satish and Arjun, and from her own combat experience.

Satish gave an appreciative whistle. 'That man sure has guts, that much is for sure. He's got an attack helicopter on top of him and perhaps fifty Red Guards on land, and he hasn't lost his nerve and made a run for it.'

Now that Alice had spotted him, she saw that there was a bit of an arm visible beneath the undergrowth. It was not going to be visible from the air, but once the Red Guard vehicles got there, it was only a matter of time before they discovered the fugitives.

Alice put her rifle aside.

'Satish, how many men do you have covering the chopper?'

'Just a two-man SAM crew and two riflemen. With the element of surprise, I have no doubt they could take the chopper down, but they cannot hold off all those Red Guards. I have two more teams with RPGs headed here, but they won't make it for the next thirty minutes.'

The buzzing sound of a large caliber automatic gun firing made Alice swivel her head around. The attack helicopter had seen something and was firing from its chin mounted turret, the rounds kicking up dust and rocks on the ground below. Alice looked through her scope and saw a frail old man stumbling along the ground. Another man was trying to pull him back under cover, but the older man had clearly lost his nerve. It was hard to be sure from this distance, but their complexion and features suggested that these were indeed the two Americans who had escaped.

She turned to look at Satish, and he just looked back, an eyebrow raised, silently asking her the question.

'Bring it down!'

As Satish relayed the order to his men, a trail of white smoke rose from the ground to Alice's left and snaked up towards the helicopter. The pilot had been so busy in trying to target the fleeing fugitives that he never had a chance to react. The missile slammed into the mid-section of the helicopter, consuming it in a giant fireball.

Alice could now see the Red Guard vehicles fast approaching the two men. She mounted the bike, with Satish behind her, and they sped towards the scene.

Alice was more than five hundred meters away when the lead Red Guard APC opened fire with its machine gun. Alice swerved her bike to the right and dove off the seat, rolling and coming up behind the cover of a large tree. Satish was concealed behind another tree. Satish's men were about a hundred meters to their left, but they too were holding their fire. Assault rifles would do little damage to the APCs.

'Over here!'

The two men heard Alice's shout and scrambled to her. Alice did not have much time to register their appearances, but they were clearly white, one a reed-thin old man whose ribs peered showed prominently through a dirty vest, and the other a younger man, perhaps the same age as Arjun, wearing a tattered leather jacket. The younger man's eyes widened a bit as he saw Alice, and he started to back up, when Alice pushed him down.

'Stay here and you may just live.'

The Red Guard APCs were now advancing steadily, and they had guessed correctly that the absence of any resistance must have meant that they were not up against enemies with heavy missiles or firepower that could threaten their vehicles. The two jeeps stayed behind, and as Alice looked, an officer was standing up in the back of one of the jeeps, speaking on a radio.

'Satish, those APCs will be on us in a couple of minutes. I have a plan.'

Before Satish could say anything, Alice had reached into

her backpack and taken out two fragmentation grenades and raced to her bike.

'Distract one of them!'

Satish peered out from behind cover and started firing at one of the APCs, and his men started unloading their weapons on it from the other direction. Caught in the crossfire, the commander manning the heavy machine gun on the turret was forced inside, as the other APC came towards it to deal with the sudden threat. Just then Alice's bike roared to life and she sped towards the second APC, the grenades in her hands. Distracted by Satish's men, the commander in the APC's turret did not see Alice until it was too late.

Alice pulled the pin from one grenade and threw it, jumping off her bike as it went careening into the APC. The grenade bounced off the APC and exploded, shredding several of its tires. Now the vehicle was effectively stranded, and Alice clambered onto its back, a handgun in one hand and a grenade in the other. The commander was struggling to take out his own pistol from its holster when Alice fired at him, sending him slumping back inside the vehiclecrashing back. Then she pulled the pin off the second grenade and dropped it into the open hatch, jumping off as it exploded.

The Red Guards in the jeeps had now disembarked, and were firing at Alice. She felt a round hit her thigh as she sought cover behind the burning APC. The second APC was now approaching and she was effectively trapped between the dozen or more Red Guards approaching her from the right and the armored vehicle bearing down upon her from the left.

The first few Red Guards were now no more than a hundred meters away and Alice could hear their triumphant shouts as they came closer. Alice leaned out and fired a burst from her assault rifle. One seemed to go down, but there were just too many of them. And as Satish's men were pinned down by the second APC even as it drove towards her, she was on her own.

The ground near one of the Red Guards seemed to explode in a burst of dust and sand and a dark figure wearing a hat rushed up, grabbing the Red Guard and pulling him down, breaking his neck in one move. Several more Biters streamed out of the hole, overwhelming the Red Guards around them. Hatter picked up another Red Guard, raising him cleanly over his head before smashing him to the ground. Several of the Red Guards were conscripts who had never seen combat, let alone seen a Biter up close. They began to panic, and that was their undoing. They fired blindly at the approaching Biters, and while many of the scored hits, only a direct shot to the head would be of any use. Within seconds they all fell to the clawing, biting attackers who had come to Alice's rescue.

The APC now drove towards the Biters, cutting several of them into ribbons them by half with its machine gun. The Biters were still not finished, but with their bodies mangled and their legs cut off, they were out of the fight.

Hatter was staring defiantly at the approaching APC, screaming in rage when the APC lurched to a halt, exploding from a direct hit. Alice heard Satish behind her.

'Thank God for RPGs. My boys got here just in time.'

Alice knew that they owed their survival to had more to it than just a handful of men armed with one rocket launcher. They would not have survived without the intervention of Hatter and his fellow Biters. Several of the Biters had fallen in the battle and their bodies lay scattered around the ground, their heads blown open by direct hits.

Alice made her thanks to the surviving Biters, and then they ambled back to their hidden tunnel and disappeared.

In spite of having spent so much time with them, and in spite of being like them in some respects, Alice was yet to fully figure out the Biters. They followed her with a loyalty that she had never experienced among humans, even humans who owed her their lives. They would throw away their lives to protect one of their own without a second thought, and unlike humans they never seemed to expect anything back in return. Alice was still young, but had seen enough of the world and of humans to know that those qualities were in incredibly short supply. People fought over power, over money, over control. Biters just fought to protect their own.

In becoming a Biter, it was strangely as if one became more human.

Alice's thoughts were interrupted by Satish.

'Let's now find out who our new American friends are, shall we?'

FOUR

'A JEEP WOULD BE NOTHING MORE than a magnet for air strikes. Why do you think I asked all my men to disperse?'

Satish said the words with a smile, but Alice had known him long enough to recognize the underlying irritation. The two Americans had proved to be a study in contrasts. The older man, who walked with a pronounced limp, was yet to utter a word. He merely kept looking around him with wide eyes, and Alice found him staring at her way too often for her comfort. Looking at his disheveled hair, torn vest and vacant expression, she wondered if he had indeed lost his mind in some Red Guard labor camp. The younger man, conversely, was all business. He had immediately equipped himself with a bulletproof vest from one of the fallen Red Guards, and armed himself with an assault rifle. To Alice's amusement, he seemed very vocal about his opinions – though Satish certainly seemed to find nothing funny in his trying to impose his opinions.felt otherwise.

'How fast can we walk? Let's take one of the jeeps and get back to this city of yours.'

Satish took a step closer to the American. He was a good six inches shorter than the blond, lanky man he faced, but

Alice's eyes, trained by years of experience, told her that the American would not stand a chance. He clearly had little experience of close combat, since he was holding his rifle in both hands. At such close quarters, he would never even be able to bring the rifle up before Satish cut his throat. She held out a restraining hand on Satish's shoulder and addressed the American.

'My name is Alice Gladwell. What's yours?'

'I am Captain Vince Hudson, U.S Marine Corps. I flew with the White Knights squadron before The Rising.'

He pointed to a patch stuck on his jacket, showing an armored man on horseback, carrying what appeared to be a spear or lance. Above the patch were the words 'White Knights' and below it were inscribed the letters 'HMM-165'.

'Vince, I have lived and fought in the Deadland all my life. Here are some things you should know. The Reds control the skies. So traveling in a large group is suicide. Traveling in large vehicles is suicide. And not listening to someone like Satish is suicide. We risked our lives to save you, but if you would rather be on your own, go ahead. I do not like to carry excess baggage.'

With that, Alice shouldered her assault rifle and began walking off.

'Hey, wait. Sorry if we started on the wrong foot. Being chased by Red Guards for a week has a way of putting you on edge.'

They took refuge in a nearby clump of trees. Satish had already radioed his men to give him advance warning of any incoming Red Guards, on land or by air. For close to an hour they lay flat against the ground, waiting for the telltale buzzing sound that would announce the arrival of an attack helicopter.

Finally Satish whispered, 'Looks like they've bled enough

for a day. Alice, it'll be dark soon; let's get into the woods and hear what Vince and his friend have to say.'

When they were in the forest, Satish passed around a meager meal of biscuits, which the two Americans wolfed down hungrily.

Alice found the old man staring at her, and finally she turned to look at him. That was when he spoke his first words.

'You are for real. So there is hope after all.'

'Excuse me?'

The old man smiled, revealing several missing teeth.

'My name is Doctor Steven Edwards, young lady. I have a story that may interest you.'

Doctor Edwards sat back, munching on his biscuit.

'I was a virologist working for the US Department of Defense before The Rising. In the days that followed, I did what many did. I hid and survived the best I could, and one day I was picked up to go and work in some labor camp in the Mainland.'

'How long were you in the camps?' Satish asked.

'I spent eight years cleaning barracks and tilling fields. At first I tried to fight back, but when I realized there was nowhere to go to and no hope for escape, I gave in. The beatings and broken teeth helped.'

Doctor Edwards' response chilled Alice. She had heard of the camps and had talked to people who had lost relatives to them, but she had never met anyone who had survived one. She now saw the scars crisscrossing the old man's body and wondered what horrors he had endured. Having grown up to think of Biters as the ultimate horror, Alice now realized that her father had indeed been right: the worst cruelty was what man could inflict on a fellow man.

Doctor Edwards continued, 'I had resigned to slaving away in the camp until a year ago, when some folks in the

Central Committee had me brought to Shanghai. They told me that they thought they could create a vaccine against the virus that turned people into Biters. Based on my background, they thought I could help.'

'Why would they single you out?'

'Because, my dear girl, I had worked on the viruses that perhaps led to this monstrosity in the first place.'

Alice thought back to the Queen of the Biters and the story she had told Alice.

'Did you know Dr. Protima?'

The old man looked down. 'I did not know her personally but I knew she was one of the researchers. Unfortunately when I did meet her, it was to harvest her dead body.'

Alice recalled how Dr. Protima had sacrificed herself in the attack to rescue Alice from the Red Guard base where she was being held. In the chaos that had followed the battle, and in wanting to escape impending Red Guard reinforcements and air strikes, Satish and his men had whisked Alice away from the base, but Dr. Protima's body had been left behind.

'I took her blood samples and got to work, thinking they were interested in only a vaccine.'

Alice explained about the vaccine Dr. Protima had given her, and Edwards looked away sadly.

'That vaccine was unstable. It saved you from becoming a Biter, but not entirely. With the labs the Reds gave me access to and blood samples from Protima, I was able to refine it.'

Satish leaned over. 'Is there a vaccine?'

'I couldn't get an actual sample out, but if I can get to a lab, I do have the details in a print-out with me. The reason we were trying so hard to get to you was that I wanted to find out if Alice was real or just a story created by people. With her blood sample and a lab I could make a vaccine that works.'

'Doctor, how did you escape?'

Vince had been silent so far, but now he chipped in. 'Not all of the Chinese are bad. As word got out about what was happening here, many of our guards were talking about whether the Biters were what they had been told. Several of them were letting prisoners escape, even against threat of execution. A young man who had lost his brother in the Deadland helped me and a few others get a spot hidden on a transport plane to Ladakh. When the doc told me what was going on, I got him along.'

'What happened to the others who escaped with you?'

The soldier's eyes hardened. 'They all died. Every single one of them. There were twenty of us, hidden among boxes of food and ammunition. We didn't have a much of a plan, but this was our best chance. When the plane landed, we tried to fight our way out. We had surprise on our side, but not much more. There were only a couple of us who knew how to use weapons, and I managed to get Doc out, but nobody else made it. We got a jeep and drove some of the way, but since then we've been walking and jacking abandoned vehicles, trying to stay alive long enough to find you.'

Something did not yet make sense to Alice.

'Doctor, why did you suddenly want to escape?'

She saw the fear in Edwards' eyes as he answered.

'They wanted a vaccine all right, but they were also doing other things. Terrible things.'

Chen saw the man in front of him pace his office, his face contorted in barely controlled anger. The Commissar had flown in from Shanghai that morning, and the last time Chen had seen him was when the Central Committee was sentencing him to a labor camp. Then Chen had literally trembled in fear – but not today. The Commissar was one of the most powerful men in the Central Committee, second only to the Supreme Commander, who had not been seen in public for years. Chen had seen the worst they could do to him, and he was no longer afraid for himself, but he still had his wife to think of, so he made an attempt to placate the Commissar.

'Comrade Commissar, we lost more than two dozen Red Guards in pursuing the fugitives. It was my decision to stop the pursuit because we accounted for most of them at the airfield, but two men were not worth losing more men over.'

The Commissar turned on him, fury showing in his eyes.

'Comrade General, what were you doing before The Rising?'

The sudden question took Chen by surprise.

'I was commanding an infantry regiment.'

The Commissar stared at Chen, his eyes boring into him.

'Comrade General, I was in charge of all our strategic missile groups. You do know the decisions I had to make.'

Chen remembered the nuclear devastation that had followed The Rising and realized where Hu was going.

'So, Comrade General, difficult times call for difficult choices and sacrifice. We have sacrificed much to preserve our people and provide stability in these trying times. China is the only nation still standing from all the nations of old. More than two hundred million people still depend on the Central Committee to keep them safe. So when two fugitives escape, it is not about two people getting away; it is about people seeing that we are no longer in control.'

Hu saw a chessboard on Chen's table and walked to it, picking up a pawn.

'I realize you have been through difficult times, but we

need men of your talent and experience in the coming struggle.'

Chen hesitated. 'Comrade Commissar, the war in the Deadland here has been fought to a standstill. For months, we have not aggressively pursued the terrorists, following the orders of the Central Committee.'

Hu continued to twirl the pawn in his hands.

'Comrade, any war is like a game of chess. You need to make your moves carefully, and sometimes there may be a long wait between moves. We have been patient, and we have been waiting for the right opportunity to make our move. Do you play chess, Comrade?'

Chen was getting more and more confused as to where this conversation was going.

'Comrade General, we were quiet in the Indian Deadland because we were hurting ourselves by trying to fight this Yellow Witch with conventional tactics. If anything, our men who fought in the Deadland came back with their minds filled with stories about the Biters and how the people of the Deadland had found a way of living with them. Then we had to spend time, effort and lives to re-educate them and re-instill the right revolutionary fervor. What a waste.'

Chen felt his throat tighten. He knew he was one of those who had been punished for going back to the Mainland with dangerous new questions about the war.

'Comrade General Chen, dangerous ideas like those make people question the reality that they have come to accept. The idea that they can gain so-called freedom can be a very dangerous one, for it makes people forget that in that freedom lies the loss of all the security and prosperity that we can provide.'

'With all due respect, there are enough veterans back in the Mainland who have passed on stories about the Biters and their Queen.'

Chen saw Hu smile, but there was little humor in his expression; just the look of a man who finally seemed to have things under control. He said, 'It is time we put an end to this. Time that we brought back the savages of the Deadland under our control. That is the key to stop the brimming unrest among the people of the Mainland. Once food flows onto their dinner tables and they no longer have to work on the farms, our people will stop thinking of freedom.'

'Comrade Commissar, we have tried. We brought to bear all our firepower, but you know as well as I do that in a guerilla campaign on their home ground, at best we will fight a long, hard war of attrition.'

Now Hu replaced the pawn, taking up another piece: the Queen.

'Comrade General, I flew down because I need you to know what is going on, so that you can use your experience in the Deadland and the trust your men have in you. We are about to enter a decisive phase in this battle, one that will change the game in our favor. A phase that has already begun with a few select operations behind enemy lines.'

Seeing Chen's puzzled expression, Hu pointed to the black helicopter at the far end of the base.

'Comrade General, it is time we stopped trying to win this war with pawns. The enemy has that half-Biter witch they call their Queen who they follow into battle. It's time that you met the Red Queen.'

Despite all that she had seen and experienced, Alice found it hard to believe that what Edwards had shared could have happened: experiments conducted on labor camp inmates to try and create hybrid human-Biters who could wage war in the Deadland, in an attempt to create an army that would not require food, water, and be immune to pain and injury. More importantly, it would not be an army of impressionable young conscripts who would go back to the Mainland with uncomfortable questions for their masters in the Central Committee about the true nature of the war they were fighting.

Hundreds of young men and women had died in the experiments, which was when Edwards refused to co-operate any further, despite all the torture he was subjected to. When he was shipped back to the labor camp, he knew that a vaccine could be created but also knew that the Chinese researchers were getting closer and closer to their dream of creating an army of hybrids.

'That explains the Biters who attacked our people. But they seemed to move and fight like Biters, without any real human characteristics.'

Alice and Satish had brought their new companions up to speed on what they had been through. Edwards seemed to be recovering both his spirit and strength with every passing hour, as he came to grips with the fact that he was finally free.

'Satish, maybe they haven't created hybrids, but if these Biters attacked your people, and they were brought in by helicopter, the Reds have found some way of controlling them.'

Alice asked Satish to get on the radio. 'We must get in touch with Danish and get this news back. If people in Wonderland know what is happening then we can work together instead of fighting each other.'

Satish's radio came alive. Satish heard Danish's voice as he put his headset on.

'White Queen, this is Looking Glass. I have some bad news. Humpty Dumpty just sat on top of the wall. He called elections and has declared that he is the new Prime Minister.

Things are pretty hot now, so suggest you not visit too soon.'

Satish slammed a fist against the ground. 'With all that's going on, Arun is still bothered about grabbing power!'

Alice sat back, wondering what she could do. It was clear that it would not be an easy job to try and get everyone in Wonderland to work together. And even more pressing, the enemy wouldn't wait until they had things together before attacking again.

Chen followed Hu to the far side of the base, passing a heavily guarded checkpoint manned by black-clad Interior Security Service men before they entered the main building. The first thing he noticed was the stench, and he brought his fingers up to his nose. He saw that Hu had put on a mask covering his nose and mouth.

'Comrade General, do you want a mask?'

The last thing Chen wanted to do was to offer Hu the satisfaction of seeing any sign of weakness.

'Comrade Commissar, I have spent enough time in the Deadland to not be bothered by a bit of the smell of death. But I do wonder why a Red Guard base has been piled up with dead bodies?'

He could hear Hu chuckling as he went deeper into the building, which seemed like a warehouse with what appeared to be prison cells lining one end of it. Heavily armed black-clad guards wearing the insignia of the elite Interior Security Service stood guard. There was not a single Red Guard conscript in sight.

'Come, Comrade General. Let me introduce you to the new shock troops ofn the Red Army who will help us win this war and bring the Deadland back into the fold of our revolution.'

Hu guided Chen towards one of the cells, and Chen struggled to keep himself from gagging at the intense stench. When he was in front of the cell, a decayed hand with two fingers missing reached out to grab him. Chen recoiled back as a bloodied, torn face slammed into the bars.

There were more than a dozen Biters inside the cell, and many of them began screaming and banging their heads and hands on the bars. Then, just as suddenly as they had started, they stopped screaming, and to Chen's disbelief, they went down on their knees. Hu tapped him on his shoulder.

'Look this way, Comrade Chen. The Red Queen is here.'

'Arun, please listen to me. We need to talk, otherwise we will have more deaths.'

Even after explaining the situation to Arun and pleading with him, Alice still faced an uphill struggle.

She had managed to get Danish to convince Arun to come to the Looking Glass. That part of the job had not been difficult at all. One of Arun's hobbies was getting time in the Looking Glass from Danish and spending hours on the radio. He had been a ham radio operator before The Rising, and while there were few people to talk to, he had actually produced a couple of very interesting connections in the short time he had been at Wonderland, including a couple of young people from the Chinese Mainland who were risking certain death or deportation to labor camps by using radios to get in touch with the outside world. From them Alice and the others had got an invaluable glimpse into what was happening inside the Mainland. They had learnt about small demonstrations and disturbances in cities like

Shanghai and about how some young men had refused to be drafted into the Red Guards to be sent to the Deadland and been punished for it.

But getting Arun on the radio had been the easy part. Actually getting him to listen to what Alice had to say was proving impossible.

'Alice, thirty-four innocent people are dead, including more than twenty children. All killed by Biters, some of whose bodies we found. All this talk of Red Guards flying in Biters is fantastic but why would I not look closer to home and ask why all the Biters in the Reservation disappeared after the attacks?'

'I asked them to hide to avoid a bloodbath till we could clear things up.'

There was a pause. When Arun next spoke, Alice knew she had already lost.

'Alice, we got everyone together and had a snap election. We cannot be leaderless in this time of crisis, and I am now Prime Minister of Wonderland. I now bear the responsibility of taking care of all the thousands of people who depend on me, and I cannot act with the impulsiveness of youth that has perhaps led us to where we are.'

Alice heard Satish snort in disgust, but the last thing on her mind was bothering about barbs thrown her way.

'What if you are wrong? Do you want to risk more deaths?'

'We have strengthened our security. I have ordered all of the recon units to come back within Wonderland's borders just a couple of hours ago.'

Satish exploded at that.

'Those are my men! You cannot order them back. Without them out there, we will get no early warning about what's going on outside.'

'Satish, you no longer command anyone,' Arun replied.

The civility had vanished from his voice. 'You ceased to have that privilege and trust when you helped a fugitive escape. All your trigger-happy antics achieve is to provoke the Red Guards – even more so on this latest fugitive rescue mission of yours. The last thing I want is to have your fugitives inside Wonderland and risk retaliation by the Red Guards. The bottom line is that we have known months of peace, and I do not want to risk that.'

Alice said, 'Arun, please listen to me. You spend so much time in the Looking Glass yourself. You know as well as any of us that the world outside that we see through the Looking Glass is far from being at peace. Please give us a chance.'

'The only thing we need to talk about is you standing trial for complicity in the murder of so many innocents.' And with those final words, Arun ended the transmission.

'Comrade General, meet Lieutenant Li.'

Chen took in the neatly pressed Red Guard uniform, the shoulder labels of a lieutenant, the thin and wiry frame, and then last of all, the face that stared back at him. The face of a young woman with yellowed skin, red eyes and a wound on her left cheek that had left a large chunk of her skin hanging loose. She snapped to attention and saluted.

'Comrade General Chen. It is my pleasure to be working under your command.'

When she extended her hand, Chen took it without thinking and then felt a stab of panic as he realized she was as cold as a corpse. He stepped back.

'Comrade Commissar, who is she? What is going on?'

Hu now had a smug look on his face, as Chen began to realize that he had been totally oblivious to some of the moves occurring on this chessboard of war.

Li answered, 'Comrade General, I lost my brother and my father in the war against the terrorists in the Deadland. My brother was killed in battle against this so-called Queen, this witch that the terrorists follow. I was in our Special Forces, and wanted to strike back against the enemy who had caused me so much pain. But as you well know, our tactics were of little use, and when the Central Committee asked for volunteers for a special experiment to help us strike back, I raised my hand.'

Chen studied Li, seeing not the half-Biter monster that the scientists had somehow produced at the bidding of the Central Committee, but a young woman who had lost her family to a war based on lies. A woman who had been a good comrade, a good soldier who had never questioned the story sold to her. Was this the future? Did human salvation really lie in making monsters of us all? Was that the solution the Central Committee had to all their problems? It would surely be expedient; Biters would not ask questions and if they followed this so-called Red Queen like they followed the young girl called Alice; they would go to their deaths without any objections. It would mean not struggling for conscripts and the war could be waged in the dark, while the masses in the Mainland once again hid behind the facade of security and stability. But how would they win the war? What could one hybrid like this and a bunch of Biters really achieve?

Hu must have sensed the emotions on his face.

'Comrade General, any chess player will tell you that one piece or one move cannot be decisive. Our Red Queen has already made a couple of important moves, but we also have other pieces in play who will come into their own when the time comes. But now, Comrade General, let me tell you of what you need to do. So far we have made a few small forays but for bigger operations we will need your men to work together with Lieutenant Li and her forces, to co-ordinate our actions. Come back to your office and I will brief you on what needs to happen next.'

Thirty minutes later, Chen was back in his office. He had grown up as the son of a loyal Communist Party member and joining the Army had seemed a natural progression. He had first started questioning what he was doing when the regime started the brutal crackdowns in 2012 on popular protests in rural areas against land grabs and official corruption. That had culminated in the second bloodbath at Tiananmen Square when it had first hit home. Some of his fellow officers had dared to talk about mutiny, and Chen remembered conversations with his wife when they began to weigh their options. The Rising had changed everything. Biological attacks by the United States, regional wars and instability and retaliatory strikes by China had made everyone forget internal issues and everyone, Chen included, had rallied around the national cause.

Then came the horror of the Biters, and Chen and his fellow officers were thrown into the forefront of a terrible new war. Several months went by in a blur of savage fighting and Chen had initially been relieved when the Central Committee was formed and announced, hoping it would mean some stability and security. Securing food and safety for mainland citizens was the declared priority, and Chen signed up when the elite Red Guards were announced. Then came one revelation after another. The fact that they were to work with Zeus, an American Private Military Contractor, and then a war that soon shifted from being one waged in defense of the Mainland to an aggressive war of counter-insurgency in the Deadland. Chen had gone along, putting aside any misgivings before the terrible threat of the Biters and the need to secure food sources for the Mainland. He had directed the struggle with brutal vigor in the Deadland, with the clear understanding that the ones he was fighting were inhuman Biters and human terrorists who were disrupting the flow of food.

And then he had come face to face with Alice and the Biters, and his conviction had been shaken. He had already paid dearly for the doubts he had expressed then. What was he to do with what he had learnt today? How did one reconcile to being part of a campaign whose first salvo had included the murder of innocent children?

'All but two of my recon teams are back within the city limits! I never thought they would fold so easily.'

The disappointment and hurt on Satish's face was clear. Most of his men were those he had commanded in Zeus for several years and then fought shoulder to shoulder with in the war against the Red Guards. To have them now effectively desert him and report back to the city on Arun's orders had come as a shock.

Alice was silent. She understood Satish's frustration but also knew that many of the men had wives and families back in Wonderland. They would not risk being cut off from them – but at the same time, they were now willingly blinding themselves to the Red Guards' next move. There were just two recon teams left, no more than a dozen men patrolling the vast expanse of the Deadland.

Vince was drawing something on the sand. Alice asked him what he was doing.

'We can figure out how to convince this Prime Minister

of yours later. Right now, the best thing we can do is to prevent another attack. I spent the last two hours talking to Satish to understand the lay of the land and how your city is situated. I flew V-22 Ospreys in the Marines for years, so I can guess where their chopper pilots will try to come in.'

Satish radioed his teams to cover two of the likely ingress routes. He and Alice would have to cover the third. As they gathered their weapons and backpacks, they saw Vince shoulder his rifle as well. Alice looked at him and Edwards.

'You don't have to join the fight if you don't want to. This is not your war.'

She saw Vince's eyes narrow.

'Alice, this is my war. My squadron was wiped out when we refused to do what Zeus and their masters wanted, and I lost my whole family in a Red Guard missile attack.'

Alice went ahead on her bike, intending to also make contact with the Biters and get them to join the battle. The problem was that they would only follow in helping the humans if she were there to lead them. Edwards was already frail and the escape had taken a heavy toll, so he sat behind her. Vince and Satish would cover the ten-kilometer distance on foot.

Alice reached one of the nearby tunnel openings that she knew the Biters used and threw a flare down. She hoped it would be noticed in time. She was about to reach their patrol area when she felt Edwards grip her shoulder tightly.

'I can see them coming.'

FIVE

ALICE WATCHED THE TWO TRANSPORT helicopters come in low and fast. She had not heard them until they were merely a few hundred meters away, but Edwards had seen them in the fading light. The moment she saw the helicopters, she ditched the bike and she and Edwards took cover behind a sand dune.

'I've never seen a helicopter as silent as these. No wonder they managed to come in for their attacks without us realizing it.'

Edwards peered around the dune's edge. 'Stealth, or maybe it's some sort of noise suppressant technology. The United States, China and some other countries had such technology before The Rising. Clearly they've been saving these for whatever they have in mind.'

Both helicopters landed as Alice kept watching in impotent rage. With her assault rifle and pistol, she would be able to do precious little against them. Edwards had been given a pistol, but it transpired that he'd never fired a gun before, so he would be of dubious utility in a fight. Even with Satish and Vince here they'd be hopelessly outnumbered.

The rear doors swung open on the large helicopters and Alice saw several figures walk out. From their shuffling gait it was obvious they were Biters. Alice raised her rifle scope to her eyes to take a closer look and saw what she had noticed before in Wonderland: these Biters were all wearing clean clothes and did not seem to have the many wounds and mutilations that Biters in the Deadland would almost inevitably have.

'Doctor, they seem to have produced their Biters, but one thing makes no sense to me. Biters would never follow a human being this way. How did they manage it?'

Edwards had no answer but kept watching as a total of more than fifty Biters filed out and stood there, as if awaiting orders. Alice gasped almost audibly as a woman in a Red Guard uniform walked out and the Biters knelt before her. The woman was wearing dark glasses and had her mouth covered in a mask, presumably to keep out the stench of the Biters.

'That's impossible! I've never seen Biters take orders from a human.'

Edwards' mind reeled, grappling with the science. 'I know they managed to inject healthy, loyal Chinese citizens to transform them into Biters. Perhaps they were able to create variations in the virus.'

Alice stayed focused on the assembled Biters. Their origin was unimportant; the main concern now was preventing them from reaching Wonderland. She did not fully understand what the Red Guards' plan was, but with the two Biter attacks they had effectively stripped Wonderland of much of its defenses. Alice and Satish, two of the most experienced in combat, were essentially outlaws; the Biters who had provided Alice's forces with much of its strength of numbers could no longer be counted on to defend Wonderland; and now the deep recon teams who served as their eyes and ears in the Deadland had been withdrawn to the city.

As Alice watched, the Biters began walking behind the
Red Guard officer. It was less than a thirty-minute walk to
the borders of Wonderland and once inside, Alice knew the
kind of havoc they could wreak. The two helicopters stayed
where they were, and other than the pilots there did not seem
to any other Red Guards on board. That was at least one
saving grace; that meant there would not be anyone to man
the Gatling guns mounted on the helicopters.

Alice heard a double click on her tactical radio. That
meant Satish and Vince were almost there, but she could not
afford to wait. She had to do something to delay the Biters.
The Red Guard officer was now striding past them, with the
Biters following her, and as Alice watched the Biters began
to disperse. If she didn't take them out as they were bunched
up, it would be almost impossible to track them all down.

Alice took out a grenade from her belt and pulled the
pin. She took a deep breath and then hurled it at the passing
group. To her dismay, the Red Guard officer either had great
instincts or was just very lucky. She looked up to see the
dark projectile coming through the air and screamed and
dove to her right. The Biters could not react with such speed
and agility and as the grenade exploded, Alice saw at least
three of them go down. It might not have killed them, but
at least they would not move any further. The officer was
now shouting orders and the Biters began to converge on
her position. Edwards had his gun out and was firing, but all
he managed to do was to distract them for a second before
they again closed in on them. Alice now had her rifle out
and was firing on single-shot mode. She took out two Biters
before pulling Edwards back with her, climbing a short hill.
Her only hope was to hold out until reinforcements came
and to trade space for kills. She saw the Red Guard officer
screaming orders and five of the Biters detached from the

main group and came around from the left. Biters who could follow combat tactics on a human's orders and flank enemy positions was something Alice had never seen, but clearly this officer had some such control over them. She knelt and fired again, felling one more Biter before retreating further up the hill.

Suddenly she heard a loud roar and saw dark shapes emerge from a hole about a hundred meters to her left. Her Biters had got the message and come to her assistance. Hatter was the first out, followed by Bunny Ears and twenty more Biters. When Hatter saw the danger Alice was in, he screamed and the Biters following him tore into the attackers. Alice watched as Hatter caught one of the Biters by the neck and nearly tore his head off. Bunny Ears had only one good arm, but he and another Biter wrestled a six-foot giant down. All around Alice, Biters were locked in hand-to-hand combat, clawing and biting each other to shreds. What was clear was that Hatter and his Biters were both outnumbered and outmatched. The Biters who followed Alice had been transformed years ago, and their bodies had all the damage and wear and tear that came with being a Biter in the Deadland. The Red Guard Biters, meanwhile, were healthy by comparison, young and fit.

They were now too mixed up together for Alice to use her assault rifle, so she handed it to Edwards and took out her favored combination for close combat: knife in one hand and handgun in the other. She ran towards the melee and saw a Biter come at her from her left. A shot to the kneecap sent him stumbling down and another to the head took him out as she ran past him, barely breaking her stride. Another Biter came at her and lashed out at her. Alice was momentarily knocked off balance, but she recovered in a second, going down on one knee to avoid the next blow and stabbing up with her knife, severing the Biter's hamstring. As the Biter stumbled, she put a bullet in his head. Alice's mind was a mask of concentration, filtering out everything other than the immediate threat in front of her, and her hands and legs moved as if by their own volition, driven by years of training and combat experience.

Another Biter went down before her and then she saw the Red Guard officer. Alice saw the officer was armed with a short sword and as Alice watched, she swung it in a deadly arc, decapitating one of Alice's Biters.

Hatter was now behind the officer and Alice saw him grab the officer's arm and bite into it. Before Alice could see what happened next, a Biter came in front of her. His teeth were dripping blood and his face was torn in several places. He lunged to bite, but Alice swiped with her knife first, catching him in the throat. Before he could recover, she shot him in the face.

She paused for a second to get her bearings. It seemed that Hatter had succeeded in taking out the Red Guard officer; and without someone to control and co-ordinate them it would be easier to pick off the remaining Biters.

Alice heard a scream and looked up, and for a second her mind refused to believe what her eyes were seeing. The Red Guard officer had a large chunk of flesh torn out of her left arm but she was hardly out of the fight. No human could have been bitten by Hatter and not been affected. The officer pivoted on one leg and kicked, making solid contact with Hatter's face, stopping him in his tracks. In one fluid movement, she turned and brought her sword up and cut through Hatter's stomach, slicing upwards as she cut through his chest. The move would have killed any human, but Hatter was oblivious to pain, and the unexpected resistance only enraged him further. He tried to claw the officer's face and she swerved out of the way in the nick of time, losing her glasses and mask in the process. Before Hatter could attack again, she had cut him off at the right knee with her sword. Hatter collapsed on the ground and she brought her sword down on his head.

'No!'

Alice ran – but it was too late. Hearing her scream, the Red Guard officer stood up to face her. Now Alice was close enough to see her features and she stopped, her mind trying to reconcile to the impossibility of what she saw before her. The Red Guard smiled.

'This is an unexpected bonus. I had not hoped to meet you so soon. Now die at the hands of the Red Queen!'

Alice brought up her gun to fire, but Li's hand shot out at blinding speed, and the gun flew from Alice's grip. She looked down to see a metallic star embedded in her right palm. Even before Alice had fully pulled it out, Li was upon her, screaming with her sword raised above her head with both hands. Alice brought up her knife to parry the blow and barely succeeded, the razor shap edge of the sword slicing through part of her left arm. Alice might have felt no pain, but she realized that she was up against a formidable enemy, so she rolled out of the way to gain some space and time to think.

Li's red eyes were glowering and she hissed in rage.

'I have heard much about you, Yellow Witch. Now I will avenge all you have done by cutting your head off and taking it with me.'

Alice had her knife ready, but she knew that her enemy would have a big reach advantage with her sword. She seemed to be perhaps only a few years older than Alice, and like the other enemy Biters she had seen, her face and skin seemed relatively unmarked. She came in again, thrusting with the sword, and Alice side-stepped her, twisting the knife into her stomach as she passed. As Alice regained her balance, she saw Li spit in contempt.

'You cannot gut me like a mere human, witch!'

This woman was unlike any enemy she had ever faced. Biters were simple to deal with; they knew nothing of tactics nor skill. Human adversaries, no matter how skilled or strong, were at a disadvantage versus her because they would tire, fall victim to wounds – she would not. However, for the first time she was facing someone like her, and she would have to rethink how she fought.

Li struck again and Alice again weaved out of the way, this time sweeping Li's leg under her as she passed. Li hit the ground hard as Alice turned to face the next attack. She did not know where this half-Biter had come from or where she fit into the Central Committee's plans, but one thing was clear. She was making an elementary mistake: she was fighting angry.

Li swung her sword again and grunted in despair as she missed and overshot and once again Alice stabbed her in the back before rolling away.

Li and her elder brother had been brought up in a Red Guard Academy since she had been five years old when her father had been called up on duty in the Deadland and her mother killed by Biters in the chaos following The Rising. The Central Committe had identified gifted children and trained them from an early age, hoping to create the vanguard of a new China when things stablized. As the war raged on, the graduates of the Academy became the elite officers of the Red Guards. With her impressionable young mind filled with tales of brutal hordes of Biters and of terrorists threatening the Mainland, Li had grown up with the certain knowledge that one day she too would serve her nation in this war.

Then as the war continued to rage in the Deadland and more and more Red Guard officers were rushed into frontline combat as Zeus units began to munity, her father and brother were sent to the Deadland to combat the menace posed by the terrorists led by some Yellow Witch. Rumors in the Academy spoke of a half-Biter monster who could not be killed. Then came the news that both Li's father and brother had perished in the fighting. At that time she had not yet graduated, but based on her skills had already been assigned to a Special Forces unit. She sent a petition to the Central Committee, pleading to be sent to the Deadland, hoping she would have a chance to avenge her father and brother. When Commissar Hu himself visited her and told her that she was to be part of a special unit to be inserted in the Deadland, she was ecstatic. When she learnt what she would have to endure, she began to have second thoughts. Then she was shown photos of the Yellow Witch, who it was said had been personally responsible for the death of her brother. She talked to combat veterans who told her about how her brother had been about to surrender, but had been killed in cold blood by the Witch. She was shown photographs of her brother's mutilated body. She had nobody or nothing to live for and she wanted to get revenge, so she signed up for the special program.

And now she finally had her chance at vengeance.

She was screaming at Alice to attack, but Alice held back, waiting for Li to commit to another strike. Alice knew that her only chance at a decisive blow was to the head and she would just wait for Li to make another mistake. Li had had years of the very best training. Alice had nowhere near that, but she had learned from years of living and surviving in the Deadland.

Li reached into her belt and hurled another shuriken at Alice. Alice ducked, the star whizzing past her. However that gave Li the time to rush forward with her sword, slicing deep into Alice's side. The sharp samurai sword cut into Alice's flanks where her belt was. Alice looked down and saw that it had sliced through the book she carried tied there at all times. The sword strike would not have finished her, but she would have had a pretty hard time trying to fight with her guts spilling out, and that would have slowed her down enough for Li to finish her off. Alice backed off, thanking the storybook named after a girl called Alice for having saved her. As Li screamed in frustration and lunged at her again, Alice went down on a knee, striking up with both hands as her knife penetrated Li's defenses and took her in the chest. As Li stopped, Alice jumped up, her elbow hitting Li's nose hard. A front kick sent Li satggering to the ground.

Seeing their leader in trouble, two of Li's Biters rushed to attack Alice, who turned to face this new threat. The first Biter was just a couple of feet away when his head disappeared in a mist of blood. The second followed an instantt later. Alice turned to see Vince and Satish approaching, firing their assault rifles. The bodies of dozens of Biters lay scattered around her. While Bunny Ears and the remaining Biters were still outnumbered, with Vince and Satish there they would thin the odds pretty fast.

Li saw the new threat and knew that she would have to abort the mission. Tempting as it was to try and gain her vengeance this day, she knew that her Biters would not last against the combined force of Biters and the trained soldiers who seemed to have appeared on the scene. She screamed at her Biters to retreat and ran towards the nearest helicopter.

A handful of Biters made it with her, but the others were picked off by Vince, Satish and Alice. Li looked down with rage as her helicopter took off and flew off towards Ladakh. The remaining helicopter was about to take off when Vince took aim and fired at the cockpit, killing the pilot.

Alice stood there, observing the carnage around her. They had prevented another attack on Wonderland, but at a terrible cost. She saw Bunny Ears and several of her Biters standing around Hatter's fallen body. She had been told that Biters had no emotions, and certainly they could not cry, but there was no doubting that Bunny Ears and the others had felt something at the passing of their comrades.

Edwards ventured from cover.

'Now I know what they were after with their experiments. They wanted to make another like you, and looks like they succeeded.'

Alice saw Vince grinning. She raised her eyebrows; what could he possibly find funny in the middle of all this bloodshed? He saw her expression and while his grin instantly disappeared, there was no mistaking the excitement in his eyes. He pointed to the helicopter the attackers had left behind.

'Look at the bright side. Now we have our own air force.'

Chen cringed as he heard the sounds of the neighboring office being trashed. When only one helicopter had come back, he had known something was wrong, and Li had rushed into the office in a rage. He looked at Hu.

'Comrade Commissar, she seems like a spoilt young girl, not your elite super soldier.'

He noted with some satisfaction the twitch of irritation

on Hu's face, but the Commissar quickly recovered his composure.

'Give her some time. In the meantime we will go and sit in your office.'

They passed the time with chess. Chen thought he had the Commissar on the ropes when he managed to trap the Queen, but then Hu surprised him by checkmating him within two moves. The normally humorless Hu allowed himself a smile as he spoke.

'Comrade General, sometimes one must turn defeat into victory. Did you see the piece I used to distract you?'

'Yes, Comrade Commissar, you made me think you had left your White King vulnerable.'

Hu got up and walked to the window, watching the building at the far end of the base, where Li was probably still taking out her anger on the office furniture.

'Comrade General, I did not anticipate that they would intercept this mission, but perhaps there is yet something we can salvage from this. These is one other possibility; a White King I have been using for small moves. Perhaps now his role can become more decisive.'

Danish was in front of his console in the Looking Glass. He had got word of the battle and while Alice had not told him the full story, since their communications were most likely intercepted by the Red Guards, the mention of a Red Queen and her Biters had him worried no end. If the Red Guards had been behind the Biter attacks, they had at one stroke found a way of driving a wedge between the humans and Biters in Wonderland and depriving Wonderland of some of its most experienced fighters.

Arjun came up behind him.

'Danish, I have a Cabinet meeting with Arun in the evening, so I thought I'd check if you needed anything from town.'

Danish asked Arjun to sit down.

'I don't know how you do it. You must not just have been a salesman, but a bloody Oscar winning actor before The Rising. You actually have Arun convinced that you're going to side with him.'

Danish had spoken in jest, but Arjun's reply was dead serious.

'When the time comes. Till then, I can't have all of us desert Wonderland. Any news from the Americans?'

The question brought a smile to Danish's face.

'Oh yes! They've got several servers up, and while the Red Guards are trying to block them, they are now communicating a lot with each other and with us over the Net. The news is that they've re-captured a couple of old airbases. After so many years, I have no idea if they can get those planes flying and combat ready, but if they do, then the battle for the American Deadland will be really interesting.'

Arjun asked him what he was planning for lunch, and Danish replied, patting his ample belly, 'I haven't had breakfast, so let's get to town and grab a bite at McDonald's.'

McDonald's was the name given to the first and so far only restaurant in Wonderland. It had been opened in the burned out shell of an old restaurant from before The Rising, but the large yellow 'M' had survived and while the food served consisted of soups, rice, vegetables and the occasional burger when hunting parties got lucky, it made everyone feel better that they had the option to eat in a restaurant again. It was one small step on the long and winding road towards normality.

A jeep pulled up outside and they saw Arun walking in.

'Hey, Arun. I'm stepping out for lunch. The Looking Glass is all yours.'

Arun sat down and fiddled with the radio in front of him. He had never anticipated that this hobby of his from before The Rising would prove so handy now. He had been a member of parliament, one of the rising young stars of Indian politics, when The Rising took place. People had said that he would one day have a shot at being Prime Minister, that he was destined for great things. The Rising had changed all that. At one stroke, he had gone from a man of considerable power and influence to one who was nothing. After The Rising, the only people who really counted were those who were strong enough or ruthless enough to survive the chaos that followed. Arun had gone into hiding in the Ruins with his family, and seen two children be taken by the Biters. They had stumbled into a settlement in the Deadland where they had lived the lives of scavengers, sending a few young boys and girls every month with Zeus troopers to serve in labor camps or farms for a modicum of security. He had been happy when Alice had emerged, leading her rebellion against the Central Commitee. He and his family had walked into Wonderland just over a year ago, but quickly his relief at returning to a more stable, safe existence had given way to mixed emotions. How could he tolerate the fact that they were supposed to now live in peace with Biters, the same monsters who had taken his children? How could he look at Alice every day, and follow the half-Biter monster she had become? Not having any alternatives, he had been content to serve for some time, and his skills with the ham radio were well appreciated, but one day he got a transmission that told him that he perhaps had a chance after all to realize the future he once believed he was destined to achieve. He tuned into the right frequency and awaited his instructions.

Edwards was holding the charred and torn book in his hands with an almost reverential air. Alice had seen Dr. Protima behave that way, but that had been because she had believed that the book contained a prophecy Alice was destined to fulfil. For Edwards, there were different emotions at work.

'Alice, when people talk of starting off on civilization again, they look at buildings, at electricity, at running water. All of those are important, but what they forget is that perhaps the most important thing to start over may be now in my hands.'

'What does that mean?'

'Our minds react to things as we see them, and usually with our basest instincts of fear, hatred and self-preservation. But a book captures the best of what people can be. A book reminds us of what is possible when we put those baser instincts aside. The ability to create something that will last beyond us, and carry our ideas to the next generation. When you get back to Wonderland, you must get them to start making books again.'

Alice played with the grass at her feet.

'I don't know when and how we'll ever get back to Wonderland. I had thought that with peace we would get a chance to create a better future.'

Edwards smiled. 'It is easy to make peace with an enemy, but difficult for ambitious men to make peace with their own greed and hunger for power. From what you've told me, that is what led to The Rising in the first place. It looks like man hasn't really learnt any lessons from it.'

Ever since the battle, Alice's mind had been on litle else other than the unexpected adversary she had just faced.

'Doctor, do you think that you can really create a vaccine that works?'

'Science can always be used for good or evil. The Central Committee is perhaps keen on creating an army of hybrids, but that same science can be used to not just create a vaccine to prevent infections among humans, but perhaps cure Biters as well.'

That made Alice straighten. 'Do you think the Biters can be cured?'

'I'm not sure, but looking at their behavior closely, I can say that they are more than just brutes. Yes, there must be some brain damage, but at the very least if we can curb their aggressive instincts, it would make co-existance much easier.'

Alice remembered what she had heard from Danish about what has happening in the American Deadland.

'Have people always reacted with so much hatred to those different from them?'

Before Edwards could reply they saw the helicopter come back for a landing. Vince had been like an excited child when he saw the prospect of flying again, and he and Satish had taken off in the captured helicopter for a quick reconaissance flight. As the helicopter landed, and Satish slipped out and ran toward them.

'Alice, Arun doesn't know how big a mistake he made by having our recon teams pull back. We barely flew out a hundred kilomteres and I could see more than a dozen Red Guard APCs on the roads. This is the first time in months they've come out in such numbers..'

Vince was soon with them as well. His eyes danced with excitement.

'I thought I would never be able to fly again. When I was

up there, it felt like I could once again make a difference, that I could once again be worth something.'

Satish slapped him on the shoulder, and Alice could tell that the earlier frostiness between the men had gone. Though she was still young, she knew that there was little that bonded two people more than being in combat together.

'Alice, the Red Guards will slowly but surely start taking control over the outlying areas. If they do, you know how easy it will be for them to form a chokehold over Wonderland. Thousands died so we could have this freedom, and now we risk losing all that to petty politics.'

At that, Edwards scoffed. 'It's an old truth. In any war, the soldiers and common people bleed, and the politicians rule over the rubble that remains.'

A few minutes later, Satish came running to Alice.

'It's Danish on the radio. He says that Arun and his so-called Cabinet have voted and they want us to return. He says that Arun wants to talk to us and has a proposal he wants to put before us.'

Alice exhaled deeply in relief.

'Thank whichever god anyone still cares to believe in that Arun has some sense after all. Let's get back to Wonderland. Once we get the doctor and Vince in front of them they will have to believe our story about the Biters being sent in by the Red Guards.'

Satish was not so easily reassured. 'Alice, I don't trust Arun one bit. This could just be a trap. For all you know, he's calling us back to arrest us and put us up in front of some court where he acts as judge, jury and executioner. I want to call my remaining recon boys in so they can go with us.'

Vince tapped Alice on the shoulder. 'We will ride in at a place and time of our choosing. And if there's trouble, we can always fly away.'

Within an hour they were joined by eight of Satish's men who were still patrolling the Deadland and the captured helicopter took off, its destination the old airport on the outskirts of Wonderland.

SIX

ALICE NOTED WITH SOME DISAPPOINTMENT that the old airport did not have any guards posted near it. The runway was still functional and with stealthy helicopters like these, the Red Guards could have landed a few hundred men there without Arun and his politician friends even knowing about it.

When their helicopter landed, Satish ordered his men to fan out and guard the entry points to the airport. The Red Guards had made extensive use of the airport to fly out labor for camps in the Mainland and to fly in supplies for their forces in the Deadland, so the defensive bunkers near the main gate were still there. When Alice checked, the gun turrets the Red Guards had abandoned after the airbase had been overrun by Alice and her forces still worked. When Satish was satisfied that they were in a defensible position, he got on the radio to Danish.

'Looking Glass, this is White Rook. I have the White Queen with me and we've flown in to pay a little visit to Humpty Dumpty.'

The mention of 'flying in' gave a surprised edge to Danish's voice, but he sent a jeep to come meet them, Arjun at the wheel. He ran towards Alice, relief apparent on his face.

'Thank God you guys are all okay. I was so worried about you being out there without much back-up. Danish filled me in on the battle but what really is going on?'

When Alice and Satish had debriefed him, they saw that Arjun looked quite worried.

'I don't know whether Arun and his friends will want to believe that the Red Guards were behind the Biter attacks. He wants to sign a treaty with them.'

Alice was dumbfounded.

'After all we've been through, does he really believe that we can make peace with the Central Committee?'

Arjun came close to her so that the Americans would not hear him.

'Alice, are you sure you want to take Vince and the doctor in to meet Arun?'

'Of course, Arjun! He may not believe me but they have just escaped from the Reds and both of saw the battle against the Biters the Red Guards flew in. They're our best chance of convincing Arun that what we're saying is the truth.'

Less than an hour later, Arun arrived at the airport for the meeting. He wore a bemused expression on his arrival at the defenses they had set up.

'Alice, surely you do not think I will try and attack all of you on my own?'

Satish cut in, 'Given how much trust you have shown in us and the fact that there has already been an attempt on Alice's life, we thought we'd prefer to meet on our terms.'

Arun looked at Satish with a trace of irritation – and then he was all business again, his smile back.

'Come on. Let's meet inside. I have much news to share with you.'

'Yes, Prime Minister.'

If Arun was irked at Satish's sarcasm, he didn't let it show.

Inside, Vince and Edwards related their stories to Arun. When they had finished, Arun looked straight at Alice.

'I have heard all you had to say. Now, for the sake of Wonderland, hear me out. The Central Committee has proposed a treaty.'

Alice cut him off. 'How can we even think of a treaty with them after all we've been through?'

'There was a time for war and warriors, and people like you and Satish did more than anyone could have asked of you in serving our people. Now it is a time for peace and for statesmen, and I know more of that world than you do. No enemy or ally is permanent, but only our interests are. If Wonderland is to survive, we must learn to adapt and forget past enmities.'

'What do you have in mind?'

Arun held up a tablet that had a message from the Central Committee. Someone called Commissar Hu had signed it. Alice scanned it, the disbelief in her voice clear when she spoke.

'Arun, how can we take their demands seriously? They ask us to stop aggressive actions in the Deadland when they are the ones attacking and provoking us. They ask us to stop all contact with the Biters when you know how much we owe the Biters in our war against the Red Guards. They ask us to open trade routes when you know that means that they will take what they have always wanted: labor to work their camps and farms to feed the Mainland. What do we get in return?'

'Legitimacy. Alice, let's face it; the world is in ruins and the only nation still standing is the Chinese mainland. They would recognize us as another nation, and commit to a ceasefire. We would get access to their technology; our people would stop scavenging for food and bare necessities. We could once again start afresh as civilized people.'

'Does having the comforts of so-called civilized living ever make up for the loss of freedom?'

Arun was now almost pleading with her. 'Alice, stop thinking in absolutes. You were born after The Rising, but before that nations fought great wars and then worked together driven by pragmatism. We can do the same.'

Alice stared. There was nothing she could say to convince him.

'My father used to say that our willingness to defend compromises with tyrants as pragmatism is what has led to our ruin time and again. We cannot compromise with the Central Committee.'

Arun sighed. He took the tablet back and said, 'I was trying to convince you because there are still people in Wonderland who look up to you, and I know how much you have sacrificed for the people here, but I am not asking for your permission. I am the elected Prime Minister of Wonderland and I have already agreed to the terms the Commissar wanted.'

'Did you even listen to what Vince and the doctor had to say? Those attacks that killed our children were carried out by Biters created by the Reds.'

'Yes, the attacks were committed by Biters, but there is no evidence that the Red Guards sent them, and as for your last battle, there is no proof of what you say other than your own testimony – and we both know you have a vested interest in making your precious Biters appear clean.'

'So why did you want us to come here? What do you want of me now?'

'You have a clear choice. Stay with us in Wonderland and abide by the new rules and I'll ensure that people don't pin any blame on you for the Biter attacks. If not, you will be evicted from Wonderland and I'll ensure that the Central Committee knows that Wonderland has nothing to do with you and your actions.'

Alice could feel Satish reaching for his gun, but she placed a hand on his arm. So it had finally come to this. After all she had done and sacrificed, she was to be sold out in a political compromise. Part of her told her to fight the decision, but she knew that even if she managed to convince some of the people in Wonderland, more than enough of its residents would side with Arun. The only thing worse than a false peace with the Central Committee would be open civil war in Wonderland.

Satish pulled her aside.

'Alice, you cannot seriously be considering what he says.'

When Alice spoke, she could not look at him. 'If we go on our own, what will the handful of us achieve in the Deadland? We cannot free those who want to be enslaved. Our best bet is to be in Wonderland so that when the time comes, we can at least be of use here.'

Satish was furious– but deep down, he knew Alice was right.

Back at the Ladakh airbase, Chen could see the smirk of satisfaction on Hu's face as he listened to the barrage of complaints from Li.

'Comrade Commissar, send me out again. This time I will smash that White Queen and her forces! How can we make peace with those terrorists?'

'Comrade Li, not every war is to be won with brute force alone.'

But that only made Li grow more agitated, so Hu stepped closer with a conciliatory wave of his arms.

'Comrade, your raids served their first purpose. The

people of Wonderland have a new leader, one we can work with. They no longer simmer in open resentment of us under the banner of the Yellow Witch. There will be once again a time when you and your troops take to the battleground. For now we will open a new front in this war.'

'What do you mean, Comrade Commissar?'

Hu looked at Chen with a broad smile.

'Comrade General, our next battle will be one based on lessons we ourselves learnt well in our history. We will smother them with our kindness, and in that dependence will be born the seeds of our ultimate triumph over these savages.'

Even compared to when the Red Guards had captured her, Alice had never felt so imprisoned. At least then her status as a prisoner was clear and she knew that, given half a chance, she would try and fight her way to freedom. Now she was bound by invisible straps. Instead of physical chains her shackles lay in the fact that she was helpless and powerless to help those she most cared about. She knew that the only way she could still help the people of Wonderland was to be one of them, not an outlaw in the Deadland. So she stayed in her room and watched as Wonderland changed around her.

The first sign of what was to come was Danish radioing her to tell her that the Central Committee had issued a message aimed at not just the citizens of its Mainland but also the people of Wonderland. The message said that after much conflict and bloodshed caused by terrorists and counter-revolutionaries, the democratically elected government of Wonderland had reached out to establish peaceful relations with the Mainland. The Central Committee welcomed this move, as it believed that the last two remaining bastions of human civilization needed to work together and forget past misunderstandings. It apologized for the violence that had been caused by terrorist leaders and renegade Zeus officers and pledged to bring about a new era of prosperity for the people of Wonderland. It went on to claim that the government of Wonderland had pledged to not give refuge to Biters.

To Arun's credit, he had not tried to defend all that the statement had said, but in the Council building where this had been discussed he had said that the Central Committee was catering to its own domestic audience. Looking at him addressing the large crowd and seeing how they seemed to lap up what he said, Alice learnt an important lesson: people got the leaders they deserved simply because people tended to follow those who projected their own fears and aspirations.

That afternoon, she had an unexpected visitor in the form of Arun.

'Alice, I hope you are doing well.'

She had no interest in exchanging pleasantries, so went straight to the point. 'Looks like your plan for Wonderland is well underway.'

'No, Alice, it's not my plan alone. It is our plan. We all share in the success of this plan for we will all reap the benefits. Don't you see that by signing this treaty we have brought peace?'

'Arun, do you really believe we will achieve peace?'

Smiling smugly, Arun said, 'Don't think I spent all those hours in the Looking Glass only fiddling with my ham radio. I've seen all the Intranet reports, including the ones the Central Committee pulls down after a few hours. The war here is very unpopular back in the Mainland as well, with people asking why their young men are being sent to die in the Deadland for no real gain. With this announcement, the

Central Committee has effectively announced an end to the war here. They will not be able to undertake any large scale military operation without it totally losing them support back home.'

At that moment, Alice saw Arun in a new light. She had believed that he was pushing for the plan only because he wanted power for himself. And perhaps that was part of it, but it was clear that he had thought it through and genuinely believed that he was doing what was best for the people of Wonderland. It was as Danish had said: the road to Hell was paved with good intentions.

Alice did not want to spend much time in the city center where she kept catching people staring at her, some looking at her with scarcely contained hatred and others asking a question with their eyes that they dared not say aloud: why was she silent? The ones who had been with her from the beginning, the ones who had felt the brunt of the fighting, felt that all they had fought for was being given away. But some of her early supporters had been shaken by the Biter attacks, and were no longer sure whom to believe any more. And then there were the more recent arrivals like Arun, who did not owe much personal allegiance to Alice but wanted to create Wonderland in their own vision.

Alice rode her bike to the outskirts, passing the abandoned Biter Reservation. On her instructions, Bunny Ears and the others had gone underground, but Alice had clearly felt their sense of betrayal. She did not doubt that Bunny Ears would remain loyal, but many others, once more wild in the Deadland, and perhaps hunted by the Red Guards, would again grow to hate and fear man.

She entered the Looking Glass to find Danish with Edwards and Vince. The two Americans had taken to spending most of their days at the Looking Glass, perhaps because it was the one way they could get a glimpse into what was happening back in their homeland.

'Alice, come over here. The Americans seem to have more servers up and running and there are several webpages now active. Some seem to have disappeared – I think the Central Committee is fighting to block them – but there are some that we can see.'

Alice quickly scanned through what the pages told her. The story they depicted was one very familiar to her, since she herself had lived through such a tale. The Americans were now waging their own war for freedom, much as Alice and her friends had waged in the Deadland. The reports she read spoke of terrible house-to-house fighting in the abandoned shells of what had once been mighty cities, of Red Guard missile strikes that killed hundreds of women and children, and of the continued menace of Biters. The Americans were fighting hard but they had two things going against them. First, with the relative peace in the Indian Deadland, the Central Committee had been able to divert its elite combat-tested units to the American Deadland, leaving the Indian Deadland to a few conscripts. Second, in the American Deadland, man and Biter were still locked in a struggle for survival.

Alice could see the expression on Vince's face, and she wasn't sure she wanted to answer the questions she knew he would have for her. However, it was Edwards who spoke.

'Alice, I can understand why Arun and the others have made the choices they did, but Vince and I need to leave.'

'Why? Where will you go? I thought you wanted to seek us out in the first place.'

Vince got up, looking out the glass windows.

'We were trying to find a place that had become almost legendary among American prisoners. A place where ordinary people were finally fighting back to regain their freedom. A place where a young girl had united humans and Biters in trying to overthrow the tyrants of the Central Committee. This is no longer that place. I cannot sit here and watch as fellow Americans fight and die while the place that inspired their struggle in the first place surrenders to the Central Committee.'

Alice didn't know what she could say or do. She had never felt so helpless before.

'Vince, how do you think I feel? But I cannot abandon these people or Wonderland. I trust the Central Committee even less than you do, but the only way I can really help my people is to be here when I am needed.'

Edwards placed a reassuring arm on Alice's shoulder.

'Alice, Arun is playing a dangerous game. If there is one thing history teaches us, it is that one can never reach a compromise with tyrants, for they inevitably mistake any concessions for weakness. The Central Committee will be plotting and I fear that in marginalizing you and your friends, and in creating a rift between human and Biters once more, they will have gained a critical advantage when they do move against you. I wish you all the best, but I am of little use here. I need a lab to work on my vaccine and Arun will not permit me one. I need to find a way back to America, and perhaps one day we can find a cure.'

Before they could talk any further, Danish tapped on the screen.

'It's a new message from our friend Commissar Hu. The Central Committee is sending a plane-load of goods as a gesture of friendship towards their fraternal brothers of Wonderland.'

Alice knew she had to get Satish, and fast.

Without their recon teams deep in the Deadland, they would get little advance warning of what exactly the Central Committee was up to. Alice could see that even Arun looked anxious. A lot was at stake, and if the Central Committee were to launch an airborne assault, it would undo everything. But Alice knew they would be far from defenseless. Within hours, Satish had a plan in place. His men were ringing the airport and the outlying areas, armed with SAM launchers. At any sign of trouble, they would shoot down the Red Guard aircraft. Vince had taken off in the captured helicopter to give them some advance warning of what was coming their way, and Arjun had gathered his internal security teams to be ready for any eventuality.

All of Wonderland was on tenterhooks, and Alice and Arun were standing near the airport when Vince's voice came in over the radio.

'It looks like a single transport aircraft. I can't see any signs of other air or ground forces.'

Arun's relieved sigh was audible.

Within minutes, they saw the faint outline of the approaching aircraft. Despite the fact that it was one airplane, Alice felt herself tense. Red Guard aircraft brought back memories that she wished she did not have, memories of the air strike that had killed her mother and sister and the other survivors from her settlement, and of the strikes that had been launched against Wonderland when she had been captured.

The black plane banked to its right and then came in, heading for the runway.

Alice saw Satish signal to one of his teams and she knew that even as the aircraft approached, several missiles would have locked in on it.

The aircraft landed bumpily on the old runway and came to a rolling halt. Flanked by several men, Arun approached the plane as the ramp behind the aircraft lowered and a solitary man walked out. Alice looked through her binoculars and saw that he was a young officer dressed in the uniform of the Red Guards. He saluted Arun and then offered his hand, which Arun shook. Then he pointed inside the aircraft and motioned to someone inside.

As Alice watched, Red Guards brought out several dozen large crates, which they left on the runway. As she watched, one of them opened a crate and Arun peered inside. She saw a smile form on his face and wondered what the Red Guards had brought with them. Within minutes, the crates had been moved to the side of the runway and the plane had taken off and returned to its base.

If anybody found it ironic that trucks captured from Red Guards killed in battle were being to transport these gestures of goodwill from the Central Committee, they kept their opinion to themselves. All the crates were brought into a field near the Council building and a huge crowd had gathered in no time, jostling to see what they contained.

Up until now, Arjun had been silent, but now he pulled Arun and Alice aside. Arun bristled a bit at having to share decision making with Alice, but a sideways glance from Arjun shut him up.

'Arun, let me and my men inspect all the crates thoroughly. Only when we are sure that they are safe should we let people get at them. Also, the last thing we need is a stampede, so get these people home and tell them that we'll sort through what's been sent and get back to them tomorrow.'

Arun agreed and the orders were soon passed out, and most of Wonderland spent that night in eager anticipation of what they would find in the crates the next morning.

'Alice, I am requesting you to help us. All we need is a small sign from you. We have more than a dozen old combat aircraft almost operational and every day we are bleeding the Red Guards dry. Our battle for liberation got a second life thanks to you and your struggle in the Deadland, but now the Red Guard propaganda says you have surrendered. They are dropping leaflets saying that Wonderland has accepted the Central Committee's terms. Just issue a statement saying it isn't so.'

'General Konrath, please give me some time to think things over.'

Alice was seething with frustration and anger at her helplessness. The American General was not asking for much, but Alice knew that having accepted Arun as the leader of Wonderland and having decided to play along with the treaty, she could not even do that much.

Vince said from beside her, 'Alice, it would be easy. There was a webcam on board the helicopter we captured. Danish and I could rig it up and we could upload your message to one of the American servers.'

Danish slammed his fist onto the desk in frustration. 'We could, but then Arun would go crazy. He comes here every day supposedly to twiddle with the radio, but I know he's keeping tabs on what we do.'

Alice was looking at the screen.

'It's not just Arun and what he may think. The Central Committee would certainly see this as an act of war, and they would react.'

Danish looked up at her. 'Alice, since when you have

been worried about what the Central Committee may or may not think?'

Alice walked out, a bitter tinge to her voice as she replied, 'I was always happy to fight to the end. But I had people I could count on, people I knew would fight by my side. How does one fight to free people who have come to like the comfort of slavery?'

Chen was sitting in his office, which had been shifted to the warehouse, and which he now shared with Li. He hated her stench, but then he had not been given any option in the matter. The one saving grace was that Li was usually out training most of the day, at the firing range or practicing close combat with her Biters. Their presence at the base was still secret, and when he went back to the cafeteria in the main building for meals he would get questioning glances from his young conscripts – questions he could not answer. Hu had expressly forbidden him from revealing the real identity of Li and her Biters. The official line, which Chen parroted, was that they were a secret Special Operations unit flown in from the Mainland. He knew he would have got many uncomfortable questions had the peace treaty not been announced. At least there was to be no more fighting in this accursed war. Chen had no idea what Hu and his masters in the Central Committee were planning, but he just hoped that he could go back home and no longer have to stain his hands with the blood of innocents; both his young men and the civilians of Wonderland.

He saw a video conference call incoming on his tablet. It was Hu.

'Greetings, Comrade General. Our token of goodwill has

reached the people of Wonderland. When the time is right, I will have another shipment for them.'

Chen was a career soldier, and understood the cut and thrust of combat, but he had no idea what political machinations lay behind Hu's latest moves.

'Comrade Commissar, dare I ask what we plan to do after that and what the orders for my men are in terms of combat readiness?'

He could see Hu smile and share a glance with someone off camera. No doubt some political officers were on hand to judge if Chen's revolutionary fervor was intact or not.

'Comrade General, we are still very much at war. The people's revolution cannot be sustained as long as counter-revolutionary forces spread the lie of democracy in savage places like Wonderland. The false idea of democracy died in the flames of The Rising. Our people need to know that there is only way to assure stability and progress, and that is for us to join together under the benevolent guidance of the Central Committee.'

Chen's eyes were glazing over. A year ago, he might have been more tolerant of such propaganda, no doubt uttered for the benefit of the political officer watching Hu, but months of torture and 're-education' in the camp had left Chen with little patience for such platitudes. Hu looked at him, a new hard glint in his eyes.

'Comrade General, do you remember our own history and how we were so addicted to opium that we did not see the occupiers for who they really were? The people of Wonderland will learn a similar lesson, but it will be too late for them to do much about it.'

The opening of the crates attracted thousands of people, and Arun triumphantly stood on stage displaying what had been sent as if this were yet another vindication of his decision. Alice was accompanied by Arjun and Satish, their contempt scarcely disguised on their faces.

Each crate had two lines stenciled on its side in large red letters:

'For our brothers and sisters in Wonderland.'

'Made in China.'

When the first crate was opened, Arun took out what seemed to be a bunch of plastic toys. Brightly colored cars, stuffed animals, and dolls in frilly dresses. Alice could hear gasps in the audience and more than one child demanded to take a closer look. Growing up in the Deadland, Alice had never really had the luxury of toys, but had heard about how children before The Rising had played with them. Seeing these bright new toys made her think of all she had missed and would never really have. Even in the relative stability of Wonderland, the best any family had managed was to fashion its own crude toys from scavenged items. For the parents of the children gathered in front of the stage, many of whom had wished they could give their children a real child's life instead of one filled with death and violence, there was no mistaking the excitement in their eyes and voices.

The buzz of excitement was renewed when the second crate was opened. Inside were fresh clean clothes, a blackboard and chalk for the school, plates and cutlery, and finally a huge supply of canned meat and food that Arun declared would form the new menu at McDonald's. At one stroke, Wonderland had regained many of the comforts that most of its inhabitants had almost forgotten.

The last crate contained the biggest prize of all: a large, slim screen.

'It's a TV,' whispered Satish.

Alice had never seen a TV before, and Arun read out some instructions that came with the TV, saying that there would be a daily broadcast for the people of Wonderland in the evening.

That evening, almost all of Wonderland gathered in front of the large TV, and there were squeals of delight as the programming began. There was a children's cartoon, something about a mouse Alice had never heard of, and then something that Satish called a rerun of an old soap opera, which to Alice merely seemed to be overweight and painted women flirting with men. But to the gathered crowd it seemed to be a miracle. For more than fifteen years none of them had watched TV, and they sat glued to it, including the ten minute capsule after the soap opera that consisted of propaganda from the Central Committee about how the 'people's revolution' was restoring prosperity and civilization.

The next day, Alice and Edwards were strolling down the main street, watching people queue up outside McDonald's for a taste of the canned meat, when they spied two young boys fighting over a plastic car. Edwards shook his head sadly.

'We never learn. Once more we sell our ideals for cheap plastic toys.'

SEVEN

T HE FOLLOWING DAYS FELL INTO a predictable routine. Most people at Wonderland would line up at McDonald's for lunch and dinner, and soon Arun found himself having to ration the stocks that had been sent. The people of Wonderland wore better clothes than they had in years and when one of the crates was found to contain bottles of shampoo and bars of soap, a small riot had almost erupted to divide up the spoils. Alice was riding her bike by the school and she saw a group of children walk by, all freshly scrubbed, wearing bright clean clothes and carrying new toys. She remembered her own childhood spent hiding and fighting in the Deadland, taking a bath once in a week, and wearing the same clothes until they wore out. She stopped to see the laughing children and wondered if Arun had been right after all. The Central Committee was certainly not demanding that people be sent to work in labor camps and so far they had made no aggressive moves towards the borders of Wonderland. Was peace with the Mainland indeed possible?

While Arun and his supporters reveled in their newfound comforts, Alice found herself totally out of place in this new world. The only life she had known had been one of fighting to survive. With no war to fight, how did warriors fit back into a society that had passed them by?

Arjun was hardly happy with the way Arun had compromised with the Central Committee, but he was too busy maintaining order within Wonderland. New clothes, toys and the TV meant that people had more things to covet and fight over. Satish sat brooding in the Looking Glass with Danish most of the time. He, like Alice, had defined himself by the war he had been fighting, and now he was just as out of place as her. Many of his men had wives and families in Wonderland and quickly lapsed into civilian life, but Satish stayed at the Looking Glass, his soldier's instinct telling him that this peace was to be ephemeral.

Meanwhile, Vince and Edwards were plotting in their own unique ways.

Vince had taken to spending most of his time tinkering with the captured helicopter, which he guarded jealously. Alice rode by the airfield, hoping to find someone to talk to. Vince was loading the helicopter up with cans of fuel.

'Hi, Vince. What are you doing?'

Vince wiped the sweat from his brow.

'Alice, there's a war on, and if the people of Wonderland are going to ignore it, then I may as well try and get to America and join up with our forces there.'

'How on earth will you get there? It's the other side of the world.'

Vince tapped inside the cockpit. There was a small computer, its screen covered in numbers and letters.

'This bird has a pretty good navigational system and a computer that uses old GPS co-ordinates. Wait until General Konrath and the others find out that some of the old GPS satellites are still operational. We could sure use some of that technology.'

Alice looked back at Vince blankly; she had no idea what he was talking about.

Vince explained, 'I've run the calculations. This bird can fly about 3000 kilometers one way on its internal fuel and the external tanks if I fly slow and easy. If I carry some extra fuel with me, I may be able to stretch that by five hundred kilometers or more. I'll have to stop along the way since I can't fly that long non-stop, but I could feasibly reach Thailand or Israel in a couple of days, depending on the direction I fly. Given that the Middle East is still stewing in its radioactive juices, my best bet may be to fly east.'

He took out a map he had found in the cockpit and showed it to Alice. It was the first time Alice had seen a map of the world and she was both fascinated by both the world's vastness, and the tiny insignificance of their minute patch of land.

'Vince, even if you make it to this place called Bangkok, your home in America is still far away across the ocean. How will you get there?'

Vince put away the map and grumbled. 'I'm still working on it, but I am not going to sit around here and become a slave to the Central Committee all over again.'

Alice's next stop was the Looking Glass. Danish and Satish had stepped out for a breath of fresh air and she found Edwards inside. He was furiously tapping away on the keyboard. When he heard Alice enter, he quickly turned around to see who was there.

'Thank God, it's just you.'

'What are you doing, Doctor?'

Edwards pointed to the screen, on which he had written a seemingly incomprehensible sequence of letters. On the table in front of him was a crumpled and dirty piece of paper that he seemed to be copying the letters from.

'I don't know if I will ever get back to America or not, but I don't need to be there physically to share some of what I've learnt. As Danish would have told you, we're restoring many of the old servers there and many websites have cropped up. Many of them are being used to pass messages between the resistance forces there, but I found that at least a couple of my old colleagues are still alive and well. I had written down some of the things I had learnt about the structure of the virus in the Central Committee's labs and am posting on a message board one of my old colleagues in America had visited.'

'Doctor, could they make a cure or vaccine with that information?'

Edwards shook his head.

'No, they would not be able to do that with this alone. To do that they would need a real blood sample, but at least all this knowledge will not be lost.'

He pressed a key and sat back.

'Well, that's gone now. What news of Wonderland?'

Alice sat down. 'I don't know how to describe it. People seem happier than I've ever seen them. They've got better food, cleaner clothes, the children have real toys to play with and they watch that box every night that seems to bring them such pleasure. Maybe I'm the one who is wrong. All I knew is fighting and distrust. Maybe I am the one who needs to change.'

Edwards smiled as he looked at Alice. Fierce Biter Queen or not, she was at her core still a young girl trying to figure out which was the right path to take.

'Alice, you don't need to change at all. I've seen the world torn apart once before when it looked like we had everything we needed to be happy. The point is that the more people have, the more they crave. That greed is what led us to ruin once before, and I'm afraid that Arun and the others never learnt that lesson.'

Alice asked the next question with a bit of hesitation, not wanting to seem totally ignorant.

'Doctor, this TV they watch so much – I don't see what's so interesting about watching some videos of people pretending to be what they aren't.'

Edwards laughed, his wrinkles creasing across his face.

'My dear, you have a way of perceiving things well beyond your age. The sad reality is that what they consider entertainment on TV is like a drug that dulls their ability to see the real world outside. The world where a bloody war still rages.'

Danish and Arjun entered the Looking Glass. Both looked quite agitated.

'Alice, we need to get to the Council building now. Arun's called a cabinet meeting and we need to be there as soon as we can.'

'What's going on?'

Arjun looked at Edwards.

'Doctor, it seems the Central Committee has sent a new message. They gave Arun a tablet, so he gets their postings directly, but we can see what they're saying here in the Looking Glass. Bring up their Intranet.'

When Edwards brought up the screen, they all read the announcement with a growing sense of dread.

The Central Committee had requested that the government of Wonderland cease all communications with the counter-revolutionaries in the American Deadland as such actions were detrimental to the creation of a peaceful people's revolution and would come in the way of further fraternal relations between the people of Wonderland and the Mainland.

Edwards whispered, 'Maybe they saw my posting.'

Arjun pretended to be throwing up, and Alice smiled.

'Arjun, it's the standard ridiculous propaganda they throw out.'

Danish just stood there, a grim expression on his face.

'Alice, I think Arun intends to do as they say.'

'You cannot let them control the Looking Glass!'

Alice had never seen Danish this angry before. His cheeks had turned red and his breathing was jagged. Worried about the old man's health, Alice gently took his hand and asked him to sit down. As much as she shared Danish's sentiments, she knew that this was an argument they had little chance of winning. Over the months, the earlier flood of visitors to the Looking Glass had dried to a trickle. When the threat of imminent Red Guard attacks had reduced, people had almost inevitably started focusing on domestic squabbles and issues within Wonderland instead of worrying about a war that seemed distant. If anything, support for the Looking Glass would have gone down over the last few days. As Edwards had whispered to Alice, people would much rather watch inane soap operas than bother about the unpleasant realities of faraway wars.

Arun had himself spent a lot of time in the Looking Glass, and Alice knew that he was fond of Danish, so he was trying his best to placate the old man instead of forcing a decision.

'Danish, they do not want us to shut it down. We are still free to see the Intranet from the Mainland and we can continue to use our internal radio transmissions. All they ask is that we not have any contact with the Americans and that their technicians will come over to install some firewalls.'

Danish spat on the ground.

'Arun, listen to yourself! Today they are trying to control what we see; tomorrow they will try and control what we think. Soon we will become their puppets. They could not win this war through arms, but now they will conquer us with their cheap toys, clothes and cosmetics.'

The audience stirred.

Vince said, 'Arun, you know that the war rages in the American Deadland, a renewed struggle inspired by your own actions in creating Wonderland. I have lived in the Central Committee's labor camps and I can tell you that they see us as no more than pawns and slave labor. Every concession we make towards them makes us weaker in their eyes, and you know what they said about bullies, don't you? They feed on weakness.'

Arun sat down, his head in his hands.

'Folks, let's get real here. Do we want a renewed war? All I'm trying to do is to keep our people safe. How will posting messages to the Americans in any way help us make Wonderland safer? Tell me that and I'll listen to you.'

And so it was done. Two Red Guard technicians flew in, and undeterred by the murderous looks Danish gave them, installed software on the computers at the Looking Glass which would prevent them from accessing any of the pages uploaded from the American Deadland. Any second thoughts or concerns the people of Wonderland might have had were silenced by another plane-load of crates, filled with food, cosmetics, and another television.

They did not have to wait long for the next move in the intricate game of chess that Commissar Hu and his masters were playing. After the nightly soap opera, a grim faced woman appeared on TV, with a red 'breaking news' scroll across the screen.

'People of Wonderland, recent investigations have revealed a most shocking truth concerning the disturbances in the past in the area known as the Deadland. These have led to much misunderstanding between our nations. Newly discovered documents show that some Zeus officers in the Deadland had overstepped their authority and had engaged in illegal smuggling of people without any knowledge of the Central Committee. They were working hand in hand with smugglers in the Mainland who were running illegal farms and then selling food to the people in the Mainland at exorbitant prices in a black market. Two of these smugglers have already accepted all charges against them and have been executed.'

There was a stunned silence among the hundreds gathered in front of the TV. Satish, who had dozed off, suddenly woke up. Arjun sensed what was coming and went to call Alice as the woman continued speaking.

'When their illegal activities were at risk of being discovered, they blamed the Central Committee and instigated the people of the Deadland against us. Then they engaged in terrorist attacks that started the unfortunate war between our nations. Now that our people are once more bound together by fraternal relations of love and respect, it's time we unmasked who these villains are. Ironically today these same men are in charge of Wonderland's security.'

Alice had now arrived, and she watched in shock as several photos appeared on the screen. There was Colonel Dewan, who had played a pivotal role in their struggle by believing in Alice and helping the resistance in the Deadland, until he paid the ultimate price by losing his life to the Red Guards. A string of officers followed – and finally there was Satish.

She saw several people in the crowd turn towards him.

Satish was now on his feet, his eyes narrowed in anger.

'Those bastards!'

A meeting followed the next morning between Arun, Alice, Satish and Arjun.

'Arun, you do realize they are lying, don't you?'

For the first time in weeks, Arun looked actually scared. He had been in his element as Prime Minister, believing he was bringing peace to Wonderland and achieving a destiny he had thought had been taken from him forever. Now his place as little more than another pawn was becoming clearer and clearer to him.

'Satish, I sought refuge here with my family and you saved us from Biters and Red Guards alike. I would trust you with my life any day. I was a politician before The Rising, so I know well what propaganda means and how it can be used and abused, but there's something I had never realized. Something that may yet prove to be our undoing.'

'What is that?' Alice asked.

'For people like me, Arjun, Satish, and others of our age, we knew what the world was like before The Rising. We know what messages are likely to be no more than propaganda and what we can really trust. We know that the Chinese were not exactly our allies and how their political system was so different from our democracy. But more than half the people in Wonderland were either born after The Rising or are too young to remember any of this. They take everything they see at face value; they are the ones most excited by the shiny toys and TV shows, and they are the ones the Central Committee is winning over with these messages.'

'They could not defeat us, so they steal our children's minds,' Arjun growled.

'Alice, we need to defuse and manage the situation. I will issue a statement that there must be a mistake and someone is trying to frame Satish.'

Alice stood. 'My father used to tell me something about why he never worked for the Central Committee despite being asked to, and why he always ensured our settlement remained independent in spite of all the difficulties we faced. He used to say that a leash, even if made of the finest silk, is still a leash.'

The meeting ended with Arun's departure. He planned to issue a statement immediately.

When he was gone, Satish looked at Alice. 'What are you going to do?'

'I think the time's coming when we'll be needed to fight once more. Spread the word among your men that they should make sure our heavy weapons are ready to use.'

Satish grinned.

'About time we did what we should have done long ago.'

As he turned to leave, Alice cautioned, 'Just don't do anything hasty. Lie low for now.'

She turned to see Arjun grinning broadly.

'What's so funny, Arjun?'

'I never cease to be amused by how you order around people three times your age, and how they listen to you.'

Later that day, Alice was called urgently to town. She raced there on her bike, hoping it was not another Biter attack. When she arrived, she found that it was almost as bad. Two of Satish's men had been eating at McDonald's when a couple of teenagers had made comments about Satish being a criminal. Words had been exchanged and before anyone could defuse things, a fight had broken out. One of the boys was in hospital with a broken nose and a large crowd had gathered in front of Arun's office, demanding that Satish's men either be disarmed or confined to barracks.

One woman shrieked, 'These men are too used to war.

They don't know how to live in civilized company anymore.'

Alice glared at her and the woman shrunk under her gaze.

'You have what you call civilized company because soldiers like them bled for you. Don't forget that.'

Arun was inside with Arjun and Satish, who seemed livid.

'Arun, these boys are our best fighters. There is no way I will disarm them.'

Arun rubbed his forehead absently, trying to deal with a throbbing headache.

'This is all going crazy. Look, can you please put your recon teams in a barracks for a day or two till things cool down? Arjun, can your men handle security till then?'

Arjun shook his head sadly. 'My boys can break up fights and help drunks home, and of course they could shoot Biters when they were in the Deadland. But they are not trained combat soldiers like Satish's men, so if there's any trouble with the Red Guards, they won't last too long.'

'But there aren't any Red Guards around, are there?'

Alice said, 'Not yet, but I'm sure we will cross paths with them soon enough.'

Back in Ladakh, Hu was seated in Chen's office, the chess set in front of him as usual, looking more complacent and smug than ever. As events had unfolded in Wonderland over the last few days, Chen had finally begun to grasp the true extent of what Hu and the Central Committee had planned.

'Comrade General, do you see now how this war is being waged and won? I don't care about those savages and their pathetic piece of land, but the fertile lands of Northern India are needed to feed our people, and we need labor to resume working on farms and in the camps back in the Mainland.'

Chen was silent, but Hu fixed him with an expectant look. Okay, if the Commissar wanted groveling and positive validation, Chen would oblige. If it helped him save the lives of hundreds more young conscripts from being thrown away in meaningless battles, he would play along.

'Comrade Commissar, the plan is certainly something I would never have thought of. It's reassuring that the Central Committee has been able to find a more peaceful solution to achieve our goals.'

Hu laughed.

'Comrade Commissar, did I say something to amuse you?'

Holding his belly, tears standing out in his eyes, Hu said, 'Who told you that there is to be no more bloodshed?' Opening his hand, he produced a chess piece. 'You see, Comrade, our game is a little bit different than a normal game of chess. In this game, the White King can be taken off the board and the game will continue.'

Arun pulled his jacket around him, trying to keep out the chill. He remembered a time when he actually welcomed Delhi winters, enjoying hot cups of tea in the heated comfort of his bungalow. In the Deadland, winters had meant nothing but misery and huddling in old, tattered blankets. So it was no surprise that the latest shipment from the Central Committee had generated much excitement, as it had brought crates packed with soft woolen sweaters and blankets. Arun had stood proudly as people had openly cheered and clapped. That one moment had brought home to him that he had finally made progress in being a true leader to his people. Wonderland may have been forged in blood and war, but Arun would be the one who brought the beginnings of peace and prosperity to his people.

The flight had also brought with it a message for Arun from Commissar Hu. The Commissar wanted to meet Arun alone to discuss some important matters. Arun had been requested to not share this request with anyone else: the message had euphemistically stated, 'Do not share broadly until we have met to prevent counter-revolutionary elements in Wonderland from sabotaging our continuing partnership'. Arun knew that the 'elements' being referred to were Alice and Satish, and he was fine with that. He had sought refuge in Wonderland like thousands of others and watched Alice and her followers wage the war that had brought them some breathing space, but while Arun never doubted her courage or skill with weapons, he did not think she had the vision needed to realize that no society could exist in a perpetual state of war. The only way out was to bring about some semblance of stability and peace. Arun was well versed enough in the ways of politics to know that the Central Committee had not been sending all their shiny gifts out of the goodness of their hearts. They would want something back in return, and he guessed that was what this meeting was about. His best guess was that the Central Committee would want to restart the farms in the plains where labor from the Deadland had once worked. When he and the others in the Deadland had been scavenging to survive, many settlements had sent people to these farms to buy some degree of security from Biter hordes. At that time, Alice's vision of these being slave camps and her offering freedom seemed compelling. Now, with a more settled presence in Wonderland, Arun believed that it could be a more equal exchange. He could promise some share of the harvest from these farms in return for assured supplies of goods that would really set Wonderland on its path back to civilization. Already he had a mental list that included more generators, bicycles to help people get around more easily, and a large screen and projector to open the first movie theatre in Wonderland – something that had been much in demand once people had started getting used to the daily dose of TV soaps.

This was what national leaders did, wasn't it? Trade with other nations to bring prosperity to their people; create a vision for a peaceful, stable society; and end long, festering wars. So Arun had slipped away at night, riding a bicycle to the borders of Wonderland and then arriving at the agreed rendezvous point. Part of him was worried at being out in the Deadland alone at night, and he nervously fingered the pistol tucked into his belt, but the excitement of a major new agreement with the Central Committee overrode that nervousness.

Arun had been so lost in thought that he almost missed seeing the sleek black helicopter that had landed a hundred or so meters away. It had arrived without making any noise, and looked like the helicopter that Vince loved to play around with. A figure stepped out, barely more than a smudge in the darkness. From a distance, in the dull glow reflected from the cockpit of the helicopter, it looked like a Red Guard officer, with the trademark slanted cap. But as Arun got closer, he was surprised to see that the officer seemed to be a woman. He had never encountered a female Red Guard before and wondered if she was an aide who had come to fetch him to meet the Commissar.

A nervous knot formed in his stomach. He did not want to be taken anywhere alone by the Red Guards. Talk of fraternal relationships was great when he was in the relative safety of Wonderland, but not out here when he was all alone.

The Red Guard officer strode toward him.

He had a tactical radio strapped to his belt, and the

frequency was set to the Looking Glass. He knew Danish would be there, and while the old man would hardly be able to offer much help, he could alert Alice and Satish. It was a sobering thought as he realized that when he was faced with imminent danger the two people he had done most to undermine in his attempt to gain power were the only two people he thought he could count on to help him.

The Red Guard officer was now mere feet away. In perfect English she said, 'Greetings, Mr. Prime Minister. It is an honor to meet you.'

Hearing her polite greeting reassured Arun and he walked towards her, still unable to make out her features in the dark.

'Greetings, is Commissar Hu here, or do I need to go anywhere else to meet him?'

The officer chuckled. Then her voice changed, taking on a harder edge.

'Prime Minister, my brother died somewhere here in the Deadland, cut to pieces by the Yellow Witch and her monsters.'

Arun stopped in mid-stride.

'I listened to survivors of his unit talk about how people like you cheered and clapped as they were hunted down by her. It was a war, I admit that, but why would you allow the slaughter of those who were willing to surrender?'

After a moment of fumbling for a response, Arun said, 'No, such a thing never happened. We always let surrendered Red Guard units go. That was Alice's order.'

'You lie!'

Li spat out the words and took another step towards Arun. He saw her reach for something at her belt and, suddenly very scared, Arun took out the one signal flare he was carrying and lit it. As he held it in front of him, he got his first look at the Red Guard officer facing him. He took in the red, lifeless eyes, the teeth pulled back in a feral grimace, and the decaying, yellowed skin. He stumbled back, the flare falling to his feet.

'What are you?'

Li picked up the flare and held it close to her face.

'I am the Red Queen, dog!'

Arun clicked the transmit button on his radio. He screamed, 'Looking Glass, I need help!'

Before he could say another word, Li had crossed the distance between them in a single leap and hit him with an outstretched palm. Arun doubled over in pain as he felt his ribs crack. He struggled to his feet as Li pivoted, cracking the edge of her palm against Arun's nose. He felt warm blood spurt out over his face and mouth and he screamed in pain. He tried to reach for the gun at his belt, but Li grabbed his wrist in a lock, applying pressure until she heard the bones snap. Arun's screams became incoherent.

Li wanted to make him suffer more, but her orders were clear as to how this man was to die. She brought him close and then leaned forward, opening her mouth to bite. Behind her two of her Biters approached to finish the job.

Danish had stepped out to stretch his legs. Sitting in front of the terminals and radio equipment for hours every day was not doing his aging joints any good. Not being able to access the American sites was frustrating but he had nowhere else to go, as he slept most nights in a small room adjoining the Looking Glass. He had decided to call it a night and sleep when he heard the scream on the radio. He rushed back inside, but he heard nothing else. Had he imagined it? He could have sworn he had just heard Arun scream. Falling down into his seat, he tried to call Arun's tactical radio.

'White King, do you copy? This is the Looking Glass.'

He flinched as he heard a low moan, sounding more like an animal in pain than a human being. That was followed by a roar that could have come only from a Biter.

EIGHT

'WHITE QUEEN, I THINK I saw some movement about a kilometer east of your current position.'

'Roger, White Knight. I'm on it.'

The moment they had been alerted by Danish to the transmission from Arun's radio, Alice, Satish and Arjun had been scouring the area around Wonderland. Arun's wife did not know where he had gone, other than the fact that he had stepped out late for a meeting. That set off alarm bells in Alice's mind, so they agreed to not only search Wonderland, but also the land bordering it. Vince was in his helicopter, using its motion sensors and heat detectors to aid in the search. Not knowing what they were getting into, Alice radioed Satish and Arjun to join her before they investigated what Vince had just spotted.

Vince reached the location well before they did and what he saw was clear. There was a heat signature in the darkness almost directly below him. From the limping way the figure seemed to be moving, it was either a badly wounded man or a Biter. He would have taken the helicopter down for a closer look but Alice had told him to stay in the air to provide warning in case this was a Red Guard trap.

Alice was riding her bicycle and so far had been cautious

in the darkness but was now pedaling as fast as she could. Arun and Satish were on their own bicycles just behind her. They had debated coming out in a jeep but Arjun had cautioned that it would make too much noise and alert any potential adversaries. From over Alice's head came the soft hum of the helicopter; she was close. Vince must have seen her on his sensors as he turned on the powerful spotlight below his copter, lighting up the figure below him.

It was Arun; Alice could recognize him from his clothes.

'Arun, are you okay?'

She dismounted from her bike and ran towards him, and then skidded to a stop when he raised his face to look at her. His right hand was clearly broken and hung limp at his side, his face was bloodied and torn, and he had several bite marks visible beneath his tattered and bloody shirt. His bald head was covered with blood and his red eyes had a vacant look in them. He looked at Alice and snarled and then took a step towards her, baring his teeth. Alice sensed Satish come to a crouch beside her, his rifle at his shoulder.

'Don't shoot,' she warned.

Alice had done this dozens of times with Biters that had joined her band, only she had never imagined doing this with someone who had been a person she had spoken with just hours ago. Removing the charred book from her belt, Alice held it above her head with her left hand.

'Stop and look at me!'

The way she had screamed her command startled even Arjun and Satish, who had never witnessed this ritual and took a step back. Arun bared his teeth and jumped at Alice, who sidestepped him and kicked him down with ease.

'You fool! Do you think I am a mere girl to be bitten? Look at me!'

Arun's eyes went to hers. He stopped.

'I am your Queen and this is the book that contains the prophecy that is our fate. As long as I hold it you will obey and follow me.'

Arun snarled again and was about to leap when Alice kicked him hard in the chest, sending him sprawling.

'Follow me or I will tear you to pieces. Look at me, look at the book and remember that you are destined to follow me.'

Arun stayed crouched, his voice a low growl, but he did not attack. Edwards had been curious about how Alice got the Biters to follow her, and she had told him her about her own experiences and also what she had witnessed among the Biters who had followed Dr. Protima. Edwards had said that perhaps it reflected the fact that even though they were now no longer fully human, Biters perhaps had one thing in common with people. Like people, Biters needed symbols to follow and believe in, and the charred copy of Alice in Wonderland had become such a symbol.

Alice knelt down and took a closer look at Arun. When Satish and Arjun joined her, he snarled at them but did not attack. Alice heard Satish draw in his breath.

'My God, who did this?'

Arjun replied, 'Probably one of those damn Biters the Red Guards seem to have following that Red Queen. Though why they would do this escapes me.'

Bunny Ears emerged from the darkness, looking first at the figure and then Alice.

'Bunny Ears, take him with you and teach him how to follow you. Keep him safe till we figure out what's going on.'

The bunny eared Biter grunted and then pulled Arun to his feet. As the trio watched him disappear into the darkness, Arjun said in a low voice, 'I may not have agreed with him, but he was not a bad man. He was just blinded by his ambition and the hate he had for Biters. Sometimes when we hate something too much, we are fated to become the very thing we hate.'

They took their time coming back into Wonderland as they swept the area where they had found Arun. Satish found indentations in the sand that could have been created by the landing gear of a helicopter but there was no way of being sure. They found some blood nearby, presumably Arun's, and a discarded signal flare. There was no doubt that Arun had come out here by himself to meet someone, but whom that had been was a mystery. Alice's mind went back to the so-called Red Queen she had encountered in battle and she found it easy to imagine her and her Biters setting an ambush for Arjun, though what the Central Committee would gain by doing this was uncertain.

Their first stop back in Wonderland was the Looking Glass, where Danish was waiting for them. When they told him what had happened to Arun, his eyes widened.

'I have a really bad feeling about this.'

Vince arrived at that moment. To Alice he said, 'So far the Reds have been playing us quite well. They've alienated you and Satish from the rest of Wonderland; they've made the humans and Biters stop working together; and they've got the youngsters in Wonderland eating out of their hands. Whatever they're trying to do with Arun has to be a part of that plan: gradually dividing people in Wonderland to weaken it.'

As if on cue, Danish spotted a new message flashing on the Central Committee Intranet. It was an invitation for the people of Wonderland to gather and watch a special news broadcast on TV that morning.

The word had spread like wildfire by the time of the broadcast, so thousands of people were gathered around the Council building, and Arjun had to bring the TV outdoors so more people could watch it. When even more people landed up, he ended up hooking up the second TV, too.

Several of those gathered asked where Arun was.

Arjun stepped up on a table. 'Folks, I have no idea what they want to broadcast, so please be silent so we can all hear.'

He made no mention of Arun. He, Alice, Satish, Vince and Danish had resolved not to let anyone else in on the secret of what Arun's fate had been until they got a better idea of what the Central Committee was up to.

Before long a red star replaced the static and then the familiar newscaster appeared. Today she looked even more somber than usual as she began her report.

'It is with profound regret that we must report the passing of one of our dear friends and a steadfast champion of the fraternal bonds between the Mainland and Wonderland.'

A buzz spread through the gathered crowd as she continued, 'Late last night, Arun Chowdhury, the Prime Minister of Wonderland, was apparently set upon by a group of wild Biters and killed. Please wait as we show photos from one of our circling drones.'

A series of photographs flashed across the screen. They were fuzzy and the night-vision optics gave them an eerie glow, but what they showed was clear enough. Arun lay sprawled across the ground with two Biters leaning over him.

Commissar Hu appeared on the screen next.

'I mourn the passing of a statesman who had the vision to see that our nations could put aside past misunderstandings and start a new relationship. It is clear that with the Zeus traitors having been exposed for the criminals they were and the so-called Queen losing control of her Biters, the people of Wonderland need security. If the Prime Minister, our dear brother, could not be protected, what will happen to ordinary citizens of Wonderland?'

Alice felt a stirring in the crowd and one or two teenage boys pointed at her and Satish. But what Hu said next scared her more than any potential disturbance in the crowd.

'Dear brothers and sisters in Wonderland, we will not abandon you in this time of need. Until you are able to secure your own borders and elect a worthy successor to Comrade Arun, I am dispatching a small force to help secure your borders and protect you from these heinous Biter hordes.'

'Dakotas at Netaji Subhas Chandra.'

It was the fifth time that day that the Americans had made that enigmatic transmission on the radio. While Danish had been unable to access the American websites, he had hidden Arun's old ham radio set when the Red Guard technicians had come, and had been using it to listen into what the Americans were saying. He had caught snippets about ongoing battles in the American Deadland and also repeated pleas for Wonderland to re-establish contact. Then had come the mysterious transmission, repeated several times every day for the last two days.

Vince asked, 'What the hell are they talking about?'

After the last TV transmission, Alice, Satish, Vince and Edwards had essentially sought refuge inside the Looking Glass. Satish's men were on edge, but he had asked them to stay in their barracks. Arjun was spending every minute passing through Wonderland, trying to soothe frayed tempers and nerves. A few young men had decided that attacking Satish would be a good idea, but Arjun had dissuaded them at the point of a gun. Wonderland was a powder keg about to explode at any minute, and Alice worried that when the Red Guards arrived they would be able to essentially take over

Wonderland with little resistance.

'I have no idea how, but the Reds have made a mistake and we need to use that against them.'

All eyes fell onto Arjun. He continued, 'They left Arun there, thinking he was dead. That Red Queen of theirs did not get transformed by being bitten. She and her Biters were created in a lab, so she probably has never seen a human get bitten and transformed. She did not know that a person looks dead and then wakes as a Biter after a few minutes. From their TV transmission, the Reds believe Arun is dead, maybe because they spotted Vince's helicopter and scooted before Arun woke up as a Biter.'

'Let's call everyone and tell them what's going on now! We must get organized and ready before any Red Guards get close,' Alice cried.

Satish shook his head. 'We will get ready, and we do need to tell people what happened to Arun, but we need to wait.'

'For what?'

'For us to be ready. I want all my recon teams back in the Deadland to act as a tripwire for Red Guards and to give us some warning, and I want my SAM teams deployed before we do anything that may get the Reds to act. But I can't do that now, not with the tensions in Wonderland. Let's wait till nightfall and get my men deployed. Then first thing tomorrow morning we can get Arun back here.'

Alice did not like the idea of waiting for one more night, but she saw reason in what Satish was saying. Armed troopers out in the streets now would likely only provoke confrontation. She also needed to get word to Bunny Ears, and that would take some time.

Suddenly Danish stood up, excitement shining in his eyes.

'I got it! I can't believe I never made the connection earlier!'

'What?'

Danish grabbed Alice by the shoulders, unable to stop himself from smiling.

'I figured out what the Americans have been trying to tell us. They would have seen Doctor Edwards' last post and I'm sure they're trying to get him out.'

Alice still had no idea what Danish was talking about.

'Netaji Subhash Chandra International Airport was the name given to the airport in Calcutta.'

Vince completed the thought for him. 'And Dakotas would refer to airplanes. Old DC-3s. It makes sense that without satellites for GPS or networks to run the navigation computers, the first planes flying are the old propeller driven ones like the Dakota. They must have made landings in Calcutta.'

Alice felt a surge of excitement. The Americans had found a way to reach what had once been the Indian subcontinent! They had found comfort in the radio broadcasts and web posts they had shared with the Americans since they told them that they were not waging a solitary war. Now there was a chance to make direct contact and, critically, to get Edwards to a location where he could help create a vaccine or a cure.

'Vince, you said you could get the helicopter to Calcutta, didn't you?'

'Yes, Alice. If I top up all the tanks and carry a bit of extra fuel, I could make it quite easily.'

'Then you must take the doctor and leave as soon as possible.'

Edwards stood up, shaking his head.

'Alice, an attack on Wonderland is imminent. We cannot abandon you at a time like this!'

Alice countered, 'That is precisely why you need to get away as fast as possible. I know that you need my blood sample and you are the only one who can help find a cure or a vaccine with it. We cannot risk you being here when the attack comes. Vince, take the doctor and get to Calcutta tonight.'

For a moment he seemed to weigh the decision. Finally, he said, 'I'll do it.'

Then he was gone, riding his bike as fast as he could to get to the airport to prepare for the long flight.

To Arjun, Alice said, 'You need to make sure the doctor gets on the helicopter and leaves safely. Danish, tell the Americans that we are sending someone to Calcutta in a way that the Red Guards won't understand even if they intercept the transmission.'

Danish nodded. 'If only I could disable the bloody bugs those Red Guards placed in our computers I could have just messaged them.'

Next Alice looked at Satish. 'We need to get ready. The Red Guards may be here any time. I doubt they will launch an all out attack at first. They have been winning this war with deceit and stealth, and they will try to continue that. I expect them to start patrols outside Wonderland and then perhaps start dictating our policies and getting people to work on the old farms in return for their supposed security. I'll go and alert Bunny Ears and the others and get Arun ready; you get your men to prepare themselves.'

Chen looked out of his window to see the black transport aircraft landing at the far end of the airstrip, well away from the prying eyes of the Red Guards at the base. Three of them had already disgorged their passengers and he had been told there was to be one more planeload. As soon as they landed, the passengers were met by Li on the tarmac and then herded into the far end of the base. Hundreds of Biters had been brought in for the coming operation and Chen felt a bit sick at the thought of what was to come. He had dedicated his life to the Central Committee under the illusion that the war against the Biters was necessary to protect what was left of human civilization. It was truly a perversity that the same Central Committee was now freely using Biters created in its labs to serve its purpose. However, all these thoughts were buried in Chen's mind, as Commissar Hu was standing right behind him, having flown in the previous night to personally oversee the operation – and while it had never been said aloud, to ensure that Chen stuck to the plan.

'Comrade General, are your men ready?'

Chen stiffened, weighing in his mind how he should reply, since the question was about the readiness not just of his men, but himself.

'Yes, Comrade Commissar, we are ready, though I must confess some of the men have been grumbling about policing duties in the Deadland when they had thought that phase of the war had long ended.'

Hu chuckled. 'Your men should learn to play chess, Comrade. That war never came to an end. We were just waiting for the right time to make our move. If my calculations are correct, the puppet government of this so-called Wonderland is now leaderless and their people are divided. Many of their youth, fed on our food and clothed in our finest fabrics, will see security in embracing us, and once more join our fold. Then, Comrade General, these savages will do as they were meant to: serve us in the farms in the plains. Food will once again flow to the Mainland, and our people will enjoy the prosperity of the people's revolution. We will win this war with little or no bloodshed, Comrade.'

Chen said nothing, but he knew that only politicians and

fools believed that any war could be won without bloodshed.

Alice watched the helicopter take off and fly eastwards. She hoped Vince and Edwards would get to their destination safely, but for now her concerns were more immediate. Satish had been getting in touch with his men, telling them to be ready. In the darkness of night, six missile teams armed with surface to air missiles and RPG launchers had moved to the outskirts of Wonderland. Arjun had also begun mobilizing his men. He knew that many of them had mixed feelings about Alice and Satish after the Biter attacks and the Red propaganda, so he told them that he wanted them to be on guard against any unrest caused by the power vacuum left by Arun's death. Despite the late hour, he had many of his men start neighborhood patrols, which ensured that if there was any trouble he would have a ready reserve of armed men to back up Satish's teams.

Alice felt a familiar buzz that she always seemed to feel at the prospect of upcoming battle. She had been told she had a keen edge when it came to combat, partly driven by years of training and living in the Deadland, and partly perhaps by her nature. Dr Protima had told her that part of the infection that turned humans into Biters activated the most primitive parts of their brain, making them hyper-aggressive. At times Alice wondered how true that was for someone who was only part Biter like her. Though she had kept it to herself, since her transformation it took a conscious effort to think strategically instead of impulsively in battle. That was what she was trying to focus on now.

'Alice, we cannot really do much if half of Wonderland thinks we are the enemy. What do you want to do about that?'

Alice turned to face Arjun.

'I am on my way now. You need to call a Council meeting and ensure as many people as possible join.'

There were still a couple of hours to go until sunrise and Alice pedaled her bike furiously as she crossed over to the Deadland. She passed one of Satish's recon teams hidden behind some bushes. She waved to them as she passed and while she did not hear them, the men whispered to themselves that when the Queen was up and about, battle would not be far behind.

She soon saw that danger was much more imminent than she had imagined. The light of a fire burned in the distance, and Alice ducked behind cover.

Poor stupid kids, she thought, wondering just how green these conscripts must be to light up a fire which would be visible for miles around. The thought that they were probably only a few years older than her never crossed her mind. She looked through the scope of her rifle and through the greenish glow of the night vision optics she saw six Red Guards huddled around the fire. Part of her felt sorry for them, but then in choosing to obey their orders they had sealed their fate. In her young life, if there was one thing she had learnt it was the fact that there was always a choice when it came to accepting tyranny. The cost of saying no might come with hardships and sacrifice, but it was never acceptable to say that there was no choice.

She would have preferred to bypass the six Red Guards, but they were directly in her path. Alice thought she could handle the six of them if she had the element of surprise, but there was no way of knowing how many other such teams had been inserted in the night in the name of providing security to Wonderland. Alice allowed herself a grin as she remembered what her father had once told her: that no matter how hard he tried subtlety was never going to be something he could teach her.

Removing a flash bang grenade from her belt, Alice began her slow approach. They were now barely twenty meters away and in the darkness did not spot her coming. If anything, sitting so close to the bright flame and staring at it had ruined their night vision. It was this that Alice would use to her advantage.

Alice pulled the pin on her grenade and threw it in a looping arc towards the men. The grenade landed just feet away from them and exploded in a dull thump, momentarily flashing more brightly than the fire.

The first two died without knowing who had shot them as carefully aimed single shots took them in the head or throat. Another Red Guard fired a wild burst from his rifle but fell as another round hit him. The remaining three men were now firing blindly, trying to pin down their attackers while they got their bearings. Alice was firing on the run, and dropped one more. Then she was amongst the two remaining men. The first fell like a chopped tree when Alice smashed his jaw in with the butt of her rifle. The last man was now screaming in terror when Alice pivoted on one foot and kicked him, sending him down. Without waiting to see if there were other Red Guards in the area that would inevitably come to the scene after seeing and hearing the gunshots, Alice ran straight towards the nearest Biter tunnel entrance, removing the branches arranged against the old drainage pipe and diving in.

It was as if she had entered another world altogether. It had been months since Alice had been inside the tunnels, but whenever she entered one, she could never forget the day this had all begun. The day she had dived into a tunnel after a Biter wearing strange bunny ears; the day she had discovered a strange subterranean world where the Biters lived with their mysterious Queen; the day when Alice discovered that her path in life was to take her very far from her settlement in the Deadland.

It was dark inside the tunnel and she lit a signal flare, holding it in her right hand. With her left hand she took out the book and held it before her. She didn't have to wait long. Within minutes of walking, a Biter appeared before her. She had been an old woman as a human, attacked and transformed in a hospital; even now she had the needle of an IV drip attached to her right arm. Her face was relatively unscathed other than a terrible bite mark to the neck, and when she saw Alice she screamed and opened her mouth to bite. Alice held the book in front of her face and screamed, 'NO! I am the Queen and you will follow me!'

The Biter retreated, bowing her head down. Alice proceeded down the tunnel. She could now hear scurrying noises all around her in the tunnels. The word would have spread that the Queen was among the Biters. After a few more minutes of walking, she saw Bunny Ears sitting in a corner. Arun was beside him, absently chewing on his fingers. Alice would have loved to be able to tell Bunny Ears to show up with Arun where and when she wanted instead of having to take them with her, but she knew such level of thinking was beyond Biters. Then again, Biters did exactly as she wanted them to. They did not debate, they did not strategize, and they did not have personal political agendas. All things considered, there certainly were times when Alice enjoyed leading Biters more than humans.

Wonderland woke up to find itself ringed by Red Guard patrols. More than once, helicopters flew close to the city and then turned back.

'Should I just have one of them shot down to make

a point?'

Arjun sniggered at Satish's suggestion. 'I don't doubt that time will come, but let's wait till we deal with our young rebels.'

More than a hundred young boys had gathered in front of the Cabinet. One of them, wearing clothes fresh from a Red Guard shipment, stepped forward.

'Arjun, why are you stopping us from joining the Red Guards?'

That morning another transmission had come in announcing an incoming message from the Central Committee. Commissar Hu had informed the people of Wonderland that the heroic Red Guards had stepped in, braving the harsh Deadland and wild Biters to provide security to their brethren in Wonderland. He had asked for a hundred volunteers to come out of Wonderland help in the patrols.

Arjun answered, 'We do not take orders from the Central Committee and certainly we do not send our boys to work for them again. Obedience to tyrants is a habit that is hard to break once formed. Today in the name of security they ask for so-called volunteers. Tomorrow once again they will start taking our people to work on their farms or labor camps.'

Jeers went up from some members of the crowd.

The young man persisted. 'Don't you get it? Those bloody Biters have run amuck again and Arun's dead. The Central Committee has done nothing but help us.'

Arjun stepped forward, bringing his face to within inches of the young man, who took a nervous step back.

'They have done nothing to help us. They seek to buy our dependence and obedience – to conquer with their cheap clothes and shampoos what they could not with their armies. They want to make us sell our freedom by making us live in fear once more.'

Another boy shouted above the crowd, 'What other option do we have? To trust our safety to criminals and smugglers?'

Suddenly, the crowd began surging forward and Satish and Arjun began backing up towards the building. There were thousands of others who had gathered to hear the morning transmission and most of them stood as mute onlookers. Yet it took only a few to start a mob.

Satish tried reasoning with the boys. 'Look, we have all fought together and lived together like a family. We need to work together, not fight each other.'

A fist shot out and grazed Satish on the chin. He calmly grabbed the wrist and snapped it, hearing bones crack. Another boy grabbed him by the hair but he kicked the feet out from under the boy. Arjun had his finger on the trigger of his gun, but he knew that if he fired there would be a bloodbath, and that was just the kind of chaos that the Red Guards wanted to take advantage of.

Two more boys tried to grab Satish and he lost his footing in the surge of the mob. Arjun had his rifle out now and was about to fire in the air, but before he could, a series of shots rang out. Everyone stopped and looked to see Alice standing there, rifle in hand. Just behind her stood Bunny Ears and a second Biter. When people saw his clothes and his bloodied face, there were gasps of horror and surprise.

'Arun,' someone whispered.

Alice walked towards the mob surrounding Satish and they melted before her. She climbed the stairs leading into the building and said in a loud, commanding voice, 'I'm glad at least you remember how to get angry and to fight. I had thought the people of Wonderland had forgotten how to be angry about all that had been taken from us by the Central Committee. But if you have to be angry, if you have to fight, do it against the real enemy, not amongst ourselves.'

There was a stunned silence as Arun stepped forward and the deception of the Central Committee became clear. Arjun told everyone about the Biters the Red Guards had unleashed and how they had divided the people of Wonderland.

Alice looked at the gathered crowd. 'I don't have time to convince each and every one of you. The Red Guards are right outside our borders and we will soon be surrounded. Who is with me?'

When Arjun and Satish stood beside her, Bunny Ears shuffled along to join them. At first only a few of those in the crowd moved – but then more and more hands lifted in the air, more and more cries of support rose up.

Smiling, Alice walked away.

'Get ready. Wonderland just declared war on the Red Guards.'

NINE

'T HE HEROIC RED GUARDS HAVE fanned out across the
Deadland to ensure that our brethren in Wonderland
can sleep secure in the knowledge that in this time of
need they are not alone.'

Someone spat on the ground, another shouted abuse,
and Arjun began to see a perceptible change in the mood of
the gathered crowd. Many of the younger folks still seemed
skeptical, but Arun's reappearance as a Biter had given
many of them reason to doubt what the Central Committee
had been telling them. Now seeing the news footage being
streamed on the TV showing aerial footage of Red Guard
units being air-dropped across the Deadland was a sobering
dose of reality. A few of them still shouted out that perhaps
the Red Guards meant no imminent harm, but then the
ominous announcement was repeated.

'We repeat our request to the people of Wonderland.
Our intelligence indicates that hordes of Biters are about
to attack. Please let Red Guards inside the city center to
help secure your homes and families and please cooperate
with them.'

It was the smartest invasion Arjun had ever seen. To
take away people's liberty in the name of providing them

security, to take away freedom in the name of fighting terror, was not a new tactic. But the Central Committee had pulled off a nearly flawless plan, the one weak link being the fact that they had not bargained for Arun having survived the attack. They still did not know Arun's fate and that element of surprise was something Arjun and the others hoped to capitalize on. Alice and Satish had already left to start coordinating the defenses, but Arjun's job was to ensure that they could prepare for the house to house fighting that would be inevitable if the Red Guards got inside the city limits. He did not harbor any delusions that everyone would believe that the Central Committee had played them all as a prelude to an invasion, but he got the feeling that he had managed to convince enough of a critical mass. More importantly, it looked like at least the threat of open civil war that had been plaguing Wonderland was finally something that was no longer hanging over all their heads.

Chen saw three more helicopters take off, laden with conscripts straight from the Mainland. Hundreds of Red Guards had been sent out overnight on their supposed aid mission. That was what they had been told in their camps in Shanghai and Beijing and he had not done anything to contradict that. He knew he could not do that with Hu looking over his shoulder, but he also knew that in not saying anything to these young men he had essentially condemned many of them to a near certain death. He felt the sting of tears and tried to blink them away. He had almost thrown away his career and his life by surrendering a base instead of having all the men there massacred, but now he had done nothing to stop the bloodshed that was about to follow. Sure, he could rationalize that his dissent would count for little, since he would likely be arrested and sent off to the Mainland, or perhaps even just be executed on the spot for treason given his previous stint at a labor camp. But rationalizing never compensated for not doing the right thing.

Hu was right next to him, smiling.

'See, Comrade General. Our plan is working like clockwork. We will get what we want without much bloodshed.'

Weighing his words carefully, Chen said, 'Comrade Commissar, from my experience this Alice and her friends will not go down without a fight.'

Hu chuckled. 'One mongrel girl and a handful of former mercenaries are all that is left of her army. How long will they last without popular support in Wonderland? If anything, once the next phase begins our boys will be welcomed as liberators.'

Li was looking at a photograph of her family. This was the last photograph that she retained of her entire family together- before her mother had fallen in The Rising, and her father and brother been shipped off to the Deadland. She wished she could cry, that she could shed a tear for what had been taken from her by the savages in the Deadland, but she had come to realize that tears were not for her anymore. Now all that mattered was carrying out her mission and avenging the deaths of her father and brother by shattering the terrorist regime of this so-called Wonderland. She had been keenly following the news reports and she knew that the people of Wonderland had cast away the yellow haired witch and her men. With her latest mission, Li would help bring the common people of Wonderland into the fold of the Central Committee, and then she would have a free hand in hunting down and killing the witch and her followers. She remembered her last encounter with the witch and reminded herself that she would not make the mistake of underestimating her again. Before Li had lashed out in haste in her quest for vengeance. This time she would operate with more deliberation and caution.

To the Biters kneeling before her, she shouted, 'Come on, glory awaits us.'

Danish was sitting in the Looking Glass, going through all the Central Committee transmissions. With all that had happened in the previous few days, he had begun to see patterns in what their propaganda meant for actions on the ground. In the last hour, the talk had shifted to one of reported imminent Biter threats to Wonderland and how the hapless and leaderless citizens were at the mercy of this new terror. He knew it was largely aimed at the masses back in the Mainland, preparing them for inevitable casualties, but it also told him the nature of the attack that was to unfold. Satish had argued that they should focus on the anti-air and RPG teams since the edge the Red Guards would have lay in their air support and their armored vehicles. Danish was no military strategist but months of studying the Central Committee broadcasts had given him some insight into how their minds worked. He knew that popular support for any military action in the Deadland was wafer thin and there had been growing unrest in Mainland cities. So any outright invasion was going to be a very risky move. Yet the Central Committee badly needed the farms in the plains and labor to work them, otherwise the discontent caused by food shortages and by having to work long hours in farms was going to push the masses in the Mainland over the edge. The Central Committee needed to control the Deadland again, but the political cost of a full-scale invasion was going to be prohibitive.

Given those constraints, Danish had to grudgingly admire the plan the Central Committee had put in place. If Arun had not been found the way he was, it was very likely that, at this very moment, Wonderland would have been on the verge of civil war. Then the Red Guards could have just stepped in, welcomed into the people's arms. If Danish's reading were correct, the Central Committee would not ideally want the bloodshed associated with a frontal assault. They still seemed to think that Arun was dead and that the people of Wonderland had marginalized Alice and Satish. All the talk of impending Biter attacks could mean only one thing.

Alice was lying down on the ground, hidden behind some bushes. There were two of Satish's men just behind her. They had ventured out more than two kilometers from the borders of Wonderland to cut off the Biter attacks that were likely on the way. There was really no way to anticipate exactly where the attacks would come from, but one thing was certain: the Biters and their Red Queen would have to be travelling together. There was no way Red Guards would be transporting a helicopter full of Biters into battle without her around to control them. That meant that there would have to be only one landing spot. Three deep recon teams had gone further ahead to warn of incoming helicopters. The Deadland around them was crawling with Red Guards and Alice and her group had already eliminated a squad of Red Guards who had stumbled upon them. Satish was with another team a kilometer to the west.

Alice's radio buzzed to life.

It was from a recon team to the east. 'White Queen, I think I see birds in the sky.'

Just then, another team called in approaching helicopters to the west.

She called Satish. 'White Rook, the birds to the west are yours. I'll watch the ones coming my way.'

She nodded to the two men with her, one of who was carrying an RPG launcher. She had considered bringing along teams equipped with SAMs, but carrying the heavy surface to air missiles would have meant losing much of the stealth they needed to get around the Red Guards teeming around them. She felt a keen sense of anticipation at the prospect of meeting the Red Queen again. She knew that the only possible outcome when the two of them met was a fight to the death, but at the same time she felt curious about whom this girl had been. What had made her hate Alice and the people of Wonderland so much? Alice closed her eyes and remembered the young Chinese girl, virtually a mirror image of her. As far as Alice knew, this Red Queen was the only other person in the entire world like her. In a different life, Alice might have liked to have the chance to sit and talk to her, to understand how she was coping with all the dilemmas and heartbreaks that came with being a young girl who could never be fully human again. Unfortunately, the only thing that they could share in this life was the moment when one of them died at the other's hand.

She heard the approaching helicopter before she saw it. She noted with some disappointment that it was not one of the black stealthy helicopters that seemed to carry the Red Queen.

The battle for Wonderland was about to begin.

'The latest news is that terrorist forces are attacking Red Guard units in the Deadland. Intelligence indicates that terrorist factions led by disgraced Zeus mercenaries and the self-proclaimed Queen of Wonderland are trying to take advantage of the power vacuum in Wonderland. Our Red Guards are rushing to the aid of our brethren in Wonderland in fighting back these terrorists.'

The statement posted on the Central Committee Intranet was clear enough. Fighting had begun. Chen closed his eyes, thinking of the young conscripts whom he had sent to their deaths. Most of them were little more than scared boys rustled up from the Mainland with minimal military training, fed on a diet of horror stories about Biters and the terrible savage humans who lived in the Deadland. They had known no better than to trust a senior officer like Chen, and he had failed them all by sending them into the meat grinder that the campaign to win over the Deadland had become.

It was a truism in most wars that young soldiers paid with their lives to uphold the lies told by old politicians, but that did not make it any easier for Chen. He saw Hu at the control center, gloating in what he thought was to be his moment of triumph.

'Comrade General, the Supreme Leader of the Central Committee has been expressing a desire to retire and dedicate the rest of his life to serving the people. If I succeed in the conquest of Wonderland, I may be offered the job, and I will reward your loyalty handsomely. How would you like to be Commissar in my place?'

Chen's smile was enough for Hu, and he returned to monitoring broadcasts. Chen found himself imagining what it would feel like to take his gun and put a bullet in Hu's head. It would take no more than a couple of seconds to end this madness. With immense willpower, he was able to control himself. But in that fleeting moment, something changed within Chen. He knew that the next time he was ordered by men like Hu to send boys to their deaths, he would not be able to go through with it.

Alice watched the smoke trail of the rocket snake out from her right, heading towards the helicopter that had just landed a couple of hundred meters away. Another recon group had already encountered a Red Guard landing and was engaged in a vicious firefight. Part of Alice wanted to wait for the occupants of the helicopter to disembark so that she could see whether the Red Queen was one of them, but she didn't want to lose any of the advantage of surprise she had. The rocket hit the cockpit, enveloping the front of the helicopter in a bloom of smoke and dust. The pilots were killed outright and several injured, bleeding Red Guards stumbled out of the passenger compartment. A few of the uninjured Red Guards had their weapons ready, searching for an enemy they could not see. Alice centered her scope on an officer who seemed to be in charge and was trying to rally his men. This was not the helicopter that would bring the Red Queen and her Biters, but the fate of the men who had just landed in it had already been sealed. Alice exhaled slightly and pulled the trigger.

Arjun was dealing with chaos of a sort he had never handled before. He had spent years living in the Ruins, leading his motley crew of `Ruin Rats' in running battles against Biters and the occasional Zeus patrol. So fighting in built up urban areas was nothing new for him or for many of the others who had joined him in their months of warfare against the Red Guards. Now, however, there was a subtle but important difference. People were no longer preparing to hide and fight in ruins that belonged to nobody other than perhaps the ghosts of their previous owners. Now they were preparing to fight for buildings they had come to consider home. All morning the TV had been carrying news reports of battles between the Red Guards and 'terrorists' and intelligence reports of impending Biter attacks. Regardless of where their trust lay, every single person in Wonderland knew a few things for certain now. The Central Committee was lying. Arun was not dead. Alice and her supporters were not trying to take over power by force. And finally, whatever the Central Committee said, people were not sure they wanted the Red Guards so close to their homes.

The positive side was that it had galvanized everyone into action. The negative was that as the old saying went, every man's home was his castle, and now every man was trying to be his own commander. Arjun knew that they would not survive long if they fought as small, isolated units, and he began to realize just how badly the months of peace had hurt their preparedness. A society at peace can be a wonderful one, but only if it never forgets how to wage war if needed.

Arjun and his men were trying to rally people into fire teams and create natural choke points among the buildings where they could trap incoming forces. The boys who had attacked him and Satish were now standing nearby, looking slightly sheepish. Arjun walked up to them. 'What's the matter?'

One of them answered, 'We all came into Wonderland with our families a few months ago. We don't know much about the tactics and tricks your men talk about. Tell us what we can do.'

Arjun sized him up. 'How many of you have killed a man or a Biter?'

Every single one of them raised his hand. Nobody could have grown into adolescence in the Deadland without knowing how to take a life.

'Then you all know most of what you need to know. I'll keep the older folks inside the city, but you are young and fast. I need you to do something that you don't need much tactics for.'

The boy looked perplexed.

'What do we need to do?'

Arjun smiled. 'You need to run as fast as you can.'

'White Rook, this is Looking Glass. Do you have a parking space ready for our cars?'

Satish heard Danish and answered in the negative. From being their window to the outside world, Danish and his Looking Glass had now effectively become their command and control center. With his access to the Red Guard Intranet and transmissions, he could provide some forewarning of what may come their way. He also had the main radio switchboard, and so was vital for team-to-team coordination. Danish had been asking where to send their only real heavy land weapons: the three jeeps that had been fitted with rocket launchers captured from downed Red Guard helicopters. Without a clear idea of where the assault would come from, Satish did not want to risk exposing the jeeps to air strikes, so they had been kept well hidden.

His group of six had already had a skirmish with a group of Red Guards, leaving three Red Guards and one of his men dead. Now he was waiting for the helicopter that was supposedly flying towards their position.

One of his men whispered to him, 'Sir, I see it. There!'

He followed the man's outstretched hand and saw a black speck appear in the morning sky. Satish's team had been closer to Wonderland's borders than Alice, so he had a SAM unit nearby and he radioed for them to come in. Within a minute, two men jogged by, one of them carrying the large tube shaped missile launcher.

'Sir, I see three choppers.'

Satish began to reconsider his options. If there had been only one helicopter, he would have ordered it shot down without a second thought, but with three incoming choppers that would be a risky proposition. Even if they managed to shoot one down with the first shot, the others would be onto them before they managed to reload. He had mere seconds in which to decide, and he barked to his men, 'Everyone, take cover! We'll get them when they land.'

Now the helicopters were close enough that Satish could see details. One was a black helicopter of the sort Vince had flown out to Calcutta; another was a larger and noisier transport helicopter; and the third was a smaller, sleek gunship. So far every indication had been that the Red Queen and her Biters flew in on the stealthy helicopter, but he had no way of knowing which of the choppers she'd be in now.

The two transport helicopters came down to land about five hundred meters away from Satish's position, but the gunship remained in the air. Satish knew the Biters inside the transport helicopter were the primary threat but if he attacked them first, he would be vulnerable to attack from the air. Making a split second decision, he ordered his men to fire their SAM at the gunship and ordered his man armed with the RPG launcher to fire at the black helicopter.

The missile snaked up towards the helicopter, and while the Red Guard pilot saw it and tried to evade, at such close range he really did not have a chance. The gunship exploded from a direct hit and its wreckage came falling down like a rainstorm of fire and metal.

On seeing the gunship fall, Red Guards began to troop out of the black helicopter. Satish screamed at his men to stop, to redirect to the other helicopter, which would hold the Red Queen and her Biters – but he was too late. The RPG hit the helicopter near the door, obliterating the Red Guards who were still trying to jump out. The few who had made it outside took cover and began firing at Satish and his men.

In the distance, he saw a female form in a Red Guard uniform run towards Wonderland, followed by dozens of Biters.

He had failed. The Red Queen had entered Wonderland.

'People of Wonderland, this is an urgent message for you. Stay in your houses and do not try and interfere with the ongoing security operation against the intruding Biter hordes. Red Guards are coming to your assistance.'

Danish sat upright as the message flashed on his screen. A second later, he got a report on the radio that the same message was being repeated on the TV news broadcasts. That could mean only one thing: that Alice and Satish's teams had somehow failed and hostile Biters were approaching Wonderland. Now it would be up to Arjun to stop them and the Red Guards before things got totally out of control. Alice had briefed him on what to do in a situation like this and he patched her in on the radio so that she could communicate directly with the frequency the Red Guard Commissar had been using for his broadcasts lately.

Chen was sitting at the control center, thinking of the conscripts running into an urban battleground for which they were neither prepared nor trained. Many of the poor fools actually thought that they were going to receive a hero's welcome.

The radio operator took off his headset and beckoned to Chen.

'Comrade General, we have an incoming transmission from Wonderland.'

Chen put on the headset.

'This is General Chen of the Red Guards. Who am I speaking with?'

The answer sent a shiver down his spine. It was a voice that had haunted him since he had looked into the yellowed eyes of a young girl who had become Queen.

'General, you should remember me. My name is Alice Gladwell.'

Hu had come up behind him and asked Chen to put the broadcast on the speaker.

'This is Commissar Hu. I want to speak to some legitimate representative of the elected government of Wonderland, not an upstart terrorist and counter-revolutionary.'

There came a laugh from the other end. 'Commissar Hu, it is rich of you to talk of democracy and elections. I have no time for small talk. Tell your men to stay away from Wonderland while we destroy this Red Queen and her Biters.'

'The people of Wonderland –'

Alice cut him off. 'They know what you have been plotting. Arun is not dead. He became a Biter and is now with us. Now call off the Red Guards or I will be forced to kill them all.'

With that Alice ended the call. Chen looked at Hu, feeling numb with fear for what was to befall his men.

'Comrade Commissar, the plan is failing. If they truly know the truth then they will not be divided; elements among them will not welcome our boys. It will be a death trap for them.'

Pulling Chen aside, Hu addressed him in a harsh growl. 'Your critics in the Central Committee were right. You had lost your courage in the Deadland, and deserved to die in a labor camp. I resurrected your career because I needed your experience, but now I see that you have no nerve left for battle after all. That witch is just bluffing.'

The men in the control center looked at the two officers with wide eyes. For a moment Chen just stood in shock; then he straightened.

'Comrade Commissar, you plot in offices, pretending the world is a chessboard and people pawns to be moved from one square to another. I have news for you, Comrade. In the real world, those pawns bleed and die, and one day that river of blood will drown you and the other old monsters in the Central Committee.'

Hu looked like he had been slapped and then recovered. He motioned to the four black-clad bodyguards he had bought with him from the Mainland.

'Comrade General Chen seems to be suffering from fatigue brought on by his tireless efforts in driving forth the people's revolution. I think he needs some rest to recover his revolutionary fervor. Kindly escort him to his quarters.'

Chen reached for the gun at his belt, but strong hands grabbed him, and he was pulled away outside the room.

Hu looked around at the terrified looking Red Guards in the room.

'Comrades, does anyone else have any doubts about

the war we are waging against counter-revolutionaries and terrorists that I can help dispel?'

Every single man looked down, unwilling to meet his gaze.

'Very well. Now, let us see how long this witch lasts against our own Red Queen.'

Neel watched the first Biters come into view from his second floor window. He was more terrified than he had ever been, and he wondered if the two boys with him were as scared as he was. Still, at sixteen he was the oldest of the three and he could not appear weak in front of the others. He had volunteered for sentry duty when Arjun had asked for volunteers and his job was to watch for Biters who were supposed to be entering Wonderland. He had a pistol in his hand, and while his father had taught him how to shoot, he had not touched the gun in the last year that they had been living in Wonderland. He now saw six or seven Biters almost directly below him and he knew that shooting at them would achieve little. There was no way he could kill all of them. He needed to get word to Arjun or one of the other adults nearby.

Suddenly the boy next to him keeled over, blood spurting from a wound to the neck. The second boy screamed in terror, only to be silenced by another bullet to the head. Neel crouched low, too scared to move. Biters could never shoot like that. Then again, he had no idea that Li was just behind the Biters, taking out targets with her rifle, clearing the path. Red Guards were going to be just behind.

Hu's plan was to let the Biters cause some mayhem before the Red Guards got to the city center and placed Wonderland under 'protective custody' until they could have an election where someone sympathetic to the Central Committee could be installed as a puppet. With everything that had happened, he hoped that enough people in Wonderland would see that allying with the Central Committee was the only way to get security. As for Alice and her followers, Hu had more than enough Red Guards headed for the Deadland to deal with them. So far his plan had gone almost exactly as he had thought it would unfold.

Arjun watched the first Biter appear on the scope of his rifle. There were four; a good number. Just as they passed a building, Arjun pressed down on a nearby plunger, detonating the improvised explosive device inside the construction. The explosion tore off much of the side of the building and obliterated the Biters.

There was no way to guard all of Wonderland's many routes, so Arjun and Satish had decided to essentially focus on defending the city center. His scouts were in the outskirts in constant radio contact with the Looking Glass, and Danish had managed to piece together a pretty comprehensive picture of the battle as it unfolded. There seemed to be about fifty or so Biters who had entered Wonderland, and other than a group of six spotted traveling as a group with the Red Queen, the others were marauding at will. That made them relatively easy targets to pick off, but it also meant that many different teams were engaged in hunting them down, leaving precious few defenders to guard against the Red Guards who were almost certainly now entering Wonderland.

Captain Tso was leading his squad of eight Red Guards into the ruins. They had been helidropped just two kilometers away and from what he had already made out from the radio reports of other helicopters being shot down, they had been lucky to not be ambushed as they landed. He motioned for his men to stop as he scanned the buildings in front of him. His men had no combat experience but Tso had spent two tours of duty in the Deadland and hated having to go into such a congested area where an enemy sniper could be hiding in every window. But his orders had been clear. They were to go into the city and ensure safe passage for the armored carriers that were to soon follow, carrying more Red Guards. He had discounted much of the propaganda that the Commissar had spouted about them going into the city to save the hapless citizens from Biters. He had spent enough time in the Deadland to know that the people there had no love lost for Red Guards, especially since the Yellow Witch had taken over command. But orders were orders, and he just hoped that he did not lose too many of the boys walking behind him.

One of them shouted, 'Comrade Captain, I see a young boy sitting there. Maybe he needs our help.'

Tso looked to see a boy of no more than ten sitting calmly by the roadside, watching them. Three of Tso's men jogged over. Something did not look right to Tso and he raised his riflescope to his eyes to take a closer look. He saw the boy's hand close around something and before he could shout a warning to his men running towards the boy, a bomb exploded near them.

When the smoke cleared, all three Red Guards were down and the boy was nowhere to be seen.

Alice was pedaling as fast as she could, towards the last location where the Red Queen had been sighted. Arjun's teams had neutralized many of the Biters and small groups of fighters were stopping advance elements of Red Guards with snipers and improvised explosive devices, but not yet the Red Queen, who was now pushing deeper into the city.

Satish had also ordered most of his men to fall back, other than a few teams he was leading left on the borders with RPGs to ambush incoming APCs. It now looked like the fate of Wonderland would hang in house-to-house fighting.

Alice spotted movement to her right and came to a skidding halt as she saw three or four Biters. She unslung her rifle and fired, bringing two down with headshots. She was about to fire again when she saw a familiar figure emerging from behind a Biter.

Alice was once again face to face with the Red Queen.

TEN

LI STOPPED WHEN SHE SAW Alice and for a second the two girls just stood there, looking at each other. Then Li motioned to the two Biters remaining with her to attack, and they started towards Alice. Li knew that they would never stand a chance, but they'd buy her time.

Alice calmly dispatched both Biters with a single shot to the head, but that had given Li the time to get off a shot of her own. Alice tried to roll aside, but the bullet grazed her neck as she came up in a crouch and raised her own rifle. Li had learnt the lessons of the last battle, and this time she would take her time to destroy the witch and not act in haste.

Alice felt something hit her neck, and while she would not feel pain like humans did, she knew it had been a close call. She had her rifle up at her shoulder and saw the Red Queen disappear inside a nearby building. Alice ran towards her, jumping over an overturned barrel and flattening herself against the wall as bullets tore through the plaster and bricks in front of her. Glancing around the corner she fired a burst, not expecting to hit much but at least hoping it would cause the Red Queen to take cover while Alice sought a new position.

Li dove as the glass shattered in front of her, showering

her with shards that tore into her face. Bloodied, she screamed in rage as she saw Alice run to the other side of the building, presumably to try and enter it through the side door. Li took out a grenade from her belt and threw it towards the door Alice was headed for. Alice saw the dark object land just feet in front of her and dove to her left as the grenade exploded. The wall she had dived behind took much of the impact of the explosion but she felt a tug at her leg. Looking down, everything below her knee was a mess of blood and skin. But it still moved normally, so she wasn't out of action yet.

Tso motioned for the two APCs behind him to stop. His squad had joined up with more than fifty Red Guards who had managed to fight their way into Wonderland and were now proceeding block by block. They had come across only two Biters whom they had shot with ease, but what had shocked them was the resistance they were facing from the human citizens. Tso had seen two conscripts walk up to wave to a woman in a window only to see her shoot them both before rockets fired by the other Red Guards had blown her apart. It seemed like every human in Wonderland was trying to fight them, and while many of them were clearly not trained fighters, in the congested city ruins Tso and his men were paying for every block they secured with blood. When he had asked for support, he had been told that an armored column was on its way, with more than a dozen APCs laden with Red Guards. The two APCs he saw behind him now were the only ones that had survived ambush after ambush with RPGs and grenades on the outskirts of Wonderland. He had been ordered to his current position to go to the help of a female Special Forces officer reportedly inside Wonderland, known by the code name of Red Queen.

Arjun had been stalking the group of Red Guards for some time. He knew they had inflicted heavy losses on the

Red Guards, but it was impossible to seal every entry route into the sprawling ruins. Also, with attack helicopters buzzing around in the skies, the defenders of Wonderland had also paid a steep price. Satish's missile teams had inflicted heavy damage but the reality was that they had only a small stock of surface to air missiles and it was impossible for them to knock down every single helicopter when the first waves of air attacks came. In the brutal fighting that had raged for the last two hours, the helicopters had by and large disappeared, after their pilots discovered that in such congested areas, with every rooftop bristling with machine gun toting men, women and children, missiles were not the only things that could bring them down. Arjun had been in a particularly vicious firefight with a dozen Red Guards, and with years of practical training in urban warfare he had lured them into ambush after ambush, thinning their ranks until he cornered the last three and he and his men killed them in close combat. But the fighting had taken its toll on his men as well. He had started the last skirmish with three hardened fighters, all of whom were now dead, and two young boys he had using as runners and scouts. In the chaos of the last battle, he had lost track of both of them. So now it was just him, following this group of Red Guards and APCs. There was no way he could hope to cause more than nuisance value before they gunned him down, so instead of attacking he was on the radio with Danish, trying to coordinate reinforcements.

'Looking Glass, where are White Rook and his pawns?'

'No idea whatsoever. They are still mixing it up on the outskirts. I imagine White Rook has his hands full there since I haven't heard from him in more than an hour.'

Arjun grunted in frustration. He had known this would be ugly, but he had never really bargained for just how unprepared many people in Wonderland were from the months of sitting around and squabbling over domestic disputes and fawning over the toys the Central Committee had sent. Other than some of his and Satish's men, and of course Alice, most of the other adults had not even fired a gun in the last year. The comforts of city living had made them forget that freedom was a fragile gift that they could be called upon to defend at any time.

The Red Guards turned a corner up ahead and Arjun took a shortcut through two abandoned buildings, coming abreast them as they passed. Then, suddenly, the Red Guards stopped. Their officer seemed to be telling them to go slow. Arjun raised his scope to his eyes and saw what the Red Guard officer had seen.

It was Alice, locked in a hand-to-hand struggle against a girl in a Red Guard uniform inside a nearby building. The Red Queen. One of the Red Guards near Arjun raised his rifle, trying to take a shot, and Arjun knew that terrible odds or not, he could not leave Alice to be attacked from behind like this. He took his last remaining grenade and was about to pull the pin when he saw dark shapes emerge from the buildings around the Red Guards. Next he heard screams from the Red Guards as they were pulled away.

Alice's Biters had come to the rescue.

Tso had ordered his sniper to take out the Yellow Witch when his men started screaming. Biters were streaming out of the adjoining buildings and at such close quarters, his men were being massacred. He shouted for the APCs to open fire and a burst from one of their turret mounted guns mowed down several Biters, but then the Biters were too close for the APCs to fire with their heavy weapons. Tso saw a Biter with bunny ears bite into one of his men and throw the bloodied body aside. The Biter then faced Tso, looking at him with his lifeless eyes. Tso had his rifle ready, but when he saw a dozen more Biters emerge from the shadows, he knew that it would be suicide to make a stand. He shouted for his men to retreat and they clambered atop the APCs as they backed down the street, Tso firing at the hordes as they rolled away. The Red Queen would have to fend for herself for now. He radioed back and heard Commissar Hu himself at the control center. Where was General Chen? The Commissar had never seen combat and without Chen to guide them, the Red Guards were stumbling along, losing far more men than was necessary. The Commissar asked Tso to take another route, saying that the Yellow Witch had to be destroyed and also that another group of APCs was on the way.

Danish was having a hard time making sense of the mass of confused radio transmissions. He had heard the term the fog of war, but had never truly appreciated it until now. The main armored forces had been stopped but at least two groups of APCs had entered Wonderland, and from the last reports the scouts had sent in, Alice was alone and right in the middle of where both armored groups were converging.

Alice felt the knife tear through her right hand, taking with it a chunk of flesh near the elbow. Li brought the knife back for another strike, but Alice blocked it, trapping Li's knife hand between the palms of both of her hands. Before Li could bring her left hand up to strike, Alice headbutted her, sending her staggering back against the wall.

After a few minutes of stalking each other through the building, Alice and Li had finally come face to face at close quarters. Both their rifles were lying on the floor by their feet, their magazines empty, and now the two adversaries were grappling hand to hand. For a minute Alice had been without her knife, losing it in the scuffle, but as Li regained her balance she snatched it back up. The two circled each other, and Alice saw that while Li's lifeless eyes betrayed no emotion, she was spitting and hissing. What had made her so angry? Li struck out again with her knife and Alice brought her left hand up, deflecting the blow, and as Li overextended, Alice turned on one foot, slamming her right elbow hard against the back of Li's head. Li crashed against a window, shattering the glass. When she faced Alice again, her face was covered with several cuts and gashes.

Alice knew that Li was a more formidable opponent than any human she could have faced. Like Alice, Li would not tire, would not feel pain, and would not stop unless Alice managed to put a knife or a bullet in her head. However, at such close quarters, Alice held the advantage. Li had been trained in the martial arts from an early age, but unlike Alice, she had not spent her youth fighting to survive every day in the Deadland.

Li snarled and lunged, bringing her knife up in an arc. Alice blocked the blow, elbowed Li in the face with her left hand and then followed through with a knife strike to the throat. Li pulled back, the knife still embedded. She felt no pain, but she wanted to scream at this witch, to tell her of all she had caused her to lose – but all she could manage was a sickening gurgle. Blood and spittle bubbled up at her mouth and she spat at Alice.

Alice turned her face away as the bloody spittle hit her and that gave Li the opening she needed. She sliced at Alice's left wrist, cutting through veins, and as blood spurted out the knife fell from Alice's grasp. Li brought her knife up, aiming at Alice's head, but Alice moved out of the way, backing up. As Li closed in, Alice pivoted on one foot and kicked, catching Li in the solar plexus. As Li staggered back, Alice rushed at her, pushing her like a battering ram straight through the window. Both of them landed on the street outside, covered in shattered and bloodied glass fragments, and as Li tried to get up, Alice smashed her head into the bridge of Li's nose, shattering it. Alice reached down and pulled her knife out of Li's neck, but before she could strike, Li managed to get her foot up and kick Alice off, and the two once again faced each other, knives in hand, circling each other.

Several bullets hit the wall around Alice and she felt at least one tear through her shoulder as she dove to the ground. A full squad of Red Guards was approaching now, guns trained on her. Li roared in frustration. She wanted to finish the Yellow Witch herself, but she was unable to speak, her vocal cords severed. So she raised her hand, signaling for the Red Guards to cease fire.

Tso ordered his men to pause. He had left the APCs behind and come through the buildings, fighting a running battle with Biters and human defenders, trying to get to the Special Forces officer he had been ordered to aid. Now he was finally close enough to look at her through his scope and he stopped in horror. She looked like a Biter. Both of them did: the Yellow Witch they had been tasked to kill and this mysterious Special Forces officer called the Red Queen. What was going on?

Alice took advantage of the momentary lull in the fighting to take cover behind a wall. There were at least a dozen fully armed Red Guards and the damn Red Queen. Armed with only a knife, Alice knew she would not last long. She tried to move to the open area to her right but a volley of fire from one of the Red Guards pinned her down.

Several of Tso's men had seen what he had and one of them asked, 'Sir, that Red Queen is a Biter. I thought our mission was to save people here from Biters.' Tso had no answer to that, but he did have a mission to accomplish. He ordered his men to fan out. They had the Yellow Witch trapped behind the wall and he would finish her. He saw the Red Queen approaching, and he felt himself pull back at the stench and recoil at her blood-covered appearance. What was a monster like this doing in a Red Guard uniform? Li held out her hand and grabbed an assault rifle from one of the men and then she started walking towards the position where Alice was trapped.

Glass crunched underfoot as Li approached. So this is how it all had to end; surrounded, outnumbered, trapped. Alice felt no regret or sorrow. She had no real life to look forward to anyways and the way she figured it, she had already died thrice. First when she had looked on as her father and his friends were massacred at their settlement; second when she had looked upon the charred remains of her mother and sister, killed in an air strike; and finally that day when she had ceased to be Alice Gladwell and become the Queen of Wonderland. She closed her eyes, thinking back to everything she had gone through. If it all had to mean something, to be worth anything, then she could not let Wonderland be taken without one last fight. If she was going down, she would take as many of her adversaries down with her. Growing up in the Deadland, she had been taught from an early age that there was nothing worse than becoming one of the undead. Better dead than undead. That had been the motto drilled into her during combat training. But in the past few years, she had learnt that there *was* something worse than that: losing one's freedom.

Better undead than unfree. She wondered what her teachers would have said to that as she stepped out, knife in hand, ready for the inevitable.

Tso heard the helicopter fly in, and looked up to see its sleek, black shape. He grinned at his men. Finally, they were going to get reinforcements, and hopefully a helicopter ride out of this hellhole. He waved to the helicopter and as the chopper came lower, the side door slid open.

Something was wrong. The man handling the Gatling gun was not wearing a Red Guard uniform. Tso screamed at his men to take cover as the gun opened fire, spitting death at the Red Guards below. More than half of Tso's men were cut to ribbons in the first burst and as the rest tried to take cover, Biters appeared from the alleys behind them. Tso knelt and shot one in the head, but there were too many of them. Tso ordered his men to retreat into the buildings and as they ran across the street, another burst from the helicopter's gun killed two more of his men.

Alice did not know where the helicopter had come from but Li had been distracted enough by its sudden appearance to give her a window of opportunity. Alice ran towards Li as fast as she could. Growing up, that had been Alice's claim to fame: the fact that she could outrun anyone in her settlement. Li tried to bring her rifle up, but she was too late. Alice held on to the rifle with both hands and slammed it back into Li's face, the butt impacting against Li's already shattered nose and pushing broken bone fragments back into Li's brain.

The last thing Li saw was the Yellow Witch looking at her.

The helicopter landed in the middle of the road and Satish and six of his men jumped out, training RPGs at the building where the Red Guard officer and his men had taken refuge. The Biters were now streaming towards the building, and Alice took out the book from her belt, holding it above her head.

'Stop!'

The Biters stopped where they were, and Bunny Ears emerged from the crowd. Alice looked at the building and called out to the Red Guards, 'Surrender now or we will kill you.'

One of Tso's men, a conscript barely out of his teens, was crying like a baby, and the other remaining soldier looked to be in shock. Tso knew he was finished, and while he might have been tempted to try and make a last stand, he did not want to be responsible for the deaths of these two boys. There had been quite enough bloodshed today, and for a cause that he was no longer sure of. Looking at the shattered body of the Red Queen, he realized that they had been fighting a war that had been based on lies. He stepped out of the building, his hands above his head, and walked towards Alice.

'I am the officer here. If you want, take me, but let my men go.'

Studying the man's nametag for an instant, Alice said, 'Captain Tso, nobody else needs to die today. We will see you to the outskirts tomorrow, but please don't come back to Wonderland and remember to tell your masters that we are free and will fight to preserve that freedom.'

As Satish's men took Tso and his men into custody, Alice walked up to the helicopter. The cockpit window was open and she looked in to see Vince, grinning at her.

'The White Knight had to come to the rescue of the Queen today, I guess.'

'Looking Glass, sector 9 is clear.'

It was now early morning, and Danish had barely slept

a single minute, hearing reports as one sector after another was cleared by Satish, Arjun or their men. Much of the previous day had been consumed by fighting, street by street, house by house. The tide had finally turned when Bunny Ears and his Biters had joined the battle. Their initial arrival in the middle of Wonderland had caused many defenders to be alarmed, and indeed a few Biters had been shot down by Wonderland's panicked residents. Remarkably, however, Bunny Ears and his band had not attacked a single citizen of Wonderland, instead focusing on fighting the Red Guards and the Biters the Red Queen had brought with her. With Vince joining the defense, they had managed to get some air support, both to attack Red Guard units and also to provide advance warning of incoming units.

By five in the evening, the battle had become one of attrition, and finally Red Guard units had begun to collapse and surrender en masse. Alice had struck a goldmine by capturing a young officer named Tso. During his debriefing with Arjun and Satish, he had confessed that the rank and file of the Red Guards had no idea about the Red Queen and her Biters. He had felt betrayed and was bitter about the loss of so many of his men for a mission that had turned out to be a lie. Tso's testimony had been broadcast on the Red Guard radio frequency and while Commissar Hu was quick to call it a fabrication, Danish had no doubts that it helped convince many of the Red Guard units in the city to give up and pull back.

The night had been one of securing the borders, mopping up any last resistance, and of taking stock of the terrible losses they had suffered.

Finally, Satish, Arjun, Vince and Alice arrived at the Looking Glass. All the men were dead tired, and both Satish and Arjun had several bandages to cover wounds from shrapnel or flying glass. The most fearsome sight of all, however, was Alice. Her hands and feet were a bloody mess and she seemed to be cut in a dozen places.

'Alice, are you ok?'

Hearing the concern in Danish's voice, Alice managed a smile. 'I'm ok. Being half undead has a few advantages.'

As they sat down, Vince told them about his journey. He had reached Calcutta, and within a day a Dakota had landed as the Americans had promised. While he had sent Edwards back to America, he had decided to come back after refueling from stocks left at the old airport.

'What made you come back? You could have gone home, Vince.'

Vince looked at Satish. 'I was a United States Marine. I saw action in Iraq and Afghanistan, and we all thought that if we ever died in combat, it would at least be while serving our nation. Instead my mates were butchered by hired guns after we were betrayed by one of our own once we refused to fly for the Red Guards. I was carted off to a labor camp, where I lived the life of a slave. So I would never give up the chance to finally fly in combat again and be what I once was. Besides, the general wanted me to come back with something for you guys.'

'The general?'

'General Konrath, Alice. He's the leader of the American resistance in the Deadland there. He is one stubborn man; I'll give him that. Do you know they lost five Dakotas and their crew before they managed to get one as far as Calcutta?'

Alice wondered why anybody would go to such lengths and sacrifice so much.

'Because he knew that the only hope for lasting peace lies in humans coming to terms with Biters. Two things can make that happen: the vaccine, which hopefully Edwards is working on right now, and you. Your voice, your story could change how people in America view Biters. Many there have heard of you but they dismiss you as nothing more than a fairy tale or myth.'

'How could I possibly get to them, Vince? You know our computers have all been disabled by the Red Guards from communicating with the Americans.'

Vince reached into his backpack and took out a large tablet.

'The general sent this. Now you can communicate all you want with the Americans.'

That afternoon, Alice walked through Wonderland. The damage and losses had been high. Despite their lack of training and practice, the people of Wonderland had fought to protect their freedom with a ferocity that even Alice had not anticipated. Whole families had perished in battle, and she had heard of small boys and girls setting off bombs that their fallen parents had laid. Despite the terrible losses, she felt a surge of hope. If there was one thing her own journey had taught her, it was the fact that liberty was secured not by a handful of heroes and champions, but when every ordinary citizen gathered up the courage to stand up against tyranny.

Bunny Ears and his Biters were waiting, so Alice approached.

'You did really well, Bunny Ears. Thank you for your help.'

Bunny Ears seemed to have lost an ear in the fighting and his face was a bloody mess, but he grunted and all the Biters knelt before Alice. Then Alice saw something that she had never seen before. People began streaming out of their houses, many still bloodied and bandaged, and they stood beside the Biters.

One of them, an old man who had served on Arun's Cabinet, spoke up, his head bowed as if not wanting to look Alice in the eye. 'Alice, please do forgive us doubting you. We are free today because of you.'

Alice raised him up.

'No. We are free today because we stood together. Let us never forget that.'

Satish had walked up behind Alice and he took in the sight before him, hundreds of humans and Biters, united in something for the first time.

'Alice, you know what you said about Biters needing symbols to follow a leader? It's not just Biters; humans need symbols to believe in as well. For the Biters, that symbol is that old book. For these people, that symbol is you.'

The rest of the day was spent beginning the monumental task of cleaning, and the Biters returned to the Reservation, though this time Alice noticed that nobody turned on the electrified fence or locked the gate.

That evening, Alice went to the Looking Glass, where Danish hooked her up via the new tablet the Americans had sent. It had a camera on it, and Alice soon found herself looking at a grizzled, bearded face.

'Alice, I am General Konrath, but you may call me Jack. Danish has been telling me about your battle, and the tale of your victory is being spread far and wide across America. Now, all we need is for you to share your story with our people. The camera will record everything you say.'

Alice spoke for the next twenty minutes, starting with her childhood, her life in the settlement at the Deadland, the day she jumped into a hole after a Biter, and then the adventure that had followed. Reliving it all left her emotionally drained, and while Biters did not cry, she knew those who heard could feel the pain that could only come from reliving the loss of loved ones.

'Thank you, Alice. One day we will meet, and our battles for freedom will become one. By the way, Danish knows of one more operation you could lead. Good night.'

Alice looked at Danish, who was grinning.

'What did he mean?'

'The Americans have managed to hack into the Central Committee's servers and broadcast systems. We can do this only once, because I'm sure the Central Committee will block all further transmissions, so we have to make it count.'

'What do you mean?'

Danish pointed to the tablet the Americans had sent. 'Reports of the battle for Wonderland are spreading through the Mainland. Many Red Guard officers have been arrested for questioning orders, and it seems General Chen is also in custody after he refused orders to assault the city. Their plan is unraveling and once those veterans are killed or carted off to labor camps, you can bet their families and comrades will seek answers. The Mainland has been brimming with discontent, and one spark is all it will take to set it off. That spark could be you. They have made you out to be either something scared conscripts have dreamed up, or an evil witch. Seeing you, hearing you in your own voice, hearing all you have gone through, hearing about the Red Queen and her Biters, could change that. Also, Satish had recorded Captain Tso's testimony. So far only some Red Guards have heard it on their radios. Now we can broadcast it to every citizen in the Mainland. But we have only a few minutes that the Americans can assure us of. So let's get started.'

Alice held the tablet in her hands after Danish had told her they were ready. The people of Wonderland were gathered around the TVs, and they saw the usual news broadcast and soap operas replaced by Alice's face. That same face was now being streamed into millions of homes in Shanghai, Guangzhou and Beijing.

Commissar Hu was in Shanghai, dreading his meeting

with the Central Committee the next morning, where he would have to explain how their plan to conquer Wonderland had turned into a bloody fiasco. He whirled around in shock as he heard the voice on TV. The most devastating salvo in this long and bloody war had been fired, not from a gun or a missile launcher, but from a small, glass covered room called the Looking Glass. That was perhaps appropriate because in any war against tyranny, the most effective weapon is not a bullet or missile but the freedom of information. Hu held his breath as Alice started speaking, her yellowed eyes looking straight at the camera.

'People of the Mainland, your Central Committee calls me a witch and a terrorist, but today I want to speak to you directly so that you may know the full truth of the war they have been waging. My name is Alice Gladwell, and this is my story.'

EPILOGUE

TWO MONTHS LATER

ALICE AND THOUSANDS OF OTHER citizens of Wonderland were at the airport, eagerly awaiting their visitors. Danish had reported that the plane had left Calcutta over two hours ago, and it could be arriving at any time. Vince was already airborne in his helicopter to watch for any Red Guards who might pose a problem, but that possibility was remote. Red Guards were seldom seen anywhere in the Deadland, though the people of Wonderland had learnt their lesson well. That lesson was the fact that freedom from the shadow of tyranny was not one that was earned or kept easily, but required constant vigilance. So Satish and his men were, as usual, roaming the Deadland in their jeeps and captured APCs, making sure that there was no danger lurking anywhere near Wonderland. Arjun and Alice had been busy helping repair the damage to Wonderland and making sure the many hundreds of wounded and displaced got medical care and new homes. Bunny Ears and the Biters still preferred to roam in the open spaces of the Deadland but every night they returned to the Reservation, where Alice would meet them and read to them from the charred and damaged book she carried.

Of all of them, only Danish felt as if he had little work to do any more. Alice's transmission had unleashed a firestorm of dissent in the Mainland. Crowds had gathered in the streets, demanding to know the truth. Friends and relatives of imprisoned Red Guards had attacked official buildings, and most disturbingly for the Central Committee, units of Red Guards had started to rise in open mutiny. Within weeks, the Central Committee had done what tyrannies often do: shut off the flow of information in the hope that would silence dissent. All networks from the Mainland were down and the TV showed only propaganda speeches of the Commissar and old footage of Red Guard parades and exercises. That did have one side benefit for the people of Wonderland: No longer slaves to soap operas beamed through the TVs, they quickly found other, perhaps more useful ways to spend their evenings.

Alice heard Vince on the radio.

'White Queen, the White Knight sees the White King approach.'

Alice strained to see a black speck in the sky, which soon resolved into a propeller driven airplane. Danish had been in daily contact with the Americans and knew that over the last month, they had converted Calcutta into a fully operational base, with a serviceable runway and a permanent detachment of Marines to guard it against any Red Guard attacks. For now, that was not really a worry, since the Red Guards seemed to have their hands more than full with the unfolding chaos in the Mainland.

The plane landed and taxied towards the old terminal

building. The thousands of people waiting burst into uproarious applause. A ladder was lowered, and a moment later Edwards descended. He smiled broadly at Alice and walked towards her, his arms outstretched.

'My girl, it can now finally be over.'

Alice had heard from Danish about how Edwards and his colleagues had used her blood samples to make a vaccine, which had already been tested on humans in America. Just the knowledge that what the Biters represented was not some supernatural evil but a disease that could be vaccinated against had proved to be a turning point in how people in America viewed Biters. Together with Alice's testimony, it had at one stroke done away with the fighting between man and Biter, and together with the turmoil in the Mainland had meant that the Red Guards had largely retreated from America as well. A cure was the next frontier, and Edwards was already working on it.

Next down was General Konrath. Alice had seen him before on video but this was the first time she had seen him in person. After they greeted each other, she and the general made a speech to the people gathered. A speech where the general reminded people that if any good had come out of the years of struggle and bloodshed, it was that people had learnt just how precious and fragile freedom could be.

That evening, the general was sitting with Alice and her friends in the Council building. He was to fly out the next morning, and the question he asked was one he had already posed twice before in the evening.

'Alice, are you sure you don't want to come along with us tomorrow morning? America was where your parents were from; that was your home.'

Alice shook his hand and smiled. 'No, thank you, General. I am already home.'

The next morning at the airport, General Konrath looked at the book at Alice's belt.

'Who would have guessed a book would have had so much power. Perhaps now we can begin to write and read books again. It would be a shame if our children forgot all that we fought for.'

'General, I've heard you were a writer before the Rising.'

The general smiled. 'Yes, I was a novelist. They started calling me General when I led the people in my neighborhood to start fighting back against the Red Guards. Alice, I am now old and tired of all the fighting. Perhaps it's time I got back to my old calling and wrote a book. It may well be the first book written after The Rising.'

'What's your book going to be about?'

Smiling, the general said, 'I still haven't thought it all through, but I do know what I'll call it.'

'What's that?'

'*Alice in Deadland.*'

Chen looked out of his one good eye to see who had come to his cell. He had already lost his right eye in the beatings that had followed his imprisonment, and his left eye was also almost closed shut due to swelling and dried blood. He could not walk very well anymore and had to be dragged out to the courtyard every morning, where he was beaten by the black clad Interior Security forces of the Central Committee. Where or how his wife was, he no longer knew. In one of his beatings, he had been told that she was also on her way to a labor camp. If that was the case, Chen prayed that she was already dead.

He heard something being dumped into his cell: a young

man in the blood-covered, tattered uniform of a Red Guard officer. The man looked at Chen and recognition flashed in his eyes.

'General Chen.'

Chen spat, a glob of blood hitting the floor, before he spoke.

'I am general to nobody now, young man. I just await the day they shoot me and end it all. Perhaps they have such a long list of people to execute that my turn has not yet come.'

Despite a broken nose and jaw, the officer spoke with a hint of a smile. 'Comrade General, you are very much still the commanding officer of the Ladakh based Red Guards. For the last month, I have been leading them in guerilla warfare against the liars in the Central Committee. We've assassinated four of those bastards and killed a dozen or more Interior Security officers, but it seems my luck ran out today. We still owe loyalty to you, General, and we were all inspired by the sacrifice you made to try and save all of us.'

Chen sat up straight, warmth permeating his body, bringing back emotions he had no longer thought himself capable of.

'What is your name, officer?'

The young man sat up, facing Chen, his back to the bars of the cell.

'Comrade General, my name is Captain Tso.'

'So what news of the outside, Captain?'

'The people rage against the Central Committee. Thousands of unarmed civilians have been killed in Shanghai and Beijing, but bullets cannot silence the cry for freedom. More and more Red Guards mutiny and follow my example. It is but a matter of time before the Central Committee falls.'

Chen smiled despite the pain. 'So it has been worth it after all. I had thought I would die a broken man who died for nothing.'

Tso smiled back. 'Comrade General, you should have been with me in Wonderland. In the midst of all the bloodshed and killing, I saw something wonderful, a view of how our nation can be and will be one day. People living free, ruled by those they choose, at peace with those different from themselves.'

A guard shouted from outside the cell, 'Shut up, you traitors! The Commissar himself is coming to meet you. I think today is the day you go to hell.'

But when the two guards outside began to whisper among themselves, Chen heard snippets of their conversation that gave away what was really happening.

'The mob's been building outside all morning. They want to free all the prisoners.'

'The Commissar has said we'll execute all of them and fly out in helicopters.'

Chen heard a few shots, which he thought meant the executions had begun. But then came the sound of assault rifles being fired on full auto. It sounded like a firefight had broken out outside the prison.

A few minutes later, the cell door opened and Commissar Hu walked in. He had lost a lot of weight and Chen noticed a pronounced limp in one leg.

'Good morning, Comrade Commissar. It seems being back in the warm fraternal embrace of the Central Committee has not agreed with you.'

Hu snarled and kicked Chen hard in the ribs.

'Shut up, you fool! Have your last laugh, for I shoot both of you traitors and put an end to your misery today!'

He called to the guards, and they entered. One of them pulled Tso to one side and the other held Chen up, holding his arms behind him. Chen looked at Tso and winked with his one good eye. For the last week, he had been carrying a razor sharp shard of glass he had picked up in the courtyard during one of his beatings. He had been trying to work up the courage to slit his own wrist and end it all. Now he knew he would get a chance to put it to another use. The man holding him was strong and young, but he was an Interior Security thug, the sum total of whose combat experience came down to beating civilian demonstrators.

As Hu took out the pistol from his holster, Chen rocked his head back, making solid contact with the guard's nose. It snapped. As the guard loosened his grip on him, Chen turned and slit the guard's throat with the shard of glass.

Fumbling with the safety, Hu leveled his gun – but too late. Chen grabbed his pudgy hand, snapping the wrist and taking the weapon from him. The guard holding Tso was reaching for his gun when Tso punched him hard in the face, sending him crashing against the bars. When he tried to get up, Chen shot him dead.

Hu was now on his knees, begging for mercy. Chen wanted to say something, to remind him of just how many lives men like him had ruined, but finally he realized that no words would do justice to the rage he felt. He kicked the blubbering Commissar down and shot him once in the head.

From outside came the heavy sounds of the Interior Security guards' boots, and the continuing sounds of the firefight raging outside the prison. Even if those outside were trying to get in and rescue the prisoners, Chen doubted they would get so far inside in time. However, he felt no fear. Indeed, he felt a sense of release wash over him as he contemplated his end. He looked at Tso and smiled as the officer saluted.

'Come, my son. Today we finally fight together one last time, but this time for something we believe in.'

As Chen took aim at the first guard to come down

the corridor, he realized that Hu had been so very wrong. Tyrannies fell not when people simply began to desire freedom, but when they had already attained one very special kind of freedom. Freedom from fear.

OFF WITH THEIR HEADS

THE PREQUEL TO ALICE IN DEADLAND

THE ACCIDENTAL QUEEN

'STAN, WHAT HAVE WE DONE?'

Dr. Protima Dasgupta was struggling to choke back her tears as she spoke to her colleague many thousands of miles away in the United States.

'Protima, I'm a bit busy. I'll talk to you later.'

Protima slammed her phone down. Even Stan, one of the most outspoken critics of the decision to use Sample Z in what the spooks had euphemistically called 'accelerated field tests', was no longer talking to her. She had spent more than twenty years of her life serving the United States Government, but it was as if her decision to leave the project and come back to India had burnt all bridges with friends and colleagues.

She walked unsteadily to the dining table and poured herself another glass of wine. She had been stupid to call Stan. It was likely his phone was tapped, but she was beyond caring now. She had argued that even if one disregarded the morality of using Sample Z on foreign populations, it was just too unstable to use yet. But of course, she had been overridden, and a week later, Global Hawk stealth drones had dropped canisters of the biological agent onto a Red Army garrison in Inner Mongolia.

Dr. Protima was not senior enough to be privy to the decision-making process, but she was senior enough to access some of the documents passed between her bosses and the men who had ordered the mission.

A shot across the bow to show them we still have an edge.

A reminder of who the superpower really is.

Those were two lines she remembered. Tensions between the US and China had reached a boiling point over the last year, with the US economy tottering and China reeling under increasing protests demanding democracy and human rights. The US had slammed the second Tiananmen Square massacre, only to be blamed by China for supporting what it called 'terrorist activity' in China to distract the US population from its economic woes. A humiliating bloody nose given to the US Navy off Taiwan had added injury to the considerable insult of the US economy having now been reduced to surviving on Chinese holding of its debt.

The fact that the garrison in Mongolia housed research facilities engaged in China's own biological warfare program was of scant consolation as Protima saw the chaos unfold on TV. When reports had come in of a strange virus spreading throughout Mongolia that turned people hyper-aggressive, attacking anyone in sight, she knew her worst fears had come true.

Sample Z had begun as a potential miracle cure for troops whose nervous systems had been badly damaged by battlefield injuries. Initial trials had been exciting, with troops doctors had given up on making recoveries to lead near-normal lives, and Protima had been exhilarated at being part of something that would help save thousands of lives. Then came the fateful meetings three years ago, when Protima and her team were asked to work on modifying Sample Z to incapacitate enemy troops, destroying their nervous systems and rendering them incapable of rational thought. A separate team had been working on another strain to dramatically enhance the strength and endurance of troops, turning them into berserkers immune to pain. Protima had warned that the differences between them were still not fully understood and the virus was very unstable. Ultimately, her objections had counted for little, and she had quit the program.

The scrolling news bar on the TV announced that there were at least ten thousand confirmed fatalities in China in the last week from the mysterious virus.

Protima turned off the TV and slept fitfully, dreaming of men with their faces peeling off, running towards her to attack her.

The next morning, she woke up to a beautiful summer morning, with the sun streaming through the windows of her hotel room. She pulled aside the curtains and saw the road already rapidly filling with the chaotic traffic that was the norm for New Delhi. She had a job interview at eleven o'clock, so she dressed quickly. She looked at herself in the mirror and for a moment she was looking at a stranger. Her grey hair was the same as usual, as were her lean, gaunt features. But her eyes, which normally sparkled with laughter, were now ringed with dark circles, and try as she might, she could not bring back the smile that had been a permanent feature on her face. After losing her husband in an accident several years ago, Protima had worked hard to recreate herself from the nervous wreck she had become, and she had almost succeeded, till the past few days.

But now she had another chance to start over. While some of her work, like Sample Z, would never be known outside a small group with the highest security clearances, she had been published widely in fields related to genetic engineering and had been given glowing references by her former bosses on the condition that she sign a very strict non-disclosure agreement. So she had no doubt she would get the job with a leading research institute using genetic engineering to improve crop yields to feed India's rural poor. Finally her experience and knowledge would be put to some good use.

She was in a taxi on her way to the interview when her phone rang. It was Stan.

'I should have left when you did. They're all dead. They're all dead.'

Protima sat up with a jolt. Stan was slurring, as if he had been drinking. 'Stan, calm down. What happened? Have you been drinking?'

'Lab 12 burned down a few hours ago. Most of the people there are dead, and the few that made it...'

Protima felt a chill going down her spine. Close friends of hers had worked at Lab 12, located just outside Washington, where Sample Z had finally been weaponized for use in China.

'I don't know if it was the Chinese retaliating for what we did or if our own government is covering its tracks...'

'Stan, stop! Please stop! We're on an open phone line.'

What Stan said next scared Protima more than she had ever been in her life. 'It doesn't matter. Nothing matters any more. What the news is saying about the outbreak in China is not even close to how bad it is. I've seen what happened to the survivors of Lab 12. Protima, it's like nothing we imagined. The media is trying to keep it quiet under government orders, but when the news breaks, it'll be too late. You need to save yourself and get the truth out. I've sent a package for you with files from our project and the orders to use it in weaponized form. There are also papers about experiments on prisoners in Afghanistan. Go and meet Gladwell at the Embassy there in New Delhi. He's an old friend and a good man.'

'You're in Washington. Why don't you get it to someone there?'

'It's too late for me now. They caught me printing out the files and I just managed to get away. They're here now. Goodbye, Protima.'

With that, the phone went silent. Protima tried calling him back, but there was no answer.

While she was waiting to be called in for the interview, Protima wondered if she would be able to go through with it. After what she had heard from Stan, she found it hard to concentrate. Her hands seemed to be shaking uncontrollably, and her heart was pounding. However, once she sat before the interview panel, she managed to control her nerves and her interview went very smoothly, but all the while she thought of Stan's call. When she got back to her hotel room, she checked the TV and the Internet, but there was no mention of the fire Stan had talked about. He seemed like he had been drinking, and he would have been hit hard by the use of their research in the Mongolia operation. Finally, she decided to get some fresh air and walked outside, sitting at a coffee shop overlooking the busy street.

It was now six in the evening, and the Delhi summer heat had begun to dissipate. Protima sipped on her coffee, contemplating her future. At the age of forty-seven, it seemed too late to make a fresh beginning, but she was going to try. She had left India more than twenty-five years ago, on a scholarship to the US for her Masters, and her work there had earned her an internship in the Centers for Disease Control and Prevention, working on studying viral strains. She had excelled there, and one day had been approached for a full-time position in the government, working on classified biological programs. Now, she would try and put that behind her. She would get an apartment, buy a car, and start afresh with her new job.

Protima was jolted out of her thoughts by the man at the next table exclaiming to a girl, 'Oh my God! Have you seen this video? They're saying the dead are coming back to life!'

Some wiseass at another table mumbled something about how he always felt like a zombie on Monday mornings, but nobody laughed.

Within minutes, dozens gathered around the young man who had the YouTube video playing on his phone. Several others were now checking the video on their own phones, and Protima saw from their horrified faces that something was very wrong. She was about to ask one of them what the matter was when the owner of the cafe shouted above the din.

'Folks, it's on CNN now. Just quiet down and let's see what they're saying.'

Protima edged towards the TV set up above the bar, and saw the familiar shape of the US Capitol Building in the background as the young news anchor adjusted her mike and looked at the camera. Protima had been in New York when 9-11 had happened, and she had seen how shaken the news anchors had been. This anchor had the same expression. Protima hushed two young girls next to her so she could hear what was being said.

'The Department of Homeland Security has said that it is premature to say whether the outbreak is a possible act of terror and has dismissed any link to the fire last night at a government lab featured in Wikileaks documents as a possible biological weapons research lab.'

The news cut to blurry mobile phone footage. The

moment Protima saw the group of men, she knew something was wrong. They seemed to be shuffling more than walking, with their heads and hands bent at strange angles, and occasionally one would violently jerk his head. Protima had seen those symptoms before, as side effects of Sample Z.

Two police officers walked into the path of the men and fired. Protima heard gasps around her as two of the men fell to the ground, their bodies jerking as bullet after bullet tore into them.

'Why are they shooting? What the hell is happening?'

Protima ignored the cries from those around her as she tried to think what might have happened. Clearly Stan had been right and there had been a fire at the lab. It was possible the vials of Sample Z might have been compromised and some people might have been infected. But why on Earth were the cops shooting at them?

That was when something even stranger happened.

The two men who had been hit by dozens of bullets got up and the group rushed towards the policemen, who ran in panic. Then the footage stopped. The anchor was back and was reading from a sheet of paper in her hands.

'The Department of Homeland Security has decided to place some affected neighborhoods of Washington under immediate curfew. Anyone seen outside without prior authorization after noon tomorrow will be presumed to be infected. They are requesting all citizens to cooperate while the authorities contain this outbreak.'

The anchor put the sheet down, and looked at the camera. Protima could tell this part was not scripted. The young woman crossed herself and said, 'God help us all.'

Protima spent a tortured night, trying to come to grips with the role she and her colleagues had played in unleashing the outbreak now devastating Washington. She tried to tell herself she had just been doing her job, but how would that make her any different from an accessory to murder? She tried calling Stan again, but his phone was switched off.

That night, as she watched events unfold on TV and the Internet, she realized there was no containing the outbreak. Cases began to be reported across the United States, and the symptoms were terrifyingly the same. Reports had been leaked of how the first infected had seemed to be dead, and then got up and attacked anyone in sight, biting and clawing them to infect them as well. Police were still maintaining their position that rumors of the infected being impervious to gunshots were unfounded, but more videos had been posted online.

When Protima went down to the lobby of the hotel, it was crammed with tourists and visiting businessmen. With the outbreak now reported in Canada and the United Kingdom, people were beginning to panic and trying to catch the first flights home so they could be with their families.

The Concierge greeted her as she passed. 'Dr. Dasgupta, a courier landed for you yesterday.'

The package was marked as diplomatic mail. She smiled, remembering Stan joking that he could never get into too much trouble no matter how insubordinate he was because he had a brother in-law in the Foreign Service. Clearly, Stan had been able to call in one last favor before... Protima stopped herself. Despite all that had happened, there was no proof anything bad had happened to Stan.

She opened the package and found a simple note addressed to her. It was in Stan's handwriting.

Dear Protima, if you're reading this letter then it's already too late for me. Just pray they have beer in heaven, or hell, or wherever people like me go.

When the pressure to weaponize Sample Z began, I got curious about what was going on. The upside is that I got my hands on these files, but the downside is that it's a matter of time before they get me. I don't know who to trust anymore. That's the reason I'm sending these to you instead of trying to get them to anyone in the government. I don't know if we can stop what is happening – it may be too late for that. But at least people will one day know the truth behind how we ruined our world.

Do as you see fit. You could try sharing it with the press, but I don't know how free our free press is any more. The people I reached out to didn't want to have anything to do with this. But do get it to Gladwell at the American Embassy. He's a good man, and he is very well-connected. He could at least help us get this to someone in the government who is not in on the conspiracy. This is all part of a plan, but I fear the men behind this don't fully understand what they are unleashing.

Take care, my friend.

Protima put the note aside and took a look at the documents, wondering how much of what Stan had written was true. As she read the first page, she grabbed the sofa behind her for support and sat down. She read non-stop for over an hour, reading each document more than once to make sure she was not mistaken about their contents.

As much as she would have liked to not believe them, the documents were devastatingly clear. There were transcripts of conversations, emails, and minutes of meetings.

What Protima, Stan and their colleagues had been working on had been a very small part of a grand plan that was both awe-inspiring and terrifying in equal measure. Vials of Sample Z had been taken to remote bases in Afghanistan for human testing. The men who had ordered the use of Sample Z in China had known its likely effects much better than Protima had realized. But in keeping the scientists out of the loop, it seemed they had totally underestimated how the virus would behave once it was transmitted from one person to another.

Protima closed her eyes, her head throbbing. Could men really condemn millions to death for a plan that called for gradual repopulation to deal with the issue of scarce oil and other resources? Could the same men seek to quell rising discontent about the ruin the financial elite had brought to the West by creating such an environment of fear that people would gladly accept any form of tyranny? Was it possible that they had managed to forge some sort of partnership with sections of the Chinese government who were struggling to contain their own people's calls for democracy? The documents in front of Protima made it amply clear that was exactly what had happened.

The final contents of the package were two small vials containing a red liquid. Protima knew what they were. The vaccines they had been working on to protect against Sample Z. They were untested, but in sending them, Stan had at least given her a shot at life.

A commotion started around her. Several men and women were standing, pointing at a TV in the corner of the lobby. The first case of the outbreak had been reported in India. With millions of people traveling by air every day, and many in the neighborhoods surrounding Lab 12 not even aware of the risks, there was no telling how far and how fast the outbreak would spread.

Now that the outbreak had begun to spread globally, Protima knew she had very little time. She dialed the American Embassy to get an appointment with Gladwell.

'They say the disease makes people into demons who cannot be killed. My cousin saw a man at the airport who bit a dozen others and the police kept shooting him but couldn't put him down. You're lucky that your destination is on the way to my home. You are my last passenger for now. After I drop you, I'm going straight there and staying put with my family till they figure this out.'

The last thing Protima needed was a talkative taxi driver. Protima just nodded, but that seemed to encourage the man.

'I gave a lift to two Army officers, and they told me they were being called up for duty. But they also said they were getting contradictory orders. Nobody in the government has any idea what to do.'

Protima didn't envy anyone who was trying to deal with the unfolding situation. Any outbreak of a highly contagious disease, let alone one with such unpredictable and terrifying effects, was best nipped in the bud. Identify the core outbreak, quarantine those infected and contain the spread till the strain was better understood. In this case, it was way too late for that. The infection had spread globally, and after what Protima had just read, it was a fair bet some elements in the government had actively aided in its spread.

As she looked out the windows, the streets of Delhi were packed with policemen. But she shook her head as she saw that they had come prepared for riot control, with batons and shields. If the outbreak spread here, they would be of little use.

As the taxi turned towards the American Embassy, the taxi driver shouted, 'There's no way they will let me get any closer. You'll have to walk from here.'

Roadblocks manned by Indian policemen barred their

entry to the approach road. Protima saw that the Marines who guarded the Embassy were now gathered at the gate, all armed with automatic rifles, and she saw movement on the roof, which could have been snipers. Clearly they were not taking any chances. As she tried to go towards the Embassy building, one of the policemen stopped her.

'This area is now closed to the public.'

Protima pleaded that she had an appointment at the Embassy but that did not seem to have any impact. Finally, she took out her American passport. 'Look at this, please. I am of Indian origin but hold an American passport. You cannot stop me from going to the US Embassy.'

The policeman looked like he was in doubt, but he was saved from having to make a decision by one of the Marines jogging over from the Embassy gates. 'Ma'am, please come with me.'

He jogged back without waiting for Protima and she walked as fast as she could. Closer to the Embassy, she saw the same emotion she had seen in the policeman's eyes. Fear.

The Marines might have looked intimidating from afar, with their weapons and body armor, but up close, most of them were very young, and they looked terrified. She was ushered into the main building, where she walked up to the receptionist.

'Excuse me, I have an appointment with the Chief of Mission, Robert Gladwell.'

The receptionist asked Protima to wait while she called Gladwell's office. Protima sat down in the lobby, which was packed with US citizens who had come to the Embassy to seek refuge and try and get home. A woman was sobbing, her head buried in her husband's chest as he tried to comfort her. Protima caught only a few snatches of their conversation before they passed her. 'Martha, all flights are cancelled. We can't get out for now. The kids will be okay...'

The TV was playing CNN. The footage showed burning buildings somewhere and Protima walked closer to hear what was being said.

'Chinese and US naval forces have skirmished off the coast of Taiwan on the same day Israel claimed to have shot down two Iranian missiles. The President has ordered all US forces to be ready to deal with the unfolding crisis, and the Department of Homeland Security has reinstated the color-coding for the threat level to the US Mainland, declaring it to be red. In a separate announcement, the Department of Homeland Security has declared that many internal security duties are to be handed to the private military contractor firm Zeus, as US military forces were needed to deal with the multiple international crises that threaten to escalate to all-out war in Asia and the Middle East. One of the first actions of Zeus has been to forcibly disband all Occupy protests, saying that they suck up precious resources needed to control the outbreak and also that crowds spread the outbreak. Many civil rights activists protested, saying private armies cannot be used to silence US citizens' fundamental rights to free speech and assembly. The spread of the outbreak continues unabated, and the Center for Disease Control has said it will stop issuing casualty figures as they are growing at such an exponential rate.'

Protima sat down, her hands shaking as they gripped the package. The plans outlined in the documents Stan had sent her were unfolding right before her eyes.

Someone coughed to get her attention and she looked up to see the receptionist. She was an aging Indian woman who had dark circles under her eyes and looked dog-tired.

'Dr. Dasgupta, I'm afraid Mr. Gladwell is unable to meet you now. As you know, things are busy here and he has some urgent matters to attend to.'

Protima felt her heart sink. 'I had an appointment with him. I just need to meet him for a couple of minutes.'

The receptionist was polite but Protima sensed she was being evasive. 'I'm sorry, but he himself has asked me to cancel this meeting. I can't help you.'

There was no way she was going away without giving the documents to Gladwell. Protima tried again, pleading with the receptionist. 'Please, please give me just two minutes with him. I don't even need to talk to him. I just need to give him some very important documents.'

'Dr. Dasgupta, I presume. Chief Gladwell asked me to apologize for not being able to meet you, but if I can help you in any way, please let me know.'

Protima turned towards the deep, gravely voice to find herself looking up at a tall, bald man built like a tank who completely dwarfed her. He was wearing a military uniform and even indoors his eyes were covered by wraparound sunglasses.

'Ma'am, my name is Major John Appleseed, and I can pass on whatever you wanted to give to Bob.'

With the unthinking trust most people had for men in uniform, Protima held out the parcel, but as he grabbed it, she paused. Stan had told her to give the package only to Gladwell. She started to retract her hand, but Appleseed held on. There was still a smile on his lips, but his voice had a hard edge to it now.

'I said I will take it from here.'

Their impasse was broken when somebody shouted and Protima turned to look at the TV. A news channel was broadcasting live from the gardens surrounding India Gate, in the very heart of Delhi. There was the sound of gunfire and of people screaming and as the cameraman zoomed in, Protima saw a group of men walking in a shuffling gait, many of them covered in blood. The camera zoomed in again and she saw that one of them had half his face torn off. More people in the reception screamed, and someone bumped into Appleseed, throwing him off balance for a second. Before he could recover, Protima was running out the door, heading into a city that, like many others around the world, was now faced with its worst nightmare – a highly contagious, deadly virus that turned people into raging monsters.

Protima managed to get a cab that took her halfway to her hotel, but the driver refused to go any further, saying it was too dangerous. Protima tried hailing other cabs, but nobody stopped. As she walked along the road, she saw that the policemen outside had disappeared. Some small shops across the street were being looted and an old man was lying on the ground. There seemed to be no law and order in sight, and she realized that she was alone and defenseless in the middle of a city that had given into terror and anarchy.

A commotion began further down the street and a man staggered onto the street. His clothes were torn and he was bleeding from a gash on his neck. He cried out to her for help but before she could cross the street, he fell to the ground. A woman emerged from the bushes behind him. She was covered in blood, with the shuffling gait of the infected, and her eyes were vacant and yellow. She shrieked as she saw Protima and began to cross the road to reach her. The wounded man, whom Protima had assumed to be dead, sat up and turned towards her. His eyes had a similar blank expression and he too screamed and got up to chase Protima.

Protima was now running as fast as she could, her heart hammering. She stumbled and fell, scraping her right knee on the pavement. She turned to see the bloodied couple still following her, and she scrambled to her feet, ignoring the pain in her knee as she started running again. After a few minutes, she stopped to catch her breath, and saw that the couple were now far behind. Protima bent over, her breath coming in jagged gasps, thankful that the infected did not seem to move very fast. Protima saw an abandoned bicycle and began pedaling it, hoping that getting back to the hotel would mean at least some period of safety for her to consider what to do next.

As she rode, she saw all around her the signs of a city that was tearing itself apart. Several pillars of smoke rose above the city's skyline and people were running all around, and every now and then she got terrifying glimpses of groups of the infected, hunting people down like packs of wild animals. There were no policemen or troops in sight, though Protima wondered what good they would have been against an enemy that could not be killed.

She finally met a small group of policemen huddled near a shop. The officer had a pistol in his hand, and the four constables with him were carrying rifles. The officer waved her down.

'Miss, you can't go that way, the entire neighborhood is crawling with Biters.'

'I need to get to the Taj Hotel.'

The officer shook his head sadly. 'Miss, from what I hear, there are Biters running wild around there. Why don't you go home?'

There was no longer any home for her. Protima got on the bike and rode in a different direction, no longer sure of what she would do or where she would go. When she had learned of the plan outlined in Stan's documents, she had agreed with his assessment that the men who had planned this were playing with fire. But now having seen firsthand what the infection did to people, she feared there was no real way to contain it. Like a wildfire, it would consume everything in its path before it burned itself out.

She had been so lost in her thoughts that she almost did not notice the black SUV just a few meters behind her and closing fast. It careen towards her and she swerved out of the way just before it could hit her bike. The front windows were down, and she could see the driver and one more man. Both were Caucasian, wearing dark suits and wraparound sunglasses. She had seen many men like them during her time in Washington. Government agents.

At first, she thought nearly knocking her down was an accident but then the driver leaned out. In his hand was a pistol. Protima was so startled that she lost her balance and the bike hit a bump on the sidewalk, sending her sprawling to the ground. That saved her life as the man fired and the bullet slammed into the wall over Protima's head. The man was shouting something, but Protima's ears were still ringing from the gunshot and she could not fully understand what he was saying.

Protima sat against the wall, shocked. No US government agents would be openly shooting at someone in the streets of Delhi.

The driver stopped the SUV and got out, walking towards her, the gun pointed at her. The second man remained in the car, but he now had a gun pointed at her as well. The man stood over her and said, 'Dr. Protima, I believe you have a package for us.'

Realization dawned on Protima as she recalled the confrontation she had with Appleseed back at the embassy. She stood up gingerly, feeling her ankle. The man's expression was inscrutable behind his dark glasses.

'Who are you? What right do you have to attack an American citizen?'

The man smiled. 'Look, Doctor, I don't want this to be any more difficult than it has to be. You're in way over your head here and you have no idea about just how far my bosses can go to get the material you have in your hands. Just give me the damn package and you won't hear from us again.'

It would be tempting to hand over the package, but could she live with the knowledge that she had done nothing? Tens of thousands had already died, and God alone knew how many more would die before it was all over. Her heart pounding, she took a step back. 'Young man, I have no doubt you could take this from me, but I will not hand it to you.'

The next thing Protima knew, she was on the ground, her head splitting with pain and warm blood flowing down the side of her face. The man raised his gun again.

'Look, lady, I don't take any pleasure in hitting old women, but I do need to do this.'

He leaned down to grab the package from Protima's hand. That was when his partner screamed from inside the SUV.

'Greg, they're coming. Hurry up!'

Protima looked beyond the man in front of her to see a crowd of at least twenty of the infected converging on the car. A couple of men in bloodied and tattered suits were mixed up with men and women wearing the rags of slum dwellers. They all had that vacant expression and many of them had blood from other victims running down the sides of their mouths. The man inside the car fired again and again, and three or four men went down, only to get back up within seconds. The man inside the car was screaming as he was pulled out and the crowd tore into him, clawing at him and biting into his face.

'Goddamn Biters!' the man in front of Protima growled. He shouted into his earpiece. 'We're under attack by Biters. Are there any other Zeus units nearby who could help?'

Zeus. Protima had heard that name before somewhere, but she had no time to think as some of the infected now came around the car towards her. The man in front of her pointed his gun at the approaching crowd, shooting several times till his magazine emptied. All he did was enrage them further, and they began to emit a high-pitched screech as they surrounded him. Protima took advantage of the situation to get back on her bike, and she pedaled away, forcing herself not to look back even when she heard the man's screams and cries for mercy.

Now all around her she saw signs of the infection spreading. There were several dead bodies littering the street, and two of the infected wrestled down and killed a large man who had tried to fight back. She realized that while they first tried to infect others by biting them, any significant resistance led them to kill their prey.

Tears were freely streaming down Protima's face as the world fell apart. When people at the highest levels of government had brought about such a catastrophe, what hope did a frail old woman like her have of fighting back?

Two more of the infected crossed her path, and she turned her bicycle sharply to the right to avoid them. Biters. That was what the man who had attacked her had called them. She wondered, as the infection spread around the world and more and more people fell to it, would people give it a name? Some terrible infections in the past had been trivialized by the names they had been given – bird flu, swine flu. What would this scourge be called? Would there even be enough people left to give it a name?

Now, further away from the open spaces around the Embassy, she had entered a congested market. Khan Market, if her memory served. The closely packed shops and cars parked in front of them had made it a deathtrap. Hundreds of Biters milled around and a few corpses lay around the front of the shops. A small group of policemen had tried to make a stand and Protima almost gagged at what remained of them – little more than the bloody shreds of their khaki uniforms.

The front wheel of her bicycle caught on something and her bike buckled under her. She was thrown forward, landing hard on the ground. The wind knocked out of her, Protima scrambled to get up, but slipped and fell again. She had attracted the attention of a few Biters and they were converging on her. She felt around and found a rock the size of her fist. The nearest Biter was now no more than a dozen feet away, a thin man with half his face ripped off wearing a bloodied and torn suit. Protima threw the rock as hard as she could, and it hit the Biter squarely on the head. He staggered back, but then he looked at her with vacant, red eyes and screamed, blood tricking down the sides of his mouth. Four others joined him and they came towards Protima.

Protima tried to scream for help, but not a sound came out. She tried to get back on her feet but a cold, clammy hand grabbed her leg. Suddenly, someone else grabbed her and yanked her back. Protima pulled away, but whoever was holding her was too strong. She found herself looking into the face of a young man wearing large rabbit ears on top of his head.

'Come on!'

He pulled her behind him on his bike and as the Biters roared in anger, he rode away at high speed.

For several seconds, Protima did not say anything. Instead

she just clutched her unlikely savior, thankful for her narrow escape. Finally, the man spoke.

'Look, I need to get to my girlfriend's place. Where can I drop you?'

Protima's mind was a blank. Where could she go that was safe? Was anywhere safe any more?

The man spoke, a tinge of irritation in his voice. 'You must have a home or a family somewhere?'

Protima started to say something but all that came out was a stifled sob. The man stopped the bike and turned to look at her, his voice considerably softer.

'I'm sorry. Things are crazy and I just want to make sure she's okay. I'll drop you wherever you want, just tell me where.'

Protima got her first good look at him and realized that he was very young, perhaps a college student, with kind eyes.

'Young man, you have done quite enough for me. Just drop me ahead near the India International Center. It doesn't yet look overrun and I can see a lot of policemen in front of it.'

He took her near the gate and as she dismounted, he smiled.

'There must be something really important in that packet you're carrying. You didn't let go.'

Protima looked at the bundle of documents she was carrying. Having failed to give them to Gladwell, did they really matter any more? Given how deep the conspiracy ran, would it have mattered even if she had been able to meet him? She wished the man luck as he rode away.

A dozen police constables stood in front of the India International Center. Normally the venue of high-profile conferences and meetings, it was more than likely that there were high-level government officials or diplomats stranded inside. That would certainly explain the security, though Protima doubted the policemen would be much use. Several of them were huddled around a radio, and they looked terrified.

One of them saw her approach and beckoned her. 'Come inside, but I doubt any place is safe now. Not after what's happening around the world.'

Protima thought he meant the spread of the infection and she told him of what she had seen in the city. When she mentioned that the Biters seemed to be killing those who tried to resist being converted, she saw more than one of the policemen visibly blanch. The one who had spoken to her pointed to the radio and said, ' It's not just the bloody monsters, the whole world seems to have lost its mind.'

'What do you mean?'

When Protima asked him what he meant, he answered, a haunted expression in his eyes.

'Some elements in the Pakistani army launched nuclear missiles against our forward areas. It seems that Iran also launched missiles at Israel. It's not clear what exactly is going on but I think a nuclear war is either breaking out, or is taking place as we speak.'

Protima stood, chilled by what she had heard. The conspiracy behind the spread of the infection was one thing. Did laying waste to large parts of the world through nuclear exchanges also figure as part of the 'depopulation' plan? And if it did, what hope was left at all for anyone?

Protima walked into the complex. People wandered around as if dazed. There were a few foreign diplomats, several people who had gathered for a book discussion and many members who had come with their families for lunch.

Now they were trapped in a city that was fast becoming a slaughterhouse. Some people huddled around a TV in the library. The news was on, and the anchor was facing the camera and reading from a prepared script. All pretense of normality had been discarded – her clothes were crumpled, she wore no makeup, and the dark circles under her eyes were obvious. As someone off-camera prompted her, she began reading.

'The infection is continuing to spread, and many cities are now totally cut off from all communication with the outside world. After the nuclear strike on Tel Aviv and retaliatory strikes on Tehran, the Middle East is in the grip of an all-out war. The Chinese government has for the first time publicly accused the United States of being behind this crisis by using illegal biological agents, a charge the US has denied. Tensions in the waters of Taiwan are high after two Chinese planes were shot down after approaching a US carrier. Closer to home...'

The woman paused and looked up at the camera, her eyes betraying just how horrified she was at the news she had been handed.

'Closer to home, rogue elements in the Pakistani military took advantage of the chaos to launch tactical nuclear weapons at two forward operating bases of the Indian Army. The Prime Minister has condemned the action and said that India will react with appropriate measures.'

Protima sat down against the wall, and while close to a hundred people were packed into the library, not a single word was said. What was there to say? Every single one of them was thinking the same thing Protima was – there was no longer any hope. It was only a matter of time before either the Biters got them or the unfolding nuclear madness claimed them.

Someone got up to turn off the TV, but several others pleaded with him to keep it on. A compromise was reached, and while the TV was kept on, it was put on mute. Protima kept staring at the screen, hypnotized. The worst nightmares of the human race were coming true, with visuals of nuclear mushroom clouds interspersed with the now-familiar images of marauding packs of Biters ravaging entire cities.

She was shaken out of her stupor by a man shouting at the top of his voice outside the library. A Caucasian man, his face reddening, shouted to no one in particular.

'I am the bloody Defense Attaché of the United Kingdom. I cannot be holed up here like an animal. Someone get on the phone to the bloody High Commission and tell them to get me out!'

Nobody stirred, and a woman tried to pacify him as his shouting gave way to sobs and he collapsed. It would take time to sink in that ranks and badges of status no longer counted for much.

A helicopter passed overhead and several people got up, shouting excitedly, pointing out the window.

'They've come to get us out!'

'Finally, we're saved!'

Protima looked out the window, and her heart sank. It was a small, black helicopter, certainly not one that could carry more than a couple of passengers. A single man stepped out, wearing black sunglasses and a dark suit. The British Attaché had raced out of the building and met the man as he approached the library. Protima strained to hear their exchange.

'Thank God you're here. Get me out. I'm the British Defense Attaché.'

The man who had just arrived fished into his pocket to take out a photograph, which he showed to the British diplomat.

'Have you seen this woman? Our aerial team saw her headed here.'

Protima felt her mouth go dry as she saw that the photograph was hers.

Getting no answer, the man pushed the diplomat out the way and walked towards the library. The British diplomat took the man by his shoulder, spinning him around.

'How dare you push me? Which government do you represent?'

The man calmly reached into his suit, took out a pistol and shot the diplomat in the head. Then he continued walking towards the library. Several people had witnessed the scene and screams rang out all around Protima as people scrambled towards the back of the library. The door swung open and the man walked inside. His eyes locked on Protima and he smiled.

'Doctor, I had hoped to meet you here. Now, will you be kind enough to hand me the package or should I take it from you?'

There was a sudden barrage of firing outside and the man turned to see what was going on. That gave Protima the time to run deeper into the library. Hiding behind a bookshelf, she saw the man talk into his earpiece.

'She's here, but looks like the Biters are at the gate. I'll get the package and be out in a minute. Bloody Biters are everywhere.'

There was another rattle of gunfire and then it stopped. Protima thought of the policemen at the gate, but for now her greater concern was survival. She went deeper into the library, people screaming and sobbing all around her. The man pursuing her was now just feet away and through the gaps between the books, Protima saw the library door open once more. She caught a glimpse of khaki police uniforms and was about to call out for help when she stopped. The ones who had just entered the library were no longer policemen,. They had blood all over their tattered uniforms, and they shuffled inside the library, emitting low-pitched moans.

The Zeus agent turned and fired at the approaching Biters, and a couple of them went down. But there were too many of them entering the library and the people inside were screaming in panic, producing an ear-splitting crescendo. Protima didn't wait to see what happened. She ran further towards the back of the library. That was when she saw the vent. She pulled it open, breaking a couple of her nails in the process, and scrambled inside, crawling on all fours. From behind her came screams and the sickening sounds of teeth tearing into human flesh. Protima kept crawling and turned a corner, finding herself in total darkness. She clutched the package tighter, and moved forward, trying to feel ahead of her with her free hand. The floor moved under her hand and she tried to put more pressure on it to see how stable it was. The next thing she knew, a whole section of the piping gave way and she fell. She hit her head on something, and then there was darkness.

Protima woke up face down in something wet, her head aching terribly. She was lying in a pool of her own blood. As she tried to get her bearings, she realized she was lying in near-total darkness with a foul stench all around her. She felt a stab of panic as she tried to remember what had happened to the package she had been carrying. She felt around her for the envelope and clutched it to her chest as she sat up. Protima reached into her pocket to take out her mobile phone. As she shone it around her, she saw that she was inside drainage pipes or perhaps sewers. She had lost all track of time in her flight from the Biters, but with the mobile showing that it was now past seven in the evening, she must have been out for several hours. She drifted in and out of consciousness for some time before she finally managed to get herself up and walk down the tunnel.

Holding the mobile in front of her like a torch, she proceeded down the tunnel. She tried to brush away the wetness around her eyes, and when she saw the red smear on her hand, Protima gasped. She had no idea how badly she had been hurt, but there was no way for her to stop and check. She had to get to... safety. She stopped herself at that thought. There was no safety for her. If the Biters did not get her, the Zeus agents would.

She sat down against the wall, trying to collect her thoughts. Her stomach was rumbling, but hunger was the least of her worries. She had to push on and hope she could find a way up to the surface soon. What she would do then she forced herself not to think about.

Something brushed past her leg and she screamed, only to realize it had been a rat. When man had finished destroying civilization, perhaps rats would reclaim what remained. She got up and walked on, flashing her mobile in front of her every once in a while. It was now past two in the morning according to the display on her phone, but down here time did not matter. It was dark, with the floor covered in slime and puddles of water. Finally, unable to walk any more, Protima curled up against a wall and slept.

When she woke up, for a minute she hoped it had all been a nightmare and perhaps she was back in her hotel room. However, the musty odor and her dark surroundings told her that her nightmare was only too real. She walked some more, but realized that unless she ate or drank something, she would not last long. Water was more important to keep herself hydrated, so she forced herself to take a drink from a puddle of water. It smelt terrible and had a metallic tinge to it, but she forced it down.

Her fear and disorientation had given way to anger. Anger at the men who had brought so much destruction upon her and millions of others. No matter what it took, she would survive and get the truth out. She pushed on and smiled for the first time in many days as she saw a flicker of light up ahead. She could not tell how far it was, but at least there was hope. Her stomach continued to growl and she felt faint with exhaustion and hunger, but she kept going.

When she came closer to the light, she screamed in frustration. The beacon of hope she had been following was a single hole about a few inches in diameter in the roof through which daylight was streaming in. Protima sat down against the wall, drained of energy and hope. She tried to get back up but her legs did not have the strength. Through the light streaming into the tunnel, she took a look around and saw what appeared to be grass or leaves lying near her feet. The wind must have carried them through the hole in the roof. She picked them up, trying to determine if they were edible. Having already drunk the filthy gutter water, Protima was beyond the point where taste mattered, but she didn't want to eat something that could make her sick or worse.

She smiled a bit as the smell brought back long-lost memories of joints smoked surreptitiously in college. Ganja leaves were abundant in this part of India, and while they could not sustain her for long, it was better than dying of hunger. She bit down on the leaves and ate about half of them within seconds, tucking the rest into her pockets for later. A short nap later, she resumed her journey.

After a few more hours of walking, she began to feel

giddy. Whether it was exhaustion or the ganja, she did not know, but she held onto the wall for support. Protima saw shadows ahead of her and called out, but there was nobody else there. She heard her husband call out to her, which was impossible. She stopped again, her head spinning, and sat down and took a nap before continuing.

As much as she knew it was messing with her head, hunger and desperation won over rational thought and Protima finished the rest of the ganja leaves over the next two meals. She thought she had been down for more than three or four days, but it was impossible to tell. More than once she saw light up ahead, only to find nothing more than small holes. She wondered what the world up there was like, whether there were any more people left, or if the whole world had now been infested with Biters. She wondered what the men who had brought this upon the world were doing now.

She sat down once again, trying to clear her head. She had found more ganja leaves, and they had left her in a dreamlike state. She knew she was hallucinating when she saw her husband, but it was beginning to feel good. She welcomed the thought that she was not alone down here. So when she heard her husband's voice, she would answer back.

That was when she heard the shuffling noises up ahead. Her mind snapped, as if waking from a dream. This was no ganja-induced hallucination.

She was not alone.

By now her eyes had begun to adjust to the dark and she saw a flicker of movement ahead of her where the tunnel curved to the left. She took out her mobile phone and held it in front of her, but its feeble light did little to illuminate whoever was coming her way.

'Hello, who's there?'

Protima regretted the words the moment they left her

mouth for her question was answered by a series of grunts and screeches. Down here, in the dark and in the endless tunnels, there was no escape. The growls and grunts ahead intensified as the Biters came towards her with increasing speed. She saw several figures moving towards her in the light her mobile threw out and she turned to run. Biters were not exactly known for their speed, but down here, trapped and with her mind numb with fear, the Biters would not need much speed to catch up with her.

She kept running, her heart pounding, trying to ignore the howling coming from the pursuing Biters. She held her mobile up to see what lay ahead and her heart sank. She was approaching a dead end. The Biters were now no more than a dozen feet away. There seemed to be at least three or four of them. For a moment Protima was paralyzed with fear, with the injustice of having her life snuffed out in a sewer. Then a thought came to her. As the Biters shuffled closer, she reached into the package she had been carrying and took out one of the vials Stan had sent. She had no idea if it would work, but if there was even a slim chance she could survive to unmask a conspiracy that had led to the deaths of untold thousands, she would take it.

The nearest Biter was now almost within touching distance and Protima gagged at the stench of decay. She opened the vial and drank its contents in one long swallow. A burning sensation worked its way down her throat, but she did not have much time to contemplate what the liquid was doing to her. A callused and bloody hand grabbed her shoulder and pushed her down. The next thing she felt was the sharp pain of teeth biting down on her arms. The other Biters gathered around her prone body, and as more of them bit into her, Protima screamed again and again. Tears were flowing down her cheeks as she felt her eyes closing. Then she saw no more.

Protima opened her eyes and sat up in a panic, expecting the Biters to be still around her. There was no sign of them. Her phone was lying by her side, and when she picked it up, the screen was cracked, but there was still a faint light coming from the display. The battery was likely almost dead and she passed the phone over her body, seeing bloody bite marks all over her upper arms and chest. The blood had largely dried, telling her that she must have been out for several hours at least. The weird thing was that while she was bloody and mangled like a freshly butchered animal, she felt no pain. Had the vaccine worked? She gathered up the courage and spoke out aloud.

'Hello, my name is Protima and I am definitely not a bloody Biter.'

As her own voice echoed back to her in the tunnel, she burst out into uncontrollable laughter. She had not been transformed into a Biter after all! As she began walking down the tunnel, she found her earlier fatigue and hunger had disappeared. She was feeling reinvigorated with a spring in her step. What had the vaccine done to her?

The Biters must have come down into the tunnels somehow, so there must be an exit. She broke into a near-run, eager to escape her underground prison.

After fifteen minutes, she saw light ahead. Part of her was wary that this would turn out to be another hole in the ceiling but she kept going, and soon she saw that it was an opening to the outside world. A small ladder led up to a circular manhole. Protima tucked the package under one arm and climbed up.

After so much time in the darkness, the daylight blinded her. When she forced her eyes open, she saw she was near the Yamuna river, with the Commonwealth Games village to her right and the large Akshardham temple complex a few hundred meters away. She was more than fifteen kilometers away from the India International Center where she had fallen into the underground tunnels. Just how long had she been underground? Her mobile phone was long out of battery and she had lost her watch somewhere down there. Between the extreme fatigue and hunger and the hallucinations brought on by the ganja leaves, she had fuzzy memories of how long she had wandered underground till the Biters found her.

As she looked around, it struck her just how silent it was. Normally, the bridge in front of her would have been full of cars and trucks, honking their horns so much one would be forgiven for believing that was a prerequisite to getting a driver's license. There would have been children flitting around the huts on the side of the road, where their parents would have been hawking whatever they could – motorcycle helmets, coconuts, magazines. The huts were there, but there were no people in sight. Vehicles were strewn all over the bridge as if a child had scattered them around after playing with them and forgotten to put them away. As Protima approached the bridge, she realized that there were people there after all; it was just that they were not alive any more. The stench of death permeated the whole area and decomposed bodies lay in the cars and on the bridge.

A school bus stood abandoned on the side of the road and Protima wondered if any of the children had made it to safety. She walked closer, and was shocked as she heard a whimper, quickly cut off. Protima called out, 'If you're in there, I mean no harm. Come out and we can help each other.'

Someone moved inside. Her hopes lifted for the first time

in days. The prospect of meeting another human being was so exciting that she threw caution to the wind and ran towards the bus. A small girl emerged first, perhaps no more than five years old. Behind her was a young woman. Both were cut and bleeding, but looked to have avoided serious injury. The little girl took a step towards Protima but the woman held her back with a hand on her shoulder, her expression changing to undisguised horror. She screamed and broke out into sobs.

'What's wrong? Are you hurt?'

The little girl was now staring at Protima and she spoke in a hoarse whisper.

'This Biter talks, Mama.'

Protima stopped, stunned at the words. That was when she caught a look at her reflection in one of the bus's windows. A gasp escaped her lips as she realized what had happened to her. She sat down on the ground, stunned. The vaccine. Was this what it had done to her? Death would have been preferable to the monster staring back at her in her reflection. She had not felt any hunger or fatigue after being bitten, and she had thought it had something to do with the vaccine. It perhaps did, because while she could still think and speak like a human, she looked like a Biter. Her eyes were yellowing, and seemed to be devoid of any expression, and when Protima tried to force a smile, she recoiled at the hideous grimace that was reflected back.

It was then that Protima realized another element of her humanity she had lost. Try as she might, she could no longer cry.

Protima jerked her head up as the familiar shuffling of Biters approached. She peered past the side of the bus and saw a crowd of more than a dozen Biters. She flattened herself against the bus, hoping the Biters would pass. The Biters walked on by, emitting growls and screeches, and

Protima kept willing them on.

That was when the little girl inside the bus coughed. The Biters stopped in their tracks. Protima was lying flat on the ground, watching from beneath the bus, as one or two took steps towards the bus. One of them, a large man with most of his scalp missing and his face covered in blood, screamed and the others began moving towards the bus. Protima knew what would happen to the girl and her mother if the Biters got to them. If the mother tried fighting back, she would be torn apart, and then the girl would either meet a similar fate or become another monster like the Biters. With all the death and devastation Protima had seen, what was the life of one little girl worth?

With that thought, Protima stopped herself. No, she had to do something, anything. She stepped out from behind the bus and stood between the mob of Biters and the bus.

The large man bared his bloodied teeth and screamed something at her. Protima was shocked as she thought she understood what he was trying to say. He was telling her that the prey inside the bus was his. He towered over Protima as he approached, the others following him. Protima felt around herself for something she could use as a weapon. Her hands felt something hard and she picked it up. She held it above her head and screamed at the Biters.

'Stand back! You will not move forward!'

The Biter was now just feet away from her and her impact on him was immediate. He stepped back as if he had been jolted by electricity. The other Biters had stopped, and one or two of them began to whimper. Perhaps it was seeing someone like them who could talk like a human, or perhaps it was the simple fact that someone had taken charge. Whatever the reason, the Biters began to step back as Protima walked towards them. At any other time, it would have seemed absurd to Protima – a pack of bloodthirsty Biters falling back before a frail old woman – but now she had only one thought in her mind: she had to save the little girl.

The large Biter got up, snarling at Protima, and was about to lunge when Protima swatted him with the object in her hand.

'I said no. No!'

Later, Protima would wonder where she got the courage and strength from, but at that moment she felt as if she could have taken on a dozen Biters in hand-to-hand combat. The Biter shrank before her as she swatted at him again.

Much later, she would come to realize that every pack needed a leader. She was the first and only Biter who had been able to order them around. The object she was holding would also become a symbol of her authority.

A roaring sound filled the sky as four jets flew towards the city center. They dived in and pulled up in steep dives, and fireballs erupted where their bombs had hit. The government was bombing what had been densely populated civilian areas.

The Biters were still kneeling before her and even the large one was now keeping his head down. She called out to the woman and the girl in the bus, but received no answer. They had slipped out. Protima doubted they could last long, but she had done all she could.

Some figures came into view to her right as a long line of Biters emerged from the nearby fields. They moved as a group now, with some sense of co-ordination. They attacked humans on sight, yet they resembled wild animals more than the monsters people had taken them to be.

Protima began to walk away, not entirely sure where what she would do next. She sensed movement behind her. The Biters were following her.

'Stop following me!'

The Biters stopped, but then they began following her again. Resigned to having the mob of Biters following her around, she kept walking away from the city.

More jets had appeared in the skies and explosions were rocking the city. In the distance, she saw something that froze her heart. A large mushroom cloud was rising into the sky. Protima did not know if this was part of the nuclear madness that had erupted between India and Pakistan or part of the desperate defensive measures adopted by governments to stave off the spread of Biters. Either way, it was clear that it was no longer safe to be above ground. She had already seen that the network of tunnels and sewers under the ground could provide some sort of sanctuary. She laughed bitterly. At least she would not have to worry about finding food or water.

She found an opening and began to pull at the heavy handle. To her surprise, several pairs of hands reached out to help her and in no time, the heavy lid covering the entrance to an underground tunnel was pushed aside. She looked at the Biters following her, now more than two hundred strong, and she saw that they were trying to communicate with her. One of them, a giant who towered over her and wore a hat, growled in a low voice. Protima could not understand the words, but he was telling her that all the Biters would follow her, and that she should lead them to safety. As his eyes scanned the sky, looking at the jets and at the huge fireballs now erupting over the city in the distance, she saw that he and the other Biters were terrified. They might have looked like monsters, but Protima began to understand that there was something more to them. She really did not want to be their leader or to have them follow her around, but there was no way she could turn them back, and besides, with the devastation being rained on the city around them, she did not have much time. So she entered the hole in the ground, and the big Biter with the hat and the others behind him followed her in.

Protima clutched the package she had been carrying close to her and realized she was still carrying the object she had picked up in the stand-off with the Biters. She burst out laughing when she realized what she had been trying to fight off a horde of Biters with.

It was a well-worn and slightly charred copy of a book she had once enjoyed tremendously. Alice in Wonderland.

THE GENERAL'S STRIPES

T HE FIRST SALVO IN THE Chinese Revolution of 2014 was typed into a Google search bar while sipping on a glass of red wine in a five-star hotel in Beijing.

Edward Johnson had come to Beijing on a business trip from his company's China headquarters in Guangzhou two days earlier. Wearing a tan suit and carrying a leather laptop case, he looked like many of the other guests at the East 33 restaurant at the Raffles Beijing Hotel – foreign business travelers staying at the opulent hotel in the heart of the capital. He had been employed with an American electronics firm as a sales director for five years and spoke fluent Mandarin, something that had quickly endeared him to his local Chinese business partners in the year he had been there. He had a doting wife and a five-year-old son, who were now back in the United States taking care of her mother, who had been diagnosed with cancer. Edward's bosses thought him a hard worker, and a stickler for detail, though his evaluations would always call out that he perhaps lacked the leadership to stand out. His Chinese business partners loved his humility and grace, and talked about how despite his senior position, Edward would always be just another member of the team.

Indeed, blending in was critical to Edward's success.

For one did not become a professional assassin by attracting attention to oneself.

Edward was indeed on the payroll of the American company, and his immediate bosses had no idea that he was anything but another dedicated middle manager. However, his real employer was Zeus, and he had been placed in China after a four-year mission in the United States where he joined his employers straight out of a commission in the US Army.

Edward, which was not his real name, had been in the US Special Forces, having seen action in Iraq and Afghanistan over multiple tours of duty. He had seen friends torn apart by bombs and rockets and then been ordered not to retaliate because the attackers were 'good' Taliban, on the payroll of supposed US allies in the Kabul regime. He had come to hate how the politicians put young men like him in harm's way and then micro-managed how they could operate. That was till he met Major Appleseed at Kandahar, where Edward had been placed in detention for snapping and shooting dead three civilians. Appleseed had told him he worked for people who wanted to change things, who wanted to take the fight to the real enemies of America. Edward joined in, partly driven by the conviction in Appleseed's words, and partly to avoid the court-martial and disgrace he knew waited for him back in the United States.

Ten minutes ago, he had received a simple text message from his wife. It said, 'The wall near our house is cracked. We should fix it when you're back home.' To anyone intercepting the message, and in China that was always a possibility, it would appear to be innocuous. In reality, it told Edward that the Great Chinese Firewall, which restricted the Internet content available to Chinese citizens, had been taken down. He typed 'Tiananmen Square' into the Google search bar on his smartphone and smiled. A day earlier, the only images he would have been permitted to see would have been those of happy, smiling Chinese citizens strolling in the square. Today, he saw what the rest of the world saw – tanks crushing demonstrators, troops firing into massed youth. Images from the original 1989 massacre and also from the more recent outbreak in late 2012. Edward copied the links and sent out an email from a secure account to a list he already had saved on his phone: a list of the most prominent political dissidents in China. He finished his wine and walked out of the hotel, planning to walk to the nearby Tiananmen Square. He figured he might as well enjoy the square while he could.

'Chen, we need you. Please help us out.'

Colonel Chen tried hard to not look into the pleading eyes of his childhood friend, Bo Liang. Liang had been an editor at a local newspaper and a published author and had done very well for himself. The two men, the soldier and the poet, had stayed in touch over the years. That was till Chen had received a notice from the Internal Security Service that he should avoid all contact with his childhood friend since he had been placed under house arrest for 'anti-national activities'. What Liang had done was to post a piece on his blog that had been mildly critical of the force used by the authorities in breaking up the protests in Tiananmen Square in late 2012. Chen had not heard from his friend for some months, and now he had suddenly called him for a meeting at a café. Chen's wife had told him to not go, since he would be watched, but Chen owed his old friend at least that much.

When Chen did not reply, Liang put some printouts on the table.

'Chen, look at these. I had blogged about them killing

a few dozen young kids, but it seems they did much more. The Net is open for some reason, and we downloaded these. There was a terrible massacre at Tiananmen, one they hushed up. They took away dozens of people and killed them afterwards. Is this why you joined the army, Chen? To kill your own people?'

At that, Chen's head snapped up. 'Liang, you sit in your cafes and air-conditioned homes and talk of democracy. Look around us and compare to the poverty we ourselves saw as children. See how much our nation has progressed. You talk of democracy – take a look at the United States. Their poor are protesting in the streets and being set upon by hired guns of the elite. With the Occupy protests, many American cities resemble war zones. Europe is in the throes of rioting by unemployed youth and one economy after another is collapsing like a pack of dominos. At least here the Army holds us together against anarchy.'

'Please then, look at this. With the Great Firewall down, we can see what is on the Internet. Please have a look and see the truth for yourself.'

Liang handed a tablet computer to Chen with the browser open to an unfamiliar website. Chen's English was pretty good and he scanned through the page – it was a posting from someone called Dr. Stan on a conspiracy forum. It read, 'The chaos around us is engineered by powerful men. The virus reported in China, the lab fire in Washington everybody is covering up. It will all lead to a catastrophe bigger than anything you can imagine. And don't for a minute think that the wars flaring up around the world are an accident. This is all part of their plan.'

Chen scrolled down and saw that many other posters had responded, most calling the original poster crazy and paranoid. Dr. Stan had never posted again. Chen handed back the tablet, exasperated.

'You expect me to believe this? The ravings of a lunatic on some crazy forum? Seeing stuff like this makes me believe the Great Firewall has its uses after all.'

Chen saw Liang's look of disappointment as he gathered his things and got ready to leave.

'Very well, my old friend. Thank you for coming to meet me. I don't know if we will meet again but good luck.'

With those words, he got up and left. Chen kept looking at the door for some time, wishing he had said something else. But in his heart, he knew he was right. The world was slipping into chaos – the Middle East was on the verge of all-out war between Israel and Iran; the US economy was tottering and social unrest there was boiling over. Closer to home, Islamic insurgents had intensified their campaign in China's Xinxiang province. The war of words with the US over Taiwan had grown sharper, and blood had already been drawn in dogfights over the straits. This was hardly the time when China needed internal strife. Chen knew only too well that the Chinese system was far from perfect, but which system was? At least the nation was prospering, and children in small towns did not have to scrounge for food or an education like his parents had to.

Chen was on leave in Beijing for the next two days, after which he had to report back to his unit near the Indian border. While the two Asian giants enjoyed an uneasy peace, Chen knew just how rapidly that could change. There were dozens of incidents at the border each year, and if it came to a shooting match, Chen and his men would not be facing the ill-equipped infantrymen the Chinese Red Army had smashed through in the 1962 war. The Indian army had grown into a modern army and the fact that both Asian giants now had nuclear weapons made any conflict much more dangerous than it had been in 1962. Chen had found Indian officers to be rational and pragmatic, but what bothered them most was their shared unstable neighbor, Pakistan. If things came to a boil between India and Pakistan, then Chen's leaders would likely ask his troops to take up an offensive posture along the border to tie up India's Mountain Divisions.

With the growing tensions around the world, the last thing Chen wanted was war between India and China. The two Asian neighbors had prospered recently, and a war would set both nations back many years.

Chen was happy to be back home so he could forget about his worries and spend some time with his wife. When he entered his apartment, his wife had already laid out dinner, and he kissed her as he sat down to eat.

After months of eating whatever their cook could rustle up at their post, Chen found the home-cooked food heavenly. He took in the smell of the thick chicken soup and smiled as he tucked into the noodles and steamed dumplings. However, he had barely started his meal when there was a knock on the door. Then another.

Only the Internal Security men would walk up to a senior officer's home and knock like this without being stopped by the security guard in the apartment complex downstairs. He had taken a risk in agreeing to meet Liang, and he hoped he could talk his way out of this.

Chen placed his hand over his wife's before she could rise to answer the door. He spoke in a hoarse whisper.

'Get inside the bedroom and lock the door.'

He kissed her again and ushered her into the bedroom. His pistol was in a drawer, but he knew that if they had indeed come for him, trying to resist would only make things worse. He forced a smile and opened the door to find two men in black suits.

'Comrade Colonel Chen, I'm afraid I have some bad news for you.'

Chen felt his throat tighten but he forced himself to not let his fear show.

'Comrades, come in. What has happened that you needed to come by so late at night?'

One of the men held a black-and-white photograph in front of him. Chen blanched as he saw the two bodies lying in a pool of blood.

'Comrade Colonel, a friend of yours, Bo Liang, met with an unfortunate accident this evening. As far as we can tell, his wife also died with him and we know of no other immediate family. The last dialed numbers on his phone were yours so we thought we would inform you so that you could help make the necessary arrangements.'

Edward smiled as he saw his Chinese colleagues talk in hushed whispers in the company cafeteria. There had been only one topic of conversation for the last five days. The Great Firewall was down and the Chinese people were lapping up information from the Internet that had been denied to them for decades. There had been an interruption previously, in early 2012, when the hacker group Anonymous had hacked into a couple of Chinese government websites. But this was on a totally different scale – the entire firewall had been compromised.

The Chinese government had been taken unawares, and at first had tried to avoid any public comment on the situation, but as the days wore on and Facebook and Google+ pages called sprouted calling for political reform and Twitter messages abounded announcingannounced protests against local corruption, the government had been forced to act. The online protests were perhaps something the Chinese regime could have hoped to ignored, but when those led to mass gatherings and protest marches, it had did not have much of a choice but to respond. The response was just as Edward's bosses had hoped. The Chinese regime had dismissed the protests as the work of `misguided terrorists' in the media and had taken in some of the protestors for beatings at police stations. That had further inflamed public opinion.

The TV in the cafeteria had been relaying news of ongoing demonstrations in Guangdong province when a news flash appeared, taking even Edward by surprise. As he listened, he reminded himself that he had no business feeling angry at his masters for not showing him the whole picture. He was a small cog in their plan. As reports emerged of a strange, highly contagious virus in inner Mongolia, with the Chinese government blaming the United States for an act of biological warfare, he realized the plan was far more dangerous than he had ever anticipated.

'Comrade Colonel, your men are ready for inspection.'

Chen straightened his back and saluted as his men snapped to attention as one. He felt a strange sense of pride as he saw the assembled men. More than five hundred of his men had been flown into Beijing over the last two days. The rest of his garrison was still at their post, but his superiors had ordered more elite infantry units back to major cities, to deal with 'potential unrest'. Chen hoped he would not have to order his men to march against Chinese civilians, and he wondered if this was a test of his loyalty, given his links to Bo Liang.

The death of his friend still stung. Chen tried to tell himself it had been an accident, but there was a voice in the back of his head telling him things he did not want to hear. For now his men would stay in their barracks near the airport, and Chen had joined them, awaiting the orders that could come at any minute.

The last week had been one of unprecedented chaos. The Great Firewall had been largely restored, but the damage had been done. Through much of 2011 and 2012, people in smaller towns had been rising up against local corruption and the fact that so many of them had been displaced to make way for the shining symbols of the new China. Many of those had been put down with brutal force. With the Great Firewall down, all those uncomfortable truths came out, and bereaved friends and relatives found a new outlet for their rage and anguish.

The President had made an appearance on live TV, vowing that he would personally crush corruption. He claimed many of the excesses had been committed by local officials without his knowledge. Chen did not doubt that, since he knew how labyrinthine the Chinese bureaucracy could be, but these assurances did not placate ordinary Chinese. Many local government offices had already been sacked and officials beaten up, or worse, and while disturbances were yet to spill over into the larger cities, Chen knew it would take but one spark to set it all alight. A part of Chen's mind also exhorted him to take a stand and to demand justice for the death of his friend, but that voice was quickly hushed by another reminding him that he had his wife and his parents back in the province to think of.

One evening Chen had sat alone and gotten quite drunk. He had told himself that ifIf he had been fifteen years younger, he would have stormed off and demanded justice for what in his heart he knew to be the murder of his friend. But he was almost forty and had a family to think of, so he needed to weigh his actions. What Chen did not realize at the time was that rationalizing one's inaction was the first step in accepting tyranny. You either stood up against tyranny or became a slave to it, there was nothing in between.

That night, he had an unexpected visitor in his room near the barracks. It was General Hong, the man who had trained him at the Academy and who had been his mentor ever since.

'Sir, you could have called me. I would have come.'

The old general waved Chen's objections aside and sat down, producing a bottle of rice wine and a handful of small packets labeled '05 Compressed Food'. Chen smiled as he saw the biscuit packets. These were the battlefield rations of the Chinese infantry – hard, dry biscuits that packed more than a thousand calories with the nourishment making up for the taste.

'Are you going on a march?'

Chen had meant it as a joke, but there was no humor in Hong's eyes as he looked at his protégé. 'We are already at war. We have been sharing these biscuits to remind everyone that we should forget the comforts of the last few years and learn to be soldiers again. Now share a drink with this old man.'

They drank in silence for some minutes, and Chen was increasingly anxious about what his mentor wanted of him. Finally, Hong looked at him.

'In two days' time, officers loyal to me will seize control of key government buildings. We will then announce that the government is working with foreign powers to create the current instability. We will help keep the peace while we can normalize the situation.' The general poured himself another drink, as if he were talking about the weather.

Chen was in turmoil. His long-time mentor was asking him to take part in an armed coup. To disobey all the orders he had followed, to turn against the same leaders he had sworn to defend.

'Sir, you're one of the most decorated officers in the whole People's Liberation Army. How can we turn against the government?'

Hong poured Chen a drink. There was a look of infinite sadness in the old man's eyes.

'Chen, I am fiercely loyal to China and would die for my nation. But I serve the people, not a few rich men and their backers. I believe our President is an honest man and he has been trying to steer our nation towards progress, but there are forces at play who have their own agenda. They are the ones who have been discrediting him and the government. There are those in our own Army and government who have benefitted much by being in power, and there are whispers of outside powers working with them to lead us down a path to war with the Americans.'

'Why would anyone want that? If they drive us to war with the Americans, what does anyone gain?'

Hong looked straight into Chen's eyes, and Chen saw an expression in the general's eyes that he had never seen before – fear.

'I don't know, but that's why we need to help restore some stability and secure the President against the forces plotting against him. Will you join us?'

Chen sat frozen in place. Joining Hong would be a huge leap of faith. His mentor was persuasive as always, and Chen did not quite know how to refuse a man who had been more than a father to him. However, joining Hong would mean throwing away his career and placing his wife in tremendous danger. He thought back to the photographs of Liang and his wife, and felt his resolve slipping. Having been a combat soldier for much of his adult life, Chen did not fear much for his own personal safety, but the thought of his wife lying on the road after another such `accident' almost paralyzed him with fear. Hong must have sensed what was on his mind.

'Chen, I have other officers to meet, so I will be on my way. I know what I am asking of you, and I would never place you in such a predicament unless our nation was facing extraordinary danger. You will know when the action starts, and your men are one of the most battle-trained units now in the capital. They will ask you to stop us, and I hope we don't have to meet on the battleground.'

With those words, Hong got up and left.

Hong's plan never got off the ground. The next morning, a Chinese destroyer attacked a Taiwanese frigate in open seas and sank it with a volley of missiles. A dogfight broke out when Chinese fighter jets attacked two Taiwanese planes that had flown to the scene. The Taiwanese government was pleading for help from the United States, but with tensions escalating between Israel and Iran, US forces were not in a position to intervene.

Chen got a sense of just how confused things were when he realized that the actions of the destroyer and the jets had not been sanctioned by the government. His friends in the government said the President was fuming because the commanders involved had acted without orders to open fire. Perhaps Hong had been right after all about renegade elements driving the nation towards confrontation.

Chen had been ordered with his men to Tiananmen Square where more than five thousand civilians had gathered, protesting human rights violations and asking for criminal action against those who had killed the student protestors at the square in late 2012. Chen had told his men to ensure that the safety switches on their guns were on and to keep a safe distance from the crowd. He did not want a nervous kid to get trigger-happy and start another massacre. He kept hoping that the demonstrators would disperse when the President came to address them, as had been promised.

Chen waited a few more hours as the crowd swelled. He noted with dismay that some were carrying pipes and bottles. The youngsters had started taunting the policemen and troops. Chen intervened quickly, but the situation was volatile and he was afraid that it could explode at any minute.

He had tried calling Hong several times that morning, but had not been able to get through. The local police who were to be the first line of defense seemed terrified and Chen doubted they would hold their lines if there was trouble. If anything, some of the younger policemen showed sympathy towards the protestors.

Edward finished his coffee at the café near Tiananmen Square. He looked at the growing crowd and shook his head sadly. He would much rather his mission be achieved with the minimum collateral damage. The Chinese troops were there, just as his bosses had anticipated, and the poorly trained police would bolt at the first sight of trouble. That would leave heavily armed infantry brought in straight from a hostile international border facing agitated civilians. Combat infantry was trained to kill, not detain or disarm civilians. Edward wondered just how well-connected his bosses were; to manipulate things to this extent would require access to the Chinese government. As he climbed up the fire escape behind the café, he knew that he would never know the full story, and he knew better than to ask questions. Curiosity might or might not kill the cat, but it would certainly lead to a short and exciting life.

Once he was on the roof, Edward opened the briefcase he had been carrying. To anyone looking at the contents, his briefcase contained nothing that would have been out of place for an executive on a business trip. Edward moved the files and papers a bit and snapped open a hidden compartment. He took only five minutes to assemble the sniper rifle.

Chen's phone rang and he picked it up, relieved to finally hear from Hong.

'Sir, thanks for calling. I've been trying to call you all morning. We are in an impossible situation here and I have no idea why they ordered my men here, but if anything goes wrong, my boys are not trained to handle civil disturbance. I've been thinking of what you said and I wanted to talk to you.'

To Chen's shock, Hong's voice betrayed panic. 'They are on to us. Someone in our group betrayed us, and they are hunting us down. I don't have much time. Take care, my son.'

With those last words, Hong disconnected the line. Chen would have tried calling him back had one of his men not shouted in alarm.

'Sir, someone's shooting the protestors!'

Three protestors lay in expanding pools of blood. Chen looked on in horror as another one fell, a mist of blood spraying from his head. Chen's trained eyes knew immediately that someone from an elevated area to the right was shooting at the protestors, and that they were using a silenced weapon. Chen scanned the buildings with his assault rifle ready in his hands.

There! He saw a glint of light from what could have been a sniper scope. Another protestor fell. Chen turned to his men.

'Make sure none of you fire. If the crowd stirs up, try and hold them back with minimum force. I'm going after that bastard who's shooting.'

Chen began to run towards the building where he had spotted the shooter, but he was too late. Some of the youth in the crowd recovered from their shock and gave vent to their fury.

'Those swine shot us in cold blood. Get them!'

Bricks and bottles began raining down on the police and soon a group of young men charged the policemen. The policemen tried to rally but two of the police fell, victims to the unseen sniper he was racing towards. A policeman thought someone in the crowd had shot his comrade and opened fire with his pistol, shooting two civilians.

After that, nobody could do anything to stop the unfolding bloodbath at Tiananmen Square.

Chen was sitting alone, his clothes drenched in sweat and blood and his body bleeding from at least a dozen cuts and scrapes. He had tried to hold his men back, but once the police fired, a few protestors had snatched guns from them and started firing at the troops. The square was littered with bodies. The sniper who had started it all was gone. Chen's wife had been calling him all day to check if he was okay, and he just grunted once in reply and then did not answer any more calls. Hong was nowhere to be found, and many officers loyal to Hong were missing. The massacre at Tiananmen Square had been a smokescreen for a wholesale purge of officers in the Army who were likely to oppose whoever was orchestrating the events overtaking China.

A TV was on in the corner and Chen saw that the entire world was being engulfed by a catastrophe of the likes that had never been seen before. Regional wars were flaring up, and the disease that he had heard of in Mongolia was spreading like wildfire. There were rumors that it transformed people into undead monsters who preyed on human flesh. Chen had dismissed those stories as the product of an overactive imagination, but now he was no longer so sure. The images of mobs of men and women hunting down others and biting them to death would have been horrible enough, but what made it even more terrifying was that the victims came back to life as monsters themselves. Several cities had been overrun by the contagion and Chen wondered if Hong had been right after all, and if there were indeed forces orchestrating such global chaos.

'Comrade, we need to talk.'

Chen looked up to see a young officer, whom he had not met before.

'Comrade Chen, General Hong told me to come to you if his plans were compromised. He is gone, as are most of the officers, but the men are ready, and they just need a leader to follow.'

'Why don't you lead them?'

The man smiled.

'My friend, I am an accountant who has never been in battle, which is why nobody suspects me of being a part of the plan. We need a warrior, not a bean counter, to lead the troops. You surely know now the kind of ruthless men we are up against, and unless we act fast, all will be lost. I don't know what their plan is and what they ultimately want, but they clearly are in the highest reaches of the government and the Army. We must act fast before more innocent lives are lost.'

Chen thought back to the hundreds of lives lost in the square earlier in the day and he looked up at the officer.

'What do I need to do?'

While Chen was sitting in his barracks planning his next move, Edward was at the airport, waiting to catch a flight out to Hong Kong. He had an onward journey booked to New York, where he would dispose of his current identity and take a well-deserved two-month vacation.

He could almost smell the fear in the business-class lounge. Most people were rooted to the TV sets, which were broadcasting details of how the contagion had spread around the world in a matter of days. The monsters now had a name.

Biters.

The major urban centers of China were still free of the scourge, but with air travel carrying tens of millions of people around the world every day, it was but a matter of time before the infection spread. Edward could only guess as to the ultimate aim of the plan but even what little he had seen was beginning to scare him.

There was a commotion outside and one of the airline employees at the reception got up to see what was the matter. When she turned to face the passengers, Edwards saw a look of fear that quickly gave way to a forced smile as she bravely tried to do her job and reassure the passengers.

'Please stay in the lounge, the police will deal with what

is happening outside.'

It would never be known how the first Biters entered Beijing. Perhaps a passenger had brought the infection with him; Edward had already read about flights landing full of Biters with the terrified crew having locked themselves in the cockpits. Or perhaps a Biter had come into the city from the countryside. As with all large cities, once the infection took hold, it spread at an astonishing pace.

Edward was at the glass door now. Blood-covered figures in torn clothes rampaged through the terminal. A man behind him screamed at him to lock the door, but when the Biters smashed another lounge's glass doors and walked in, oblivious to the shards, Edward knew that hiding was not an option. He was not going down without a fight.

As the first Biters approached the business-class lounge, he shouted at the waiters to get knives from the kitchen. He armed himself with two carving knives and met the first Biter as he smashed through the glass into the lounge. Edward slashed him across the throat and kicked down the next Biter before stabbing him through the heart. He heard a gurgling noise behind him and turned to see the first Biter get back up, a gaping hole in his neck where blood spurted out. The Biter bared his teeth and advanced on Edward.

Edward dropped the knife, a terror like he had never known before taking hold of him. How did you fight an enemy you could not kill? He closed his eyes and screamed as the Biter grabbed his hand and bit down hard.

Chen had fallen asleep within minutes of getting home at three in the morning. However, it was anything but a sound sleep. He kept dreaming of bloodied corpses and of mobs surging towards him. He heard loud booms and for a minute he thought he was dreaming it. Then his wife shook him awake.

'Huahei, look out there!'

Chen looked out the window to see the night sky light up in the distance with bright bursts of flame. As another explosion sent up a crimson plume, he knew what he was looking at – an attack from the air. The explosions seemed to be coming from the direction of the airport. However, there was no return fire. There was no way an enemy could attack the Chinese capital without its formidable anti-aircraft defenses firing back. What was happening? He picked up his phone as it rang. It was an unfamiliar voice, but the words Chen heard electrified him.

'Comrade, the contagion has spread to Beijing. The Biters overran the airport and we had to destroy it from the air. There are more Biters headed to the city. We need you and your unit to deploy now. A truck is on the way to fetch you.'

Chen's wife had turned on the TV and he saw that the contagion had consumed much of the world and now was at the doorsteps of China's major cities. China's lack of freedom worked in its favor now. Unlike major Western cities, the entrances to Chinese cities were closely guarded. With rising tensions, crack Army units had been positioned outside most cities to guard against escalating civil protests, and while nobody had said it out aloud, the real possibility of a military coup. Together with the network of spies in various communities, the Chinese leadership was able to get word of the emerging outbreak before many other nations.

The President was on TV now and Chen felt an emotion he thought he had forgotten – patriotism.

'My fellow people. Today I speak to you as our nation confronts an enemy we have never fought before. Nation after nation has fallen to this scourge, but we will resist till the very end. As I speak, units of the People's Liberation Army are racing to intercept these infected hordes before they breach our major cities. To civilians caught outside major cities, we will be broadcasting safe zones where you can enter the cities and seek sanctuary. Our nation has been divided, but now the time has come for us to unite in facing this threat. If we fight shoulder to shoulder as comrades, we may yet survive. But if we do not, one thing is certain. Our nation will cease to exist.'

Chen passed through a city in panic as he rode to join his unit. People were boarding up their homes and even at five in the morning nervous crowds were gathering outside. One of the young men began to clap as the Army trucks sped past to meet the oncoming hordes of Biters. It was soon taken up by many others, and an old man emerged from a group, wearing a crumpled old uniform with rows of medals on his chest. He caught Chen's eye and shouted out, 'Go get them, boys! All of China depends on you today.'

Chen spent the rest of the ride thinking about everything he had seen and heard. Minutes later, he was in front of his men.

'Sir, I hear we cannot kill these Biters with bullets.'

Chen stormed up to the young infantryman and grabbed his helmet with both hands, pulling him close till his face was inches away.

'If not with bullets, then we will rip their fucking hearts out with our bare hands.'

He loosened his grip on the shaking soldier and addressed all his men now arrayed before him.

'I know many of you have been troubled, and after what happened yesterday, I cannot blame you. There will be a reckoning one day for those innocent lives lost, but now we are all that stands between those monsters and the millions of people in the city. Fight like this is our last day on Earth because it may well be.'

The first Biters came within the hour. There were six of them, all dressed in bloody remnants of Army uniforms. Some of his men hesitated to fire at those wearing the uniform so Chen fired on full auto. One of the Biters dropped as several rounds tore into him. Chen lowered his rifle and then recoiled as the fallen Biter got up, blood covering his torso, and joined the others in walking towards the troops. Some men took a step back and Chen knew he had just a few seconds before his men gave into full-scale panic. His men were well trained, but they had never fought an enemy who could not be shot dead.

He had already heard how other units had panicked and tried to run. That never worked. The moment one of them was bitten, the contagion spread, and within minutes, a disciplined platoon of crack troops was turned into bloodthirsty and mindless Biters.

Chen ordered one of his men to fire an RPG and within seconds the rocket snaked out towards the approaching Biters. It exploded in their midst, scattering all but three of them.

'Did we get them?'

Chen did not answer the man who had asked the question but brought up his rifle scope to his eyes to take a closer look. The Biters who had been torn apart by the rocket were not dead yet. One of them had his leg taken apart by the rocket but his torso was still trying to crawl towards them, his mouth open with blood and drool streaming out of it.

Another had lost much of one side of his body, but both halves were flopping around. As horrified as he was, Chen had just learned an important lesson. Even if the Biters could not be killed, they could be stopped.

'Take their legs apart! Aim low and fire on full auto!'

A volley of rifle fire on full automatic targeted the three approaching Biters and all three of them went down, their legs shredded. What remained of them continued to move and wriggle around on the ground, but they were no longer an imminent threat.

'RPG!'

At Chen's command, another rocket streaked out and obliterated what had remained of the Biters. For all Chen knew, their body parts were still moving, but they were not getting any closer and for now, that was victory enough. A cheer went up as his men realized that the enemy they were fighting could be defeated after all. He turned to smile at the men and shouted loudly enough so that they could all hear him.

'Every bastard thinks he's tough till we put a few rounds into him. If they come again, just remember to shoot low and anyone who hits them in the balls gets a drink from me.'

A few chuckled but then his radioman's face turned ashen.

'Sir, scouts are reporting more of them.'

'Deploy into fire teams of six men. One RPG and five riflemen. Shoot only for the legs and then mop them up with rockets.'

As his men began to deploy, he saw the hesitation on his radioman's face.

'What is it?'

'Sir, aerial recon is reporting that there are hundreds of thousands of Biters headed this way. We just got news that Guangzhou has been overrun, and all radio contact has been lost with the city.'

'Sir, we are out of bullets for the sniper rifles.'

That was the last thing Chen needed to hear. All day they had picked off Biters at long range with their snipers. He had ten specialized snipers with him, and they had fired and fired again till their fingers bled and their guns overheated to dangerous levels. But Chen had known it would never be enough. The People's Liberation Air Force had been flying all day as well, but China was a vast nation and the PLAAF was already dangerously overextended.

War had broken out in the Middle East, and with all seemingly lost, Iran had launched nuclear missiles at Israel. Chen had heard that the Middle East was now a radioactive wasteland. India and Pakistan were trading blows as well, and then had come the news that some fool in Taiwan had ordered missiles fired at the mainland. The Chinese had retaliated with a fury, unleashing a barrage of missiles and air strikes. What the Biters could not accomplish in terms of wiping out civilization, it seemed humans would finish on their own. But for now, Chen had more immediate concerns. He had heard back from the Air Force that short of using tactical nuclear weapons, there was no way they could hold the Biters back.

The one silver lining was that news had spread along the line on how to stop the Biters. It was simple really.

Aim for the head. Only the head. That was the only thing would bring a Biter down for good.

So Chen's snipers had been busy for over an hour, shooting down hundreds of Biters from more than two kilometers away. The problem was that they were now out of bullets and there were still thousands of Biters shuffling towards Chen's position. Chen ordered his riflemen to take position, but he did not have high hopes. They could not guarantee head shots at long range, and if the Biters could get close enough, he knew they would be overwhelmed by sheer weight of numbers. Chen thought back to his days in the Military Academy and smiled at the irony of it all. The Chinese Red Army had made itself infamous for its near suicidal 'human wave' tactics which had come as such a nasty surprise to the Americans in Korea. Now the same Red Army faced the prospect of being overwhelmed by sheer numbers, but this time the oncoming wave was hardly human.

Some of the men pointed to the sky as two jet fighters swooped in low, releasing bombs over the approaching sea of Biters. As the bombs exploded, a wave of fire expanded from the point of impact. Even from a kilometer away, Chen could feel the extreme heat they unleashed.

'Was it a nuke?' one of the nervous men whispered. No, it was not a nuclear weapon, but a napalm bomb dropped right in the middle of the approaching Biters.

For a few seconds, all that was visible was a wall of fire and Chen heard cheers. Those disappeared when the Biters emerged from behind the flames. Some of the Biters were on fire, yet they shuffled on, stepping over the burnt bodies of their comrades. Any normal army would have collapsed under the firepower unleashed against them and the devastating losses they had suffered, but the Biters were unlike any army Chen had imagined.

Chen sighted his rifle and took aim, sending a bullet through a Biter's head. A couple of men whistled appreciatively at his aim.

Chen tried to put up a brave front and turned to look at his men.

'Just take off their heads. Not much to it.'

A few of his men took aim and fired and a couple of Biters went down from direct hits to the head. It was but a small victory, but Chen knew the war was far from over, and he was no longer sure he would live to see it through to its conclusion.

'Blow the bridge.'

Chen watched as the explosive charges were triggered and the bridge went down, taking with it several dozen Biters. It was now almost dark and they had retreated well into the residential areas of Beijing. Any further and the Biters would be among the millions of civilians now cowering inside the city.

There was no counting how many Biters had been destroyed in the fighting that day but they kept coming. Many Army units had been overrun, further adding to the ranks of the Biters, and finally Chen had received orders to retreat, destroying all bridges and mining all approach roads along the way. A row of tanks in the distance were heading out to meet the Biters, but he doubted they would achieve much. He had already heard tales of tanks that had destroyed hundreds of Biters, then run out of ammunition and gotten bogged down. Heavy armor was of little use against a seemingly never-ending sea of Biters. Once the tanks ran out of ammunition or got bogged down, the Biters would just bypass them and carry on.

The Biters did not seem to feel tiredness, fear or pain. They kept coming, and several more cities had fallen. Beijing, Shanghai and a handful of other cities were still intact, but he had already heard that with Beijing under greater threat, the government had been flown out to Shanghai. His men were dead tired, and terrified. Many of them just wanted to get home to their families, and Chen thought of his own wife. Yet he knew that he could not allow them to leave their posts. One or two units further to the East had scattered and Chen had heard about several desperate last stands by small units. A dozen men could not hope to last long against the Biters.

Chen had managed to keep his men operating as a cohesive unit, and other than four men who had died when one of their RPGs misfired, he had suffered no other deaths. Most of his men were however dehydrated, and many of them had swollen and bloodied fingers from the constant firing. More than a dozen were wounded due to misfirings and weapons that had overheated, and in more than one case, exploded. Chen had tended to some of the wounded himself, and his uniform was soaked in blood.

For all that, Chen looked at his boys with pride. They had not broken and run as had so many units. For all their misgivings about the regime and their role in Tiananmen Square, they had done their duty to the people of China. They had fought the battle of their lives, not for a flag, not for politicians, but for the millions of ordinary people who counted on them. So, despite every muscle in his body screaming in protest, Chen walked among his men, whispering words of encouragement to each one.

When he was done, he sat down heavily and looked across the river. The horizon was dark with Biters. It was a matter of hours before they reached Beijing and he was not sure they would be able to hold them.

Chen drank some water and thought of how much the world had changed in just one day. Much of the world was lying devastated. The Middle East was largely gone, wiped out in a day of tit-for-tat nuclear exchanges. India and Pakistan had traded their own nuclear blows and their major cities had been hit. Biters had swept through much of the world, and it was unclear if there was any organized government left. In all the chaos, the Great Firewall was down, but as Chen looked at the laptop screen in front of him, he realized news from around the world had not been updated for over six hours.

The latest updates chilled him. The US Government had decided to use tactical nuclear weapons, air burst weapons, on cities that had been totally overrun by Biters. Other nuclear powers – Britain, France, Russia and India – had followed suit. It was a desperate last measure to deny the Biters control over human cities. Chen wondered how many hundreds of millions had died in one day around the world.

One of his men started sobbing and Chen looked up sharply, planning to give the man a lecture. Instead, Chen just stared at the sight he saw, and tears began to stream down his cheeks. Just over the horizon, four giant mushroom clouds billowed over the earth.

'There is someone here to see you.'

Chen sat upright, sweat pouring off his face, and his wife placed a gentle hand on his chest, trying to calm him. There were a dozen people sharing their apartment, and many of them looked on as Chen got up to see who was at the door.

With the people that had streamed into the city, Beijing was now home to more than thirty million people, and residents had opened their homes to the newcomers. Three days had passed since Chen and his men had held the line long enough for tactical nuclear weapons to be used to finally secure Beijing. There was no telling whether more Biters would come. China had been home to well over a billion people and only a hundred million were reckoned to be safe. But for now, they had bought themselves some time. Enough time to airdrop thousands of mines around the cities and to ring Beijing and Shanghai with armored forces to hold any further attacks.

It was now a foregone conclusion that any further massed attack by Biters would be met with nuclear strikes. There was no news from the outside world. The Internet was now down, as were phone lines.

A man in a black uniform was waiting for him.

'Sir, I am to get you to Shanghai immediately.'

A few hours later, Chen was waiting in front of a nondescript office in Shanghai. He had put on his uniform, since he was meeting someone at the very top of the government, but he was beyond caring about the reek of sweat and dirt, the tears in a couple of places, or the dried blood all over the front.

The door opened, and he was ushered in. Two old Chinese men were seated at a table, and next to them, surprisingly enough, was a Caucasian man. One of the Chinese men, an old man with ribbons across his chest, nodded at Chen and asked him to sit down.

'Comrade Chen, we thank you for your heroic actions in helping to secure Beijing. Now only Beijing and Shanghai remain, but we will make a new beginning, thanks to the bravery and sacrifice of men like you.'

Chen swallowed hard as the rumors he had heard were confirmed. Only two cities remained intact in all of China. True, that meant that perhaps a hundred million or more had survived, but what about the billion more who were not inside the secure cities? How many billions had perished or become Biters around the world?

The old man continued. 'In the chaos, we suffered terribly. The President and his cabinet perished in an air crash as they were being flown to Shanghai, and so now we are trying to re-establish order. As you can see, we are putting past differences aside and are joining hands with like-minded American friends. Together we will usher in a New World and begin afresh. Our nation, our civilization, is the only one left intact from all the nations of old, and we will begin to spread civilization again through the world. Unfortunate as the circumstances are, perhaps it is our destiny to be the ones who reclaim our planet in the name of human civilization. But first, we must secure our cities and feed the millions of civilians that depend on us. For that we need men like you.'

'Comrade, what could I do to help?'

The second Chinese man spoke.

'We are bringing the old government and armed forces into one single command structure, called the Central Committee. We need our Chinese soldiers to keep order in our cities, but we will need other forces to seek out survivors in other parts of the world and to secure resources and food for our people. In that, we will be helped by the forces that our American friends have at their disposal. A highly trained force called Zeus. We will bring their forces and ours into one command, and we need capable men to lead them. Our aerial reconnaissance indicates that there are two major areas where there may still be land to grow food and where there may still be human survivors who need our help – the Midwest of North America and the Northern plains of India.'

After all that he had seen over the last few days, Chen replied without a second thought, 'Comrade, where can I serve and who do I report to?'

The old man chuckled.

'You are everything I had read about you – a committed soldier to the core. No, Comrade, your days of reporting to others are over. As of today, you are a General.'

The man stepped forward and pinned a medal on Chen's chest, and a set of stripes on his shoulders. Chen was too stunned to say anything.

'Comrade General Chen, welcome to the Red Guards.'

A BUNNY'S LAST WISH

'OF ALL THE THINGS ANYBODY has ever done to impress a girl, dressing up as a bunny must be the weirdest and stupidest plan. I do hope she's worth it.'

Neil smiled and playfully threw some water from the sink at Jiten. 'She is not just any girl. She is the one.'

Jiten shook his head. 'Dude, I hear you and I'm sure she's special but please take a look at us. She's rich, she's good-looking and we spend our spare time serving pizzas and washing dishes.'

Neil was not dissuaded. He had heard it all before, and it did not bother him. He might not have had much, but one thing he did have was boatloads of determination. He was only eighteen, but having grown up in an orphanage had matured him much faster than others his age. He had quickly learned that if he wanted to do something with his life, he would need two things – education and money. So he had studied his butt off and got admission into one of the best colleges in New Delhi, and he worked two part-time jobs to pay the fees and save up for a professional degree. He did not know much about what was expected or even whether he would be good at it, but his dream was to get an MBA. For Neil, it was simple – he wanted a job. A job that made sure he no longer had to worry about money; a job that helped him get rid of the label of being a nobody that he had carried ever since he had been born; a job that paid him enough and gave him enough respectability for someone like Neha.

But for now, he still had to get her to date him. The very first time he had seen her, up on stage during a college function, he could have sworn a voice whispered into his ears that she was the one. He had had his share of crushes, but with Neha, it was different. He would hang around after class, whiling away time over cups of tea so that he could see her finish her class and get into her chauffeur-driven car. He signed up for an extra credit in Philosophy and suffered through incomprehensible lectures on Kant and Plato just so he could sit behind her. Of course, she had never noticed him. Neha was one of the most popular people on campus, and he was an outsider. Most of the kids came from privileged families, with cars, flashy phones and late-night parties they attended together. He was the poor orphan from a different world.

With half the college queuing up to be Neha's boyfriend, on the face of it, Neil's chances were slim. But he was not one to give up so easily. So a few Google searches later, he had found out something that nobody else knew. Neha was a volunteer for the Make-A-Wish foundation, and so Neil had offered to volunteer there as well. Six months had passed, and then he had been called up for his first wish – to accompany a five-year-old with leukemia to meet her favorite movie star. The movie star had agreed and Neil and another Wish Granter were to accompany the child and her family from their humble home on the outskirts of Delhi to meet the star in a hotel.

When Neil had first seen the little girl with her hair all gone to multiple sessions of chemotherapy, something in him changed. He realized that while he had started this all as a ruse to get closer to Neha, he wanted passionately to help these kids – to give them the joy that came with fulfilling their wishes, to bring some hope into their lives, if even for a day. Joy and hope that nobody had brought into his when he was growing up in the orphanage. Every time one of the kids smiled, it felt like in some way he was making up for all the nights he had cried himself to sleep at the orphanage. So he had dived into his volunteer work with a vengeance and in the New Year's party, he was given an award for being the most active and enthusiastic Wish Granter in all of Delhi.

That day, Neil learned another lesson – that sometimes just doing what was right eventually got you more reward than any amount of scheming and planning. He sat at the same table as Neha that night, and they immediately hit it off. She saw not another boy from college wanting to get into her pants, but a gentle, sincere boy who gave so much of his time for a cause she so dearly loved. Neil learned that Neha had lost her mother to cancer, which had made her embrace the work of the Make-A-Wish foundation with such fervor. They stayed in touch, and within days, Neil got the news that for the next wish, he was to partner with Neha. In some secret corner of his mind, he wished that Neha had requested specifically for him to be her partner. The more prosaic truth was the Wish Granter paired with her had fallen sick and they had picked Neil at random, but that did not bother Neil; he saw this as a sign from God that the wheels were finally turning in his favor.

Of course, that also meant that he had to go dressed as a giant bunny. It seemed that the little girl they were to help that day was a huge fan of the book Alice in Wonderland, and wanted Wonderland to be enacted for her. She was to be dressed as Alice, Neha was to be the Queen, and of

486

course, Neil was to play the part of the role of the rabbit who led Alice down the hole. Neil knew he looked silly in the oversized bunny ears. He was tall and lanky to the point of looking gaunt, and the large, floppy ears only made him look even taller and thinner. But it would make a sick little girl smile, and yes, it would allow him to spend time with Neha. After the wish, he had planned on asking her out for a coffee, and pleasant thoughts of their first date occupied him as he rode his bike to the girl's home, where he and Neha were to prepare a Wonderland-themed birthday party for the girl and her friends.

Neil had been riding his bike for almost thirty minutes when he first got a sense that something was wrong. Normally, in the middle of a Saturday afternoon, traffic should not have been so bad, but now cars were backed up as far as he could see. The girl's home was in a compound of low-rise apartments just a few kilometers away from where he was now, near the Delhi zoo, but with the state of traffic that he saw around him, there was no way he was going to make it in time.

Loud music sounded to his right and an auto-rickshaw pulled up. The driver was smiling and singing along, and when he saw Neil stare at him, he turned the music down. 'Don't look so serious, young man. We'll be stuck here for quite some time.'

'Why, is there an accident or something up ahead?'

The auto-rickshaw driver looked at Neil as if he were an idiot. 'Don't you watch the news? The demons are loose now. I hear they think the bloody Delhi Police will stop them. All they know is how to take bribes.'

Neil leaned closer to see what the man was talking about, and caught a whiff of country liquor. There was a half-empty bottle nestled against the man's legs. No wonder he was babbling about demons. The man saw Neil's expression and pointed to the bottle. 'My friend, you also go and get a good drink before the demons come.'

One of the cars inched forward, and Neil maneuvered his bike through the gap. He managed in this fashion for a few minutes, moving perhaps a few hundred meters, when he saw that the road ahead was blocked by a police jeep. Three nervous-looking constables were standing in the middle of the road, diverting traffic. Not able to move further on his bike, Neil got off his bike and walked towards them.

'What's happening? Why are you blocking the traffic?'

One of the policemen, a kind-looking old man who looked like he had been pulled out of retirement, stepped forward.

'Son, we're just following orders. It seems there's trouble up ahead near the Taj hotel. Officially they haven't told us what's going on yet, but if I were you I would go and spend this time with your family.'

Neil thought back to what had happened in Mumbai a few years earlier when terrorists had attacked a number of hotels and other targets. His heart sank since he knew that Neha's home was close to the Taj.

'Is there a terror attack going on?'

The policeman shook his head.

'No, son, it's worse. Have you been following the news about the strange disease that showed up in China?'

Neil got most of his information from the Internet, and sure, he had heard about how a new virus was supposedly taking hold, and how some people were spooked about it. But then, that was the media's job, right? To make everything seem like the end of the bloody world was in sight. He still remembered how they had drummed up SARS, mad cow, bird flu and God knew how many other epidemics that were supposedly going to kill millions, and of course, nothing happened. Plus, the news from the US was just a day or two old – surely no virus could spread so fast? And even if it did, why would the cops be so paranoid?

He took out his phone to call Neha to check what was going on. There were several unread notifications on his Facebook and Twitter icons. As he watched, the count seemed to increase steadily. With slightly shaking hands, he opened up Facebook and scrolled through the status updates of his friends.

'What the hell is going on in Delhi? Isn't traffic bad enough on normal days?'

'They say it's a virus? I think the only virus has affected the traffic lights.'

'Maybe the cops just want some bribes to let us through. Recession must be hard on them as well. J'

But then the messages started getting more somber.

'My bro came home and says he saw something on the road near his school. He won't stop crying and he's scared stiff. WTF is going on, please?'

'I stepped out to buy some Coke and the cops are now telling everyone to stay in their houses and lock their doors. Are there terrorists around?'

'Stay safe, guys. The government has declared a state of emergency. How can they do that without even telling us what's going on?'

'One of the news channels got an interview with a guest at the Taj. He was babbling about monsters.'

At that point, Neil stopped, a knot forming in his stomach. He had dismissed the auto-rickshaw driver's comments as the rants of a drunk, but what was really going on? What was this talk of monsters?

Then he saw the status update that galvanized him into action. It was from Neha.

'I'm scared. I can see these... things... walking outside. There are some cops firing at them. I'm alone and my dad's at work. Don't know what to do.'

Neha was alone, and in danger. Monsters or no monsters, Neil was not going to leave her alone at a time like this. He responded to her update with a simple comment.

'I'm coming for you.'

He revved his bike and tore through the police barrier. One of the cops grabbed at the bag that contained his props and in the struggle, managed to snatch the bag away, leaving just the large bunny ears in Neil's hands. Needing both hands free to control his bike, Neil put the ears on top of his head and rode off towards Neha's home as fast as he could.

A thin boy wearing pink bunny ears was hardly the sort of one-man army movies or novels would portray, but today Neil George was angry enough to go to war with anyone who was threatening Neha.

Neil didn't have to go far before he saw the first signs of trouble. He needed to take a right turn near the Old Fort to get to Neha's home, but the road was blocked by people running across the road from the government colonies to the left. Many of them were well-dressed and perhaps the families of the officials who stayed in the apartments, but there were also some pavement dwellers and even some policemen. One of the policemen took one look at Neil and shouted, 'Have you lost your mind? Don't go any further.'

Neil didn't have time to ask anyone what was happening,

since the crowd seemed to be seized with a wild panic. While he waited for them to pass, he took a quick look at his phone. There was a new update on Neha's Facebook page: 'Neil, don't come here. They are all around.'

Neil started his bike and rode straight past the fleeing crowd. Neha was clearly in great danger and he was not going to leave her.

Neil had progressed only a half-kilometer further when he first saw them.

An elderly man staggered to the side of the road, blood all over his clothes. His white hair was covered in red and his face was barely visible behind a mask of blood. The man was moving slowly, as if in immense pain, and before he could consciously think about it, Neil had stopped the bike near the old man.

'Do you need help?'

The man's head snapped up and Neil realized that something was terribly wrong. The man's eyes were yellow and vacant and his lips were drawn back, making him look more like a snarling dog than a human being. Neil noticed the foul smell, like that of dead rats, and he wondered what was wrong with the old man. That was when the man growled and lunged at Neil, trying to bite him.

'Holy shit!' Neil almost fell off his bike in terror but recovered his wits in time to start his bike and speed away. Now other bloodied figures emerged from the colony. They were all shuffling along in a slow gait and as Neil caught a glimpse at one or two of their faces, he saw the same lack of expression. They snapped and clawed at him with their teeth or clawing in the air as he passed.

Neil was more scared than he had ever been in his life. What the auto-rickshaw driver had said came back to him and he wondered if these were actually demons. A couple of the Facebook posts had said that someone in the government had announced that this was the result of the virus that everyone had heard about sweeping through the US, but Neil wondered how a virus could possibly turn people into the inhuman wraiths he saw all around him.

He swerved his bike to the right just in time to avoid three of them coming at him and rode down a side street. An overweight man ran onto the streets and right into the path of the three Neil had dodged. One of them clawed at the fat man's face, drawing blood. As the man clutched his bloodied face, another one bit into his shoulder. Blood spurted out in a fountain and the man went to his knees, as another one of his attackers bit him.

When Neil found an isolated patch hidden by a clump of trees, he stopped his bike. He retched and retched again as he remembered the blood, the fat man screaming as he was bitten and the sickening fetid odor.

Neil sat there for some time, wondering what was going on. Just then, his phone rang. It was Neha.

'Neil, please don't come here. They're calling them Biters. They attack any person they see, and once they bite you, you become like them in a few hours. They're saying on TV that the government is trying to quarantine parts of the city to contain the spread of the virus.'

'Where are you, Neha? Are you okay?'

'I'm hiding in our apartment. The Biters are all around the colony and I don't think they've seen me yet.'

Hearing Neha's terrified voice was like a splash of cold water. Neil was still scared, he still did not understand how a virus could have caused so much carnage, and he didn't know how he was going to get through the rampaging Biters to get to Neha's home. But hearing her gave him something to focus on, something that took his mind away from just how terrified he felt.

'Neha, stay there. I'm less than a kilometer away, and I'm coming to get you.'

Around the next corner, Neil saw a scene straight out of a movie. An aging policeman was standing with a rifle in his hand, shepherding dozens of terrified people into a high-rise apartment building. Neil had no idea if that guaranteed them any safety against the Biters, but in a city where everyone seemed to have lost their mind, this one policeman's selfless act of bravery stuck a chord.

A crowd of Biters, at least twenty strong, advanced towards the policeman, who had by now sent the last of the civilians into the building and turned to face the Biters. Neil had slowed his bike down, waiting to see what happened, praying that perhaps the policeman would stand a chance. The Biters were advancing, fanning out like a pack of animals to encircle their prey. The policeman showed no sign of panic, indeed he moved deliberately, and with, for lack of a better word, dignity. He knelt and brought his rifle up to his shoulder. As the Biters came in even closer, Neil sent up a silent prayer for the old man.

The policeman fired and Neil smiled as one Biter went down, spurting blood from a direct hit to the chest. The policeman fired again, and another Biter went down, this time with a gaping neck wound. The policeman might have been incredibly brave, but he was certainly not suicidal. Neil saw that he was buying time, and with every shot was moving closer to the building where the door was still ajar, and those he had saved were cheering him on. The old man fired twice more and two more Biters went down.

Then Neil saw something that in one fell swoop took away all the hope he had harbored. The first Biter who had been shot was now sitting up, and despite the bloody mess on his chest, got up and began walking towards the policeman. The second Biter, with a grotesque hole where his neck should have been and his head hanging slightly to one side, was also sitting up. The policeman dropped his rifle and Neil could see that the old man's lips were moving rapidly in prayer, but there would be no saving him today. The Biters ripped into him in a frenzy, and they tore the policeman apart till there was nothing but a mess on the road.

The people shut the door but the Biters were banging on it, and Neil knew it would be a matter of time before the door gave way. Something snapped inside Neil, and he felt a surge of anger. He picked up a metal rod lying on the side of the road and drove his bike as fast as he could towards the Biters. He swung the rod with all his strength. It connected with a satisfying thud and a Biter fell, his head smashed in. He did not get back up. Neil knew he did not stand a chance against all the Biters, but, having extracted revenge for the policeman's sacrifice, he swerved away towards Neha's home, the rod now tucked under his arm.

Most roads were blocked by bands of Biters and he took another detour through the normally busy Khan Market toward Neha's place. The market was deserted, other than Biters roaming around and bodies lying in the street. That was when he saw a group of Biters crouching over a prone figure. It was a thin, elderly woman, and she seemed paralyzed with fear, clutching a large package to her chest. Neil swooped in, and once again, his rod did its work, splattering the brains of a Biter on the pavement.

'Come on!' Neil grabbed the old woman with one hand and pulled her towards him. She seemed to have recovered her wits a bit and sat behind him as he sped away. She was mumbling something, clearly in shock.

'Look, I need to get to my girlfriend's place. Where can I drop you?'

There was no reply, and Neil was beginning to get irritated, knowing that every second with her was a second wasted.

'You must have a home or a family somewhere?'

The woman just sobbed, and Neil realized that he was perhaps being too tough on her.

'I'm sorry. Things are crazy and I just want to make sure she's okay. I'll drop you wherever you want, just tell me where.'

She looked at Neil, and he saw not just fear, but sadness in her eyes, as if she had lost something or someone of immense value. 'Young man, you have done quite enough for me. Just drop me ahead near the India International Center. It doesn't yet look overrun and I can see a lot of policemen in front of it.'

He took her near the gate and as she dismounted, he smiled.

'There must be something really important in that packet you're carrying. You didn't let go.'

As she walked into the Center, Neil turned his bike and drove towards Neha's home, hoping she was still okay and wondering if he would be able to protect her.

The last few hours had been so chaotic that Neil had almost run straight into the dozen or so Biters now crossing the road. Neil ditched his bike just in time and lay flat on the grass near the sidewalk. If he had not been so terrified, he might have found it amusing. The Biters were crossing the road single file, slowly, deliberately, displaying better traffic-safety consciousness than the good citizens of Delhi.

For the first time, Neil got a longer look at the Biters, and he was surprised at what he saw. In the initial chaos, the Biters had seemed rabid, attacking people at random. He now saw that they were moving with some sort of co-ordination. The group that had just passed had perhaps been members of one family or one neighborhood, and seemed to be moving together, with the adults in front and back and children in the middle.

Before proceeding to Neha's home, Neil fished out his phone and checked the news. What he saw froze his heart.

There were unconfirmed reports of nuclear war in the Middle East and tactical nuclear exchanges between India and Pakistan had already taken place. North Korea had lobbed missiles armed with chemical weapons at Seoul and Taiwan and the Chinese mainland were trading missile strikes. Biters were roaming freely in all major cities in the world and most governments seemed paralyzed by the sudden chaos. What had begun as an outbreak of some sort of deadly virus was heading towards a climax where the world melted in a nuclear holocaust.

Neil clicked on the Facebook icon and saw that updates were now scarce. People were perhaps just too busy trying to stay alive... or... Neil didn't want to contemplate what might have happened. A day earlier, they had been sharing an update on their new dress, or a bad grade in a test, or their mood. There were a couple of updates on the page of Make-A-Wish India, one posted by Dr. Joanne Gladwell, who was one of the senior volunteers at the foundation and took care of a lot of their fundraising activities.

'Calling all friends. The US Embassy staff and families are all headed to a safe zone near the Domestic Airport.

The Indian Army has secured the area and is calling on all civilians to head there.'

The airport was at least an hour's ride away, and Neil considered the corpse-littered street ahead of him. He could just get on his bike and make straight for the airport. The Biters, as horrifying as they were, did not move too fast, so there was a good chance that he could get there in safety. Or he could still try and get to Neha. He weighed it for a few seconds. Sure, he had called Neha his girlfriend to the old woman, but that was wishful thinking. Neha was someone he had a bad crush on, but to be perfectly honest, she was not even a close friend. He looked at the last update from Neha on Facebook.

'Neil, they are in the apartment downstairs! Don't come, please. I want you to be safe.'

That made up Neil's mind for him. Here he was, worrying about his pathetic little life, and there was Neha, in imminent danger, trying to keep him safe. It did not matter whether she was his girlfriend or indeed, whether they would ever get a chance to form any sort of relationship. There was a relationship bigger than one formed by love, lust or relation. That was the fact that they were all human, and if people were to have any chance of surviving, they would have to stick their necks out for each other.

Neil hefted the metal rod in his hands. Till that morning, he had never struck another person, even in a schoolyard scrap. Neil had always been the one to walk away. Other boys in the orphanage had only paid lip service to the sermons doled out by the Catholic nuns who ran it, but without a family or much to call his own, Neil had embraced their teachings. He wondered how what he was seeing around him squared with all that he had been taught about good and evil. In his young mind he reconciled himself to the fact that the devastation unfolding around the world was a sign of the End Times, and that now was the time when good and pious people would have to step up and help others.

He waited till the last of the Biters was out sight and then mounted his bike for the last stretch of his ride to Neha's home.

Neil had been a pretty keen cricket player as a child, and he tried to block out the blood and splattered brains, instead pretending that he was playing a game of cricket and dispatching each delivery out of sight. He held the thick metal rod in a two-handed grip, almost perpendicular to his body, in a stance that would have been more at home on a baseball diamond than a cricket pitch, and waded into the Biters outside Neha's home.

He had arrived to find a good half-dozen Biters clawing at the door to the stairwell that led up to her apartment. The apartment downstairs had been torn apart, and other than huge bloodstains around the floor there was no sign of the inhabitants. The rod made solid contact with another Biter's head, this one a middle-aged woman who had an iPod dangling around her chest, the earbuds still in her ears. As the Biter fell, her head cracked open and Neil took a breather. Fueled by rage and adrenaline, he had waded into the Biters, and now three of them lay at his feet. But that still left three more closing in on him, drooling and growling, and his shoulder felt like it was on fire. He resolved that if he got out alive, and if anyone made movies ever again, he'd write to them telling them just how unrealistic their fight sequences were. He could barely breathe, and had to muster every single ounce of strength left in him to lift up the rod again and smash it against a Biter's head. He missed but made solid contact with his shoulder. The Biter, a big man in a bloody, torn vest, roared and clawed at Neil's hand, drawing blood.

'Shit!'

Neil looked at the growing trickle of blood on his forearm and backed away. He had no idea if the virus or whatever made people into ghouls could be transmitted by a scratch, but he figured he would find out soon enough.

'Sissies scratch. Men do this!' The normally mild-mannered Neil's face was a mask of rage as he swung his rod again and smashed open the Biter's head. The two remaining Biters looked down at the carnage around them, and for a second, Neil hoped that they would decide to cut their losses and find easier prey. Instead, they roared in fury and advanced on him again.

In his duels so far, Neil had learnt an important lesson. He could break their hands, smash their knees, crack open their ribs, but they would keep coming. The only thing that stopped them was smashing open their heads. So he had quickly overcome his squeamishness and started aiming only for the head. The first time he had made solid contact and taken off a Biter's head, he had screamed aloud.

'Off with their heads!'

Wearing his bunny ears and having set out to enact Alice in Wonderland, he though it only appropriate and he was repeating that battle cry as he took on the remaining Biters.

The rod he was carrying was covered with blood and other gore that Neil did not want to think about. Neil swung his rod at one of the remaining two Biters and missed, slipping on the blood on the floor. He tried to recover his footing but fell hard on his back, the rod rolling a few feet away. Neil backed away as the two Biters steadily advanced on him. Both had their blood-stained teeth bared and were a mere couple of feet away when they staggered back as a thick foam enveloped them. Neha stood in the doorway, a portable fire extinguisher in her hands. She sprayed the Biters again and then screamed at Neil.

'Come on!'

He grabbed the rod and the two of them ran out of the apartment building, leaving the two Biters behind. Neha got on the bike behind Neil and they sped away.

'Where do we go now?'

Neil knew the answer to that. The problem was getting there in the fading light with millions of Biters rampaging through the streets of Delhi.

They had stopped at an abandoned gas station to top up Neil's bike for the remainder of the ride to the airport. In the twenty minutes since they had left Neha's home, they had seen plenty of Biters roaming in the streets, but moving at speed, they had managed to get this far without incident. The remainder of the trip to the airport would require them to get on the highway, where Neil hoped they could pass unmolested, but they would not have many opportunities to top up his fuel tank, which was nearing empty. So he had taken the risk of stopping to pump gas into the bike, the rod that had served him so well in his other hand. Neil caught a glimpse in the mirror ahead of him, and he scowled.

'I forgot I'm still wearing these silly bunny ears.'

He was about to take them off when Neha's hand gently tousled his hair. Her touch sent a jolt through him.

'I think you look cute in these.'

Neha laughed but then Neil noticed a change in her tone as she touched his shoulder.

'Neil, you're bleeding!'

Neil looked at his hand, still bloody from the scratch he had suffered at Neha's apartment. 'Relax, it's just a scratch.'

'No, I mean up here.'

Neil caught the tension in her voice and took a look in the mirror near him. There was a red patch on his left shoulder. He dropped the rod and peeled back his shirt. His shoulder was covered in a thin film of blood. He wiped some of it away to reveal puncture wounds.

'Neil, did they get close enough to...'

Neha did not dare complete the sentence, but the moment Neil saw the wound, the same thought had burned itself into his mind. Had he been bitten? He could not remember it, but then the struggle below Neha's apartment had been so savage that he had not really been conscious of much other than swinging his rod at the nearest Biter he could see. He had assumed the pain in his shoulder was from the exertion of the fight. But now, looking at the wound, he was beginning to have doubts. He looked at Neha, his eyes filling with tears.

'How long do I have? Have you read anything on the Internet?'

He could see that Neha was starting to cry as well and sobs racked her body as she tried to turn away. 'Maybe it's just a cut.'

Neil got up, holding her shoulders so that she was forced to look straight into his eyes. 'How long do I have?'

Neha spoke in little more than a whisper, seemingly forcing each word out. 'They say that the speed at which the infection takes hold depends on how deep the bite is and the number of bites. Some people with minor bites thought they had got away but became Biters after three or four hours. People who are bitten repeatedly turn pretty much immediately.'

Neil looked at his watch. He had been bitten perhaps thirty minutes ago. Even assuming he had a couple of hours, the best he could hope was to get Neha to the safety of the airport, and then what? He had met many brave boys and girls during his work with Make-A-Wish, and he had marveled at their strength in the face of terminal illnesses. He found his knees buckling and realized that he did not have that same strength. Of course, they had months or perhaps years to go – he did not even have one day.

He just sat there for a few seconds, Neha squatting in front of him, her hands on his shoulders. His mind was numb, with fear, with self-pity, with regret for all the things he would never be able to do. He looked up into Neha's tear-filled eyes, and felt a renewed resolve. Neha must have seen the change in his expression.

'What's wrong?'

He stood up, and finished filling his bike's tank, and then looked at Neha.

'If I drive really fast, I can probably get you to the airport in thirty minutes. So we should still have time before anything happens to me. But before that, will you grant me one last wish?'

Neha burst into tears. 'Neil, maybe it's just a cut...'

Neil held her shoulders and she hugged him.

'You know better than that. Now, we don't have a lot of time. Will you fulfill my wish?'

Neha fought back her tears and nodded.

'I was thinking of asking you out for a coffee after the party today. Will you go out with me on a date? I don't have much money, I don't look like much, but I do have these funky bunny ears and I am currently the world champion in the game of Biter Swatting with my rod here.'

Neha laughed and hugged him tight.

'Lead the way, my bunny-eared hero. Where shall we have our date?'

And so they sat in an abandoned Pizza Hut. They didn't eat or drink anything, but just sitting there, holding hands, made Neil forget, if only for a moment, what he was faced with. For that fleeting moment, he was living his dream.

They talked about their families, their dreams. Neil told her about how he was saving up to go to a good college, maybe get an MBA. Neha told him about how she hated being always told what to do, and being expected to join the family business after an MBA, and how she would much rather become a journalist. They talked about their likes and dislikes, about movies, and music, and friends at college, and then Neil took a look at his watch. It had been just fifteen minutes. The most magical fifteen minutes of his life. But now he had to get Neha to safety. He got up, but she stopped him.

'Your wish isn't yet over. There's something left.'

Then she leaned close and kissed Neil.

The highway looked like a giant junkyard, with abandoned vehicles littering it. There were bodies strewn among them, but Neil tried to focus on the path ahead as he maneuvered his bike between the vehicles. They had seen groups of Biters when they had left the city center and taken the road to the highway, but they have been traveling too fast for the Biters to catch them. Now, hemmed in by abandoned cars on all sides, and in the fading light, he was forced to trade speed for safety, and there was no telling what lurked behind the next car. Neha was acting as the lookout, and once or twice she yelled out warnings of approaching Biters, but in both cases, it turned out to be a case of nerves, made worse by shadows being thrown around them.

Then she screamed, but even before the words left her mouth, Neil saw the danger. Two Biters had come out from behind a car to their right. With three abandoned cars blocking the way to their left, they did not have enough room to avoid them. One of the Biters was a frail old man with his face largely ripped off below the nose. The other was a younger man, wearing a bloodied Mickey Mouse t-shirt. Neil told Neha to be ready to grab the handlebars when he told her to, and then accelerated his bike, speeding towards the Biters. He turned the bike sideways at the last moment and kicked out at the older Biter. The momentum of the bike , more than Neil's strength or aim, sent the Biter sprawling. The other Biter was coming towards Neil, bloodied mouth open, ready to bite, when Neil screamed at Neha to steer the bike.

'Mickey Mouse, meet Bunny Ears.'

With that, he swung the metal rod over his head and crushed the Biter's skull in one blow. The older Biter was scrambling to get back up, but by then Neil had sped away down the highway.

For the next ten minutes or so, they rode in relative peace, and with fewer cars visible on the road. Then up ahead Neil saw some vehicles moving at high speed. There were a couple of SUVs and what looked like five large Army trucks. The windows of the lead SUV were rolled down and rifles stuck out at least one window.

'They look like Army vehicles. Maybe they're also heading for the airport.'

Just then, Neil was racked by a violent coughing fit, and he barely managed to bring the bike to a stop before he fell off. Neha had fallen and scraped her knees, but she hardly noticed the pain as she ran towards Neil.

Neil was now on his knees and continuing to cough. The front of his shirt was now coated with blood and his hands were beginning to shake.

Neha started to cry, but Neil got up and pushed her towards the bike.

'Not yet, not yet. I have to get you to safety. I may not last till the airport but I can get you to those Army trucks.'

Neil drove faster than he had ever driven before, with Neha clutching him tightly as he bore down on the vehicles he had seen. He saw someone lift the flap on the rear truck's cab, and a rifle peeked out. Neil wanted to shout at them to not shoot, but when he opened his mouth, more blood came out. He would just have to take his chances. He increased his speed and came alongside the lead SUV, motioning frantically for it to stop. A man in military uniform pointed a rifle at Neil.

'Sir, I will shoot if you do not move away from this convoy.'

Neha shouted back, 'We need help. I'm trying to get to that safe zone at the airport, and my boyfriend needs medical help.'

The man with the rifle turned to talk to someone inside and then another face peered out, a familiar face. Then the convoy came to a halt and a man in an Indian Army uniform ran out from the SUV. He addressed Neha.

'Ma'am, were you with the Make-A-Wish Foundation?'

When Neha nodded, he pointed back to the SUV.

'We really don't have space in there for anyone, but Dr. Gladwell recognized you from the foundation and is asking that we take you along. Anyway, the airport is gone, so we're going to another army shelter nearby, and you had best come along.'

He took Neha's hand and was pulling her when she looked at Neil. 'Can you help him?'

The soldier looked at Neil, pity in his eyes as he took in Neil's bloodied clothes and his yellowing eyes. 'Ma'am, I'm really sorry. We can't do anything for him any more. We need to get going.'

When Neha hesitated, Neil took her hand. 'Please go, Neha, and take care of yourself.'

He was saying the words in his mind, but he realized they were coming out all garbled as more blood came out of his mouth. He felt another sharp stab of pain in his chest and he pushed Neha away. The soldier half dragged her to the SUV and then the convoy drove away.

Neil sat down by the side of the road, watching the vehicles disappear into the distance. He coughed out more blood and then lay down, unable to sit any more. His body felt like it was on fire, but he smiled one last time. He had managed to get Neha to safety, and she had called him her boyfriend, had she not?

With that last thought, Neil George relaxed, closed his eyes and awaited what was to come.

WE'LL NAME HER ALICE

'BOB, I NEED SOME AMERICAN Chopsuey NOW!'
Robert Gladwell put the phone down with a
sigh. He might be the second-in-command at the
American Embassy in New Delhi, but when it came to
his wife, Joanne, there was no question who was in charge.
Especially when she was cranky, sleepless and in the middle
of a very tough pregnancy.

They had been in New Delhi for close to two years, and
Gladwell had been through enough Third World postings
in places like Bangkok, Jakarta and Riyadh to appreciate the
real richness of cultures and relationships that lay beneath
the surface.

He told his secretary that he was going to take a slightly
longer than normal lunch break and as he told his driver to
head to their apartment in the city's Diplomatic Enclave,
he called ahead to order some Chinese food. He had long
realized that the Chinese food available in India was nothing
like what he had tasted in the US, or indeed during his trips to
China when he had been on a trade delegation. It was spiced,
fried and tossed in ways that were possible only in India, and
the crispy noodles with oversweet sauce ambitiously named
'American Chopsuey' most Americans would have found

neither American nor Chopsuey. But who was Gladwell to argue with a pregnant woman's cravings?

'Dan, after lunch, I think I'll stop by for the briefing at South Block.'

Gladwell put down his phone after telling his Personal Security Officer in the car following him about his plans and thought about just how much things had changed. A year ago, security would no doubt have been tight, but he would not be tailed by a contingent of officers from both the US Diplomatic Security Service and India's Special Protection Group, even when he headed out for a quiet family dinner.

The world was imploding fast – tensions in the Middle East had reached a fever pitch, and the attacks on Israeli diplomats in New Delhi in early 2012 had proven to be just a small preview of what was to follow. Attacks on US and Israeli diplomats had occurred through the rest of the year around the world, and the finger of suspicion had always pointed back to Iran. Israel was itching to bomb Iran, and the US efforts at holding it back were fast slipping. Being in India put Gladwell and his team in an especially uncomfortable place. India, while allied to the US, had important commercial interests in Iran, and was also reeling from constant attacks from terrorists based in Pakistan, a nation the US was relying on to allow some sort of orderly withdrawal from the festering mess that was Afghanistan.

Just thinking of it all gave Gladwell a headache, and he was not looking forward to the afternoon's briefing by India's External Affairs Ministry, where they would share intelligence about how rogue Jihadi elements were dangerously close to getting control of Pakistan's nuclear arsenal. Gladwell had seen it all before, in files sent his way by the CIA, but the leadership back in the United States was choosing to stay strangely mum about it all. If all of that was not bad enough, then there was the recent virus in China that had led relations between China and the US to hit rock bottom, and the occasional skirmishes between Chinese and Taiwanese forces did not help. Between Jo's mood swings and the chaos at work, Robert Gladwell looked forward to the pint of beer he had been promised by an old Army buddy who was in town later that evening.

'Hey, Dad, don't tell me Mom wanted that Chopsuey crap again!'

'Young lady, you watch your language.'

Gladwell waited to see the expression on his ten-year old daughter's face gradually change from one of amusement to one of concern. Gladwell rarely lost his temper, but she knew that it wasn't a great idea to make him do so. Finally, he smiled and ruffled her hair.

'Put your school bag in your room and help me set the table, and to make up for the Chopsuey, we'll have some ice cream after lunch.'

Jane whooped and ran more than walked to her room, as Gladwell went to meet his wife, Joanne.

Dr. Joanne Gladwell was six months pregnant and now very much showing it, but she still insisted on participating in the one thing beyond her family that she was passionate about – the Make-A-Wish foundation. She had a Doctorate in Literature and had taught for some years, but gradually found it hard to sustain a teaching career with the constant moves that came with being the wife of a Foreign Service Officer. So she channeled her energy and passion into volunteer work. As Gladwell walked into their bedroom, she was reading up on some of the fundraising plans for the foundation.

'Sweetheart, how're you feeling today?' Gladwell leaned over and kissed her on her forehead, lovingly playing with her blonde hair. Jo held his hand and made him sit down next to her. 'What are you looking at?'

Jo smiled as she answered. 'At my knight in shining armor, my bearer of American Chopsuey.'

Gladwell laughed and got up to set the table.

'Sweetheart, I'll rush through lunch a bit as I have a meeting to get to. By the way, how's the little one?'

Jo grimaced a bit.

'She's kicking, as always. This one will be a real firecracker.'

Jane had been a dream pregnancy and a real angel to bring up. Their second child, a girl, as they had learned in an ultrasound back in the US, was quite the opposite. Jo had terrible morning sickness in the early months, and now, the little one never seemed to stay still.

A rushed lunch later, Gladwell was at the meeting, but it was the press conference in the evening that he dreaded more.

'Mr. Gladwell, what can you tell us about what is happening in China and what is your reaction to the Chinese government's accusation that this virus is the result of biological warfare by the United States?'

Gladwell had been wondering when the question would be asked. The first thirty minutes of the press briefing had been routine questions about the Middle East and the situation in Pakistan, for which Gladwell had stock platitudes ready. But the China situation was one where Gladwell had received no instructions or briefing from his bosses back in Washington. All he knew from intelligence reports was that an unknown virus was raging in China, with the epicenter being a remote military installation in Mongolia. The Chinese had tried to hush it up, a tactic that backfired when the virus exploded after three days. Reports were sketchy, and Gladwell personally thought stories of frenzied victims attacking others were over the top. He wished the Ambassador had been around, but he was on a vacation back in the US, and Gladwell had been left holding the fort.

He took the mike. 'I'm sorry, but I have no information to share on that beyond what Washington has already shared.'

An hour later, Gladwell was seated at a pub with Joshua Abernathy, a face from his past life. As often happened with close friends, there was no need for small talk, even though they were meeting after a dozen years. After hugging each other and ordering drinks, they sipped their beer in silence and only when Gladwell started his second pint did Joshua speak what was on his mind.

'Things are going to get real ugly. You thought of getting your family somewhere safe, with Jo being pregnant and all?'

'Aren't you overreacting? India and Pakistan have been playing these games for years, and even if the shit does hit the fan in the Middle East, we should be safe here.'

Joshua put his mug down and his eyes were creased with worry. 'That's not what I'm talking about. You do remember what I did when I left the Army, don't you?'

Gladwell still didn't know where Joshua was going with this, and motioned to Joshua to wait as he ordered another round of drinks.

'Bob, you need to pay attention, please.'

That got his attention, and Gladwell looked at Joshua, curious as to what had spooked his normally unflappable friend.

'I joined Zeus, a PMC. Private Military Contractor. After Bosnia, when we left the Army, my skills were useless in the civilian world and I wasn't as smart as you were to be able to study and become a diplomat. Zeus contacted me, and for a while it was fun. I ran protection duties for VIPs, hooked up security for international summits and so on, and it paid well. But then it got ugly.'

Gladwell waited as Joshua paused to take a sip, and then continued, an edge to his voice.

'My bosses seemed too well-connected. As I got deeper into the organization, they would regularly meet folks at the State Department and even the White House. Then I was transferred to their Special Division, which, as I quickly learnt, did a bunch of black ops that could be denied by the people ordering them as no US forces would be involved. Stuff like illegal renditions, and hits on targets in countries we'd normally consider friendly.'

Bob could see his friend was worried, but none of this was news. PMCs had mushroomed in the 90s and the War on Terror had provided them a lot of scope to peddle their wares to the highest bidder. Some had grown to have resources to train and equip whole armies for tinpot dictators. But then Joshua continued.

'There are Zeus operatives crawling all over this city. I left Zeus a year ago when I couldn't handle their dirty business any longer, but I still have contacts there. They're all over the Middle East, China and Asia, and it can't be a coincidence that trouble is being stirred up there.'

'Zeus may be powerful but they can't be doing all this on their own. That sounds too far-fetched.'

Joshua leaned over. 'That's what I'm trying to tell you. There are folks in our own system making this happen.'

Joshua's words stayed with Gladwell, but he found it hard to believe that elements in the government could have been engineering this level of chaos. Sure, he was no babe in the woods, and he knew that politicians and business interests were not above dirty tricks to suit their agendas, but something on this scale, with such global ramifications –

that did not make any sense.

He spent the evening at home, playing on their PS3 with Jane and then helping Jo decorate the room they had already assigned to their new baby. At night, as had happened for a few weeks, they sat together and debated baby names

'Alexis?'

'No, sounds too strong. I want a nice, feminine name.'

'Lucy?'

'Too common.'

And on it went till they had added a couple of additional names to their already long shortlist.

'Bob, this guy's refusing to go away. Sorry to bug you on this but could you help out?'

Gladwell groaned and got up from his desk. He couldn't blame his secretary for asking him to help. This Major Appleseed had been coming to the Embassy for two days, flashing all sorts of credentials, and asking for information that he had no right to ask for. So now Gladwell would have to take on the unpleasant task of turning him away.

For all the pain he was causing, Appleseed was a serving officer in the US Army so Gladwell did him the courtesy of calling him to his office and asking for some coffee to be served. As Appleseed walked in, Gladwell saw that the bull analogy was quite appropriate given Appleseed's bulk. As he began speaking, Gladwell found himself taking an instinctive dislike to him. He was eager and friendly in the manner of a pushy car salesman.

'Morning, Gladwell. Am I glad I got to meet you instead of trying to convince those bureaucrats down there to help me out. This person of interest I'm looking for has registered at the Embassy and I'm hoping you can make my life simple and tell me where she is.'

Gladwell kept his tone pleasant, but his voice had an edge to it. 'Major Appleseed, as others have explained to you already, we cannot share details of where a particular US citizen is staying in Delhi because you have no apparent need to know.'

When Appleseed fished inside his coat pocket for some papers, Gladwell waved them aside. 'You have personal letters from some senators and a supposedly verbal instruction from the Vice President. Unless I have something more formal than that, I am not going to compromise the privacy of a US citizen.'

Appleseed's smile disappeared, to be replaced by a look of disdain. 'Look, Gladwell, I was just trying to save myself time. I can get what I need in a couple of days.' As he began to walk out the door, he turned to look at Gladwell. 'I see your desire to play Boy Scout has not gone away. I've seen your Army files, and if I were you, I would get with the program. The people I work for will need people they can trust, and will have no patience for those who stand in their way.'

Gladwell stood up, barely controlling his anger. 'Major, I have seen *your* files and I can see why you picked up the moniker of the 'Beast of Kandahar'. With the human rights violations you are accused of, you should be in jail. I suppose your political connections are bailing you out, but I have no room for them here. Goodbye.'

As Appleseed slammed the door on the way out, Gladwell sat down, trying to calm down. Appleseed had struck a nerve, one Gladwell had tried to keep buried. As a young officer straight out of training, he had been on a peacekeeping mission in Bosnia, with orders not to intervene unless his men were fired on. They had stumbled upon a group of masked gunmen who had lined up several dozen young men and boys and had begun to execute them. After repeated pleas over the radio to get permission to intervene, he had acted on his conscience and ordered his men to open fire. Eight of the gunmen were killed but instead of being rewarded for saving dozens of civilians, Gladwell found his military career in tatters, especially when it was revealed that the gunmen were on the payroll of a US Private Military Contractor with links to powerful senators. The case was buried and Gladwell was given an honorable discharge. A change in administration gave him the opportunity to rejoin the government but this time as a diplomat, determined to not let such perversities of foreign policy happen again. With people like Appleseed on the loose, and what his friend had mentioned about Zeus operatives, he was not so sure that he or anyone else could come in the way of the sort of evil that Appleseed and his masters represented.

As he headed home, he wondered who Appleseed had been so interested in. He hadn't even bothered to ask his staff, but then it was the principle that mattered. Gladwell closed his eyes and tried to wish away the throbbing headache.

'Honey, I'm sorry, but you need to listen to me when I tell you something. You are not going out today. Am I clear?'

Gladwell had shouted much louder than he had intended to, but the accumulated stress of the last two days was beginning to tell on him. Jane sulked and ran sobbing to her room. 'You made me miss my ballet performance in school. You know how much I've prepared for that.'

Gladwell winced as she slammed the door to her room, but he had already vented enough at her to take her to task for this display of defiance. He felt a hand on his shoulder.

'You're beginning to scare me. First you tell me not to step outside of the home, now Jane, and why on Earth do you have a gun in our house? Will you please tell me what's going on?'

Gladwell took his wife's hand in his and slumped against her, finally feeling himself unable to bear all the pressure and tension he had been under for the last two days. He asked Jo to sit down, and she sat down on his lap, trying to calm him down.

'Do you know all the stuff that's on TV about the virus in China and reports about something like it in the US?'

When Jo nodded, he continued, finding that sharing what was plaguing him made it a bit easier to bear, though he was now passing on a terrible burden onto Jo. But if things were going to unravel as fast as he feared, she needed to be prepared.

'The news channels are downplaying it, making it seem like something like bird flu or swine flu. But it's not, it's much, much worse.'

'Do you mean worse in terms of people dying from it?'

Gladwell fumbled for a while, trying to put into words what little he had learned. 'This virus does something to people. It doesn't kill them, but it changes them. They start attacking others. I don't know much more, but I do know they are about to declare martial law in some parts of the US.'

He could tell by the expression on Jo's face just how difficult she found it to believe this. 'I'm sure they'll cure it. It's just a virus...'

Gladwell cut her off. 'Jo, I don't know a lot, but I've read some cables that show it's spreading faster than anyone thought and its effects are like nothing anyone's seen. Then you have half the planet going to war at the same time, and nobody has a handle on things any more. I heard the first cases in India are being reported so I want you guys to stay home.'

'What happens now?'

Gladwell stood up, gathering his coat. He was now on more familiar ground. While the danger was very real and imminent, he knew the emergency evacuation procedures were in place and his government would not let him and the other Embassy staffers down.

'Don't worry, sweetheart. If the shit does hit the fan, they'll get us out.'

'I'm sorry to disturb you personally, Madam Vice President, but nobody seems to be seeing the gravity of the situation. There are cases in India now and the media is still largely ignoring the spread. All I'm asking is that we authorize an emergency evacuation of the families of Embassy staff here. I and a skeleton staff will stay behind.'

Gladwell had sent many cables to Washington making the same request, and many of his colleagues around the world were making similar pleas. What was puzzling was that nobody in Washington seemed to care. It was as if they thought they could wish away the crisis by denying it existed. So Gladwell had taken the risky gambit of going all the way to the top. One of his mentors had been a White House staffer, and while he was unable to help directly, he was able to at least set up this call.

Deborah Henfield's voice boomed over the speakerphone.

'I am Deb Henfield, the Vice President of the United States and I say that there is no imminent crisis based on all the information I have.'

With that, all of Gladwell's worries were dismissed out of hand.

In just one day, things had spiraled horribly out of control. Many large cities in the US were now affected by the virus, and the government had reacted with a media blackout. Bizarrely, the Armed Forces had not been called out to help deal with the crisis, supposedly because they were needed to deal with crises overseas, Zeus had been appointed to deal with containing the unrest and chaos in the US. Regional wars had broken out all over the place and it looked as if the whole world had lost its sanity at the same time.

Gladwell's phone rang. It was Brigadier Randhawa, an Indian Army officer whom he had befriended during his stint in Delhi. The Brigadier was as blunt as ever. 'Bob, our governments don't give a fuck and things will go downhill soon. I have my men ready with our families to get to our base in Manesar. If you want, we'll pick you and your people up.'

Gladwell thanked him and hung up. Randhawa was a highly decorated soldier and was part of the National Security Guard, India's elite commando force, and if there was one place where safety could be found, it was with him and his men.

The next thing he did was to call the head of the Marine detachment at the Embassy. With outbreak cases reported across India, Gladwell had already asked the Marines to be ready for any eventuality.

The Embassy was already full of anxious American citizens, many of them now stranded. Several international flights had already been cancelled as authorities panicked. At first, a few had been outraged at what was happening back in the United States, especially since Zeus mercenaries were in charge of law and order in the US. But now everyone had bigger things to worry about. Rumors that the first cases had been reported in Delhi had sent everyone into a panic and Gladwell was increasingly torn between staying at the Embassy to hold things together or getting home to be with Jo and Jane.

He also saw with increasing irritation that Appleseed was back at the Embassy. As a serving Army Officer, he had every right to be there, but what irked Gladwell was the fact that he was bringing in a gaggle of black-suited men, who were on paper US citizens in Delhi on business trips. Again, going by the book, there was nothing Gladwell could do to stop them, but the fact that their employer was Zeus told Gladwell where Appleseed's true allegiance lay and also made him even more concerned.

'Dr. Dasgupta is here to meet you.'

Gladwell normally would never have entertained a meeting request at a time like this, but this lady had called multiple times and had said that it was a life-and-death situation. He had done background checks on her and he could not figure out what had made her so anxious to meet him. She had recently resigned from some government-funded lab to come back to India.

He finished a couple of emails and then was about to tell his secretary to send his visitor up when his phone rang. He sat down when he realized the call was from the White House. The President had been largely invisible in the preceding days and the VP had been the public face of the government. Remembering his last conversation with her, Gladwell hoped that she was not too ticked off.

'I am calling you on an urgent national security matter that you need to know. We have been tracking a person of interest called Protima Dasgupta who we believe to have links with terror groups. Do not meet her or allow her access to the Embassy. We have men on the ground who will deal with her.'

Then she hung up, leaving Gladwell flabbergasted. He found it odd that the Vice President would call about a matter like this, but then he also knew that he was hardly privy to all the classified operations sometimes going on under his nose. The last thing he wanted in the middle of all this chaos was a terror suspect loose in his Embassy. He dialed his secretary.

'Tell Dr. Dasgupta that I'm busy and I cannot meet her today.'

When his mobile phone rang, it was Jo, and she sounded terrified.

'Bob, they're calling these things Biters, and I've got calls from friends saying they're right in the middle of Delhi.'

'Sir, do we open fire?'

'No, Jim, just get us home. Randhawa asked us to link up with his convoy on the way to National Highway 8, and we don't have much time.'

The SUV sped through the streets of Delhi, and not for the first time, the driver ran over a Biter who got in the way. Under normal circumstances, Gladwell would have been horrified at the thought of running over people in his rush to get home, but things were anything but normal.

In the minutes following Jo's call, all hell seemed to have broken loose. There were rumors that Biters were all over central Delhi, and Gladwell tried one last time to get through to his superiors and ask them to send help, but nobody was picking up the phone. The news was reporting that the President and Vice President had already been evacuated and that the US mainland was now teeming with Biters. Then came the news that tactical nuclear attacks had been launched on Indian Army targets by Pakistan, and that India was in the process of retaliating.

Gladwell took an hour to ensure that the staffers got transport home, in many cases relying on the Marines to stop taxis for them. He wished there was more he could do for the US citizens at the Embassy, but after talking to Randhawa, he was told that there were only five trucks, and there was no room for others. Gladwell had agreed on a rendezvous point with Randhawa and asked all his staffers to get there with their families. He only hoped most of them would get there safely.

Gladwell had initially been skeptical about the rumors about the Biters being bloodthirsty monsters who could not be killed. But in the ten minutes since they had left the Embassy, he was more scared than he had ever been before. All around him, small groups of Biters, covered in blood and grotesque wounds, roamed through the city at will, attacking anyone they saw. He saw a couple of police posts that had been overrun, and his stomach had churned at the sight of what had remained of the policemen.

The SUV screeched to a halt outside Gladwell's home and the two Marines at the back stepped out, their assault rifles at the ready. The driver was also armed, but he kept the engine running as Gladwell sprinted inside and came out a minute later with Jo and Jane. As he herded them into the vehicle, Jane saw a trio of Biters walk towards them and she screamed. That got their attention and they increased their pace.

'Get inside now!'

Jane was now crying in terror and had to be bodily lifted inside the vehicle. The driver backed away and began the journey to the highway where they were to link up with Randhawa. In theory it was only a twenty-minute drive, but now they were going to drive through a city teeming with Biters.

'Sir, the road's too blocked with cars. There's no way we can proceed!'

Between the driver's increasingly panic-stricken updates, Jane's continuous sobbing and one of the Marines' loud prayers, Gladwell was having trouble concentrating on keeping all of them alive. This was the third dead end they had hit in the last ten minutes, and he was beginning to regret having taken the SUV in the first place. True, they comfortably fit into it, but with the streets littered with abandoned vehicles, it was that much tougher to find a way through the maze. On the flip side, they had managed to store some stocks of drinking water and canned food in the trunk, but Gladwell was pretty sure by now that they were at more imminent risk of dying at the hands of Biters instead of thirst or hunger.

The first time he had seen one of the Biters' victims get up and join in the rampage, his heart had nearly stopped. He had turned around to see if he could somehow shield Jane, but he found her watching with tear-filled eyes. He did not know if he could protect her physically, but he knew he had already failed to shield her from the horror unfolding all around them.

There were bodies strewn around this stretch of the road, as a company of troops, who had rushed into action without knowing what they were up against, had been torn apart. Gladwell had noticed a couple of things so far – one, that the Biters massacred anyone who tried to resist, and second, that for all their terrifying invulnerability to bullets, they could be killed. Two Biters lying in pools of blood near the scene of this battle told him that. But for now, he could not contemplate what that weakness must be, since there were at least a dozen Biters bearing down on them.

'Back off, we'll find another side street!'

Gladwell was trying to sound confident, but he knew that they were lost. In trying to get around the maze of cars and trying to avoid large groups of Biters, they had strayed too far from the main roads, and were now trying to find their way through a warren of smaller side streets. The two Marines had their rifles ready, but there was no way they were going to roll down the windows. By now Jane had pretty much cried herself into silence, and truth be told, the one who had most kept her wits about her was Jo. She had her left hand on her belly, saying soothing things to their unborn daughter, and in her right hand was a map of Delhi, with which she was now trying to guide them. She caught Gladwell looking at her and he just smiled and patted her knee. He wanted to tell her how proud he was of her strength and how looking at her was making him feel braver than he really was, but for now that little gesture said more than he could have hoped to have said in many minutes.

'Go straight and then turn right at the next traffic light. We should get onto a major road and then you can find your way to the highway.'

'Yes, Ma'am.'

The SUV careened down the narrow street and for a moment Gladwell thought that they had finally got a lucky break. The street seemed to be abandoned. That was when the four Biters ran into their path.

If the driver had maintained his speed, he could have run over the lead Biter, but he panicked and swerved the SUV hard to the left. They hit one Biter and flung him to the side but brought the SUV to a halt. As he fumbled with the keys to start the engine again, the other three Biters started banging on the windows.

This was the closest Gladwell had come to a Biter so far and he looked at the bloodied face staring at him from just a few inches away, separated only by the glass of the window. The man was wearing what had once been perhaps an expensive pair of designer sunglasses, but now the shattered remains of those hung from one ear. His eyes were vacant and drool and blood were streaming down his mouth. He had been bitten several times on his neck and shoulder, and blood from those wounds joined that from his mouth to almost completely cover the front of his shirt. He was banging on the window with both hands and, not able to make much headway, he began banging his head against it.

Gladwell was carrying his gun, a small .25 Guernica he had acquired a license for a few months ago after the attacks on diplomats intensified. The glass cracked as the Biter kept banging his head against it, and without thinking, Gladwell raised his gun and fired a single round straight into the Biter's forehead. The Biter rocked back and fell onto the pavement, and as blood seeped out of the single hole in the middle of his head, he did not show any signs of getting up. Gladwell screamed to the Marines in the rearmost seats.

'Shoot them in the head! Aim for their heads!'

Galvanized into action by Gladwell's words, the Marines selected single-shot mode on their M-16s and fired a single round each into the heads of the Biters attacking the rear windows. Both Biters went down and did not get back up. By now, the driver had recovered enough of his wits and started the SUV again.

Everyone sat in silence, watching the alleys around them for any further signs of Biters. Gladwell gripped his pistol in both hands, scanning both sides of the road. He knew that they still had a long way to go, but at least they had learned one important lesson – Biters could be defeated.

'I can see three more cars!'

The cry from Jo got everyone's attention. They had proceeded relatively unmolested for the last fifteen minutes and were now close to the rendezvous point agreed with Randhawa. This was at the point where the road intersected with the National Highway, and Gladwell was heartened to see three cars already there. His spirits rose at the thought that the staffers and their families had made it. There was no sign of Randhawa, but then Gladwell expected that they would make slower progress in their trucks. One of the Marines opened the door as the SUV stopped and was about to step out when Gladwell stopped him.

'Not so fast. Something doesn't seem right.'

He recognized at least one of the cars as belonging to his staffers, but there was no sign of anyone there, and a couple of the cars had their doors open. He asked the driver to keep the engine running and stepped out, followed by one of the Marines. The other Marine stayed in the vehicle to provide some cover for Jo and Jane in case there was any trouble.

Gladwell had his gun in his hand, and try as he might, he could not stop his hand shaking. He had seen combat up close in the Balkans, but that was many years ago, and he had been facing men, ruthless mercenaries but men like himself, who would bleed and die, not ghouls of the sort that now roamed through Delhi. Something moved behind one of the cars and he readied his gun, holding it in both hands, both to steady his aim and stop his hands shaking. He motioned to the Marine to give him cover and then he peered around the car. He was in no way prepared for what he saw.

It was, or rather had been, Jonathan, a young staffer at the Embassy who had been there for less than a year. His blond hair was matted with blood and his lean, dimpled face that had once set many a woman's heart aflutter at Embassy parties was pulled back in a grotesque grimace. His eyes were closed and his breath came in ragged gasps. The front of his shirt was covered in blood. As Gladwell leaned closer to see if he was okay, his eyes snapped open, and instinctively Gladwell took a step back.

Jonathan's lively blue eyes were gone, replaced by a yellowed stare that Gladwell had seen earlier in the Biters that had attacked their SUV. Jonathan's mouth opened, and for a second Gladwell hoped that he might say something, that his humanity might yet be preserved. Instead, he emitted a low growl that was more animal than human. He bared his teeth and snapped at Gladwell, who jumped back. Gladwell's gun was pointed at the figure in front of him, but Gladwell could not bring himself to shoot someone who had till a few hours ago been a friend.

He stumbled back towards the SUV, almost bumping into the Marine, whose eyes widened as he saw the figure shuffling towards them. He had his M-16 raised, but Gladwell could tell by the hesitation in his eyes that he was also having trouble pulling the trigger.

A group emerged from the side of the road. There were two more staffers, their wives and, most horrifying of all, their four children. They shuffled towards Gladwell, teeth bared, their clothes and bodies covered in blood, and Gladwell gave up all pretense of bravado.

'Run!'

The two of them sprinted to the SUV and he could tell

by Jane's haunted expression that she had seen everything. He got into the front seat and asked the driver to pass the cars and get on the highway. He called Randhawa. He heard the soldier's voice on the third ring, but had to strain to hear what Randhawa was saying as every word seemed to be cut off by loud pops.

'We're fighting our way through an absolute mob of Biters. Get on the highway and wait for us. We'll catch up soon enough.'

'Sir, we can't just wait here in the middle of the highway. We'll be a magnet for Biters for miles around.'

Gladwell knew that there was a lot of truth in what the Marine had said. But the people gathered around him were waiting for him to make a decision. It was one thing to decide on matters of protocol sitting in his air-conditioned office, quite another to be making life-and-death decisions in the middle of a warzone.

Waiting for Randhawa and his men left them exposed since Randhawa was at least twenty minutes away and his last conversation had been interrupted several times by the sound of automatic fire. On the other hand, their chances of survival on their own were slim. He did not know the exact location of the base they were headed towards and even if he got that from Randhawa, he did not fancy his chances of getting there in one car with four armed men. The outlying areas of Delhi they would have to pass were slums. Once the contagion had taken hold, it had taken mere hours to spread through those packed shanty huts. The local radio channels had stopped broadcasting an hour ago but the Internet still seemed to be up and Jo had read out heartwrenching updates on thousands of Biters from these slums spilling over into posh condominiums built in the suburbs. The impoverished and the elite had become one as a bloodthirsty mob of Biters that was consuming everyone in its path and fast spreading towards the city center.

'We wait.'

Gladwell stared down the young Marine till it was clear who was in charge. Then he got to work, half-forgotten training and half-remembered instincts taking over. For a second, he was brought back to a misty morning in Bosnia.

Then, as now, he was a reluctant warrior forced to fight to save innocent lives. There were two big differences. One, he was no longer a twenty-two-year-old who believed he could not be touched, and second, he was now fighting for his family. The first made him less impulsive and the second made him determined that if the Biters got to Jo or Jane, they would do so by stepping over his corpse.

He asked for the SUV to be parked near the side of the road on the large flyover. That ensured they could not be attacked from behind and also that they would have the advantage of height. Neither of the Marines had seen combat before and Gladwell gave them sentry duty, hoping that they would be too busy to be afraid. The driver was a Diplomatic Service agent who had served in the Middle East and quickly got the Marines in place.

Gladwell felt a hand on his arm. It was Jo. 'Bob, ask the Marines to give me and Jane their handguns and tell us how to shoot them if we need to.'

Gladwell didn't know what to say. His family was in as much danger as the rest of them but he had never contemplated little Jane and his own Jo carrying guns.

Jim, the driver, cut in. 'Sir, she's right. If there are as many Biters out there as they say, we'll need every gun we can get.'

And so they began the wait for Randhawa and his men, watching the roads and slums nearby for Biters.

They did not have to wait long. Their position overlooked the Radisson hotel, and one of the Marines shouted out a warning that he had spotted some movement. Looking down from their vantage point, they saw the first of the Biters appear from among the decrepit shops that surrounded the area and then several more appeared from the shattered front door of the Radisson. As Gladwell watched, their numbers continued to swell till many hundreds of Biters streamed out of the buildings, heading towards the city. Gladwell's first thought was that they seemed to be like a swarm of locusts, consuming everything in their path, but he knew they were much more dangerous, for with each victim they swelled their ranks till they were too numerous to stop or fight. He looked around him and realized that with their modest numbers and firepower, they would not have lasted more than a few minutes if that mob of Biters had been headed for them.

Deciding quickly that discretion was the better part of valor, he asked everyone to get down, and they all sat with their backs pressed to the side of the road, hearing the thumps and growls of the Biters as they passed under them. Gladwell had put down his gun and was holding Jo's hand with one hand and Jane's with the other. He had never been a particularly religious person, but this seemed like as good a time as any to send up a prayer for the safety of his wife, his daughter and their unborn child.

They had been waiting for about ten minutes when Jo whispered, 'Some of them are on the highway.'

Gladwell didn't know if they had been spotted, but a

group of about twenty Biters had detached itself and turned onto the flyover where Gladwell's group was huddled. With the SUV partially obscuring them, Gladwell wasn't sure they had been spotted yet, but if the Biters got much closer then there would be no option left but to try and fight it out. Gladwell looked to Jim, aware that of all of them, he had perhaps the most field experience.

'Jim, what do you reckon are our chances of taking them out before they get too close?'

Jim's face bore a grim expression as he answered.

'Not too good, Sir. If those were twenty humans, even trained soldiers, we could have ambushed them now and taken out half of them in the first salvo before they got a shot off. But we need headshots, and they're about two hundred meters out. At that range, we can forget scoring head shots with our handguns, and the two boys with the M-16s aren't exactly trained snipers either.'

'Then we hide as long as we can.'

They huddled against the SUV with Jim lying flat on the ground behind a tire, watching the Biters as they approached. All of them were trying to be as still and as quiet as they could, and then Jane brought her hands up to her nose, trying to stifle a sneeze. Everyone looked at her in dread, the two seconds seeming like an eternity. As the moment passed, they all spontaneously broke out into smiles. And then it happened.

Jane sneezed.

The Biters stopped, looking right and left, and then Gladwell's heart stopped. One of them looked straight at the SUV and roared, and they began shuffling towards the SUV as fast as they could.

'Marines, fire at will!'

Gladwell's roared command galvanized the two Marines

into action and they stepped out from behind the SUV, their M-16s at the ready.

'Single shot only. Aim for the head. Only the head.'

As the Marines took aim and began firing at the approaching group of Biters, Gladwell and the others took aim with their handguns. Gladwell ensured the safety was off on Jane and Jo's guns and steadied Jane's hands, pointing them towards the Biters.

'Sweetheart, don't worry about the heads. At this range, we won't hit them with pistols. Aim for the legs so we can at least slow them down. Take a deep breath, count to three, aim and fire, and then repeat. Don't fire blindly or too fast.'

And then the group opened fire in a deadly volley that would have massacred any human opponents. With the Biters, it had less of a dramatic effect. The two Marines were trying their best, but with the Biters moving, most of their initial shots missed their targets. Some hit the Biters in the chest and neck, and sent them staggering back till they resumed their approach. Then one of them scored a direct headshot and the Biter went down for good. The group cheered, but it was a small victory.

That still left almost twenty Biters now closing in on them. Jane and Jo were firing away and Gladwell noted with dismay that most of their bullets were pinging off the pavement around the Biters. With human adversaries, even such near misses would have sent them scampering for cover, but Biters did not seem to care. He was about to say something when he saw how badly Jane's hands were shaking.

He took aim, focusing on a large Biter closest to them, a man wearing only a pair of shorts, his bare torso covered in blood and gore. Gladwell fired two rounds, one smacking into the Biter's thigh, the second hitting him in the stomach. The Biter doubled over for a second and then straightened up and made straight for him. Jim and the Marines had been busy and at least three Biters were down but now they were less than fifty meters away and it was a matter of time before the Biters overwhelmed them.

That was when Gladwell did something quite extraordinary. Under normal circumstances Gladwell would never have worked up the insane courage to do something like this, but all Gladwell could think of was protecting his family and so he stepped into the middle of the highway and began to walk briskly towards the Biters. Jo screamed out his name and he did not look back as he replied.

'Keep shooting!'

He was now less than ten feet away from the nearest Biter, a thin man wearing a bloodied Superman t-shirt. Gladwell shouted back, though he would have no recollection of what he had said, though much later Jo claimed he had said something along the lines of 'Eat shit and die'. Gladwell felt a stab of fear as the Biter came closer, and he tried to give him a name, to think he was a living, breathing enemy who could be killed, not some undead monster. So this one naturally became Superman.

As Superman howled, Gladwell put a bullet through his forehead, sending him flopping down on the road. Gladwell was hardly a crack shot, but at such close range, he did not need to try too hard. Another Biter, this one a woman with flowing long hair now matted with blood oozing from her neck, took his place and came towards him. Gladwell missed with his first shot, which hit her in the shoulder, but the second put Rapunzel down for good. Another Biter went down from a headshot, and he turned to see that Jim had joined him. The two Marines had also come to join them and at such close quarters, they were putting down Biters with almost every shot. A large Biter, who towered over him, came so close that Gladwell could smell his putrid breath and see the yellow gore on the corners of his mouth. He put a bullet in his mouth and as the Biter staggered back, Gladwell kicked him in the gut and shot him in the head.

Gladwell was suddenly aware that the Biters were no longer just in front of him but beside him. In the chaos of the battle, he was no longer facing a mob of Biters but in the middle of one. He shot another Biter down and took a step back as two more Biters reached out towards him.

That was when both Biters fell, their heads cracked open by direct hits from large-caliber weapons. The deep rumble of heavy engines rose and Gladwell looked up to see several trucks and one SUV. Men in the black commando fatigues of the National Security Guard jumped out of the trucks and began mowing down the Biters with precisely aimed shots to the head. The bearded and turbaned face of Randhawa peered out from the passenger side window of the SUV.

'Gladwell, I thought you were a diplomat but you would put bloody John Rambo to shame. Come on!'

As Gladwell shepherded Jo and Jane into Randhawa's SUV, he turned to see the two Marines and Jim looking at him with an expression he had not seen before. Till now, he had been the ranking diplomat. Now, he was respected. In the new world that faced them all, this was one of the subtle changes they would all come to adapt to – the ranks and badges of the past meant nothing. Respect, and indeed survival, had to be earned in blood.

They sat in silence for a few minutes, each of them quietly taking in how everything had changed. Gladwell was glad to see that a few stragglers from the Embassy who had arrived late had been picked up by Randhawa's convoy. In all, they numbered about a hundred men, women and children, all headed towards the relative safety of Randhawa's base.

Jo and Jane were in the back of the SUV with Randhawa's wife and child and four armed commandos, and Randhawa had decided to drive the SUV himself, asking the driver to take a break in the back of one of the trucks. The terrified young soldier had saluted gratefully and jogged back to one of the accompanying trucks.

Unable to contain his curiosity any longer, Gladwell asked Randhawa if he knew any more about what was happening in the world. Randhawa looked at him with bloodshot eyes. 'It's really the bloody end of the world, that's what it is. First we have these Biters crawling out of every frigging corner, and what they haven't ripped apart, we will ourselves.'

When Gladwell asked what he meant, he got a chilling account of the multiple nuclear battles being waged. Contact with much of the Middle East had been lost as Iran and Israel engaged in a last orgy of mutual nuclear annihilation that engulfed much of the region. Chinese missiles were flying into Taiwan and India and Pakistan were at each other's throats. Gladwell closed his eyes and sat back, wondering if this was all a bad dream, if he would wake up and find that his biggest worry was fetching American Chopsuey for Jo at odd hours. He opened his eyes, and seeing the abandoned vehicles littering the highway, he realized that the world he had come to take for granted had indeed died. What would arise in its place was a terrifying prospect and he wondered how long he could keep his family safe.

Thunder rumbled and Randhawa flinched before recovering. Randhawa grinned at him, and not for the first time, Gladwell wondered how he could manage to smile at a time like this. 'Never a better time to get out of the city.'

Gladwell looked back and saw smoke rising in the distance from numerous fires that had broken out. He shook his head sadly. Even when human civilization was threatened, man's baser instincts could not be tamed. The soldiers in the back were talking about how they had seen looters rampaging through the streets and with no apparent law and order, raping and pillaging at will. While Randhawa's convoy had fought its way through a large mob of Biters, they had gunned down an equal number of human looters who were rampaging through nearby shops. Someone spoke out on the radio.

'Sir, I see a bike approaching us at high speed.'

'Who's driving it? Are they armed?'

Gladwell could sense the hesitation in the man's voice as he answered Randhawa.

'Sir, there's a young woman in the back, and it's being driven by a kid wearing... rabbit ears of some sort.'

Randhawa slammed his fist on the steering wheel.

'Just what we need. Some drunk kid out on a joyride wearing silly ears. If they come closer, tell them to back off.'

As the bike moved towards them, Gladwell's hand tightened around his gun. The boy's shirt was covered in blood and his face had a desperate look that Gladwell didn't like. One of the soldiers in the back pointed his rifle at the boy.

'Sir, I will shoot if you do not move away from this convoy.'

The girl sitting behind the strange boy with bunny ears raised one of her hands and pleaded.

'We need help. I'm trying to get to that safe zone at the airport, and my boyfriend needs medical help.'

Jo murmured behind him, 'Oh my God, could that be Neha from the foundation?' Jo pushed down the rifle the soldier had pointed at the bike and pleaded with Randhawa to stop. 'Please, please stop. I think I know that girl from the Make-A-Wish Foundation. We can't just leave them here.'

They were tight on space and Randhawa seemed to be mulling the question over in his mind. Finally, he barked into the radio. 'Stop, everyone stop. One of you in the back go and check who they are.'

One of the soldiers disembarked and went over to the bike, which had stopped alongside the SUV. He talked to the girl, and started to lead her back to the SUV. The girl was sobbing and pointing to the boy, whose eyes had started yellowing. Now that they had stopped, Gladwell and the others got a closer look at him. There was no question about it – he was transforming into a Biter, yet he had somehow got this girl to safety, knowing he was doomed. Gladwell felt a lump in his throat. In the middle of all the madness and hatred, this simple act of sacrifice reminded all of them that being human was still worth clinging on to, still worth fighting for, still something to be proud of. Gladwell thought he saw Randhawa's eyes moisten as well, but the grizzled soldier blinked it away, though he did give a curt nod of respect to the boy. The girl was still sobbing uncontrollably as Jo took her in her arms and then the convoy sped on towards its destination.

Gladwell was surprised, though perhaps he should not have been, that the first predators they had to fight off were human.

With the outbreak came a lawlessness that nobody had ever planned for. Initially there was some looting, but soon people realized that money was of little value any more. Prison doors lay open. Serial killers, sociopaths, rapists – the worst of man came out to wreak their havoc.

Three days into their stay in the base, Gladwell and Randhawa had started seeing small groups of civilians escaping from the madness in the city. They had taken them in, though soon enough supplies and food would be a real issue. Then came those who came not to take refuge, but to prey upon a well-stocked settlement. A settlement with food, supplies and women.

The first attack had been smashed before it had really unfolded. Ten men armed with swords and cleavers had tried to enter the complex at night. The American Marines and Indian commandos, by now trained to aim for the head after all their battles with the Biters, had mistaken the intruders for Biters and felled four with headshots before the others screamed in terror and ran away into the night. The next attack had been more serious, with two jeeps full of armed men, members of a paramilitary unit that had decided to use their weapons and training to their advantage. The firefight had lasted more than thirty minutes before they were driven off. But after that, attacks by looters ceased. Word had spread that this particular settlement was occupied by people not to be messed with easily. In the second attack, Randhawa had been seriously wounded, and by consensus, Gladwell was appointed the leader of their small settlement.

That night, Gladwell sat down next to Jo, who was singing to her unborn daughter, hoping that innocent rhymes would register with her instead of the gunfire and screams that she heard all day.

'How are you doing?'

'She seems to like the noise. She's been kicking all day.'

Gladwell kissed her lightly on the head and then sat down to take stock of their situation. They had plenty of ammunition, but at the rate at which they were attracting new members, they would have to organize some sort of effort to get food. By now, nobody believed that things would get back to normal. Gladwell had organized small patrols to scour the neighboring areas, and they all spoke about Biters running rampant. The Internet was down, and there was nothing on TV, but they did manage to pick up radio transmissions from military channels and from private radio operators.

The picture they painted was terrifying. Most of the world had been laid waste by the wars that had erupted, and by the Biters. There were reports that many governments had authorized nuclear airbursts over major cities in a last-ditch, desperate attempt to wipe out the Biters and reclaim the cities. Gladwell shuddered as he considered what would be happening to the human survivors left in the cities.

The ground shook and he wondered whether on top of all the other catastrophes they had endured, an earthquake was next. That was when Jo screamed out to him. He rushed to her, and Jane came into the small room that they shared with three other families.

A mushroom cloud billowed over the city of Delhi. There had been air strikes on the city for the last couple of days and Gladwell had assumed it was another one but the cloud told him that Delhi had joined the list of cities that had succumbed to this madness.

One of the soldiers had told him that if governments were indeed using air burst nuclear weapons then the risk of residual radiation was small. Moreover, they were almost fifty kilometers away from the city center. That was little consolation to Gladwell as he held his family tight and watched another mushroom cloud join the first one. When they stepped out of the room, all the people in their group were standing there, tears in their eyes. If any of them had still hoped that they might go back home, there was no question of that now.

Gladwell heard someone mumble next to him, 'We killed the world. It's all dead land out here now.'

That evening, their settlement was eerily quiet. Randhawa was still unconscious and Gladwell realized that no matter how low people felt, Biters and human predators would not stop coming. So he spent several hours making a schedule of who would be on guard duty and also scheduling firearms classes for everyone. In the new reality they faced, they would need every single one of them to be able to fight if needed.

Mentally and physically drained, he joined Jo at night. As he walked in, Neha, the young girl they had picked up on the highway, left.

'How's she holding up?'

Jo looked tired and miserable but managed to smile.

'Poor girl's been through a lot. Lost her family and then the young man who got her to us. At least we still have each other.'

Gladwell hugged Jo and sat next to her on the floor. He was due for sentry duty in two hours' time, so he wanted to get as much rest as he could. He ran his hand gently over Jo's stomach.

'How's the little one doing?'

'Still kicking and jumping around.'

'Thought of a name?'

Truth be told, Gladwell was so drained that he no longer had the energy to debate names. He was happy to go with whatever Jo chose.

Jo thought of the bunny-eared young man who had got Neha to safety despite knowing that he was doomed and of the wish they had set out to fulfill. She had heard people start referring to the world outside as Deadland and the name had stuck. While she did not want her daughter to be born into such a world, she was not yet ready to give her hope. So she thought of a name that would pay homage to the brave man wearing bunny ears, a name that harked back to childhood tales of a more innocent time, a name that would hold out the promise of a land filled with wonder, not death.

She looked at Gladwell, her mind made up.

'We'll name her Alice.'

ABOUT MAINAK DHAR

MAINAK DHAR IS A CUBICLE dweller by day and writer by night, with thirteen books to his credit. He has been published widely by major publishers in India like Random House and Penguin, but took the plunge into self-publishing with the Amazon Kindle Store in March 2011 to reach readers worldwide. In his first year on the Kindle store, he sold more than 100,000 ebooks, making him one of the top selling self-published writers worldwide. He is the author of the Amazon.com bestseller Alice in Deadland and you can learn more about him and his writing at www.mainakdhar.com.